"Kimberly Cates writes with a unique blend of beauty, magic, and power that never fails to touch me deeply."

—Linda Lael Miller,
bestselling author of *The Last Chance Café*

"Kimberly Cates is an extraordinary storyteller."

—Jill Barnett,
bestselling author of *Sentimental Journey*

PRAISE FOR
KIMBERLY CATES

AND HER POWERFUL CONTEMPORARY NOVEL
OF LOVE, FRIENDSHIP, AND FAMILY

Fly Away Home

"Kimberly Cates is one exceptional storyteller. . . . Her stories are just as riveting and unforgettable in a contemporary setting as they are in a historical one."

—*Romantic Times*

"A beautifully written romance that shimmers with the haunting magic of Ireland."

—Kristin Hannah, author of *On Mystic Lake*

"Relationship drama fans will want to fly away with this warm, contemporary romance with a bit of the supernatural. . . . A stirring tale of love."

—Harriet Klausner, Bookbrowser.com

Books by Kimberly Cates

Angel's Fall
Crown of Dreams
Gather the Stars
To Catch a Flame
Only Forever
Morning Song
The Raider's Bride
The Raider's Daughter
Restless Is the Wind
Stealing Heaven
Magic
Briar Rose
Lily Fair
Fly Away Home
The Mother's Day Garden
Lighthouse Cove

Published by POCKET BOOKS

Kimberly Cates

Lighthouse Cove

POCKET **STAR** BOOKS

New York   London   Toronto   Sydney   Singapore

An *Original* Publication of POCKET BOOKS

 A Pocket Star book published by
POCKET BOOKS, a division of Simon & Schuster, Inc.
1230 Avenue of the Americas, New York, NY 10020

Copyright © 2002 by Kim Ostrom Bush

ISBN: 0-7434-1887-5

First Pocket Books printing November 2002

10 9 8 7 6 5 4 3 2 1

POCKET STAR BOOKS and colophon are registered trademarks of Simon & Schuster, Inc.

For information regarding special discounts for bulk purchases, please contact Simon & Schuster Special Sales at 1-800-456-6798 or business@simonandschuster.com

Cover art by Rod Wood/Wood, Ronsaville, Harlin

Printed in the U.S.A.

To Serena Coppula with love, as she embarks on her own future in photojournalism. May you and your camera have a lifetime full of adventures.

I believe in you.

1

This was the last place on earth Jacqueline Murphy wanted to be. She brushed back wisps of caramel-colored hair that had pulled loose from her no-nonsense ponytail. Eyes so intense and crystal blue they didn't seem real swept over the scenery surrounding her. She homed in on a perfect shot, snapped it from every angle with her camera, then let the familiar weight of her battered Leica swing down and hang from its strap around her neck.

Waves crashed, white-capped, against the shore, clusters of children squealing in delight as they darted through showers of silvery spray, their parents joining their frolics in the bright summer sun. Raw bundles of hormones disguised as teenage boys bodysurfed to show off for blanketsful of bikini-clad girls. Old women and men strolled along the beach hand in hand, age unable to diminish the softness a lifetime of love had left in their eyes.

Beautiful, most people would call the scene. No trained eye needed to appreciate the jeweled colors, the gleam of salt spray, the glorious sight of the edge of the world, washed clean by waves and sunshine. But the beauty didn't fool Jack for an instant. She saw the warning in the distance—the solitary white spire of the lighthouse pointing skyward from its narrow isthmus of land, a single, shadowy eye staring out across the shipwreck marooned on the shoals beyond. Jack could almost hear it whisper "they once thought this place beautiful, too."

She shivered in spite of the warmth of the sun, and stared at the retired lighthouse/bed-and-breakfast that had been her home this past week. What had the crusty former keeper and owner of the place said when she'd ushered Jack through the green painted door of the stone house attached to that soaring round tower?

"Two hundred fifty years this old girl has watched the sea play cat's paw with the ships that sailed here. One minute, skies so bright blue it seemed storms would never come again. Next minute a gale so fierce it could blow the beard right off a man's face. Two hundred ships ran aground on those shoals, wrecked in spite of Mermaid Lost's warning. Almost every old family on this stretch of coast lost someone they loved. We had the ship's names carved on the face of that boulder near the telescope on the cliff's edge. Just so we never forget."

But Jack doubted anyone really needed a reminder etched in stone far out on some deserted cliff. She'd found that loss carved itself where you couldn't hide from it. In your memory. In your heart.

"Something for everyone on this stretch of coast," proprietor China Pepperell had boasted, her windburned face more lined than a map of New York City above her yellow nor'easter.

"Not for me," Jack had hedged. "I'm just here to do a favor for an old friend. I plan to be on my way as soon as possible."

But the older woman had just chuckled. "That's what my great-great-grandfather Captain Rake Ramsey said when he sailed in. No pirate born would want a home port like this. But God laughs when people make bold claims like that. The notorious pirate fell in love, and, well—I'm here, so you can guess the rest. His ship was the first one to wreck on those shoals. My great-great-grandmother was birthing their second baby, and she'd nearly died the first time around. The midwife claimed the only thing that held her tight to life was the clasp of her husband's hand.

"The authorities hereabouts were hungry to bring Rake to justice, and the whole coast knew of his love of his wife. Though Emily begged her captain to stay away, and promised she'd find him in Jamaica soon as she had the baby she was carrying and it was strong enough to travel, the captain wouldn't listen. The instant the midwife was called to the lighthouse, the soldiers laid their trap.

"Terrified that they would capture her husband and hang him, Emily did the only thing she could to warn him. In spite of the birth pains tearing at her, she climbed up the stairs to the top of the tower. Doused the light. Prayed he'd stay away. She could have been hanged herself for giving him warning. But her sacrifice was all in vain.

"She should have guessed that nothing would keep him from her side. Onward he sailed, blinded by the dark. He ran his ship into the reef, every soul aboard lost.

"When Emily heard the terrible sounds of the ship

breaking apart, she let go of life. Some people claim they can still hear her voice at night, calling her captain's name."

"She should have drowned the idiot herself," Jack muttered. "She risked her life to save him and he had to fling himself into the fire anyway. What use is nobility and honor and that wild, passionate love stuff if you still end up dead?"

Or alone.

The image of a face flashed into her mind—chocolate-dark eyes blazing with heat, rugged features taut with desire, passion so hot she still felt the imprint of his hands on her skin. She'd been so eager to grow up, show the world what a bold adventurer she was, she'd flung herself headlong into that summer romance with all the passion in her twenty-year-old heart. She'd shown the world all right—that she was just one more gullible kid.

She'd gotten burned. So badly she'd never been tempted to put her hand back in that particular brand of fire again. She'd deep-sixed the painful memory the way she had so many others. So why hadn't it stayed buried?

What in the world had made her think of the affair after years of barely remembering the man had ever existed? China Pepperell's mad, romantic tale of love and loss? Absurd. Love had nothing to do with those crazy two weeks she'd spent in that wide, quilt-covered bed. She'd just fallen victim to a bad case of hormones like so many other young kids did. Then she'd grown up.

Jack grimaced, shoving away the dark mood she could ill afford. Legends like the pirate captain's were highly overrated. She had little patience for grand, heroic gestures. They didn't inspire her or make her misty-eyed. They made her mad as hell. But then, she was definitely in the minority when it came to that. Take Ziggy, for instance.

Trust Ziggy Bartolli, photojournalistic ace and mentor extraordinaire to love this strip of Maine coast, she mused. Pirate ghosts wailing in the night to give him his daily jolt of adrenaline. Tales of love that lasted beyond the grave for his ridiculously romantic soul and a pub a mile away where he could dazzle people with his war stories. In the eight years since Ziggy had taken her under his wing, a heartbroken kid so desperate to earn her stripes she was going to charge into a hot spot without the backing of a press agency or the protection of a press pass, little about the man had changed. Ziggy had always adored Mermaid Lost's kind of ambience. Jack shunned it the way she had the sheik in Tambiza who had offered Ziggy a thousand camels if he could convince Jack to be his sixth wife.

Yes, Jack thought in resignation. If there was a heaven, Ziggy Bartolli was looking down at her right now with that smug satisfaction her partner had always showed on those rare times he'd gotten the better of her. She should have told him to go to hell instead of caving in and swearing to come here to Mermaid Lost. She *would* have told him to go to hell, except, as usual, Ziggy hadn't played fair.

But this time the wily photojournalist had outdone even his scheming, manipulative, brilliant self. Jack had always claimed he'd do anything to get his own way. But even she hadn't expected him to go this far. She'd never thought Ziggy would die.

She closed her eyes, the peaceful Maine coastline shifting into the suffocating heat of the Congo, the blaze of orange from two dozen gun barrels stark against the night. Heart pounding, breath-stealing adrenaline rushed through veins, sensations familiar as bedtime stories for Jack and Ziggy as they bolted away from the latest batch of revolutionaries, toward the helicopter that would fly them out of the bush. Precious rolls of film jammed the pockets of their khaki photographers' vests. Pictures the latest regime would go to any lengths to be certain the rest of the world would never see.

"Helluva story, princess," Ziggy gasped, ducking down to clear the rotary blades. "Did it again, didn't we?"

She'd always hated it when he'd started gloating before they were out of the woods. Figured he was tempting fate. This time, fate had bitten back. Hard. When a bullet slammed into Ziggy's chest.

"Want you to promise me something," Ziggy whispered, his voice weak, blood oozing from beneath Jack's hand. "Book . . . wanted to have it finished for . . . anniversary. Present for Shaara."

It was all Ziggy had talked about when they were in the jungle—the publishing contract he'd gotten for a book full of photos depicting his favorite place in the world. The place where he and Shaara had honeymooned, vacationed, renewed the special relationship they'd forged when he'd stumbled across his future wife in the deserts of Egypt trying to save her young sister from being stoned to death for loving the wrong man. An honor killing, the men of the country called it. Jack had never been able to think of anything less honorable than murdering a seventeen-year-old girl for daring to fall in love.

"Go to . . . lighthouse," Ziggy had pleaded. "Summer pictures only ones I still need. Have to . . . finish the book. Spent so much time . . . away from her. Chasing wars with this damn camera. Need her to know . . . always thought there would be time for us to . . . spend there together. Wish I hadn't . . ."

Spent a lifetime racing around the world, struggling to capture other people's lives on film, other people's joys, other people's tragedies, other people's loves and losses instead of building a real life of his own?

"Shaara knew what kind of life you lived before she married you. She knows you love her."

"Knew I'd never quit work no matter how many times I promised. Always got this . . . wistful look in her eyes when I talked about . . . retiring. Going to live near Mermaid Lost. Jack, need you to catch the lighthouse on film, show her what I dreamed for . . . for both of us. Promise me."

"I promise."

"Been trying to get you to go there for years. Never expected it to happen this way. But . . . it'll do you good, Jack. You're always going . . . the ugliest places in the world. Never take . . . a break. When you do what we see in this business you have to . . . wash your eyes clean sometimes or you'll go mad."

She would have preferred the oblivion of madness to the excruciating reality that filled the weeks after Ziggy's death. Reality from which there was no escape, no blessed distraction of work or physical danger to dull the pain. It was pure nightmare telling Shaara that she'd never see her husband alive again, seeing her at the funeral, her exotic face so full of quiet dignity. But then, Ziggy's wife was no stranger to the harsh edges of life.

During that hellish week Jack had spent helping settle Ziggy's affairs, a barrage of stories had been splashed across every television, every newspaper, courtesy of the pilot's point of view. Editorials about the grim cost Ziggy Bartolli had paid for working with a woman partner in countries where women were mere chattels to be crushed at will beneath men's feet. Maybe it wouldn't have hurt so much if Jack's own father hadn't written the most scathing editorial of all.

Jack closed her eyes, trying to blot out the picture of Frank Murphy's florid face at the funeral, his crumpled suit dusted with cigar ash, his bushy white brows lowered over eyes that burned like zealots she'd faced down in deserts half a world away.

"I told you this would happen, didn't I, Jacqueline?" the memory of her father's voice pounded in her head. "But you wouldn't listen! And now a good man is dead! Was it worth it just to take a few mediocre pictures?"

"Miss?" A strange voice jolted Jack back into the present. She shook herself, in an effort to clear her head, and found herself back on the coast of Maine staring into the features of a fresh-faced young woman and the blond man beside her, their faces both creased with concern. "Are you all right?"

"I'm fine," Jack said sharply.

"We were just walking by and we saw you taking pictures. You looked like you knew what you were doing, and we thought . . . well, we're on our honeymoon, and we wondered if you might take our picture." The girl held out a disposable camera, hopeful.

Jack wanted to shove it back at her and get the blazes out of there, but she'd learned early to stand her ground in front of a charging elephant—whether the elephant was a bull with sharp, gleaming tusks or memories that hammered her from the inside out.

She took the camera, pointed to a cluster of rocks. "Stand over there. That should make a good shot." They each slipped their arms around the other's waist and gazed into each other's eyes, the lighthouse in the distance a perfect backdrop except for the wreck that edged the frame. *How many couples who honeymooned*

here had ended up like that old ship on the rocks? Jack wondered, as she squeezed off the shot.

When had she gotten so cynical? Shaara and Ziggy
had stayed together. They would be together still if she
hadn't . . .

Jack thrust the camera back at the couple, brushing
aside their thanks. She turned, trudging through the
crowd. Maybe that was why she felt so edgy in this
place. In the world of Mermaid Lost everybody had
somebody—families with flocks of children, old couples, still dancing to the tune of their old romance.
Even the lifeguards clustered in pairs, laughing.

Jack had no patience for the uncharacteristically
wistful sensation tugging in her chest. And she would
have died of embarrassment if anyone in this crowd of
strangers suspected that something more vulnerable
lay hidden beneath the hard-driven journalist she'd
worked her whole lifetime to be. Jacqueline Murphy—
unflinching under the threat of bomb blasts and
machine-gun fire, able to leap tall buildings and capture the most dangerous of stories in a single bound.

Jack grimaced. How many times in the past few
years had Ziggy teased that she was becoming a legend
on her own. So cool under fire it seemed impossible
that she could be so detached and yet capture the pulsing heart of any situation she photographed. The ice
queen who never let herself be swept up into the
whirlwind of emotions that threatened to destroy the
sanity of any combat vet—whether they wielded an
M16 or a camera. If only those determined to lionize
her knew the truth, Jack thought. She'd just been
burying her emotions, storing them up until Ziggy's
death yanked them to the surface. From the night
she'd first marched into the smoky press bar half a
world away in Paris to the day she'd arrived here at

Mermaid Lost, Ziggy could have attested to the fact that the force that had driven her was the same as many a man joining the French Foreign Legion. One badly bruised heart.

Good lord, was she insane? Thinking about a two-week affair after nine years had passed? Or was it inevitable after Ziggy's death, to remember the force that had brought them together? She didn't know. But two insignificant weeks still had the power to unnerve her. How strange. Unexpected. She winced, hating to admit even to herself that she'd found a crack in her emotional armor.

Time to go back to the lighthouse, she resolved, far away from crowds and laughter and sunshine. It felt so awkward to her, so strange out here among people safe and laughing. When had peace and leisure become her enemy, more dangerous than the strafing of machine-gun fire?

Somewhere, somehow, her world had turned upside down. Quiet was the enemy now. Because with the quiet came remembering.

2

———◆———

The staircase spiraled up into the light tower, patches of late afternoon sun streaming through the closely webbed vine pattern transforming the wrought iron into an exquisite, immovable circle of lace. Flat on her back on the stone base at the foot of the stairs, Jack shoved with her feet, trying to squeeze her body into a smaller space as she searched for the perfect camera angle to capture the strength and beauty and unexpected bit of whimsy that led to the light far above.

She stopped short, her head banging into one of the posts anchoring the staircase to the floor. Muttering low, she wriggled one hand up to rub at the bump on her head. "It would be just my luck to get stuck and have to be cut out of here with a blowtorch," she grumbled. "Wouldn't the guys at the press club just love that. I can just hear it—'Knew her head was getting too big. Not only does she manage to get herself into a spot she can't get out of, but she destroys a historical treasure in the process.'"

It was China Pepperell who had talked her into

taking shots of the lighthouse interior, painting images of the place as a home as well as a landmark. And Jack had acquiesced figuring that even if the pictures weren't much use for Ziggy's book, she could hand them off to the older woman as a sort of payment for kindnesses lavished on Jack no matter how many times Jack argued against them.

A burning ache tightened the muscles in Jack's neck. She grimaced, muttering aloud. "China will be pleased. If I end up in traction, she can come to the hospital to visit and there'll be no escape for me. There I'd be, trapped like a rat in one of those hospital gowns that leave your backside bare, and she'd be bound and determined to keep me compan—*whoa!*"

Jack grappled with her camera as sunlight suddenly streaked just the way she'd wanted, lighting up the cylinder of the tower, making it mystical, an unexpected work of art.

Her heart fluttered as she lowered the camera back onto her chest. She lay still for a moment, just enjoying the sensation of a mission accomplished. She'd have to remember this feeling late tonight when her bumps and bruises were clamoring for attention, and every muscle in her body ached from lying so long on the cold stone. She was just trying to wedge herself back out through the opening between the stairs' iron supports when she heard a knock on the lighthouse door.

She grimaced, knowing full well who it would be. The thing she liked best about staying at Mermaid Lost was its isolation. The worst challenge was the fleet of Pepperells that made their way up to their old homestead whenever the mood struck them.

They always came bearing gifts. Chocolate cake, casseroles to put into the freezer, books and articles about points of interest that might help her with her project or bundles of candles when it looked like a storm might knock out the electricity. She'd spent a third of her life in places where people had barely heard of electricity, but she hadn't had the heart to tell them that. Not when she'd figured out their motives a long time ago. They were afraid she'd be lonely.

Wanting to be alone—now, that was a concept the Pepperells couldn't begin to understand. Packed into the lighthouse tight as pickles in a jar, China's six surviving sons quarreling madly, hosting a constant stream of in-laws and children and friends the family had known for generations, they probably couldn't fathom the charm in solitude. Couldn't understand how Jack craved it. But alone was the one place she could let her guard down, allow her restless mind to empty itself of the blur of violence and greed and courage she'd seen. The one place no one could ask anything of her—not a scrap of food, not a forbidden book, not secret, safe passage out of a hellhole somewhere in a country with a name most people couldn't pronounce.

Or worst of all, her own mother, asking her to come home and pretend that the disaster of her childhood had never happened, that they'd really been that picture-perfect family that had smiled out of the photos in the engraved Christmas cards they'd always sent.

Jack would have loved to lie still on the cold stone floor, ignore the insistent knocking at the door and wait until her visitor went away like any normal person would. Unfortunately, she knew China Pepperell wouldn't give up that easily. The woman had a key and the irrefutable innkeeper's excuse that she was bringing fresh towels and sheets and would be checking supplies to see whatever else her guest needed.

No, there was nowhere to run, nowhere to hide.

Jack would just have to get rid of her as quickly as possible. She managed to shinny out from under the base of the stairs and scramble to her feet. Shoving her hair out of her eyes, she went to open the door.

She should have been irritated, but it was hard to hold on to that emotion when you came face-to-face with China Pepperell. The woman was sixty years old, but it seemed nobody had bothered to tell her. She was twice as spry as any twenty-year-old Jack had ever met. She'd faced the loss of her husband, buried two of her children, and scraped out a hardscrabble life on this weather-beaten stretch of coast. But she bustled around with boundless enthusiasm, mothering anyone who crossed her path, laughing and teasing, enjoying the fun with as much gusto as any of her six remaining sons.

"And so, my girl, how are you on this lovely day?" she asked, grinning over her stack of thick, fluffy towels.

"Fine."

"Fine? What kind of a poor excuse for a word is that? It tells me nothing useful, except that you've no intention of telling me how you really are."

Jack stifled a sigh. The woman had unerring accuracy in judging other people's moods, maybe an ability she'd honed in a lifetime of trying to judge the weather. Jack figured her best move would be to change the subject.

"I've been following your suggestion. Taking pictures inside the house, here."

"Most important thing of all, to my way of thinking. Show that this place was someone's home. A family lived here, laughed here, loved here. And some were buried from here," she added wistfully. "People see this place like a picture postcard, frozen, empty. Just a pretty shell. Never forget how alive it was, Jack, when the light still burned and the ships sheared off, afraid of the shoals."

China's storm-gray eyes grew distant, dreamy, and Jack sensed she was remembering her own boys racketing up and down those iron stairs, or their beds, all six of them crowded into the single room they'd shared. Even Jack could almost hear China's hot-headed brood of boys squabbling, chasing each other, horsing around until China blew the sea captain's whistle she still wore around her neck, a gift from her father to keep order among her own mutinous band of little sailors. Jack felt a twinge of guilt that she was only trying to humor China by taking a few shots inside the place and had no intention of using the images in Ziggy's book.

"Can I see what you've got so far?" China asked. Jack rarely showed people her works in progress—felt almost rabidly protective of the pictures before she felt ready to have them displayed—doubtless a result of years of her father's constant criticism. Ziggy had done his best to drive back what he'd affectionately dubbed her "paranoia." But Jack had never been able to get past the sick sensation she'd felt as a child when Frank Murphy dug through her drawers or her coat pockets, coming up with the little packages of pictures she'd gotten developed at the nearby five-and-dime.

Her stomach still felt hollow at the memory of how his lip would curl in disdain. "Play with your Brownie camera all you want, little girl. You might be able to take pictures at your own kids' birthday parties without cutting off anybody's heads, but you'll never be good enough to photograph anything else."

Once she'd gotten old enough, she'd found the perfect place to hide her work—inside the boxes of Kotex pads in the closet of her bathroom. That was one place she was certain the mighty Frank Murphy would never have the guts to look.

She couldn't help smiling even now at what a resourceful little cuss she'd been.

"Jack?" China's voice broke in. "I promise, I won't say a word. I just want to see—"

"I'm sorry, China. Really," Jack said. "But I never show my work until I think it's ready. Once I do, I promise you'll be the first to get a glimpse of it."

China didn't bother to hide her disappointment. "Well, then, I guess I'll just have to be a little patient. I've waited out hurricanes, Jack Murphy," she said with a wink. "I can sure as hell wait out you."

Jack chuckled.

"Thought I'd make up your bed and so forth," China said, trying to look official. It might have worked if it hadn't been for the twinkle in her eye.

"You know as well as I do you're just making up an excuse," Jack teased. "I should make you do up the bed just out of spite, but I'm feeling particularly gracious today, so I'm letting you off the hook. Just leave the stuff on the table. I'm a big girl. I can even make my own bed now."

"Maybe you should let someone else do for you once in a while. Maybe it would do you some good to be mothered just a little, even by an old salt like me."

"We've been over this before, Mrs. P.," Jack said, suddenly wanting to get the woman out of the house. China had touched a nerve. But then, the woman knew it. Family was China Pepperell's life, always had been. She couldn't conceive of anyone wanting to live alone.

"The boys pulled up a fine catch in their nets today," China said, deftly changing the subject. "And their babies, well, they dug up a whole mess of clams.

Thought we'd have a clambake down on the beach. Will you come?"

Jack sighed. "You have to be the most stubborn woman I've ever met."

"Besides you, you mean?"

"China, I don't want to offend you or hurt your feelings, but I've told you as plainly as I can that the whole family outing thing—it's just not my scene."

"It's not an outing, it's a clambake. You could come when you want, and leave when you choose. It would do you good to actually talk to a living human being besides me."

"And whichever of your boys and their children you send up in an effort to charm me?"

China didn't even have the grace to blush. "A handsome lot they are, aren't they? If only you were a bit younger, Asia isn't spoken for yet."

"Asia is seventeen!" Jack exclaimed.

"A pity. You'd make fine children, handsome as you both are."

Children—back to that subject again. Another one of China's favorites—the glory of motherhood. "We've covered this before," Jack said slowly, deliberately, as if talking to a very slow child. Slow—that was something China Pepperell definitely was *not*. "I don't want children. I've never wanted children."

Except for one brief, sweet space of madness when she'd wondered what it would be like to hold a baby with chocolate-dark eyes and a crooked grin, a voice inside her whispered. But she wasn't about to let China home in on that old chink in her armor.

"I'm no good with children even when I can't avoid interacting with them," Jack insisted.

"Interacting? My lord, what a word! You just play with them. Plunk your behind down on the sand next

to 'em and ask what kind of castle they're building."
China must have noticed the tightness around Jack's
mouth. This time it was Mrs. P. who sighed.

"My boys, they keep telling me I shouldn't pry into
your private life, darlin'. It's not usually my way."

Jack almost had to laugh in spite of herself at the
sudden, prim light in China's eyes. Not China's way to
pry into people's lives? Jack thought wryly. It was practically the woman's full-time occupation. Not only was
China Pepperell sure she knew what was best for herself. She knew what was best for everyone else as well.

"It's just—there's something about you." China's
voice gentled. "You remind me of myself, I guess.
Hardheaded. So determined to prove you can stand up
to any storm. There's anger in you. That's what you'd
like everyone to see. You're as ready to jump into any
fight as any one of my boys, God bless 'em. But you use
your words instead of your fists."

"Actually, I do kickboxing to keep myself in shape."
Jack tried to joke. "Nothing like whacking a giant
punching bag to get your frustrations out."

"Strike out all you want, Jack, my girl, but it won't
work. Maybe it gets out anger, but it will never get you
free of the hurt. That's what's really inside you. Pain.
You and I both know it's true. And Ziggy. He knew it,
too."

"Ziggy talked about me?" She winced instinctively.
"God, can't he ever keep his mouth shut—" She
stopped, the stark reality of Ziggy's death slamming
into her chest afresh. Ziggy—one of the few people
she'd ever allowed herself to love. Even though it had
made her mad as hell.

"We got close over the years, Ziggy and I," China
said. "Think he liked me because I could always tell
when he was bullshitting me."

It should have shocked Jack, hearing such crude language coming from a little old woman's mouth. But it didn't. It fit with China somehow. The shortest, most succinct way to say something. No mincing around the edges of it, just diving in, headfirst.

"When he put one over on me, he figured he'd really gotten away with something," she shared, her eyes soft with affection and with loss. "But he wasn't bullshitting when he talked about you. He worried about you."

"Yeah, well, he was wasting his time. I'm fine."

China gave a snort of disgust. "Fine. There's that word again. Why not come down to the beach at five tonight. You can be 'fine' there, too."

Jack closed her eyes for a moment, imagining the scene all too clearly: China's sons bantering among themselves, telling off-color jokes while their wives tried to hush them up because of the kids playing nearby; the older children grumbling because they had to keep the wee ones from toddling into the water; the younger kids oblivious, frolicking on the strip of beach near the tumbledown boathouse where the old keepers had kept their rescue boats twenty-odd years ago.

Caleb, the most solemn and dreamiest of the children, one of Seth's brood, would be gathering shells and making a sweep of heaven on earth, arranging the starfish he found in constellations on the sand. Even Jack hadn't been able to entirely shut out the winning eight-year-old who'd accompanied his father on missions to the lighthouse more often than any of the other Pepperell children.

The boy had the soul of an artist, here on the wild Maine coast, and the spirit of adventure that had made sailors centuries ago sail in uncharted waters, even though they feared they might fall off the edge of the world.

"We'll see," Jack averred. "If I get all my work done here, I might come down."

They both knew she was lying.

"Well, you're always welcome."

For a moment Jack thought she'd finally won. That China was going to turn and go. But the woman had one parting thing to say.

"Jack, God doesn't always give us the families we wish for. Sometimes, you have to go out into the world and build a family for yourself."

"I told you, I don't want—"

"Children, I know. But there's more to a family than that. It's anyplace that you can feel safe, loved, sheltered from the storms. Where you can be yourself and never have to be afraid."

Jack had to question that one. Young Asia must dread the cuffs his older brothers dealt him on a regular basis. The way they tormented him about his seasickness. It would have been easy to dismiss China's little grain of wisdom if Jack couldn't also remember scores of acts of kindness she'd seen.

Seth casually putting his own broad body between Asia and the worst of the wind. Rick lending the kid his car for a big date. The bruises and black eyes the whole Pepperell crew had proudly displayed after some muscle-bound tourist and his band of jerk friends had decided to amuse themselves by fighting with one of the locals.

Nobody but Ziggy would ever have put himself between Jack and trouble. Not because Jack didn't have friends, but because she'd never let them try to help her. Except for Ziggy. And now he was gone.

"You can make a family out of so many things," China said. "Friends, people you work with. People like us. We Pepperells are always ready to take one more onboard. Like to sail with a full crew. We always have."

For an instant Jack let herself wonder what it would be like to be taken in to China's raucous, loving family. To belong at Christmas dinner and birthday parties and clambakes on the shore, instead of enduring the torture of holidays at the Murphy family table. Everyone trying to think of something to say. Pretending they were just like all the other families carving turkeys up and down the block.

There were other places people had tried to take her in. The most impoverished huts in Africa. Tents nomads pitched in the desert, the way their ancestors had hundreds of years before. In India, where people had so little but offered what they possessed with joy in their hearts.

Come in—she could hear them offer in a score of different languages. *Warm yourself by our fire, fill your stomach with our food, cool yourself after your long, hot journey.*

They'd been offering so much more. Jack had nibbled on a bit of food so as not to offend them. She'd rubbed her hands by their fire, working the feeling back into stiff, half-frozen fingers. She'd drunk deep of their water or their wine, and left gifts to make up for whatever she took. Payment. And yet, you couldn't ever pay for the welcome in those simple people's eyes, the openness of their hearts, their courage at ushering others into their humble homes, risking mockery, cruelty, possible danger.

They'd awed Jack. Touched her heart. Showed her without words things she could never possess. Lives in many ways far richer than the one she'd chosen.

Maybe that was why she'd never been able to get her fill of shooting pictures of them—the simple people touched by war or famine. People who still dared to show decency even when they were surrounded by strife.

People China Pepperell would understand, belong with, far more than Jack ever could.

She smiled and nodded, not really hearing China say her good-byes. Jack closed the door, leaned against it for a moment before turning back to the interior of the lighthouse. But the glow of sunshine was gone, blocked by some wayward cloud. The house was silent again, still.

Just the way she liked it, Jack reminded herself. Maybe she'd eat her solitary dinner out by the cliff, or up at the top of the light tower, where the whole world spread out before her in a blanket of buildings and people and coast, stretching so far away.

3

Thunder crashed overhead, the weather-alert radio China always insisted be left on spitting out yet another rash of storm warnings through bursts of static. Jack flicked the radio off as she slipped wearily out of the closet she'd turned into a makeshift darkroom. Yeah, yeah, it was going to storm. But for once she was grateful the weather had given her an excuse to shut down operations, her equipment flickering on and off as the bad weather came rolling in.

One of the challenges of staying out on a cliff miles away from civilization was that the power lines were strung so far they were bound to take a beating. But this time, Jack had to admit, the imminent power outage was just as well. Her usual laserlike concentration had flown out the window, landed somewhere back in the middle of her talk with China Pepperell, or out on that strip of sun-kissed beach along with that glowing honeymoon couple or the old man and old woman, their faces still bright with love.

Happily ever after—okay, so her nine years of experience had taught her it *could* actually exist—for a select few. But not very many. Not for her. When she'd pulled out of her parents' driveway that long-ago summer on her mission to fill her portfolio, she'd been so sure of herself, so certain she was strong, tough, determined. What she'd really been was completely gullible, embarrassingly naïve. Now, whenever she thought about the girl she had been, she wanted to shake her until her teeth rattled. Tell her what an idiot she'd been, leaving herself open to the kind of pain her blind adoration for a man had earned her.

"You should've been falling on your knees in gratitude when things blew up instead of crying yourself sick," Jack grumbled to the kid she had been. "Things worked out the way they were supposed to. You realized your childhood dream. How many people get the chance to do that? If you'd married Tom Brownlow, you just would've ended up limiting yourself for him, ended up resenting him. And you would have despised yourself for selling out. You got just what you always wanted. And he made his own choices, too."

Maybe so, a voice prodded her, but his choices had promised disaster. Jack had seen firsthand what happened when people sold themselves out. Nobody won—not even if their reasons were the kind the world would call "noble." She only had to look at her mother to know that.

But then, Tom must have gotten something out of the situation or he wouldn't have plunged in. Who knew? Maybe he'd gotten what he'd wanted, after all.

At the moment, Jack just wished he'd get the blazes out of her head.

A knock sounded on the door. Jack made a face. Doubtless, China or some of her crew coming up to deliver armfuls of candles and oil for the kerosene lamps, and warn her it was going to rain. As if she couldn't see through the windows the storm clouds racing across the sky.

And of course, the "Pepperell of the day" would plead that she come down the narrow cliff road to weather the storm in the cozy rooms above the pub.

You never know when the storm could wash the lighthouse road out. You might not be able to get down from the cliff for days.

Ah, Jack had to resist saying, *but that was the beauty of it. No one could get* up *the road, then, either.*

Thunder clapped again, and she hurried toward the door. Seemed like the kind of storm where China or some of her brood could get stranded up here. That was the last thing she needed.

Another knock on the door. Must be the most eager of the Pepperell brothers. If Asia got stuck up here, she'd surely lose her mind. As his brothers were always saying—seventeen-year-old Asia could talk the shine off a brass doorknob.

"I'm coming," Jack called. She fumbled with the knob, swung the door open.

She blinked hard. Whoever it was, it sure wasn't Asia. The figure who stood with his back toward her was no gangly teenager. His body was unmistakably that of a man as he looked back toward the SUV parked in the lighthouse driveway. The wind molded his navy blue jacket around broad, hard-muscled shoulders that weren't strangers to hard physical work. Wavy black hair just a little too long skimmed a leather collar turned up against the wind. Long, runner's legs filled to perfection jeans worn soft and pale blue in all the right places, while scuffed boots braced hard against the buffeting of the wind.

Something about him tugged hard inside Jack—the

instinctive pleasure of an artist glimpsing a truly intriguing subject to capture in clay, on canvas or film. A challenge to see if her talent or creativity or inner vision would be strong enough, skilled enough or patient enough to do justice to so fine a subject.

For the first time since she'd trudged up to this lighthouse, Jack felt the burn of real enthusiasm in her veins.

The man turned, the stormy skies casting his face in shadows.

Jack flicked on the porch light, froze, excitement plummeting to cold shock as she stared into blazingly familiar brown eyes.

She hadn't faltered when rooftops had blown off mere yards from where she stood, but only years of practice kept her legs steady now. Tom Brownlow stood before her, as if she'd conjured him out of thin air.

Relentlessly masculine planes and angles framed a darkly tanned face far more mature than the one in her memory. A square chin jutted defiant at the world, its pure stubbornness belied by the unmistakable sensuality of his mouth. But it was his eyes that confused, tempted, entranced—dark, sensitive, strong, no stranger to either laughter or trouble, willing to stare either one full in the face. Yet bullheaded, too, stubborn enough to be blind when the truth was too brutal, unwilling to let other people make their own choices when in his so-wise opinion they might get hurt. That was one flaw Jack had never been able to forgive him.

What was it an African woman had once told her? That you could summon up evil spirits by dwelling on them in your mind. The man standing in front of her wasn't exactly evil, and was definitely too solid to be a spirit. In spite of that, Jack wished like hell she'd learned the African woman's spell for sending him back to wherever he came from.

Most aggravating of all was the differences in their reactions. While she felt as if she'd just been hit with a baseball bat, Tom looked past her into the lighthouse, so preoccupied it was as if he didn't see her at all. "Sorry to disturb you with the storm coming and all, but I was wondering if you had any rooms to rent?" he asked so civilly Jack wondered if she'd hit her head harder than she realized rummaging around under that staircase.

Time spun backward, images flashing in her mind like a slide show spun out of control.

A blazing hot Kentucky night when she'd just turned twenty-one, her lungs clogged with smoke she couldn't cough free. Soot and grime coated her skin, jeans and tee shirt while the stench of burned fur and panic swirled up from the crumpled, bleeding form clutched in her aching arms. Pain searing her toes as she kicked the metal door to the vet hospital with all her might.

She remembered footsteps, hollow beyond the steel door, shadows beyond the glass windowpanes of someone approaching.

Tears flowed down her cheeks, her hand burning where the terrified animal had bitten her before it realized she'd come to help. But even then, Jack had feared she was too late. The black-and-white Border collie weighed down her arms, blood oozing in spite of Jack's makeshift bandage, silky, furred head drooping as if the pup were too tired to hold on.

"Someone's coming. They're going to help you," Jack murmured to the animal, hoping she was right.

The clinic door swung open, a man in his mid-twenties towering over her, dark eyes exhausted in a face that could have made Mel Gibson jealous. Sexy features, intense, dark eyes, a mouth mingling the sensual and the sensitive above a stubborn, square-set chin.

"Help her!" Jack had croaked, thrusting the dog into his arms. "You have to help her. Something fell on her back legs, trapped her in a barn hit by lightning."

Dark eyes probed hers so deeply Jack could feel it in her toes. "You went into a burning building to save your dog?" he said, admiration in his face.

"Not my dog. A stray. I was taking pictures for my portfolio. Shooting an abandoned barn in the storm. Lightning struck the building and the whole thing turned to flame. I heard her crying, ran inside. She's nothing but skin and bones and terrified of everything."

"Except you." Warm, rich—his voice was as bracing as a quick shot of bourbon. Was it that sound or her ordeal charging into the burning building that made her suddenly light-headed?

"What's your name?" he demanded.

"Jack. Jacqueline Murphy."

He signaled her toward an examining table. As gently as possible, she set the collie down on its smooth, cool surface. "That was a damned brave thing to do," he said, taking a length of hot-pink stretchy gauze from his pocket and deftly twisting it around the dog's long muzzle to keep it from biting. "It was also a damned stupid one. You know nothing about this dog's temperament, its medical history. In its panic, it could have gone for your throat."

"Just my hand," Jack muttered under her breath, but the vet didn't hear her, he was too busy rummaging around on a nearby tray. Glass clinked, metal thunked softly, stiff paper underneath the instruments crackling.

He grabbed a hypodermic needle, drew medicine

into it from a clear glass bottle, then threaded the needle into one of the dog's veins. His mouth tightened in empathy when the dog gave a whimper. The vet murmured soothing words, stroking the collie as he finished with the injection.

"That should help with the pain," he said. Setting the syringe aside, he looked up at Jack, a deep crease between his dark brows. "I'm Dr. Tom Brownlow, a student here. Please tell me something, Jack Murphy. Tell me this dog didn't bite you."

Jack shoved her bloodied hands into the folds of her tee shirt. "I had to pull the dog to get her free from a wagon axle that had smashed down on her legs. I would have bitten me, too! So what? I'll heal."

She started as he grasped her wrists in both of his large, strong hands, drawing her fingers from the soot-smeared folds of her tee shirt, revealing them to the bright institutional lights blazing overhead.

Jack's own stomach churned a little as Tom Brownlow turned her hands over, revealing a pattern of puncture wounds, deep and filthy and oozing.

"Yeah. You'll heal all right," he said, deftly flushing the wounds with warm water. "But not until you've gone through a hell of an ordeal on your own."

"What are you talking about?"

"This dog is a stray," he explained gently. "No tags. No owner. No . . . rabies vaccine."

Even Jack knew what that meant. Her knees threatened to cave. He grasped her by the arm, eased her down onto a chair. "You're going to need a series of rabies shots—two weeks' worth."

Jack felt the blood drain from her face, her paranoia about needles kicking in full force. "I guess it will be worth it, if the puppy gets to live."

His face darkened.

"What is it?" she demanded harshly.

"One more problem we're going to have to sort out. The dog is a stray," he repeated. "That means there's no one to pay massive medical bills or help her through a long, grueling recovery. I hate the system as much as anyone, but the bottom line is that it doesn't seem fair to put the dog through the pain and suffering of surgery when we'll have to put her to sleep in the end anyway. There will be no one to help the dog learn how to get along with that mangled hip of hers. Seems more merciful to put her out of her misery as soon as possible. I'm sorry."

And Jack had known he really was. What neither one of them had expected was just how much more they would have to regret before the next two weeks were done.

Jack shook herself inwardly, trying to clear away the memories, focus on the present, as strange and surreal as it was. But the images from the past were still vivid. Her insistence that "Gracie" was her dog. The conspiratorial compassion in Tom's eyes that told her he knew she was lying. She'd had to assist in the surgery, since Tom was the only one left at the clinic. She still remembered the shape of his hands, long-fingered and deft like an artist's, as he set what was broken, stitched what was torn, healed what was hurting.

And later, while Gracie was recovering in his apartment, Jack had felt that tender touch on her own skin. She stared at him, trying to grasp the fact that nine years later, maybe a lifetime later, Tom was standing before her again, real again. And while he'd caused Jack's memory to flood with painful memories, her presence hadn't made Tom so much as flick an eyelash.

Don't let yourself get tangled up into some kind of a knot over this, Jack warned herself. *You don't have time or energy with the book deadline and Ziggy's death to deal with. So what if the man turned up on the doorstep of this blasted lighthouse? He can just go right back where he came from.*

She forced a smile. "Sorry, Tom. No room at the inn," she said, her voice sounding absurdly nonchalant even to her own ears. But then, she'd had lots of practice hiding her feelings. Plenty of times her life had depended on it.

Tom stiffened at the sound of his own name, his gaze finally fixing on Jack's face. He paled as if he'd seen one of China's ghosts. He took a half step back, recognition flashing into his eyes. "J—Jack? Is that . . . you?"

"Yeah, it's me. What a surprise, huh?" That should win the Pulitzer for understatement of the year.

He stared at her as if her face were a puzzle whose pieces didn't quite fit. As if he'd never seen her before. Maybe he hadn't. She could see his face shifting, emotions streaking across features even more stunningly handsome than she'd remembered. Was he recalling how horrified he'd been, discovering that she'd run short of money and was camping out in her '69 Mustang, hoping to capture that elusive masterpiece of a photograph that would open the door to the press corps, make people take her seriously? Too proud to ask her parents for more money, too stubborn to admit defeat.

He'd offered to let her crash at his student apartment until her wounds healed up, fully intending to do the honorable thing and keep his hands off of her. She was so damned young, unprotected; what he hadn't figured on was the hunger inside her, the eagerness in her or that she'd fall in love. How he'd be her first lover, and she'd be wild to learn all the sensual secrets of her newly awakened body and his harder, more experienced one.

"I was just coming to see if this place had been rented," he explained.

"As you can see, the lighthouse is taken—all mine for the next two months. I'm afraid you're out of luck. There are lots of places down in the village. You might be able to find someplace there."

"The village? No." He tensed. "No, thanks. I don't want to stay where . . ." He hesitated, and Jack sensed he wasn't going to finish what he'd started to say. "It's so—you know."

Actually, she had no idea what he objected to. Mermaid Lost was charming, nothing like those tourist traps Jack thought anyone should try to avoid like a bad haircut.

Jack shrugged. "Well, it's up to you," she said.

"Jack, how . . . how are you? How have you been?" he asked, as obviously unnerved as she was.

"Fine." The word had barely slipped out when Jack started imagining China's reaction to it.

"Listen, I don't mean to be rude, Tom, but I've never been real big on talking about old times. And, I'm in deadline hell. Howitzers aimed at my head from all over New York. So, sorry there's no room for you here. I'm sure you can find someplace to stay down in the village, at least until the storm passes. Guess I'll say good-bye." She started to shut the door, wanting a solid piece of wood between herself and memories his appearance was dredging up.

Tom's hand shot out, flattened on the door, held it open, his face harder, darker than she remembered it. "Wait. Please, Jack. Just give me a minute." He let his hand fall away from the wooden panel, squeezed his fingers into a fist, then released it. His eyes flashed once more to the vehicle parked on the crushed-shell driveway.

Jack's stomach sank like a cold stone. Someone was waiting in the car. Who else could it be besides the rest of the happy family? The woman Tom had chosen to marry leaving Jack brokenhearted and alone. The child that had been born seven months after Jack had left Kentucky, Tom and her dreams behind.

Jack scoffed inwardly. To think there had been a time she'd actually thought Tom was more tuned into people's feelings than any other man she'd ever known. Obviously wrong again.

"You could have saved yourself a lot of trouble by picking up the phone and calling to make a reservation before you drove all the way out here. Too bad you're inconvenienced, but when you just drop in somewhere on a whim, you're bound to be disappointed once in a while."

"I'm not just wanting to stay here on a whim," Tom protested. "There's a reason I need to stay here."

"Need to?" she cut in, wanting to get him the hell off the cliff as quickly as possible. "No, Tom—*I'm* the one who *needs* to stay here—and in peace and quiet. I'm doing a book about this place. I promised a friend that I would finish it on time. That's two months from now. So—"

The face she'd once loved tensed, as if his request were as difficult for him to stomach as it was for her. "I don't want to stay here," Tom admitted. "Hell, I'd rather be anywhere on God's earth than be here, even if you were three thousand miles away."

Why should it bother her that he wanted her on the other side of the world? Jack thought, oddly irritated. Wasn't that exactly where she wanted him? Back where he belonged, knee-deep in Kentucky bluegrass with all the wounded creatures he was always taking in.

"Jack, I don't want to be here, but my daughter does." He said it sharply, quickly, not hesitating for an instant, but then, he'd had years of medical experience. He knew if you were going to rip open an old scar it was better to do it quickly.

"This is the one place in the whole world Lucy wants to see."

Lucy—the little girl's name. She tried not to remember how much the child's existence had tortured her, how she'd spent her first few years racing around the globe trying not to wonder if the baby had Tom's dark eyes, or Tom's crooked grin.

"I'm sorry to disappoint you—and your daughter. But Lucy"—she forced herself to say the name aloud—"will have to just see the lighthouse some other time. I'm sure if you or Laura talk to the innkeeper, Mrs. Pepperell, there will be another time you and your—family can stay at Mermaid Lost."

"Laura's not in the picture anymore. We divorced five years ago."

Jack felt a rush of irritation. It had only taken him three years to get Laura's number? Too bad he hadn't figured it out when it could have made a difference.

Tom's jaw clenched, and he blinked fiercely, as if the wind had blown something into his eyes. He swiped the back of his hand over them, and Jack stilled, sensing something inside him, deep, far beyond that iron control.

"Daddy?"

Jack started as the word vanished in an uproar—a sudden thud, a high pitched cry as a small figure in yellow crashed into the antique milk box on the stone steps, knocking a tin pitcher full of wildflowers to the ground. Metal banged against stone, a small head clunked against a wooden pillar, a blur of little arms and legs flailing in the dim light. Tom wheeled, swooping the small bundle up into his tender grasp.

A little girl—small for her eight years—stared warily at Jack from her perch in her father's arms, embarrassment darkening freckle-spattered cheeks. With one bandaged finger, the child shoved a pair of thick, clear-framed glasses back up onto her small upturned nose. The glasses made her translucent green eyes seem far too big for her face.

Jack didn't move, but inside she reeled as if she'd just taken a blow to the solar plexus.

The child peered out at the world like a lost fairy, her solemn face framed against the crisp folds of her father's blue shirt. Jack tried not to flinch. The little girl was wearing a yellow tee shirt with one of those "Save the World" mottoes on it—a circle of endangered species frolicking about with smiles on their faces in hopes of a kinder, gentler world. Just the kind of thing Jack would expect Tom's daughter to wear. But it seemed the animal-loving banner on the shirt and the dimple in her left cheek was the only way the child resembled her father.

She'd seen Laura only once, in Tom's apartment the night "happily ever after" had fallen apart, and yet she'd never forgotten the face of the woman who had altered her life forever.

If someone flashed her a handful of photos of the exquisitely lovely Laura Willoughby and this child at the same age, Jack was sure she'd feel hard-pressed to tell them apart. The shoulder-length, tawny-gold hair, caught back in sparkly butterfly barrettes. The one slight difference between them was the light sprinkling of freckles dusting the little girl's delicate nose and the pair of clear-framed glasses that accented her expressive eyes. But Jack would bet the child's mother just covered a matching set with a fine layer of makeup. The girl clutched a wad of pink blanket sheepishly under one arm as she peered warily at Jack.

"Are you okay?" Tom asked, brushing at the child's dirt-covered knee with his free hand.

"Yeah," the girl said in a small voice. "At least this time I didn't break my glasses. I didn't break anything else, either. Good thing or this lady might not let me stay in the lighthouse. Right, Dad?"

"That's uh, what this lady and I are trying to clear up right now. I thought I told you to stay in the car until things were settled, Lucy."

But the child didn't seem much concerned about her father's gentle scolding. In spite of her age, Lucy snuggled against Tom, according him a level of fatherly trust Jack could scarce imagine possible.

"The thunder's getting close now," Lucy confided. "And it's dark. Real dark."

Tom glanced over his shoulder to where the lighthouse gardens lay, their colors blurred and dim. "You're right. It did get dark," he soothed. "I hadn't noticed or I wouldn't have left you out in the car."

Lucy flashed him a little smile.

"I'm sorry about knocking your pitcher over," she said to Jack. "Sometimes I clunk into stuff, especially when I'm running around after dark."

"No damage done," Jack said, unable to deny the genuine contrition in the little girl's face.

"Lucy, this is Jack—ah, Jacqueline Murphy," Tom introduced. "Jack, my daughter, Lucy."

The elfin face grinned. "Is this your lighthouse, Jack? It's the prettiest one we've seen all day."

"No. Mermaid Lost isn't mine. I'm just staying for a little while."

"Like Daddy and me, then. You're just visiting."

"No," Jack denied. "Not exactly."

"We can't stay at the lighthouse, Lucy. Jack has a very special job to do while she's here and not much time to do it in," Tom hastened to try to explain. "She travels all over the world. So her time here is very important."

"Oh."

Jack felt an odd twinge at the shadow that fell over the child's face. Lucy regarded her for a long moment in silence.

"I guess you don't go home much," Lucy said at last.

"Not much," Jack agreed. "I travel all the time. I have to go where there are things that people want pictures of." She stunk at explaining things in a way that a child could understand. But Lucy was staring up at her, her brow crinkled in concentration, her eyes intent and a little bit sad, as if it were strangely important to the little girl to try to understand.

"Like—well, the Pyramids," Jack ventured. "Even if I wanted to, I couldn't take pictures of the Pyramids here. I have to go where they are, in Egypt."

Obviously Jack hadn't cleared things up any. Lucy looked even more somber than before.

"Actually," Tom interrupted, "that's why Jack is here right now at this lighthouse. She's making a book about it."

Alarm streaked across Lucy's face, the little girl grabbing at Tom's arm. "But she can't do that! Mom is making a book about this place. That's like—like copying on a test, isn't it, Dad?"

Laura Willoughby writing a book? Jack had never figured the woman had written anything more than her signature on her daddy's charge card. Her surprise must have shown on her face.

Was it possible? Tom looked even paler, his face more tense than it had been a moment before. "It's not like copying at all. Jack's book is nothing like . . . Mom's. Jack's will be for grown-ups. Your mom's is—"

"It's for kids," Lucy informed Jack earnestly. "She's working so hard on it, I bet it will win all kinds of prizes and be in all the libraries and stuff." She sniffed, wistful. "It's taking a long time, though. Good thing she left me part of the story before it got finished so I can read it and pretend like she's with me."

So the child hasn't seen her mother in a long time then, Jack thought. Obviously Tom had custody, rare in itself. Weren't dads usually the ones trying to maintain relationships with their kids on occasional weekends and alternating holidays? There was no way Tom was spiteful enough to keep his daughter from having a relationship with her mother. Or was he? How would she know anymore? Eight and a half years could change people. She realized that every time she looked into the mirror.

Jack wondered what the story was. Tom tensed even more than moments before, the porch light revealing changes in him—a harder angle to his jaw, as if he were braced against a blow, deep lines etched at the corners of his eyes, bracketing his mouth, furrowing deep into his brow. What had changed him?

The changes in Tom couldn't be denied. He was a far different Lancelot from the man she once knew—no longer bright with enthusiasm, fresh, young, eager for battle. This man had seen the dragons win, suffered battles lost, learned just how hard it was to pick himself up and try again.

Tom shifted from foot to foot, obviously uncomfortable. "Jack's working hard on the book she's writing," Tom explained. "That's why we can't stay here at the lighthouse."

Jack winced inwardly at the child's crestfallen face. Tom had put Jack in a rotten position with his daughter, but the truth was that he was the one who had messed things up. It was too bad the kid was disappointed, but it wasn't Jack's fault.

Lucy looked up at Jack solemnly. "If you let me come in the lighthouse, I promise, I won't even talk if it would disturb you. Working on books is a real hard thing, I know. You can't do it with kids bothering you.

"I wouldn't care what lighthouse I got to see, except, well," Lucy straightened her barrette, confiding, "my mom stayed here when she was a little girl."

Jack tensed, hating the sharp intrusion of Laura's presence into this place Ziggy had loved. Hating the vividness of Tom's face and Lucy's pleading eyes now inextricably linked with Mermaid Lost. One more reason to finish this project as fast as possible and get out of Maine for good.

Lucy peered up so hopefully Jack doubted that even the most hard-hearted journalist in the world could have completely resisted her. "I even know what bed my mom slept in," Lucy said, shifting her glasses to rub at one eye as if it were irritated by dust, then blinking to clear it. "I'd just like to peek at it."

Jack caught a glimpse of Tom out of the corner of her eye, old pain and new irritation stirring. She would have sent him packing and taken pleasure in it if it hadn't been for his little girl. Jack turned her attention to the kid.

"Go peek all you want to, Lucy," Jack offered. After all, what could it hurt? She could have a quick look around, and then she could get back into the car with her father and drive away from Mermaid Lost without even looking back.

"Really? Can I?" Lucy's cheeks flushed with excitement as she glanced up at her father, asking for permission. Tom nodded, his face filled with a mixture of love and pain and regret so sharp it made Jack's heart hurt in spite of her fierce determination to keep her distance until father and daughter were gone.

Jack expected Lucy to bolt off the instant she got permission. But those great green eyes stared up at Jack with an earnestness far beyond her years.

"I promise I won't touch anything," Lucy assured Jack. "I'm real, real careful." She frowned for a moment, uncertain. "See, I drop things sometimes, or knock them over. I don't mean to, it's just, sometimes it's hard to see—you know, in the gray times, when it's just getting dark."

Jack winced at the memory of the child's flushed face when she'd fallen minutes ago, the shame in it, the humiliation. Emotions Jack's father had incited in her whenever he got the chance. The last thing Jack wanted was any kind of shadow over the kid's brief pleasure here tonight.

"The lady who used to live in this place had eight boys. Six of them grew up here," Jack reassured. "There's not much around here anyone can break."

Lucy's eyes flickered with gratitude. "That's good to know," she said, giving Jack a smile, all the sweeter because it was so grave. Lucy turned, her hair a waterfall of tawny gold down her back as she walked carefully down the hall, mindful of everything around her as she turned the corner and vanished from sight. Jack was the first to admit she knew nothing about kids. Still, there was something about Lucy's behavior that seemed just a little off-key.

"Jack, I appreciate this—" Tom shook her from her thoughts, his voice low. She could hear shades of that sincerity she'd once been certain was Tom's alone. But that had been a long time ago when she'd believed in happily ever after.

Did Tom see those shadows in her eyes? He chafed, ill at ease. "It was kind of you to let Lucy poke around in here. It will mean a lot to her."

"I'm not a complete monster, you know." She wasn't sure who she was aiming that information at— Tom or herself. "You still should have called first. You could have saved us both a fair amount of discomfort. I didn't want to see you again."

"I know. Don't blame you. If I had known you were here . . ." Tom gazed down at her with eyes wounded as his daughter's, but without the blessing of Lucy's naïveté. Jack steeled herself against him as he spoke. "I guess I don't know anything about you now," Tom said. "I barely even recognized you when you opened the door. You've changed, Jack."

"I certainly hope so after eight and a half years!" Jack tried not to mind the disappointment in his eyes. "I was a starry-eyed kid back then. I've seen the real world since."

"Maybe too much of it." The insight astonished her, annoyed her. She curled in on herself even tighter.

"You can't see too much of what's real. Closing yourself off from the ugliness doesn't mean it's still not out there."

"But you can't stare into that kind of ugliness all the time," Tom argued. "I still volunteer at the animal shelter, take care of their abuse and neglect cases. It's important work, and I'm glad I can do something to help, but if I never did anything else, I'd get so depressed or so hardened to it I wouldn't be able to stand myself. I know it's necessary for you to do what you do. But if I were in your position, I don't think I could do it all the time."

"Well, that's where we're different. Luckily it doesn't bother me at all," Jack said with a wave of her hand. "I have a high tolerance for cynicism. But there are plenty of people even in my line of work who would agree with you. My partner used to tell me—" She stopped, startled at herself. Since the day Ziggy had died, she'd been trying to avoid speaking of him at all costs.

Even so, she couldn't deny the truth, at least to herself. Ziggy had always been insisting she needed to get a different perspective from the one she found at the end of her viewfinder.

"Maybe I should go find Lucy," Tom said, looking even more uncomfortable. "I don't want her to—uh—get into trouble on her own."

He was genuinely worried, as if the kid could get lost or something! The lighthouse wasn't nearly that big or confusing. Simple rooms, simply furnished, with obvious paths to follow back to the front door. But then in the brief time since Tom Brownlow had come into Jack's life, she'd seen plenty of evidence how careful he was, how fiercely protective, how eager to shield anyone he judged to be less competent than he was. Trying to balance things exactly, control every variable so no one could stumble or fall, even if they needed to after a long, wild run. Obviously that much hadn't changed about him, unfortunately for his little girl. But there was something more, something deeper, more dangerous just beneath the surface.

Her eyes narrowed as she watched Tom walk away, following his daughter. Something was wrong. She sensed it the way she had the ambush in the Congo, something just out of whack to send her intuition spinning. Ziggy had dismissed her nervousness the night he was killed, and she'd lost him because of it. But this time was different. Whatever trouble was stalking Tom Brownlow and his daughter had nothing to do with Jack, wasn't her problem. She'd known Tom a lifetime ago. Loved him for a time beautiful as it was brief, painful as it was wondrous. Then she'd let it go. Blocked it from her mind so that it held no power over her, no regrets, no self-loathing, no lingering of grief in a heart she'd closed up tight.

So maybe his unexpected arrival here had put a few cracks in that hard, desperately needed shell. She'd seal them back up the instant he drove down the lighthouse road and out of her life where he belonged.

She tipped her head to one side, listened to footsteps echoing through the stone lighthouse, Lucy's careful, soft movements. But Tom's heavy strong tread pressed into something far deeper than the stone hallways and bright-scrubbed rooms. Memories even Jack could no longer control. She tried hard not to feel the imprint of his hands on her body, the heat of his mouth mating with hers, the wild passion of first times, first dreams, first heartbreaks. And the hard-edged, fiercely determined expression on his face that long-ago night he'd walked away and left her alone.

4

Tom followed the muffled sounds of his daughter's footsteps, and tried to mask the feelings rolling through him. Disillusionment, disappointment, his shock at seeing Jack again. Beautiful, God yes, she was still beautiful, with that lithe, willowy body and small, firm breasts he could remember just filled his hands. The deceptively delicate oval of her face was just a trifle thinner, while those wide fiercely intelligent eyes were still so blue a man could swim in them.

Most unnerving of all was her damned defiant rose of a mouth, so soft and sexy it stunned a man when she snapped out her opinion, made him want to argue with her just to see the fire ignite in her eyes. Passionate, bursting with life and enthusiasm and determination to make the world a better place, never afraid to disagree or fight for what she believed was right. Jack was still the strongest woman he'd ever known.

And yet, all her strength, sexiness and raw capability had been sweetened eight and a half years ago by just a touch of naïveté, a soft heart few would ever be allowed to see, all too easily wounded by other people's sorrows.

But the woman who had met him at the lighthouse door was far different than the Jack he remembered. Nothing but a stranger, whose face vaguely resembled the girl he'd once loved, but whose eyes belonged to someone else entirely. A grown woman, cool and steady, without passion, without light, without that rare eagerness to embrace life that had been Jack's alone.

He wished he hadn't seen her, had never known just how much she'd changed. But there was no way he could close his eyes to the differences in her now. No way he could hold on to his belief that she was out there in the world somewhere with her camera, living life to the fullest. Making a difference, opening people's eyes to the good in the world, inspiring them to change what was bad—affecting people's hearts and minds the way she'd dreamed of doing since she was a kid. He'd wanted that for her so much. But it was as if every glimpse she'd had of a tiny Armageddon somewhere in the world had shaved away another piece of the woman he'd known and left someone else in her place.

And if his feelings about Jack weren't unsettling enough, he had other emotions to deal with as well. Most disturbing of all, a stealthy sense of guilt, self-loathing at the relief he couldn't quite stamp out when Jack had firmly said no to Lucy's request to stay at the lighthouse.

It was true that he'd tried his best to grant Lucy's wish. Did that mean that he was a rotten father because he couldn't help but be grateful things had turned out the way they had? They weren't staying here. They would be leaving Mermaid Lost. One small but vital blessing.

He and Lucy could just climb back into the SUV, pop

another installment of the Harry Potter books into the tape deck, and drive away. Away from this lighthouse holding a Jack so very altered, worlds different from the girl who'd abandoned her camera on an isolated hill to help a dog she'd never seen before. Away from the streets and sea-swept cottages Laura had loved before her life spun out of control. Away from people whose minds were full of memories of her, people who might know secrets Tom had tried to keep, truths he had tried to shelter Lucy from.

No matter how hard he tried to conceal things, Lucy would eventually learn the truth. He knew that, with a cold, sick dread. But not yet. Lucy had already been through so much. She had enough to sort through without adding even more. She wasn't ready. And neither was he. He had to have just a little more time.

And the last thing on earth that he needed was for Lucy to sense he was keeping something from her. She had always had both the gift and the curse of being able to key in to his moods too easily. And the grim months of tests and specialists, hospitals and painfully fading hopes, had only honed her ability even more sharply until almost nothing got past those solemn green eyes.

Sometime during the past months since her diagnosis, Lucy had started trying to take care of *him*, comfort him, soothe him. *It's not so bad, Daddy. You don't have to worry.*

He didn't have to worry, she was always insisting. She'd be fine. She'd train the dog. She'd get to listen to books on tape and could just lie there, imagining, and never even have to turn the page. She'd already counted the steps to her best friend Jenny's house. Three hundred and twenty-seven, as long as she didn't see Mr. Larson's new puppy and get so excited she lost count.

"Hey, there, Kitten, what do you think of the

place?" he asked, using the pet name he'd given her when she was a tiny little thing, toddling around with a kitten's boundless curiosity and wide, busy eyes.

"I think this is the one Mom described in her book even though it's changed. You can see where the big beds used to be, all in a row. The carpet's lots darker there. And there's the window the boys always fought over. See those little hooks up there, near the ceiling? That's where they'd hang the curtain when Mom spent the night here. So she had her own private place, just like a princess. They always gave her the window so she could be close to the sea."

Lucy went to the casement, opened it, and leaned against the stone sill. "Bet if it wasn't all stormy, you could see all the wrecks out there. Lots and lots of them, with pirate treasures inside."

"I don't think you can see the ships, sweetheart. At least, not the pirate ships. They were made of wood, and sank a long time ago. The ocean would have gobbled them up."

"Oh, they're still out there. Mom said." Her face glowed with a child's absolute certainty. "In her book, Abigail was going to bring the treasure up."

The "book," one more project Laura had been obsessed with for a few weeks, before she threw it into a bottom drawer, abandoned as her interest leaped to something else she'd never finish. Hobbies she'd abandoned almost as carelessly as she had mothering their little girl.

Bitterness left a bad taste in Tom's mouth. Leave it to Laura to make this as complicated as possible once she walked out the door, to leave behind subtle poisons to make it even harder for Lucy to understand what had happened to her family.

Had she really forgotten the spiral notebook half-filled with scribbles in that drawer where Lucy had found it? Or had Laura left it there on purpose, hoping to worm her way into Lucy's heart and mind, even when Laura was no longer around.

Tom wished to hell he had found the tattered notebook before Lucy had and burned it. But it was too late to get rid of the thing now. Lucy treasured the ratty mess of a half finished story as if it were priceless. The handwritten pages were crumpled and smeared now, read and reread, the picture of Laura tucked inside it dog-eared. Lucy's greatest treasure except for her beloved pink blanket with the bunny Tom's mother had embroidered in the corner. Lucy had spent years now, sleeping with that notebook tucked safe under her pillow, dreaming about the mother she couldn't remember.

Thank God, Tom thought.

The story about summers at Mermaid Lost lighthouse had become Lucy's only contact with Laura—a shadowy Laura, a ghost—one that might soon transform back into someone very, very real.

Tom stifled a curse as a clap of thunder startled him, so loud the windows rattled. Lucy jumped. "That scared me," she said, with a shiver. "Daddy, do you think pirates were ever scared of storms?"

Storms like the one Laura might well bring back into Lucy's life? Tom thought, tensing. But he fought to keep his emotions hidden from his too-perceptive daughter.

"They must have been scared," he mused. "They knew what storms could do to their ships. How the winds and rain could blow them off course. It's all right to be afraid as long as you keep sailing."

Lucy shot him a long-suffering glance. "Daddy, I'm asking about pirates, not about me. I'm not scared."

Thin fingers rubbed at her temple, a sure sign she was getting tired, needed to rest her eyes, not that she would ever admit it.

Tom made an effort to bury the worry gnawing inside him. He ruffled her hair and smiled. "You know you don't have to be scared," he said. "Not ever." *I'm scared enough for both of us,* a voice inside him whispered as the rain came pouring down.

The suddenness of it startled him almost as much as the sudden thudding of footsteps rushing toward them down the corridor. Jack appeared in the doorway, breathless.

"I'm really sorry to have to cut this short, but you'd better head out before the rain really hits."

"But—but I haven't been up in the tower yet," Lucy pleaded, her desperate wish to see the place obviously overriding her innate shyness. "I wanted to lean on that little rail Mom talks about and look for the pirate ghosts. I promise I'll hurry."

"There won't be enough time for you to get up those stairs and still get down in time to leave the lighthouse before the storm hits. The road down to town is dangerous enough when it's just dark," Jack said to Tom more than to Lucy. "And in the rain it can be downright treacherous. Or nonexistent. Every so often, it washes out completely."

Jack felt more than a twinge about disappointing Lucy. Tom could see it in her face. But they'd both feel a lot worse if they got stranded up here on the cliff together for who knew how long. He had enough ghosts to battle, enough threats to face without adding one sharp-eyed photojournalist to the list. Jack might as well be a stranger, considering all the time that had passed, and yet—one who'd made a fortune delving beneath the surface of people's hearts to find the bleeding core underneath. And that was a place he wanted no one to probe.

"Hey, Daddy?" Lucy's eyes lit up, a little guilty, a little hopeful. "Maybe it's too dangerous already," she suggested. "Maybe we'd better just stay here until the storm is all over."

"Nice try, kiddo, but Ms. Murphy has already nixed any idea of having company. And we still have to find somewhere to stay for the night," Tom said, folding his hands gently over her narrow shoulders and urging her toward the door.

With any luck the storm would hold off long enough for them to drive someplace far enough away that there was little danger of someone seeing Lucy's face and recalling the troubled girl who had once made this her summer home.

But in spite of his efforts to herd his daughter along, Lucy hung back. Her gaze darted around the room, and Tom could feel the intensity in her, her desperate attempt to commit the place to memory. That trapped sensation Tom hated welled up inside him.

Okay, so he was a selfish jerk, being grateful that he could get her out of here so quickly. And yet, he knew all too well the kind of damage that could have been done if they'd stumbled across the wrong person who had said the wrong thing. Things he'd spent the past eight years trying to protect her from. Somehow, he'd find a way to make up for her disappointment about not staying at the lighthouse.

He had to take hold of her hand to gently, firmly, lead her toward the exit, Lucy hanging back as much as she could, trying, Tom knew, to squeeze out one more minute. He stopped at the green painted door, turned, struggling to figure out what to say to the woman watching him with such worldly-wise eyes.

"Thank you for letting us come in, Jack. It was . . ." Good to see her? It hadn't been. "Take care of yourself," he finished instead.

Her chin bumped up a notch, a poignant reminder of the determination, the strength and courage in her that he'd once admired. But that was before he'd learned how dangerous it could be to run with the bit in your teeth, before he'd seen how many lives could get trampled on the way.

"Taking care of myself is what I do best," she said, almost as if she could sense his censure of the kind of life she chose to live.

She oozed success, intelligence, ambition. But she hadn't always been so hard, so cold, so sure of herself.

Regret clenched inside him. What if he hadn't done it? What if he'd stopped her instead of sending her away so many years ago, found some other way to . . . ?

But there hadn't been any other way, Tom reminded himself with ruthless honesty. Even then they had been too different, chafing against each other, tempers flaring. The hard truth was that he'd only known Jack for a couple of weeks. Maybe he'd never known the real Jack at all. This woman, all hard edges and cutting wit—she exhausted him. Disillusioned him. What kind of wife would she have been? What kind of mother?

No, there was nothing soft in Jack anymore, no sign of the deeply caring woman who'd come away from a burning barn with a stranger's neglected dog in her arms. No sign of the Jack who had confided in him that she'd bungled lovemaking the first time she'd tried it, almost embarrassed because she didn't quite know what to do and she hated it when people knew more about anything than she did.

"Good-bye, Ms. Murphy. Thank you for letting me

see your house," Lucy said earnestly. "Don't worry about the rain. You couldn't help it."

Absolution from an eight-year-old. Jack looked at Tom's little girl, nonplussed.

"Good-bye, Lucy. Have a great trip with your dad. Now, you need to hurry."

She looked as if she wanted to shove them out the door and give the car a push down the hill. But even Jack couldn't bring herself to be that rude.

Later, Tom would look back and wish she had. The moment he and Lucy started out the door the rain changed, shifted, the pattering drops drenching them in a deluge of cold water before they got three steps from the door.

"Come on, Luce, run for it!" he urged her, but Lucy hung back, wide-eyed, afraid. The sky was a mess, wild black and green, clouds swirling, waves crashing.

Shipwreck weather, Laura had called it.

Still, the storm had just started. Surely they could make it down to the mainland before the road got too bad. He managed to maneuver Lucy into the car, helping her open it because he knew in the dark she had trouble seeing the handle. He slammed her door shut and then ran around to his own side. He flung open the door, meant to slide into his seat when a hand closed over his arm.

He turned, saw Jack, her hair plastered to her head, rain running in miniature rivers down her pale face.

"It's too late," she told him.

"We'll be okay. This thing has four-wheel drive. It can get through anything."

As if in answer, lightning split the sky.

"It won't do you any good if you can't see and veer off the road. It's a twenty-yard drop with rocks at the bottom."

"Daddy, the car's getting all wet inside."

He could hear Lucy's worried cry.

He looked at Jack, then tried to make out what had once been a ribbon of crushed-shell road. The rain gushed down, already making rushing streams out of the ruts.

If Tom had been by himself he would have taken the risk, at least attempted to get off of this slender finger of land. Especially if it meant getting away from Jack.

Tom's stomach tightened. *It's dangerous to stay here,* a voice inside him whispered. He'd known of the risk even before he and Lucy had pulled out of their driveway back home. *Here at Mermaid Lost there were too many chances for things to get even more tangled up than they already were.*

Stop it, Tom warned himself. He didn't have to worry, at least not for tonight. It was obvious Jack knew nothing of Laura except for that brief time years ago when they'd faced off in his apartment. Jack didn't know about Laura's past here at the lighthouse, not her illness, or the ultimate price it had cost them all. No, that much was safe, at least.

With one last, longing glance at the barely visible road, he surrendered. "Grab your suitcase, Lucy," he said. "Looks like you're going to get your wish to stay at Mermaid Lost after all."

Lucy snatched up her overnight bag, then fumbled with the car door. Tom fought the urge to run and help her.

Let her keep doing things for herself, the doctors had cautioned. She has to learn new ways to cope and she *will*, as long as people around her don't convince her that she is helpless.

Tom wondered if the doctor, with his two perfectly

sighted children, had any idea how hard it was to do what he was asking.

Lucy gave a skip of excitement when she thought no one was looking, and Tom knew she'd try hard not to gloat when she knew that Jack didn't want them there.

Maybe this whole fiasco would turn out all right after all, Tom thought. After everything he and Lucy had been through lately, spending one night under the same roof as Jack Murphy should be no big deal.

In fact, maybe in a way their meeting could give him a closure he hadn't even known he needed. As for this Jack Murphy—the one he'd met tonight—he would never have loved her at all. Might not even be able to like her.

When had she lost the Jack he had known? he wondered. Where had she been when she peeled away the layers of her passion for life and threw them away?

He'd lost her eight and a half years ago when he sent her out of his life. It was ridiculous to feel the change in her so deeply tonight. Almost as if he had lost her all over again.

Lucy scrambled back to the lighthouse, stumbling and sliding on the rain-slick ground as Tom dug the rest of their bags out of the car. He caught his breath as she almost went down once, twice, heaved a sigh of relief as she disappeared into the green painted doorway.

But before he could turn back to the car, he stiffened, a crash sounding nothing like thunder erupting from the house.

"Luce!" Tom dumped the leather bags into the fresh mud and sprinted toward the house. Lucy was sprawled in a tangle of table and chairs and mud-sodden brochures about the lighthouse, a glass figure of a lighthouse shattered around her. He froze, not wanting to startle Lucy into jerking around, cutting herself on the broken glass.

Jack was already moving toward Lucy.

"Don't move," Jack ordered, surprisingly low, calm, as she picked her way through the wicked shards of glass and lifted the little girl free of it. Lucy blinked back tears, her small face crumpling in that bewildered, chagrined look Tom hated.

"You didn't have to run *that* fast," Jack said, awkwardly brushing tears from under Lucy's reddening eyes. "It's not like I was going to lock the door on you if you didn't get in quickly enough. Oh, well. It's just a little accident."

"No. Not a little one." Lucy sniffed. "A big one and they just get bigger and bigger."

"Next time you'll be more careful," Jack said.

"I can't be more careful. And there've been so many next times I'm sick of it. It's my stupid eyes. They don't work right and even my glasses can't fix them."

Lucy flung the glasses across the room, blessedly landing them on the couch cushions.

"Lucy," Jack said, stunned at the desperation in the child's outburst. "It's not that big of a deal."

"Yes it *is* a big deal! The biggest deal ever. You know why I wanted to come here, to see the lighthouse and lots of other stuff?" the child demanded, suddenly so woebegone it broke Jack's heart. "Because I'm going blind and not even my daddy can stop it."

5

⚭

Lucy's cry echoed in the sudden, terrible quiet of the room, Tom stunned to silence at his child's revelation to a stranger, Jack dead still, mute. Her expression might even have been funny under different circumstances, Tom thought. One of the few times in life when Jack Murphy didn't know what to say.

Tom held his arms out instinctively for his little girl, and Lucy came to him, sobbing softly as he gathered her tight to his chest. She buried her face in his shoulder.

"I threw my glasses away. I wish I could throw them away forever and ever."

"I know, baby," Tom murmured. "I do, too."

He stroked her silky hair, drinking in the warmth of her, the sweet, fresh scent of baby shampoo on her hair, wishing he could make time stand still. "Let's not think about that right now," he suggested. "Let's just think about which room you're going to sleep in tonight and what the ocean will look like when you peek out the window."

Lucy snuffled, rubbing her eyes against his shirt,

leaving damp, teary places behind. She lifted her head, and looked into his face. "Do you think I could sleep where Mommy did? Where I can see the ocean all night and hear it sing to me?"

Tom shot Jack a pleading glance.

"Sure," Jack agreed uncomfortably. "I sleep all the way on the third floor. As long as you don't take that room, I don't care where you sleep. Make yourself at home—for tonight, anyway."

Tom crossed to retrieve the hated glasses from the couch, then tenderly settled them on his daughter's freckled nose. She grimaced, but didn't protest. "How about if you head upstairs and stake out your new digs?" he suggested. "That way Ms. Murphy and I can get a few things settled. House rules and stuff."

Lucy wiped her nose on the sleeve of her shirt, and gave Jack a look that would have melted Tom's heart.

"Thank you for letting me and Daddy stay. I'm sorry I broke your statue and threw my glasses. I just get mad sometimes, no matter how hard I try not to."

"Don't worry about it," Jack said. "Sometimes I get mad, too."

Lucy smiled back, and disappeared up the stairs, leaving heavy silence in her wake.

Jack spoke first. "Tom, I—I'm so sorry about Lucy. I can only imagine how hard this is for you."

Hard? That was the understatement of the year. And yet, Jack's empathy touched him. Until she squared her shoulders, tipped up her chin.

"I'm afraid Lucy's condition doesn't change my decision," she said. "I'm sorry, but I have to get this book done, and there's no way I can do it with people rattling around in my personal space. She's welcome tonight, but tomorrow you'll both have to go."

He stared at her, wishing she'd been different, softer,

more compassionate, ready to fight for what was right, like a little girl who was going blind spending the week of her dreams here at Mermaid Lost. But then, he was remembering Jack as she had been—soot-smeared and smelling of smoke, her hand bleeding from a dog bite. He doubted she ran into burning buildings like that anymore, and if she did, he was sure she never forgot her camera.

"I understand," he said, running his fingers through thick, coffee-colored hair.

He wished to hell he didn't. The Jack he'd known was gone, but then so was the man he had been—eight and a half years ago when he couldn't get enough of her lithe, generous body, her wild, brave spirit and that all too brief passion that had changed them both.

Candlelight cast shadows on Jack's bedroom wall, drafts from the onslaught of storm rattling the windows and making the flames waver on their wicks. But even though the candles flickered, Jack preferred the scent of beeswax and the soft glow so like the primitive places she loved, rather than the hard glare of the battery operated lantern China kept in the room for just such emergencies.

It came as no surprise, the lights going out up here on the cliff. And yet, somehow tonight the darkness made the walls seem closer, the air thicker with the presence of other people in her space.

With every breath she took she was aware of Tom Brownlow and his daughter just one floor below her. True, they had been quiet for hours now, the soft sounds of voices, the rhythm of footsteps, the clink of dishes being washed and dried and put away finally stilled. But somehow those long-faded noises haunted Jack even in the silence.

The two of them must be long asleep by now, and Jack wished that she could join them, but sleep was the one thing she couldn't do.

It wasn't that the meeting with Tom had unsettled her *that* much, she reassured herself. It was just one of those nights she'd become familiar with during her years of globe-trotting with her camera. Nights when every fiber in her body pulled tight, every sensation heightened until it grew almost painful. Light and noise, taste and smell, even the feeling of clothes touching her skin rasped against her nerves.

At least tonight she knew where the edginess was coming from. Lucy Brownlow, wide green eyes that wouldn't always be able to see, a desperate plea from a father who couldn't shield his daughter from the darkness that was stalking her.

And the hard, practical decision Jack had had to make so that she could do her job. It hadn't been easy to lay the truth on the line with Tom, tell him that he and Lucy would have to leave in the morning. Jack just didn't want the boundaries to get blurry, leave room for yet another uncomfortable scene.

But maybe she was losing a little bit of her edge. Her decision *had* bothered her, and so had the battle-weary expression in Tom Brownlow's eyes.

Jack caught her lip between her teeth, fighting the shiver of awareness rippling through her, as if his mere presence could breach the floor between them and leave her physically aching for hands on her skin, hot breath at her throat, kisses so deep she felt like she was melting.

Ridiculous, Jack grumbled inwardly. She didn't even know Tom anymore, after eight and a half years. She was burning up because of the memory of a man who didn't exist anymore and sex that probably hadn't been as great as she thought it was, embellished as it had been by time.

Even so, it was far too easy to remember what it felt like to press herself against Tom's hard body, feel the tantalizing brush of his chest hair against her nipples. Reach down between them and find him there, full and ready and wanting her. In her years of worldly experience had any other man's touch even come close?

No. Because she'd been twenty. In love with love. Scooped up on Sir Lancelot's charger and rescued as if she'd been starring in some sort of fairy tale. And she'd believed in one soul mate for everyone, love charted in the stars binding hearts so strongly that mere human mistakes couldn't screw things up.

It had been wonderful to believe so completely—a roller coaster ride of pleasure, excitement, fulfillment and dreams. That was, until the roller coaster crashed into a hard wall of reality.

Jack cursed under her breath. The last thing she needed at the moment was a nightlong instant replay of the hours she'd spent in Tom Brownlow's arms.

She would have killed for the oblivion of sleep or for Ziggy's dry humor to at least distract her. He'd been the only person she'd ever been able to bear knowing about her restless nights. Not that there was any way she could've kept the secret from him even if she'd wanted to, considering how many nights they'd spent together on assignment out in the middle of nowhere.

Ziggy had never made a big deal out of it when she was on the ragged edge. He hadn't tried to comfort her or tell her it was okay. He'd just laid his hand on her shoulder. Listened if she wanted to talk. Stayed silent if she didn't. But either way, he'd sit quietly on guard until she'd drifted to sleep.

Once she'd asked him how he'd known what to do.

He'd told her he'd had dark shadows, too, until he'd started filling the leather bag he wore around his neck with talismans of his own.

His medicine bag—he'd believed in it so strongly. Jack couldn't even count how many times she'd seen his fingers smoothing over its bumpy surface, as if assuring himself that the treasures inside the bag were real.

He'd challenged her to start a bag of her own, even given her a lovely one he'd made with his own uneven stitches. He'd put a picture of the two of them inside it, the image, the day she'd conned him to take her with him on an assignment when she had no experience, no agency to publish her work, only a desperate need to get on with her life and leave memories of lost love behind.

But she'd never followed through with Ziggy's suggestion, never filled her own bag with things to believe in. She told Ziggy it was because she didn't have time. But she knew the truth. The magic in a medicine bag had always been rooted in the owner's belief, faith in that power for good. Somewhere on the journey she'd traveled, she'd lost the ability to believe in anything except herself—and since that fateful day in the jungle, she'd lost even that.

She paused for a moment, half-tempted to go to her bottom drawer, dig beneath the piles of clothes to the small box she kept there. Ziggy's bag was there, now. She only wished, somehow, he'd been able to leave a little bit of his faith behind, too.

Jack crossed to the window, tried to peer out, but the view was too small. On impulse, she grabbed one of the battery operated lanterns, then blew out her candle and stole silently into the hallway.

As she made her way through the silent house, she

hoped Tom and Lucy were asleep in the two rooms she'd given them below, unaware of her restlessness.

The wildness of the storm called to Jack, drawing her up the wrought-iron stairs, spiraling round and round until she climbed as high as she could go.

She pushed the trapdoor open, stepped up onto the narrow platform where the keeper of the light had kept vigil on nights like this two hundred years before. Warning ships away from the shoals, rescuing the crews of vessels that had veered too close to the treacherous rocks off Mermaid Lost.

The thick windowpanes that had once protected the precious light from the dousing winds and rain rattled now, the narrow walkway around it slippery and wind-battered and, to Jack, completely irresistible. Jack opened the portal and slipped outside into the wild, primitive beauty of the storm.

She fought back shivers as icy rain drenched her and crossed the few steps to the very edge of the walkway. Leaning over the guardrail, she stared out at the waves piercing their silver-white breasts on the rocks, imagined the lighthouse keeper trying to keep control of his wild domain, warn ships off to safety, rescue those who strayed too close to the rocks. A weathered savior in oilcloth and tall rubber boots.

She wished one of the old keepers could sweep in now, pull her free of the memories Tom Brownlow's presence had unleashed in her tonight, eased the deep ache she felt for the child she should have hated. The child Laura had been pregnant with when she staggered into Tom's apartment years ago. The child Tom had unknowingly fathered before Jack had come into his life.

What a rotten trick of fate—the two of them arriving at Mermaid Lost. Leaving Jack with one more set of emotions to deal with when she was already holding herself together with duct tape and baling wire.

If she hadn't been dealing with the aftermath of Ziggy's death, seeing Tom again wouldn't have affected her nearly this much, she assured herself. It was all ancient history, two weeks of craziness brought on by overactive hormones—and, maybe, the novelty in the way Tom had treated her, with kindness, respect—at least until it looked like those dreams of hers were going to put her in harm's way.

Even before he'd shown up at Mermaid Lost, she would have admitted that there were times she'd thought of him while she'd roamed in faraway places. The occasional dream she'd wake up from with a start, sweat-sheened and unfulfilled. The brief sting when she saw a dark-haired man bending tenderly to kiss some other woman. Or the tiny ache in the middle of her chest, that pride should have blotted out—pride at her independence, her self-sufficiency, her strength.

Of course there had been memories that burned, actions that had made her blush, regrets she hadn't been able to completely get free of when it came to her first real love affair. Didn't everyone have a certain awkwardness concerning that time in their lives?

But actually seeing Tom again shouldn't have rocked her the way it had. And seeing the daughter that had cost her so much—even that shouldn't have unsettled her so deeply. It wasn't as if she'd had delusions of still being in love with Tom after all these years.

A gust of wind buffeted her, and she gave a sigh of disappointment. Time to head back inside. The storm was waning now, just a whisper, but she could sense it, feel it. Just the slightest dip in the wind's force, the once-heavy drops of rain easing. Soon the sky would clear, the ocean calm, the sun would shine, the storm past.

The storms inside her would pass, too. In time, she'd find a woman back to the way she used to be. She'd find confidence again, brazen courage. She'd find the fierce drive to excel that had always been a part of her. She'd find that certainty she'd once had that she was doing the right thing in the work to which she'd devoted her life. She'd banish Tom Brownlow back to where he belonged, the shadows of a past she'd done her best to forget. And once she'd managed all that, maybe, just maybe, she'd be able to forgive herself for what had happened in the jungle the night that Ziggy Bartolli had died.

Jack combed her fingers through her towel-dried hair in an effort to tame it down a little as she made her way downstairs. The storm had left her in dire need of a cup of tea, but feeling at least a little bit better. The night would be over before she knew it. She could get the Brownlows out of here and—

She paused, her brows lowering in confusion. A pale half circle of light spilled through one of the bedroom doorways. Was Tom awake? Jack wondered, her cheeks heating at the wicked memories she'd been having the past few hours. Her stomach tightened, as if some part of her feared that if Tom Brownlow caught so much as a glimpse of her he'd be able to see those intimate images in her face.

Nothing to worry about, the voice of reason nudged her. That wasn't the room she'd given Tom. His was the dark one across the hall. The room with a candle still lit was Lucy's.

Lucy's? she thought in alarm, remembering all too clearly the little girl in a heap on the floor surrounded by shards of glass, or on the porch scattered with wild-flowers from the tin pitcher she'd upset.

Jack felt a stab of irritation. What kind of idiot would leave a candle burning in an eight-year-old's room? Especially one who was going blind! One bump of a table, and Lucy could set the whole house on fire!

Jack started toward the room, intent on creeping in and blowing the candle out. But two steps into the room she stopped, staring.

Lucy lay sleeping in bed, the silk edging on her ragged pink blanket tucked up against her cheek. Beside her, a solitary figure sat in a chair, keeping vigil. Tom's elbow was crooked atop the arm of the chair, his chin propped in the hollow of his hand, long fingers splayed on the lean plane of his cheek. He'd always been mouth-wateringly gorgeous, with his quarterback's body and his poet's eyes, dark with both strength and compassion. He wore pants from a set of surgical scrubs and an old football shirt, so worn his tanned skin peeked through a smattering of holes in the material. Jack remembered just how that skin felt, like hot satin, smooth and taut.

The dark waves of his hair lay in disarray against the muscular column of his neck, his lashes thick and dark, the dimple, so like his daughter's, just a smudge on his left cheek. Most women would have found him incredibly sexy, and yet, the instant Jack caught a glimpse of his face, any hint of such fantasies faded.

The candlelight on his face told secrets Jack sensed he would rather no one else know. It stripped away that "everything is okay" façade he fought so hard to show his daughter, leaving him starkly vulnerable and confused, shoulders bowed as if he carried the weight of the world upon them—or maybe just the weight of one little girl whose sight was slowly slipping away.

His emotions stripped naked, he sat lost in his private sorrow. Wanting to spare him the knowledge she'd seen, and herself the discomfort of having to respond, she started to back out of the room. She winced in pain as she hit the corner of the door with her hip, the hinges betraying her with a soft creak.

Tom straightened, turned, those deep, dark eyes burning into her.

"I'm sorry," Jack stammered, crossing her arms over her chest, as if to shield her own most secret, tender places. "I didn't mean to disturb you. I was just coming down to get a cup of tea, and saw the light burning."

And so, what? Jack thought, her cheeks afire, she'd just stopped in to have a little chat?

"I didn't think it was safe to leave a lit candle in a kid's room," she tried to explain, "so I—"

His gaze lasered in on her with quick, hot anger, any suggestion he wasn't taking stellar care of his child an obvious flashpoint. "You thought I'd left it burning next to Lucy's bed?"

"Well, I—I don't know. Maybe."

Tom's jaw set, hard. Glancing one more time at his daughter, he stood and paced to the door. He smelled so clean, of soap and shampoo from the shower he'd taken hours before. But his eyes were harder than she'd ever seen them. "I take good care of my daughter, Jack. I always have."

"I didn't mean to suggest you didn't. I just—you've got to admit it's strange to leave a candle burning like that."

"Strange? I suppose so." He seemed to shake himself inwardly, his rugged cheekbones dark with what Jack sensed was embarrassment. "It would be rude to burn the lighthouse down, especially after you gave us shelter from the storm." He struggled to force a smile onto his lips. The end result was more potently sexy than any smile she'd seen on any continent on the globe. Jack swallowed hard, averting her eyes. Unfortunately, her gaze snagged on the tear in his jersey that revealed the shadowy dimple of his navel. Jack looked away quickly, staring at a picture of one of China's grim-faced forebears as intently as if she expected the old sea captain to shinny out of the mahogany frame and come back to life.

"I should have given you one of the lanterns," Jack said. "I like to burn candles when the lights go out, so I just didn't think about it." She wasn't about to admit she hadn't thought of it because she'd been too busy trying to get far away from Tom and his daughter as she could—as fast as she could. "I left my lantern out in the hall, if you want it."

"Take the candle so you can get back upstairs without breaking your neck. Those stairs are awfully steep."

Jack's chin bumped up a notch, her pride piqued by his overprotective tendencies—she'd been living here for a week, doing just fine. Hadn't fallen down the steps once yet. In fact, she'd been doing just fine for the past eight and a half years in war zones that would turn his blood cold.

But before she could snap out her usual defensive quip, she caught a glimpse of pink bunny blanket and baby-soft cheek. The last thing she should do at the moment was bite the man's head off in an effort to preserve her pride and independence. In a way, it was astonishing that he could be concerned about someone else when he was drowning in troubles of his own. It was a rare quality. Special. She'd never tried to deny Tom possessed it, even when she'd been hell-bent on hating him.

His gaze traveled down her body, the soft, red folds

of the floor-length silk tunic so different from usual garb that no one could help but notice. Jack felt an irritating flush of feminine pleasure when his eyes lit up in appreciation. "What is that you're wearing?" he asked, touching the sleeve with one finger and sending a spray of sparks across her still-damp skin. "Is it from one of the places you've traveled?"

"India," Jack said, drawing away from his touch, determined not to let him sense how the mere brush of his hand had disturbed her. "Relief groups are trying to help start cottage industries there, giving the women materials to weave in their homes to help support their families. I fell in love with this one."

"It suits you," Tom murmured, low in his throat. His lashes dipped to half-mast, and he couldn't seem to keep himself from catching the hem of her sleeve with his fingertips, this time not quite brushing the skin beneath. But he didn't have to, Jack realized in consternation. Awareness still trickled through her veins.

"I always imagined you wearing clothes like this," he said, rubbing the silk between his thumb and finger, his eyes suddenly soft. "Traveling in countries I couldn't even imagine, eating food I'd never taste. I thought you'd be happy."

She didn't want to know that he'd been thinking of her at all. Nor did she want to see the disappointment in his face. As if she hadn't lived up to his expectations for her.

"I am happy," she insisted. "Deleriously so. Photojournalism was everything I hoped it would be."

Tom's gaze flashed up to hers, and for an instant, Jack sensed he thought she was lying. Let him think what he wanted. He'd be gone by tomorrow afternoon. She searched for a way to beat a graceful retreat.

"Well, you've got a long drive tomorrow. No sense

in my keeping you up. Since everything's okay with the candle and all I'll just go grab my tea," she said, sweeping around in a swirl of flame-red silk and memories she wished she could brush away like the shadows that clung to her bare feet.

"She's scared of the dark." Tom's voice startled her, the tones so changed, raw somehow, but unguarded. More like the man she'd once known.

Jack froze, stunned by his abrupt explanation. She hadn't expected one. Hadn't wanted one. She'd figured he was as anxious for her to leave as she was to make an exit.

She turned back to face him. "You don't have to explain," she said, fingering the silk fastening at the hollow of her throat. "It's none of my business."

But Tom's eyes only grew more determined. Maybe she didn't want to hear, Jack thought, but that didn't seem to matter. He went on, his voice low so as not to wake his sleeping daughter.

"Even before we found out she was going blind, Lucy was afraid of the dark. It started when she was three, just after Laura left. One night she woke up, screaming. I got her this little night-light—one with Winnie the Pooh flying, holding on to a bunch of balloons, hoping it would help. But whenever she'd wake up alone, she'd start sobbing her heart out."

"Tom, I—" She wanted to stop him. But Tom continued, as if he hadn't even heard her.

"We worked through it. She'd be fine as long as I got up the instant I heard her first cry and started talking to her as I walked to her room. And as the years passed, well, sometimes she'd even forget to put the night-light on. But since the diagnosis—"

Tom looked away from Jack, swallowed hard. "I want to make sure my face is the last thing she sees when she goes to sleep and the first thing she sees when she wakes up. When it happens, I don't want her to be alone."

When it happens. . . . Tom's words echoed ominously in Jack's head. No question what "it" was: The darkness no night-light could ever drive back.

Jack's heart gave an unfamiliar squeeze of emotion, but she did her best to quell it. *Life is full of heartache,* Jack reasoned inwardly. She'd seen plenty of it before on the faces of people she'd photographed.

Yeah, a voice mocked her. *You snapped a few great pictures, told the people how sorry you were. Left the kids a few American toys and the old women warm scarves for their heads, and then you walked away. You never looked back, and you sure as heck never had to stay there, helpless, and watch—*

"You know," Tom said, staring down at the polished hardwood floor at his feet. "When she first got sick, I wanted to fix it, somehow. That's what I do. Who I am. A doctor. Okay, I heal puppies and horses and cows, but Lucy—she thinks I can work miracles. Make anything all better. She had complete faith in me, but I failed her."

"You didn't fail her. I remember you well enough to know you'd move heaven and earth to help her."

"We saw specialist after specialist. Got one pair of glasses after another. And the tests they ran—I thought they'd never end. I didn't want to tell her, didn't want to give up hope. Even when I knew the truth. One night when I was putting her to bed, she grabbed my hand, looked me square in the face. She said, 'My eyes aren't going to get better, Daddy. Not ever.' It wasn't a question. She wasn't looking for reassurance that everything was going to be okay. She knew the truth and she wanted to make it all right for me."

He gave a raw little chuckle, love etched in his handsome face. "She kept telling me not to worry. She'd be fine. Maybe she could teach Gracie to be a Seeing Eye dog."

"Gracie? You still have Gracie?" Jack reeled at the information. She closed her eyes, remembering it all so clearly.

She'd shown up at the clinic with the injured Border Collie in her arms, swearing she'd take care of whatever Gracie needed. In the end, Tom had ended up taking care of Jack.

She fingered the pale, faded scars on her hand. He'd taken her in at the same time he'd taken care of Gracie, insisting that the dog needed constant care, and they couldn't both stay in Jack's old Mustang.

It had been so damned easy to fall in love with him—his laugh, his big heart, the way he'd made her feel sexy, beautiful . . .

When their love had crashed and burned, she'd had to leave behind the dog she'd rescued from the fire. She intended to move heaven and earth to get herself a press job. And she had within months of leaving Kentucky. But you couldn't take a dog with you when you were flying into Somalia one week and Bosnia the next and only crashed at your lame excuse of an apartment long enough to stock up on boxes of film and make plane reservations for your next assignment. Tom had promised he would find a good home for the dog. But keep the dog himself? She could hardly imagine it.

"She and Lucy are inseparable. You should see them together—" he stopped, and Jack turned away, hoping he hadn't seen the hot flash of vulnerability in her eyes.

She went to the half-moon table tucked under a

portrait of China's sea captain father. Running her finger over the smooth curve of wood, she put distance between herself and her emotions, cooling them, untangling them until they were smooth and soft and far away.

She'd gotten good at it over the years, but this time it was harder, somehow. Maybe because in spite of regrets and ambitions and the passing of time she could still remember caring about Tom Brownlow more deeply than she'd let herself admit for a very long time.

But even if she did feel bad for Tom, she couldn't do anything about it. Ziggy had been pure magic at reaching out to people in trouble. And Tom—that had been his gift as well. But it had never been Jack's. She had no idea what to say. What to do.

You could give that little girl her wish and let them stay at the lighthouse. It would just be for a little while.

No way. Jack brought herself up short. She was already exhausted after one sleepless night filled with memories of Tom. She wouldn't be able to take a picture worth the effort to develop if she were dead on her feet.

You could work it out, a voice inside her whispered.

But she wouldn't. She'd survived this far by setting ironclad boundaries and never crossing them. Better to be flat-out honest about her own limitations than to scramble around out of guilt, trying to be something she wasn't.

"Once we both knew Lucy's prognosis, that she'd lose her sight God only knew when, I couldn't stand knowing how much she would miss seeing. A world full of beautiful things."

And ugly ones, Jack thought, looking at Tom's face, untouched by the sights that she'd seen in her travels.

"I wanted to fill her up with colors and landscapes and images she could hold on to. I wanted to squeeze a lifetime's worth of historical sites into her memory.

Show her all the wonders she could imagine so she wouldn't miss anything.

"It was ridiculous, in a way. I know," he said, "but it was my way of making sure this illness took as little as possible away from my little girl. When I told Lucy I'd take her on this trip, told her she could see anything in the whole world she wanted to, I thought she'd pick Disneyland or Paris or a ranch in Montana where she could ride horses and play with all the animals. I never imagined she'd want to come here. Maybe I should have suspected it, but—" He sighed. "It's that damned notebook Laura left in the bottom of the desk drawer. A half-finished story set here, at Mermaid Lost. Lucy's always been fascinated by the place."

"Laura's never taken Lucy here when she was with her?"

"Laura . . . isn't in Lucy's life anymore," Tom said.

Jack stared, almost certain she heard him mutter "thank God."

He cast a brooding glance back at Lucy, asleep under the covers with her pink blanket still cuddled to her cheek.

Tom swore, low. "What am I doing?" he murmured. "You didn't need to hear all this. And I sure never intended to talk about it. I guess it's just been a while since I've had a grown-up within earshot."

"Just don't make a habit of sharing confidences around me. It makes me twitchy." It was a joke. Sort of.

Jack started to walk away. She wasn't fleeing anymore, just making a necessary exit. She grabbed up the candlestick and started down the hall toward her room.

"What about your tea?" Tom asked.

"Don't want it anymore." Jack didn't slow a step. *Don't want the tea?* she thought. More like there was no point.

She'd used the warm brew in a hundred different countries to calm her nerves, soothe her, help her center herself and find peace. But she knew she wouldn't find peace tonight, no matter how hard she tried.

Better just surrender and go up to her room, count the hours until Tom and his daughter drove back down the crushed-shell driveway and back out of her life where they belonged. In fact, if she were smart, maybe she could arrange it so she wouldn't even have to see them in the morning to say good-bye.

Her camera. She couldn't begin to count the number of times it had come to her rescue—not only a passion, a job, but a damned good excuse when she needed it. Entering her bedroom, she crossed to the little captain's desk tucked into the crook of a gable, and grabbed a piece of paper and a pen.

Going out to get some early shots, she wrote quickly. She paused, nibbling for a moment on the end of the pen. What else should she say? *Have a nice trip? Good to see you again? Sorry your wife turned out to be as much of a witch as I always thought she was? Hope you find a miracle and Lucy doesn't go blind?*

Jack's fingers clenched on the pen until they ached. What else should she say to Tom in the note?

Nothing.

There was nothing left to say.

6

∞

Jack walked along the edge of the cliff, her tennis shoes soggy from slogging through the aftermath of the storm. She'd been out since the sky had just started to turn silvery around the edges. Too early to actually snap any pictures, but giving herself plenty of time to scout out a likely place to set up before the sun actually started to paint the sky.

She'd found tidal pools full of crustaceans and a few shingles blown from one of the lighthouse's eaves. The remains of a wooden sailboat that hadn't been seaworthy for years had edged its way onto the beach. But no matter how carefully she framed the compositions that made up her "after the storm" collection, there was no denying it. Somehow, the shots she had taken that morning felt flat.

Or was it just that last night seemed far more vivid. The sounds of movement drifting up to Jack's bedroom from the floor below—muffled voices, soft laughter, a strange melody Jack so rarely heard. Even the strain she sensed in Tom hadn't been able to mar the beauty of it for Jack, the rare jab of envy—for whom? The daughter so certain of her father's warm, generous love? Or some faceless woman not so restless or driven or damaged as Jack, who could be a part of that world if she chose to.

Jack's mind filled with images of candlelight painting the planes and angles of Tom's face, Tom filling the room with his strong, masculine body, his soulful eyes so changed from when Jack had first known him.

But now, hot embers of anger sparked beneath the surface of Tom's gaze, confusion and betrayal and doubt. He'd always believed in the innate goodness in people, in fate, in God. That as long as he gave enough, loved enough, fought hard enough to do what was right, some benevolent hand from above would reach down to stand up broken soldiers and smooth down raging waters and set little lost sailboats safely on sandy shores. Or make certain his baby girl could see.

But he questioned that big-time now. Jack always had.

She rubbed her wrist with the fingers of her other hand, remembering the brush of his fingertips on that sensitive skin. She hadn't wanted it to feel so good when he touched her. Preferred it when she could convince herself that he was just an unimportant "blast from the past" she couldn't wait to shove out of the house. That he had never really mattered.

But he had mattered—enough that she hadn't been able to sleep while he was in the house, enough that the briefest of touches had reminded her all too vividly of sultry Kentucky nights, flower-scented breezes through open windows, times when night was too long to wait for and kisses seemed to go on forever.

It was all a long time ago, Jack reminded herself. *No wonder you're getting all nostalgic, though.* It's been—who knew how long—since she'd allowed herself the luxury of even one of her brief, practical relationships: two busy people grabbing dinner and a few fast kisses before rushing off to their next assignment.

There was no denying that what she'd had with Tom even those few brief weeks had been so much more.

Yeah, the cynical voice inside Jack muttered. *Like your first ride on the Ferris wheel when it's all dangerous and wild and exciting, before you realize that half the lights aren't working, the paint's all chipped and the guy who put it together stopped evolving somewhere around the time of Neanderthal man.*

I suppose things could be a lot worse, Jack told herself. *After all, I made it clear Tom needed to leave as soon as they got up. There's no denying the kid is already playing hell with my concentration. Why should I be feeling guilty about sending them on their way? Lucy did get her wish, spent the night in her mother's room. Stayed in the lighthouse. Everybody wins. She goes off wherever she and Tom are going, her wish granted, and I get left in peace to finish this book as soon as possible so I can go back to my real life.*

Her real life. Dodging bullets, smuggling to the outside world rolls of film holding controversial pictures, the rush of adrenaline through her veins reminding her what it felt like to be alive.

Finally she'd walked well out of earshot, watching the sun rise until she was certain Tom had to have left the lighthouse. After all, he was as anxious to get out of here as she was to have him go. Maybe even more so, Jack's intuition nudged her as she remembered the edginess in Tom's face.

Get a grip, Jack. She brought herself up sharply. *Whatever is wrong, it has nothing to do with you.*

So what if he'd let her crash at his apartment when she'd been sleeping in her car. So what if he'd convinced the M.D. to let him give her the rabies shots himself so she wouldn't have to run back and forth to a doctor's office? So what if he'd risked losing his "no pets" apartment by nursing Gracie back to health in the warmth of his bedroom? That was all ancient history. And she'd paid in full for it, hadn't she? When he'd walked out of her life?

She shoved her hair off her brow, and tugged her Barbour raincoat more securely in place. Time to head back. Surely Tom was somewhere on the turnpike by now.

But as she broke through the tangle of brush, to the clearing near the lighthouse, she stared, scarce believing what she saw. A child, dressed in jean overalls and a purple sweatshirt disappearing over the perilous edge of the cliff.

"Freeze!" Jack bellowed in the voice that could stop seasoned guerrillas in their tracks. "Not another step!" She strode toward the cliff, seeing the culprit's pale face bob up, peek over the rim of rocks.

She expected one of the Pepperell grandchildren, unruly little pirates that they were. No fear of water or rocks or anything that swam or crawled in the ocean or on the shore. But the eyes that stared back at her, wide with alarm, didn't belong to any of China's crew. Lucy Brownlow's little face was framed by jagged rock, a deadly drop of blue sky behind her, just waiting for one misstep to plunge her to the stones below.

She stormed toward the little girl, stretched out her hand. "Grab on," she ordered, and Lucy did as she was told, her small fingers cold against Jack's own. Jack expelled a breath she hadn't realized she'd been holding, once she got the girl back up on solid ground.

"Exactly what did you think you were doing?" Jack snapped. "Can't you see how dangerous that was?"

Most kids would have resorted to defiance or crying. Lucy just straightened her narrow shoulders. "I was being careful," Lucy replied. "I just—I wanted to see if there was treasure on that boat."

"Treasure?" Jack echoed, leaving no doubt she thought the kid was out of her mind.

"Like the one in the book my mom's writing," Lucy said, her cheeks warming. "No one ever found the pirate treasure of Mermaid Lost. That's what it says in chapter ten. 'And it lies there, still.' "

Jack had to bite her tongue not to crush the kid's illusions about "the book," if only to keep Lucy from putting herself in danger. "Have you ever thought that maybe the treasure is make-believe?" Jack asked. "Stories aren't always about things that really happened. Most of the time they're just made up."

"Like fiction, you mean."

Jack did a double take at that big word coming out of a little kid's mouth. "You know what fiction means?"

"I read lots. Aunt Debbie always said I was going to wear my eyes out. Maybe I finally did." Lucy nibbled at her bottom lip.

Jack wasn't sure what to say. She decided to bail and defer to an expert. "What does your dad say?"

"He says Aunt Debbie was just teasing. She cries now when she sees me reading. She thinks I don't see her, but I do." She stopped, eyed Jack with distrust.

Some people would've tried to draw the girl out. Jack was relieved she'd gone quiet. "Where's your father?" Jack demanded, just managing not to add what she was really thinking: *And what is he doing letting an eight-year-old wander around out here all alone?*

But for once it seemed someone could read Jack's mind instead of the other way around. Lucy's chin stopped quivering, her soft brow wrinkling as she glared at Jack. "My daddy's still sleeping. He's tired 'cause he sat by my bed all night."

Because his little girl was afraid of the dark, Jack remembered, her irritation fading just a little. "Well, maybe we should march inside and wake him up so he can keep you from doing something foolish like climbing on cliffs."

"No!" Lucy cried, stubbornness and defiance vanishing, her eyes pleading. "Please don't do that! He—he'll get all mad at himself instead of getting mad at me. He already worries all the time. I promise I won't go near the cliff again. I'll just go sit in that chair over there and won't move an inch if you won't tell on me. Cross my heart."

Jack knew the girl would do just that if she agreed. It was obvious the girl took her promises very seriously. Besides, Jack supposed she could take some shots around here, keep an eye on Lucy surreptitiously until Tom finally came out. It wouldn't be that big a deal.

"Okay. In the chair. And don't move an inch."

Lucy nodded in abject relief. With one last, longing glance at the beached sailboat, she scurried over to the white painted Adirondack chair and settled herself on the wooden slats. She tucked her knees up to her chest, wrapped thin arms around them and perched her chin on her folded arms.

Jack tried to go about her business, but there was something about the way the little girl sat there that unnerved her, as if Lucy were trying to make herself so small she could disappear. Maybe Jack had been a little hard on her. After all, if Jack had been let loose on her own on this strip of coast as a kid, the cliff would have been the least of the trouble she would have gotten into.

Yeah, she argued inwardly, but *she* wouldn't have been going blind.

Jack stole another look at Lucy. She drooped like a scolded puppy, so wistful that even Jack's usual steely resolve gave a resounding crack. Okay, so how bad could it be to watch the kid for a little while? Let her experience the shore the way she obviously burned to? It wasn't as if Jack were getting any work done at the moment anyhow.

Jack strode over to the chair. Lucy peered up over her folded arms, her face still hidden. She was a little scared of Jack. Jack could tell. Hardly any wonder when she'd practically snapped the kid's head off. Jack sucked in a deep breath, tried not to notice that the little girl was looking at her with eyes exactly the same as Laura's, the woman Jack had hated for eight and a half long years.

"So," Jack began, feeling lost as if "kid-speak" was a foreign language. But over the years, she'd become adept at communicating in rare dialects all over the world. Surely, if she tried she could manage to figure this one out as well.

"So," she began again. "You wanted to see that sailboat close up, huh?"

"Yeah."

"Something about treasure?"

"There's a treasure on one of the boats that wrecked here. Mom said so in her book."

And, obviously, whatever Laura said in "the book" must be gospel.

"Well, the treasure would have had to be here a long time ago, when your mom stayed here. How else could she have written about it?"

Bursting another of the kid's bubbles. Not a very auspicious way to start a truce.

"Maybe that boat was there then, too."

"I can guarantee you that it wasn't. In fact, it wasn't

beached up on that shore even last night. It was probably just junked on one of the islands and washed ashore in the storm."

Lucy frowned. "Maybe it has treasure in it anyway. I need one real bad."

Need treasure? What for? Jack wondered. Did Lucy think that she could find some miracle cure if she just had enough money? Tom didn't look as if he were in financial trouble. Sure, his car was a few years old, but it was nice. Had been expensive when it was new. No, Jack doubted that was it.

"You couldn't fit a treasure on that tiny boat without sinking it all together. And what do you need treasure for anyway? Looks like your dad takes care of you okay."

"I can't tell you," Lucy said, with blunt honesty.

"Sorry to disappoint you, but there can't be any pirate gold left out here on Mermaid Lost. All the big wrecks except that old steel boat have vanished underwater where you can't reach them, and the steel boat is from World War Two. There wasn't any pirate gold then."

Lucy's face fell. Her eyes filled with tears. *Oh, no!* Jack thought, panicky. Was there anything more alarming than a crying kid? She scrambled for something to stem the tide.

"Maybe there isn't any gold in the sailboat," she said. "But I can show you a way to make the water look like gold instead."

Lucy was smart enough not to trust her. "It's mean to lie to someone just because they're a kid."

Jack started, taken aback, all but leveled by the steadiness in Lucy's eyes. "I'm not lying." Not that she'd have had any compunction about doing so, if it would have kept a kid from wailing around her. In cases of emergency, you had to do whatever worked. "See how the sun is shining on the water? If we find just the right spot on the shore and adjust the lens settings just right, we'll be able to make the reflection from the sun sparkle off of every little wave."

"Could I . . . take the picture with me when I go?" Lucy asked.

"I suppose that could be arranged." She could get a mailing address from Tom and send a copy of the photo to Lucy.

"Then whenever I wanted to remember what gold looks like, I could hold the picture and remember. This is what gold feels like. And smells like! All crispy and warm, like this morning." Lucy closed her eyes and drew in a deep breath, as if trying to fill herself up with everything that was the color gold.

The fierce concentration on Lucy's soft features tugged hard at the place Jack's heart used to be.

"Gold tastes like apple pie. Did you know that?" Lucy asked.

"No. But . . . I think if gold had a taste, that's what it would be."

Lucy's voice dropped, low. "Do you think you could remember all the colors in the world if it got dark for a real long time? Years and years and years? Or do you think you'd forget? Forget red and blue and green and all the rest of them?"

A thin sliver of horror drove itself into Jack's heart at the question. The very concept that one day all the colors that made up her world could vanish into dark, lifeless shadow. Lucy was waiting for an answer, watching Jack's face carefully, as if to detect if Jack was going to be honest or cover up the truth, protect Lucy from it the way the grown-ups in the little girl's world must want very much to do.

"I'm not sure," Jack said, trying to imagine her world colored with nothing but gray.

"I'm not either," Lucy said, satisfied. "But I'm going to try real hard to memorize all of them. Like, burying a big box of crayons in my head so I can color pictures inside me when my sight is all gone. It's hard, though. What's blue look like? How does orange feel? And pink—how does pink smell? What makes it different from purple?"

Jack couldn't begin to explain. She only knew that the subtle blending of hues had been at the heart of her world for as long as she could remember.

Suddenly Lucy gasped, pointing. "Look! There's two whole rainbows painted in the sky."

Jack's gaze followed the direction of Lucy's finger, saw that the child was right. The image was exquisite; skies with silver-edged clouds, glittering like butterflies' wings, bars of sunlight piercing holes in them, sprinkling the water with light, the beached sailboat, picturesque on the shore as if God's own hand had arranged it for the photograph. And twin rainbows, arching magically across the sky.

Jack's breath caught, and she motioned to Lucy. "See if you can catch that rainbow," Jack urged, struck by sudden inspiration. Her hands flew over her camera, setting shutter speed, adjusting lenses, snapping picture after picture from every vantage point she could. Lucy climbing on a boulder, eyes fixed on the colors above her. Lucy's hands reaching for the bright ribbons of sky color as if they were tails on a kite.

Satisfied at last, Jack let the camera dangle from its strap around her neck. She'd caught it all, knew these were some of the best shots she'd taken of Mermaid Lost.

"Did you make the water turn into gold?" Lucy asked hopefully.

"Yes," Jack assured her. She'd done more than that. She'd caught the very essence of Mermaid Lost, the shimmering spirit of this place. Something so fleeting it chilled her to think how easily she could have missed the opportunity. And somehow Lucy had known. The little girl had known it was magical, a perfect image to keep. Did Lucy Brownlow have a photographer's instinct? Or was it just that every image the little girl saw was precious because the ability to see them was going to be snatched away from her forever sometime soon?

Had Jack's eyes softened just a little? Whatever the reason, Lucy grew braver. "Could I—could I touch it?" she asked, gesturing to the camera.

Jack had come close to severing the limbs of people who got their prying little fingers too close to her precious Leica. But something about the way Lucy looked at it, as if it held all the wonders in the world, made Jack pause for a moment, consider.

"Okay. Be really gentle."

Lucy glanced up at her, beaming. "Really? Can I?"

"Don't give me time to change my mind." Jack found herself smiling at the kid.

Lucy reached out, slowly, reverently, as if the camera was the Holy Grail. Maybe to her it was.

"Lucy!"

They both nearly jumped out of their skins at the sound of Tom's voice.

Lucy turned, guiltily, shoving both hands behind her back.

He strode toward them, his hair tumbled in unruly dark waves across his forehead, his faded scrub pants and old football jersey wrinkled from sleeping in them all night. Imprints of wrinkles from whatever he'd slept on—a stray pillow or just the sleeve of his own shirt—had pressed a web of fine lines into the lean plane of his left cheek. His eyes were red, dark circles underneath them. How long had it been, Jack couldn't help wonder, since the man had gotten a decent night's sleep?

"Lucy, what are you doing, running around out here alone? You know better than to go off like that without telling me."

"I'm sorry that you worried about me, Daddy. But I just wanted to come out and . . . and go exploring before we had to go away. It was too dark to see anything last night, and when I looked out the window the morning was so perfect, I just *had* to see it. Please don't be mad at me."

Tom didn't look mad, Jack thought. He looked exhausted, overwhelmed, still buzzing from the shock of waking up and finding his daughter gone.

"I'm not mad. I'm just . . . confused. I thought I'd made it clear that Ms. Murphy needed to work, and we weren't supposed to disturb her."

"I didn't disturb her. She disturbed me," Lucy offered, then cast her eyes down, guilt painting her cheeks deep pink. Jack could almost hear what the kid was thinking: *Terrific, now he's going to expect me to explain and I'll have to tell him I was climbing around on the cliff. Mad won't even come close to what he is once I do that.*

"Actually, everything worked out in the end," Jack surprised herself by coming to the little girl's rescue. "Lucy found a double rainbow and helped me get some terrific shots. I took a few with her in them. I think they'll be good. Maybe I could use some of them in the book if you'll sign a waiver saying I can."

"Me?" Lucy cried, amazed. "In a book? Really?"

Tom tried to look stern, but even Jack wasn't fooled for an instant. "Wouldn't that be rewarding you for disobeying?" he asked his little girl.

Lucy grabbed his hand, in complete certainty that she wouldn't be turned away. "But Daddy—maybe Mom would look at it, 'cause it's about her favorite place in the world. Maybe she would see that I'm not a pesty baby anymore and come see me."

Tom stiffened, a flash of something in his eyes before he shifted them out to gaze at the broad sweep of ocean. "There's time to talk about this later, honey. I want you to head inside and pack up. We need to get out of Ms. Murphy's way."

He was hiding something, Jack knew instinctively. Or more accurately, he was *trying* to hide something. Lucy was so tuned in to his moods, he wasn't fooling her for a minute.

Lucy's enthusiasm faded, and she caught her lower lip between her teeth. What was it about the mere mention of Laura that could drive a wedge between these two?

"I'm sorry, Daddy, I just . . ."

Tom scooped Lucy into his arms, held her tight, too tight for an instant, as if he were trying to shield her from some peril no one else could see. "Nothing to be sorry for, sweetpea. I think it's a great idea, having your picture in a book. We'll have to buy a dozen. One for Grandma, one for Aunt Debbie, and one for . . . what's his name? That boy who's had a crush on you since the first day of kindergarten?"

Lucy smiled, but this time it was stiff around the edges, where moments ago it had been bright and real and full of sunshine. "I'll go get my stuff," Lucy said, climbing out of her father's embrace. "I'll hurry. I promise."

This isn't your business, Jack told herself firmly. *Keep your distance the way you always do.* But somehow, Jack couldn't stand by and let Lucy leave Mermaid Lost, her eyes filled with guilt and confusion, this strange, palpable barrier between her and the father the little girl so obviously adored.

And a part of her couldn't bear the thought of Tom climbing back into that car alone, heading off to a marathon of sleepless nights, too-short days, and the terrible isolation of being alone with Lucy, watching his daughter slide into darkness. It wasn't as if Jack wanted to get involved; it was just that maybe knowing there was someone else around would help. She could give him a bit of a break for a few days, let him build up his inner strength before he headed off into a future neither he nor Lucy had chosen.

The man was dead on his feet and once, a very long time ago he'd been kind to her. Maybe she didn't have Ziggy's gregarious, generous nature, but Jack *did* pay her debts. That's all this was. It had nothing to do with Tom Brownlow's strong hands or his poet's mouth. It had nothing to do with how long it had been since Jack had felt a man hold her in his arms and let herself be a little, just a little vulnerable. In fact, when was the last time she'd dared to surrender even that much? Eight and a half years ago under the rainbow quilt Tom's grandmother had made him?

Don't do it, Jack, a voice warned her. *This is way dangerous, and not in the way you can usually handle—snake fangs and crocodile jaws and really pissed-off revolutionaries. Those you can handle—but this . . .?*

"Just a minute." Jack jumped, startled by the sound of her own voice. Tom and Lucy both looked at her. Jack hoped like hell she could think of something to say. "I was just thinking . . ."

She wasn't *thinking* at all—and that was dangerous.

"Maybe you could stay here a few days."

"Really?" Lucy gasped, her eyes wide and so hopeful, Jack winced.

"It's very . . . generous of you," Tom began, shaking his head. "But we couldn't impose."

"You wouldn't be imposing. Actually, you'd be doing me a favor. I've been struggling with the project I was working on. Was afraid it would just be one more book full of pretty pictures. But the shots I took today, with Lucy in them—they had something special." At least that much was true.

"No, Jack. We've stayed here a night. That's enough."

"No it's not, Daddy! I could stay here forever and never get tired of it. I read the papers in that rack by the door, the ones that tell you all the stuff you can do for fun around here. There are pirate caves and places you can swim, and you can go look for whales on the ocean. I've never seen a whale. What if someday, they're all gone and I never got to see one?"

"Lucy, Ms. Murphy is just trying to be nice. We can't take advantage of her."

"Time to disabuse you of that notion right now," Jack said briskly. "You can ask anyone who knows me. I'm *never* 'nice.' Everything I do is based to a greater or lesser degree on some self-serving motive. And this is no different." Jack put space between them, trying to make the boundaries of this offer clear. It wouldn't do to have either one of them thinking she was some kind of Good Samaritan, with a soft heart hidden beneath a crusty exterior.

"Lucy wants to stay and explore the area. I need a subject to give the photographs more life. That doesn't mean we'd have to be glued together at the hip. The more natural the poses the better. The two of you just go about your business and I'll go about mine. I'll just take shots whenever we happen to be in the same place and I see something I like."

One thing Jack was certain of—Tom didn't like anything about this offer. He looked edgy as a horse in a box canyon, with a pack of wolves closing in.

Guilt stung Jack. She hadn't meant to paint Tom into a corner. Maybe she shouldn't have brought the subject up with Lucy right here, her freckled face brimming with hope and delight.

Lucy threaded her fingers through Tom's. Any other child would be jumping up and down, begging, whining, coercing their parent any way that they could. But Lucy stood silent, peering up at him with her heart in her eyes.

Tom didn't have a chance against Lucy's quiet plea, Jack thought with a tug of sympathy.

"Maybe we could stay for a few days," Tom agreed, reluctance still shadowing his face.

Lucy sucked in a quick breath. "Honest? I'll be good, Daddy. Really good. And I won't make a mess, or leave my tennis shoes where anyone could trip on them, and when Ms. Murphy takes my picture I won't put on my cheesy smile—you know, Daddy, that one I always do when I take school pictures."

"Good," Tom said, "then Ms. Murphy will only have to worry about tripping over *my* shoes in the hallway. But then, they're the size of canoes, so she'll be more likely to see them, instead of your itty-bitty ones."

He was trying to tease her, make her smile, and Jack couldn't help but admire him for it. Her own father had never been one to suffer in silence. Those few times Frank had been hoodwinked or bribed into doing something he hadn't wanted to, be it a family dinner, a movie he thought was stupid, or a school program in which Jack had the starring role, he'd made sure everyone knew he was miserable. And he'd made absolutely certain that, by the end of the night, they were even more miserable than he was.

Lucy didn't even giggle at Tom's joke. She flung her arms around his waist and hugged him with all her might. "You're the best daddy in the whole world!" she said fiercely.

Why did those words fill Tom's eyes with such pain?

Her only excuse had to be temporary insanity, Jack thought as she worked in her darkroom hours later. What had she been thinking, asking Tom Brownlow and his daughter to stay under the same roof with her? She liked living alone. Needed her space. The noise and clutter—just their being in her personal space would make her so edgy that by the time they were ready to leave Mermaid Lost, Lucy would probably be pushing on the SUV's gas pedal herself.

The image of the little girl's pink tennis shoe on top of Tom's "canoes" made Jack chuckle. But that was the only thing that had Jack laughing. There was nothing funny about the other effects Tom's presence was having on her. An unaccustomed flutter when he came into the same room—just surprise, of course, not being used to company. The way the low rumble of his voice made the hairs at her nape prickle, and the absurd times she actually caught herself ignoring whatever she was doing to watch Tom and Lucy together.

What was that motto she'd always taunted Ziggy with? No good deed goes unpunished. By the time the Brownlows' little visit was over, Jack would probably be cured of any lingering altruistic impulses for life.

Tough as Jack was, she couldn't deny the hard

truth—that no matter how sexy Tom Brownlow was, or how reluctantly she felt the renewed stirrings of attraction for him, it hurt when she looked at Lucy and saw shades of Laura Willoughby staring back at her. Hurt deep down in a place Jack had all but forgotten. She'd blocked so much of that long-ago summer out of her memory, the joy and the pain and the sharp sense of betrayal. The torture of picturing Laura's baby in Tom's arms, Laura in Tom's bed, Laura clinging to him in that disgustingly helpless way that had made her want to slap them both.

It wasn't Lucy's fault that she looked like her mother; even so, the memories made Jack edgy, angry. Vulnerable. Reminded her too sharply of losses she thought she'd gotten over a long time ago. And now she'd ushered the kid into her life for the next few days.

Maybe she had been crazy, Jack thought, and yet, she knew in her gut that she had made the right decision, not only for Lucy, but for the book that would be her gift to Ziggy's memory. Satisfaction stole through her as she watched the prints she'd taken this morning appear like magic, comforted herself with the fact that she *had* told the truth about her selfish need for Lucy to stay.

Lucy was just the element her images had been lacking. Yes, it was lovely to see postcard-perfect shots of sunsets and sunrises and rainbows arching over picturesque lighthouses. But to see the wonder through a child's eyes made it more accessible, more alive. You could feel the salt breezes tugging at Lucy's curls, sense the strength of the stone light tower in contrast to her innocent, freckled face.

Maybe China had been right all along, wanting Jack to capture the "human" side of Mermaid Lost. Lucy gave the lighthouse something tangible to protect, to shelter, to keep safe from storms. The beacon no longer shining out over the ocean to nameless boats and face-less sailors, but also to a single little girl who was lost in her own high seas, needing guidance on her own very difficult journey.

If you went to a place that was all dark for years and years and years do you think you'd remember what red looks like? Lucy's wistful voice echoed in Jack's head, painting her own thoughts with a completely new color.

How did you help an eight-year-old remember the color of grass? Or a perfect blue sky? Or twin rainbows with their luminous, fleeting hues? How could you remind her of the subtle pink in the heart of a seashell, all satiny, worn smooth by the sand? Or the chocolate-warm glow of love in her father's dark eyes?

The mere possibility of Lucy losing all that chilled Jack to the bone. She shouldn't have cared so much. She couldn't deny that she did.

7

A soft knock on the darkroom door shook Jack from her thoughts, and she couldn't help realizing how strange it was. No one ever interrupted her when she was working in the darkroom. Anyone who knew her would've expected nothing short of an explosion when she opened the door. Looked like there were still some boundaries to set with her houseguests.

She opened the door, found Lucy waiting. "Daddy's on the phone with Grandma and there's somebody at the door. I didn't think I should open it."

Uncertainty wreathed the little girl's face, a desperate desire to please, get things right. Jack figured the discussion about darkroom etiquette could wait.

"It's a really short lady and a bunch of boys." Lucy might as well have said "pirates bent on pillage," the way she shuddered, reminding Jack of the days when all boys had cooties. However, the first glimpse of China Pepperell's wild crew might make any eight-year-old girl nervous.

"The biggest one was climbing up the trellis and two others were trying to pull him off."

And China probably hadn't said a word. She was the calmest woman alive when it came to dealing with out-of-control boys. Probably because all the shouting between her own sons had made her half-deaf.

"It's the lady the lighthouse belongs to," Jack said, wiping her hands on her jeans as she crossed to the door. Lucy hovered a few steps behind her like some shy woodland creature ready to bolt if one of the "pirates" got too close. She was too curious to beat a well-advised retreat, and too wary not to leave herself an avenue of escape. She was trusting Jack to look out for her. It unnerved Jack to be trusted that way.

"No one tells better stories than China does," Jack said, in an effort to soothe Lucy. Lucy brightened with interest.

"Better than *Lassie Come Home* and *Black Beauty?*" Lucy asked.

Jack chuckled. "Not necessarily better, but different. China's stories are about real people and real places and things that happened a long time ago."

Jack opened the door, and the dull roar that always accompanied a visit from China's grandsons poured into the quiet of the stone house.

"Well, now, Jack," China said briskly. "I'm glad to see that you've weathered the storm just fine. The road's intact, praise the Lord, and Asia will be coming to fix the shingles. Looks like you'd lost a few of them in the gale. But when I saw that strange car in the drive I couldn't help wondering who it belonged to." China paused. Eyes keen from watching the waves for her son's fishing boats to come in sharpened as she saw the unfamiliar figure lurking behind Jack.

"What have we here?" China gentled, obviously

sensing Lucy's reticence. "A new visitor to Mermaid Lost? Don't tell me you finally took my advice, Jack Murphy, and invited someone so you wouldn't get so lonely up here?"

Jack thought about setting China straight, but it was easier to let her think she'd won this time. "This is Lucy," she introduced, but didn't move so the suddenly interested Pepperell boys could get a better look at the new kid. If Lucy wanted to draw closer, Jack figured she could do it on her own. "She's going to be staying here for a few days."

"It's a relief to me to know you're here, Lucy," China said in that voice that charmed every child she came in contact with. "I told Jacqueline it was no good, being out at this lighthouse alone. Why, my great, great aunt Hetty went stark, raving mad when she and her husband were alone up here one terrible winter in 1847. Weather was so bad she didn't see another soul for almost six months. A city girl, she'd been, used to company and all the pleasures to be had. But out here, all alone, well, she couldn't cope. She played the same tune on the piano, over and over and over again, month after month, until round about April, she finally jumped right out of the tower window. Sometimes folks can still hear her playing."

What is China trying to do? Jack thought. *Give the kid nightmares?*

"I read about that in the papers on the table," Lucy said eagerly, edging out of Jack's shadow by a few steps. "You have three ghosts here."

China smiled like the "kid charmer" she was. "There are three ghosts that we know of. Aunt Hetty, the pirate captain, and his love, Emily. But I'd wager others will come back to haunt the place, people who have been most happy here, or most sad."

"Ah, China," Jack said, feeling completely awkward and inept. "Don't you think she's a little young—?"

"I'm not a baby," Lucy protested.

"Of course you're not," China snorted. "Kids are complete little ghouls. They love this stuff, right, Lucy?"

Lucy agreed enough to step completely into the light streaming through the green painted door. "There's lots of stories about Mermaid Lost. A pirate treasure and shipwrecks and . . ." The child faltered, fell silent and Jack stiffened instinctively, both suddenly aware of the laser intensity of China Pepperell's stare as it locked hard on an unimpeded view of Lucy's small face.

"Speaking of ghosts, why, if you don't look just like one from my past. Someone I always thought would come back." China reached out, touched Lucy's hair as if to prove the child was real. Lucy stiffened at the contact from a stranger.

China shook herself, made a wry face as she dropped her hand back to her side. "I'm sorry, darlin', I'm just a silly old woman who needs to get her glasses checked. I just wasn't expecting—I mean, you remind me of a girl who used to stay at Mermaid Lost sometimes when my own sons were little boys. But she'd be all grown-up now. She's been gone for a long, long time."

"My mommy used to come here," Lucy offered. "She wrote down that her mom and dad had a summer house on the shore. But my mom liked this place best. She was an only child like me, and she wanted some kids to play with, I bet. She stayed up in the dormitory room with a curtain hung up, and the boys let her sleep next to the window 'cause she liked to hear the sound of the waves."

"Lord above!" China breathed. "You're Laura's little girl?"

Jack's stomach sank. China had known Laura Willoughby? She must have, obviously, considering Lucy's chatter the night before, and yet, somehow Jack had managed not to connect the dots. She'd considered Mermaid Lost Ziggy's place, and had come to like China and the other Pepperells in spite of her best efforts to keep them at a distance. But China's reaction to the little girl changed things somehow, in a way Jack knew she'd never be able to alter. Now, there was no denying that Laura had claimed this place as her own. Laura had stayed here, and not as a casual visitor. It made Jack vaguely sick, feeling the other woman's presence here so suddenly, so sharply.

"What a small world." China grinned. "Why, Jacqueline Murphy, I didn't know that you knew our Laura."

Jack's smile felt rubbery. What she knew of Laura wouldn't be fit for the woman's eight-year-old daughter to hear.

"Actually, I knew Lucy's father," Jack hedged. Knew him in the biblical sense, but in the end, hadn't known him at all.

"You knew Daddy?" Lucy piped up, eyes brightening. "But you didn't tell me. Neither did he."

"It was a long time ago." Jack tried to evade. "Just a few weeks when your dad was still in vet school. He took care of . . . uh, my dog."

Jack stiffened, all too aware of China's brief, uncharacteristic silence. The old woman regarded Jack a little too intensely, as if trying to read the undercurrents in Jack's voice.

"He's really good at that, isn't he?" Lucy bubbled. "He can make anything in the whole world better."

Anything, Jack thought with a stab of sadness, *except his beloved daughter.*

"Lucy?" Tom's voice rang out as he came down the

stairs, phone call obviously over. "Grandma sends her love—" He stopped as he saw the crowd at the door. China and her grandsons, who were now, by some miracle, silent.

Lucy turned to him, flushed with excitement. "Daddy, you didn't tell me you took care of Jack's dog!"

Tom's cheeks darkened, his gaze flashing to Jack's. "Oh. Yeah. I did. It must have slipped my mind." Not much else had. The man looked so uncomfortable Jack knew damned well there was one person he wasn't fooling. China would be full of questions the next time she got Jack alone. Terrific. Just terrific.

Yeah, China, Tom and I had the hottest affair of my lifetime—a real volcanic eruption of passion. And you've got to admit, the man's still a babe. No love handles on that man, no soft beer belly; he looks just as hard and delicious and over-the-top sexy as he did the first time I practically dragged him into bed.

Jack could only hope Lucy was too excited to notice the abashed light in Tom's eyes. Kids seemed to have the most inconvenient radar sometimes. But the instant Lucy spoke again, Jack knew that their former sexual escapades were the last thing on Tom Brownlow's mind.

Lucy grabbed Tom's hand, tugged hard, urging him to look at her. "And Daddy, you'll never guess what else! This lady knew my mommy!" She jabbed a finger at China as if she'd just pulled a rabbit out of a hat.

Or a snake, by the expression that flashed across Tom's face before he shuttered it away.

"Is that so?" Tom's lips tightened, his tanned cheeks paling just a shade. Jack could feel him fighting not to give himself away. But he'd always been lousy at hiding things.

"She says I look just like when mommy was a little girl," Lucy enthused, turning back to China.

Tom forced his lips into a wooden smile. "You have the same hair and the same eyes. You figured that out yourself, remember?"

"Yeah, when I found that picture of her in the bottom of the drawer."

Tom tugged at the neckline of his jersey, but it seemed China was too caught up in the pleasure of unexpected memories to notice his discomfort.

"So you're the man who finally carried Laura Willoughby off to his castle," China said.

Tom looked almost sick.

"You had plenty of competition, I'd wager. My own boys adored her. I almost thought Seth would marry her, but she left before he could ask her. I always figured her father had something to do with whisking her away, selling the beach house before things could get too serious. And for once I agreed with the old man. Seth and Laura weren't suited. She needed someone more polished than a fisherman's son. You look as if you're better fit for Laura. Successful. Polished. But still, a sturdy-looking man, built strong in all the right places, and I should know. Have six grown sons of my own."

Jack jumped in, trying to cover for Tom. "This is China Pepperell, Tom. Her family has kept the light here at Mermaid Lost for the last two hundred years."

"You must be the Pepper Lady from Mommy's book," Lucy exclaimed.

China laughed, hunkering down to Lucy's level so they could talk eye to eye. "You're the very picture of Laura. My boys won't be able to believe their eyes when they see you! And just where is your mama right now? Down combing the beach for treasures, I'd wager my life."

"My mom isn't here," Lucy faltered.

"We're divorced," Tom explained. "Have been for years." An edge of bitterness crept into his eyes. Jack sensed just how hard he fought to quell it, to spare his daughter.

China's wrinkled cheeks washed pink, her features filling with sincere regret but not, Jack noticed, surprise. "I'm sorry to hear that. But I'm glad as can be to meet the two of you. Seems so right, don't you know? Laura's daughter, back here at Mermaid Lost, right where she belongs."

"We won't be here very long," Tom cut in. "Just a few days."

"Then our Lucy will have a lot of people to meet in a dashing hurry. My boys will want to get to know you. Every single one of them was crazy in love with your mother at one time or another. Even my youngest used to follow her around like she was a fairy princess come real."

"I don't think—" Tom began.

"And you and I, Lucy" China barged on, "you and I will have a tea party out of the tea set my great-great-grandfather brought back on one of his voyages to China when the sea was still dark and dangerous, and only the bravest of men dared to sail."

Lucy glowed. "My mom had tea out of those cups?"

"And so shall you, I promise. And the word of a seafarer's lady can never be broken. Wait until you see all the treasures the captains in our family brought back over the years. Masks from Africa and jade carvings from the Orient, and elephant tusks longer than a grown man's arm, all carved so fine and delicate they look almost like lace."

Lucy nibbled at her lip, that nervous habit Jack was already becoming too familiar with. "Elephants are going extinct, you know," Lucy confided to China. "It's wrong to keep their tusks when the elephants still need them."

China smiled at her warmly. "And so it is. It's a good thing that our tusk was brought over years and years ago, when there were still lots of elephants tramping about."

Lucy seemed to mull it over, and her attraction to China won out over her ecological concerns, for the time being, at least. "I suppose it's all right to keep it, then."

"We'd have a hard time giving it back," China said. "Where would we find the right elephant? Besides, he was a boy elephant, from the size of the tusk, and he'd look mighty silly with a bunch of flowers and pretty Chinese ladies all over his tusks when he was trying to chase off lions and tigers. I'm afraid he'd be the laughingstock of the jungle."

"The savannah," Lucy corrected solemnly. "Elephants live in savannahs. There wouldn't be any room for them under a rain forest canopy."

"Big words, for such a small girl," China said. "Maybe we can work out a trade. You teach me about savannahs, and I'll teach you about all the wonderful places our family's ships used to go."

"It's nice of you to offer," Tom interrupted, "but I doubt Lucy and I will have time for it. There are so many things she wants to see on the coast, here, and we don't have much time."

"We've got lots and lots of time," Lucy protested. "We don't have to go back home for three more weeks, remember?"

"But we won't be here all three weeks, honey. Remember all the other places I want to show you."

"But you said I get to pick this trip. And I want to see the flower tusk and drink out of the tea set."

"As it happens, the boys and I were going on an adventure right now. Maybe you'd like to join us and see what the storm has blown in. Sometimes, after a gale, bits of the old wrecks underwater are carried in by the waves."

Cal, the dreamer among China's brood of grandchildren, came to lean against the doorjamb. "I've found lots of stuff. Barrel rings and coins, and once, I found an old metal box with a whale tooth in it. It had a picture carved in it of a whaling ship and sailors with harpoons. If we find something today, you could take it home."

"Please, Daddy! Please can I go?"

"Lucy, no."

Jack stared at Tom in surprise, the finality in his voice startling her. "Tom, I've known China ever since I've stayed here, and I have—had—a friend who'd spent every summer with the Pepperells. I know China will take good care of Lucy."

Tom glared at her, something stark flashing for just a heartbeat in his eyes. "I'm sure that—that you mean well," Tom said to China, "but there are special circumstances with Lucy."

Circumstances? Jack thought. The circumstance was that Lucy needed to have all the adventures she could before time ran out, and there was no one on the coast of Maine better suited to show her the time of her life than China Pepperell. "Tom, China's raised six sons of her own here and more grandkids than I can keep track of. Lucy couldn't be in safer hands."

Tom winced visibly, schooled his face into unyielding planes. "I'm sure you're right. And I'm grateful to you, all of you, for wanting to include Lucy, but this isn't a good day."

Something told Jack there wouldn't be a good day—ever.

"It's a great day," Cal argued. "It's not every day you get a rip-roaring gale like the one we had last night."

China seemed to sense Tom was adamant, too. She smoothed Cal's cowlick with one gnarled, weathered hand. "We'll do it another time. Can't just pop in on people and expect them to drop their plans, can we, boys?"

Tom's rigid shoulders relaxed a trifle. "It was kind of you to ask. I appreciate it. Really. Lucy and I just need some time alone. That's what this vacation is all about."

Lucy looked up at him, bewildered. "I thought it was about me seeing lots of new things and saving them up for when I go blind."

A shock went through China. Jack could feel it. China looked down into Lucy's eyes, so perfect, so fragile. Jack was sure she saw tears glitter on China's stubby lashes.

"I'm sorry to hear of your troubles, Miss Lucy," China said, touching the little girl's cheek. "But this is a lovely place to fill up on, so many things to see. I'm sure you and your dad will have a marvelous time, just the two of you. Mr. Brownlow, if you ever do change your mind, I'd be in pure heaven to spend a little time with such a wonderful girl."

China leaned down, whispering conspiratorially into Lucy's ear. "All boys I've had, and my grand-babies—boys, every one. Don't mistake me, I love the rowdy little pirates, but once in a while it would sit just right in my heart to have tea with a little girl."

"I'm sorry, but that won't be possible," Tom insisted stubbornly.

"Well, it's up to you, after all. Now the boys and I had better be on our way. Their dads will sail in from checking the nets in a few hours, and they'll be wanting to see the day's catch."

With that, China rounded up her brood, driving them before her like a mother hen in a nor'wester. The other two boys raced off ahead, heedless, but young Cal glanced back at Lucy, disappointment in his face.

Jack shut the door, not knowing what to say. She shouldn't say anything at all. Lucy wasn't her daughter, after all. If Tom wanted to tell her she couldn't go off with the Pepperells, well, that was his right, wasn't it? She'd said everything she could, told him China was completely trustworthy. It was out of Jack's hands.

She'd just turn around and beat feet back to her darkroom, and the complete isolation it would bring.

Jack froze, midstep, unable to ignore the woebegone little girl before her. Lucy looked as if someone had just snatched the last piece of birthday cake out of her hands for no reason at all.

Memory flared in Jack, that sensation she knew so well—bewilderment, hurt, helplessness. Maybe Tom wasn't like Frank, but this time, he was cruising awfully close to being a dictator.

"Hey, Lucy," Jack said. "Why don't you go up to my room. I've got a package of cookies from England in my bottom drawer for you to try. Your dad and I have some things to talk about."

"Could I take the cookies upstairs and go out on the tower balcony?" Lucy asked. "I wouldn't get crumbs anywhere, and maybe I could see that boy with the sticky-up hair and his grandma on the beach."

"No!" Tom snapped. "You're not to go out there unless I'm with you. It's too dangerous and you can't always—"

Tom stopped, his cheeks dull red, eyes filled with both stubbornness and regret.

"I know I can't see good sometimes. But the light's

real bright now and I'd be careful. I wouldn't fall off like that Hetty ghost woman. I'd be careful."

"I said no. This isn't up for discussion, Luce. Do you understand me?" He stopped, touched the little girl's stiff shoulder, didn't turn away from the hurt in those wide green eyes. "I'm sorry. You're just too precious for me to lose. You're my treasure, you know. Like the ones you read about in those books of yours?"

"It's boring being a treasure, locked up tight all the time." Lucy's lower lip thrust out stubbornly. Jack ached as it quivered.

"Why don't you go up to my room, then while I talk to the dictator here?" Jack ignored Tom's sharp glare and Lucy's puzzled expression. "There's a great view and lots of stuff from other countries lying around. I think there's even a book about that savannah you were telling China about. And don't worry about the crumbs, kiddo," Jack said. "You can't hurt anything up there."

"Are you sure there's nothing she can get hurt on? Solutions or X-ACTO knives or—"

"She's not going to touch anything she's not supposed to. She's a good enough kid to respect my things, aren't you, Lucy?"

"You don't have to tell me what a good kid she is! I've raised her for eight years."

"Then trust her, dammit!"

Lucy's eyes went wide at the swearword, but a hint of a smile softened her mouth, the kid obviously seeing Jack as a sudden and unexpected champion in her battle to wriggle out from under her father's too-cautious hand. Lucy headed up the stairs, but Jack could feel the child's disappointment at being denied the adventure with China and her crew.

Tom stood, rigid. Jack figured he had some idea as to

what was coming. They faced off, eyes snapping with temper, silent as they listened to Lucy's footsteps fading away.

Jack confronted Tom, hands on hips. "Okay, exactly what was that about?"

"What?"

"Breaking the kid's heart by forbidding her to go with China. She would have had a great time, been absolutely safe."

"Safe?" Tom choked. "What do you know about keeping Lucy safe? Keeping any child safe? If you had your way, you'd probably have Lucy rappelling down the side of the lighthouse tower as if it were a cliff or something. Wasn't that always your motto? No fear? Well, sometimes there really are things to be afraid of, and it's my job as Lucy's father to keep them from hurting her."

"Keeping what from hurting her? China adores kids, any kids, and she obviously knew Laura when she was growing up. Lucy's dying to hear about her mother. And she's got every right to."

"Don't tell me what 'rights' my daughter has. I've been taking care of her since she was too tiny to walk. I've watched over her every day of her life, bandaged up every skinned knee, got her arm put in a cast when she broke it. I've sat up with her at night when she had bad dreams. I don't have to explain my decisions to anyone."

"Not even to her mother? Doesn't Laura have anything to say about her own daughter?"

"She lost that right five years ago when she—" Tom stopped, swore. "You don't understand, Jack. But then, how could you?"

"Because I've never had a child? Maybe that's true. But I *was* a child once upon a time. A child with a father who tried to keep me locked up in a little box. Not as a treasure. But locked up, nonetheless. It's a rotten way to grow up."

"Don't even try to compare me to that bastard of a father you had!" Pain cut deep across Tom's handsome face, and Jack felt it as if she'd turned the knife on herself as well.

"I know you're not like my father. You love Lucy. Anyone can see it. But chains formed out of love can chafe just as badly as the dictatorial kind my father tried to bind me in. And leave scars just as deep. You say I can't understand? Try me. I'm listening."

But there weren't enough words to soften the pain in that darkly handsome face. It surged to the surface, taking Jack's breath away.

"There are things I don't want Lucy to know. Things that could hurt her."

"About Laura? What is it? Unless she's an ax murderer, I figure Lucy could handle it."

A harsh laugh tore from Tom's throat, so unexpected it was as if he'd changed in an instant to another man—someone Jack could never know. But she'd seen eyes like that before, in bombed-out villages no one could ever rebuild.

"It's none of your business, Jack. If you can't handle that, maybe Lucy and I should just go."

She should have called him on the threat and run. Let him pack his battered duffel bag, his little girl and her pink bunny blanket up into the SUV and floor it down the driveway in a spray of crushed shells.

She wasn't up for all this emotional upheaval. God knew, she had enough to deal with on her own. And yet, the image of Lucy and Tom speeding off shot an unexpected jolt of alarm through Jack. Lucy being whisked away from the place she wanted so much to see. Tom speeding back to some secret place inside him where he wrestled with Lucy's illness all alone.

What the hell was wrong with her? Jack wondered, amazed. Wasn't that what she should have wanted? The two of them out of here? "The kid's already disappointed," Jack said. "The last thing I want to do is take this time away from her."

"Then try to remember Lucy's not your daughter."

A pain she'd tried to forget twisted somewhere deep inside her. Jack met his gaze, for once, too raw to conceal her emotions. "You're right," she said hoarsely. "She's not my daughter."

As if that were something she could ever forget.

8

Tom stared at Jack's rigid back as she crossed to her darkroom, entered and shut the door, locking the world out, locking *him* out. Not that he could blame her. He felt sick at what he'd just said to her. Okay, so he'd been angry. Defensive. And she'd hit one hell of a nerve—specifically to make her point, if he knew Jack Murphy.

Even so, Tom knew he'd never forget the glimpse he'd had of the stark vulnerability that lay behind those sharp, intelligent eyes. Ghosts of a past they'd both been sure she'd gotten over long ago. A crack in the armor that had seemed impenetrable a mere hour ago.

He'd judged her as distant and cold when she'd really only been trying to hide the hurt he'd dealt her in the days when she'd been young and impulsive, so loving and brave he'd fallen in love with her within days.

She'd seemed so competent and together and strong in the recent hours they'd spent together. She'd tried to act tough to cover her kindness to Lucy and show Tom she was fine. But he should have guessed something deeper lay beneath. Jack was still far too proud to let anyone guess how bruised he'd left her heart.

And as if he hadn't done enough damage way back then, he'd had to douse her old wounds with acid, been the most heartless son of a bitch imaginable when he'd been cornered.

Lucy is not your daughter . . .

But she could have been . . .

God in heaven, how many times in the first years of his baby girl's life had Tom wished Jack had been the woman who had borne his daughter?

He winced, struck by the sudden sharp memory of the future he and Jack had planned, so young, so full of hope that anything seemed possible. A game preserve in Africa—he'd tend to the wildlife there, while she'd capture the perfect beauty of the place so that those who saw the pictures would fight to preserve the creatures who lived there.

Adventure, wonder, work with meaning. They'd dreamed it all. While he'd resolved that he would find a way to keep her safe, protect her no matter how stubbornly determined she was to charge into the lion's den. He'd find a way. She'd never guess. Or else, he'd realized grimly, they'd have fights that the native peoples would still be talking about in a hundred years. But it would be worth it, to have a woman like Jack in his life.

Sure, she was strong, but there was another side to her she didn't even know of. A softer side, with a gift for wonder and eyes that could see beauty other people missed. Maybe that was what he'd loved most of all.

She'd blushed, so damned uncertain, when he'd whispered to her about the children they would have, how they'd grow up on the savannah, wild and self-reliant and free.

"I—I never . . . never thought much about babies," she'd confided, far more nervous than she had been when they'd discussed tracking man-eating tigers. "They scare me a little."

He'd cradled her against his chest, awed at how much she trusted him. "We can learn together. You have so much to give, Jack."

"What do I have that could possibly matter to a baby? I can't sit still for five minutes. I'm always getting in trouble. I watched my mother give away so much of herself. I'm far too selfish for that."

"So your kids won't have any reason to feel guilty. You can give our children independence, courage, a spirit of adventure. You'll be able to understand their restlessness and show them how a woman can be strong, take care of herself, and not accept a life so safe you feel half-dead."

She'd peered up at him with such astonishment, such sudden hope, he could barely breathe. "Really? You really think so?"

"Don't listen to the doubts other people put in your head, Jack. Somewhere in here you know the truth." He splayed his hand on her heart. "I believe in you."

In that instant, he'd seen his babies born in her eyes—sparkles of possibility where once there had been self-doubt.

"It's not life the way I imagined it," she'd confided, and for an instant fear lanced through him, fear that he'd disappoint her, limit her, and that someday she would hate him for it.

"Nothing's set in stone," he'd said, and meant it. "I mean, I want kids. I always have. But we don't have to decide right now. I want you to be happy."

"It's not the way I imagined my life," she breathed again. "It's so much more." Tom could still remember the fire her fingertips had lit inside him as she touched his throat, his cheek. "You can show me how to love," she'd whispered, pressing her lips to his chest. "You're so much better at loving than I am."

He'd promised her he would. Promised her everything they'd dreamed of. A life of adventure. A love nothing could threaten. Babies she'd never even dared dream she could hold. He'd seen wonder set her face aglow, a softness, a trust in the future he'd never seen before. One she'd believed would have no boundaries. One where he prayed he could keep her safe without her ever guessing his love was fencing her in. They'd work it out, he'd told himself. Once they were married, she'd see that what they shared was too precious to risk in daredevil schemes, no matter how rewarding the work, no matter how important the issue she wanted to capture on film.

It had seemed so simple, for that frozen moment in time. A future beyond his wildest dreams just within his grasp.

She'd trusted in him for that precious scrap of time. Until reality had slipped in. Until the truth had slipped out and she'd seen his secret fears for her. Until sparks had flown and dreams had been in danger and he'd made a choice he would never have imagined.

Accepted his duty? Or had he been a coward even then, with a life holding more boundaries than Jack could bear? So confined that she couldn't breathe there?

It had haunted him for years, that single question.

Why had he done what he'd done? Chosen what he'd chosen? Honor? Practicality? Duty? Or had he been too small a man to embrace Jack's wide-open world?

Whatever the reason, the result was the same. She'd trusted him with all that she was. He'd made her believe he was man enough to take it all in, let her be free, stand beside her without holding her back.

And then, just when she'd believed the most, he'd taken it all away.

He'd still had a daughter to hold, to love, to marvel over. Innocence and wonder and bright little-girl smiles. Pain, yes, he'd had pain and loss and fear. But even if he could have gone back, changed things—banished Laura from his life and forgone the terrible price she had cost him—even if he could have drained that misery from his life, he never would have. He had Lucy. What did Jack have? The life she'd insisted she wanted? The career that had drained so much joy out of her face? Eyes that had seen things that had scarred her deep inside where she'd let no one reach to comfort her? What did she hold in her arms when night came except emptiness where the dreams they'd woven that long-ago night should have been?

"Dammit, it wasn't as if I wanted to hurt her," he muttered under his breath. "Not back then. Not now. As for Lucy—I just couldn't let her go off with China Pepperell. Risk someone telling her—"

"Telling me what, Daddy?"

Tom stared, appalled, at the small figure standing at the foot of the stairway. "Lucy! You're supposed to be upstairs."

"I heard the door slam. I knew that Ms. Murphy was—well, gone."

Tom could see Lucy steeling herself for one of their rare arguments. "Daddy, you broke the rules."

"The rules?"

"You promised whenever you told me no you'd always explain why. But this time you didn't even try and I can't figure it out by myself even though I tried. That China Pepperell lady was nice and she wanted me to go with her and see things I'll never have a chance to see again. And my mom knew her so she wasn't really a stranger. I thought we came all the way here so I could have adventures and going wrecking with them would have been the best kind I could even imagine. You sounded all prickly and mad but nobody did anything wrong at all."

Tom winced. "I can't explain this time, Lucy. You'll just have to trust me."

Like Jack had eight and a half years ago? I'd fail Lucy, too, in the end. The truth would come out and I wouldn't be able to stop it. Just as it had with Jack—

But Lucy stood her ground before him, reminding him for a moment far more of the woman in the darkroom than her mother, stubborn in her quest for truth. "But if you don't tell me what's the matter, you don't trust me, do you?"

He'd encouraged the kid to question. Her logic today dismayed him.

"Sometimes things get complicated." He stopped at the expression on his daughter's face. She'd dealt with her parents' divorce, her mother vanishing from her life and the threat of impending blindness. She had to be thinking "How much more complicated could things get?"

Thank God she has no idea, Tom thought.

"Remember when you went over to Jenny's house and her baby-sitter let you watch that movie I wouldn't allow you to? You had nightmares for a week because it just wasn't right for girls your age?"

Lucy flushed, embarrassed. "There was a big dog in the closet and it had bloody teeth."

"You made me check inside your closet for a week. I

said you shouldn't watch movies like that because I wanted to keep you from getting upset, having bad dreams. You knew it wasn't real, but once the scary parts got in your head you thought there were monsters everywhere."

"But what if there *had* been a dog in the closet?" Lucy reasoned. "At least if I knew it was in there, I could keep him from biting me. Wouldn't it be worse if I opened the closet and didn't even know a monster was inside?"

That's what I'm afraid of, Tom thought miserably. *That you might stumble on monsters that will change the way you look at me forever.*

"I promise I won't let anything hurt you," Tom said, wishing keeping Lucy safe was just that simple. But he knew that sometimes monsters slipped out, no matter how hard you tried to keep them locked away. Nightmare dogs with bloody fangs, people you wanted to forget, old mistakes resurrected when the piper demanded that you pay up at last.

She peered up at him, looking more hurt than defiant. "You're still breaking the rules," she insisted. "Keeping secrets. The only other time you did it was when the doctors said I was going blind. Whatever secret you have now must be something really bad."

Tom's fingers curled into fists, his heart lurching. Cornered by an eight-year-old with no good way out. "Lucy, *I'm* the grown-up here. I'm supposed to protect you from things like—well, like violent movies and too much sweet stuff that will make you sick."

"Yeah, but then you tell me it'll make me sick. You won't tell me anything about what's making you act funny now."

Tom stroked her hair, winced when the familiar gesture didn't fool her.

"Do dads ever get scared?" Lucy asked. "Of ghosts and bloody fanged dogs and things?"

He wanted to lie. But already he'd told more half-truths than he could handle. "Sometimes."

There were plenty of ghosts he was scared of—especially here, in this lighthouse. Images of Laura swirled around these halls, biding their time with a patience that turned his blood cold. Glimpses of the Jack Murphy-who-might-have-been haunted him. Made him want to shake her, take her in his arms, make her feel joy instead of exhaustion, force her to trudge through thick walls of misery because she didn't know how to stop punishing herself for something he couldn't guess. Something that had happened in the wild places she'd run to? No question, Jack had secrets of her own. But puzzling over them now would just make Lucy more suspicious and confused than she already was. She'd sense he was hiding something, fear the worst with the vivid imagination of a child.

He looked down at his solemn-faced daughter and winced inwardly. During the endless car ride to Maine, she'd babbled on for hours about the lighthouse and Mermaid Lost, her cheeks flushed with delight, her eyes twinkling with anticipation until it had seemed every star in the heavens were trapped beneath her lashes. Now, shadows gathered in the green depths and her soft pink bow of a mouth turned down at the corners.

Tom hunkered down so they were eye to eye, let love and regret show in his face. "I'm sorry things haven't exactly turned out the way you hoped they would here, sweetheart, and I know a big part of that has been my fault."

"You've been acting like that porcupine we found tangled up in an old fishing line."

"That bad, huh? How about if I try to do better? Come on, Lucy," he urged. "Let's not waste any more of the day being mad at each other. We can explore the beach, just you and me. Who knows what we might find?"

Shark teeth or giant shells, old fishnets or sparkly trinkets tourists had dropped. Anything Mermaid Lost might hold except his memories of Jack Murphy loving him or the even more daunting shadow looming large—the secret that just might make his daughter hate him.

Sunshine streamed over the storm's footprints, a drift of broken branches, tangled fishermen's nets, the small, battered sailboat even Tom could tell would never be seaworthy again. Hours spent combing the shore had by turns delighted and dismayed Lucy, her emotions at the moment changeable as the Maine skies.

His own feelings were even more unmanageable. He wished to God he could understand them. Tom watched Lucy retrieve yet another starfish stranded on the sand, cupping the tiny creature carefully in her palm as she crossed to the lapping ocean waves, released it into a foamy crest.

He felt as trapped as the tiny sea creature by a nagging guilt that was growing by leaps and bounds, the morning's altercation between him and Jack playing over and over in his head.

She thought he was a jerk. A dictator—her accusation echoed in his mind. The knowledge stung. He'd seen the disgust in every line of her expressive face, the sharpness in her narrowed eyes, the curl of her fingers tight into her palms, like fists, poised to fight what she saw as injustice. But even if she thought he could rival Atilla the Hun, why should it matter so much?

A week from now she'd be out of his life and he'd never see her again. So why should it chafe at him so much if Jack Murphy thought he was a control freak? A father who laid out his decrees with no explanation to anyone—especially his daughter? Maybe he *had* been too cutting with his angry response. But the bottom line was that he didn't owe Jack any explanation at all for his decision not to let Lucy run amok with a tribe of wild boys and their sixty-year-old grandmother clambering around on cliffs where a single misstep could mean a terrible fall to jagged rocks below. Lucy's sight had suffered in the months since her diagnosis. Her perceptions sometimes just enough off to make her stumble on stairways or trip over tree roots she should have been able to avoid easily enough. Hell, she'd crashed and burned twice since they'd gotten to the lighthouse.

But right now the obvious dangers were the least of his worries. Far more treacherous, insidious perils than broken bones threatened Lucy when she was in China Pepperell's presence, and in Tom's experience broken hearts took far longer to heal than cuts and scrapes and arms bound in casts. He winced as Jack's image rose in his mind. Sometimes, even when it came to people with the strongest spirits, broken hearts never fully mended at all.

Tom clenched his fists, his brow furrowing as he watched Lucy shield her eyes with her flattened hand, charting the starfish's course as it swam away. A hint of wistfulness still clung to her freckled face, but the worst of her rare spell of pouting had faded. After hours of sunshine and exploring she was obviously better, so why did he still feel like hell?

"Daddy?" She approached him, not at a run, rather slowly, deliberately.

"What is it, Kitten?"

"What's a dictator?"

He should have seen that question coming. Lucy had devoured new big words from the time she'd been three years old. "A dictator is someone who makes people do what they want them to, instead of letting them decide for themselves. Like, well, remember that show we watched together on the History Channel? The one about Hitler?"

Lucy nibbled at her bottom lip. "Why did Ms. Murphy call you that?"

"She thought you should be able to go and play with the other kids. She thought I was being unfair. So she got mad and called me that name. You get mad sometimes, don't you? So do I. You don't always mean exactly what you say."

"She looked like she meant it a lot. Her eyes looked all hot and her face got red."

She'd been scarlet—until the moment he'd flung out his coup de grâce and her face had gone waxen pale.

"I've been trying to figure out in my head why she was acting so funny. Do you think that maybe the reason Ms. Murphy got so mad that you wouldn't let me go was because she likes to be alone all the time? If we'd gone with the Pepperells, she would have had the lighthouse all to herself again."

"You think Jack—I mean, Ms. Murphy wanted to get rid of you?"

"I just was thinking if she's alone all the time like she says, there's nobody around to tell her 'no.' Maybe she's just not used to it."

Out of the mouths of babes, Tom thought. He brushed away a patch of sand clinging to his daughter's cheek, touched by Lucy's efforts to understand—both him and

Jack Murphy. Jack not used to people telling her no? The problem was more likely that Jack was far *too* used to it. Tom thought with a surge of respect for the woman who'd gone toe to toe with him that morning. Eight and a half years later, he could still remember stories Jack told him of her father, Frank Murphy, trying to control her, undercutting the independence Jack craved like air to breathe. Trust Lucy to stumble on the reason the scene this morning still haunted him. Jack had looked at him as if he were some kind of monster, a Simon Legree who had brought her own childhood's trauma flooding back to her. It made him feel cruel and small and he'd hated it.

Tom stilled for a moment, astonished at the ache he felt someplace deep at that certainty. Part of him was still mad as hell at the woman. So why should he care? And yet, even sharp and defiant and flinging into his face truths he'd far rather deny, there was one thing about Jack that was inescapable. She made him feel more alive than anyone else he'd ever known. *A little like stepping on a live wire*, he thought, trying hard not to be amused by the image.

"Daddy?" Lucy shook him from his thoughts by tugging at his sleeve. "You're thinking so hard your face is all scrunched up. How come? Can't you tell me what's the matter?"

"I was just thinking about what you said—about Jack not being used to people telling her no. I think it's the opposite, sweetheart. I think people tell her no all the time, but she can't just give up when they do. Not considering what she does in her work."

"She takes pictures of stuff," Lucy said, bemused. "People like to get pictures taken, at least if someone tells them to smile in time."

"The types of pictures Jack's been working on here

aren't the type she takes most of the time. Pictures of lighthouses and ocean scenes and little girls with freckles." He cradled her cheek in his palm for a moment. "Jack takes the kind of pictures you see on the news at night or in newspapers or magazines. Sometimes she shoots photographs of things that are nice, but most of the time she captures things that aren't nice on film, things we need to know about even if they worry us or scare us."

Lucy quieted for a moment, and Tom could almost hear the wheels whirring beneath her silky blond curls. "I think I know the kind of pictures you mean. Ones like that baby gorilla crying when the poachers killed its mom?"

They'd been working together on a science report on endangered species when Lucy had stumbled across the picture on the Internet. He'd just been gone an instant to get a Coke. When he'd returned, she'd been staring at the horrific image, crying as if her heart would break. She'd been inconsolable over the powerful camera shot—the baby gorilla, all too human in its grief, being torn away from its mother's body. He had hoped that with the passage of time Lucy had forgotten it. He should have known better.

"Yes, sweetheart," he said gently. "Pictures like that one. Except most times it's not animals Jack takes pictures of. It's people who are in trouble."

Lucy digested that for a moment, scuffing at the sand with the toe of her tennis shoe. "I wouldn't like that kind of job. Doesn't it make her sad?"

Tom turned his gaze away, trying to hide the ache that had reverberated through him when he'd seen shadows darkening Jack's once eager face. "I think it does make her sad. But Jack takes pictures anyway. Pictures of people like those poachers, people who are doing something to hurt others. She hopes that if good people see them, we'll fight to change things."

"Like the collection I took up in my class to send to the gorilla foundation after I saw what those bad men were doing?"

"Exactly like that. Jack's pictures make people mad at men like those poachers. The people who are doing wrong don't like that."

"She must be really brave. Those men hurting the gorilla looked meaner than monsters, and they didn't even have bloody fangs."

"She is brave. And she cares very much that people and animals—that everyone is treated fairly."

"I get it now!" Realization dawned on Lucy's face. "You weren't being fair when you didn't want me to go play with those boys on the cliff, so she thinks you're a dictator!"

Somehow this wasn't the direction he'd been hoping this conversation would go. "I suppose she does," Tom admitted, "but then, she's not a mom or a dad. She doesn't understand about kids."

"But she was a kid once, wasn't she?"

Hadn't that been Jack's point exactly? Tom closed his eyes, remembering all too clearly the hushed confidences Jack shared with him in bed, under cover of darkness when he couldn't see her face. She'd told him tales of her father's iron control, how he had broken her mother's spirit, but never, never Jack's. Tom hadn't been old enough then, to wonder why Frank Murphy had been so hard on his daughter. No question Jack's father had had a mean streak. Jack had claimed her father hated her for her defiance, liked his women to be elegant, soft-spoken and lovely, like the First Lady he'd named her after. She'd been the exact opposite of Jacqueline Kennedy in so many ways. And yet, did something else lie behind his tempestuous relationship with his daughter? Had the tough guy reporter been scared to death, watching Jack grow up, fearing her growing fascination with dancing on danger's sharpest edge?

If that were so, would Lucy resent Tom forever for refusing to let her run wild on the beach today? A pleasure denied seemingly for no reason—just because her father said so. One chance to have the adventure of a lifetime—a chance that would never come again. Kids got wounded so easily, and they had a long, long memory.

After a moment, Lucy spoke. "Daddy, I like Ms. Murphy a lot. Don't be mad 'cause she called you a name. She just wanted me to have fun."

Tom peered down at Lucy's face, his baby girl, always wanting to soothe places that hurt, bandage wounds people couldn't see, bring smiles out of secret sadness. She'd gotten that trait from him. It hurt him, sometimes, knowing he'd passed that curse on to his daughter—understanding too deeply, sensing too much of other people's pain as well as one's own.

He straightened, suddenly struck by an idea. "What say we go to that little grocery store we passed on our way here. Pick up some stuff and then head back to the lighthouse, make dinner? Some of my famous lasagna? We can invite Jack to eat with us to smooth things over."

"You think she'll make up with you just 'cause we make her some food?" Lucy's fine-drawn brows arched doubtfully. "I think she's lots tougher than that, Daddy. Even if you do make better lasagna than Grandma."

Tom chuckled, and gathered Lucy close, her sweet innocence warming the cold places dread had left around his heart. "It's worth a try, anyway, don't you think, baby? Even tough war photographers have to eat."

"Daddy, if she's always running around weird places, who knows what she's had to munch on. I saw a picture in a geography book once of people on this strange island eating great big bugs and smiling like they tasted like candy bars. And the scientist who came to study those people, he had to eat bugs too or else he'd insult the island guys. Who knows? Maybe feeding her something great like lasagna will be a bigger deal than I thought."

Tom set Lucy back on her feet, gratitude welling up inside him when she slipped her small hand into his. Whatever bumps she'd gotten today were fading. She wasn't angry with him anymore. But Lucy was right to doubt the potential success of the peace offering they'd planned. Jack's anger would probably be much harder to crack than Lucy's was. He'd probably be lucky to get Jack to take a bite of the meal, no matter how delicious the pasta and sauce smelled.

Even so, Tom felt better as he started toward the lighthouse, clipping the length of his long stride to match Lucy's shorter one. He wondered where Jack was now. Her small rental car was still gone from the driveway. She'd peeled off down the road as soon as she'd been able to refill her camera bag with supplies after their fight that morning. She hadn't eaten breakfast, and, knowing Jack, she hadn't bothered with lunch either. God knew the woman needed a decent meal.

Maybe he wasn't rash enough or optimistic enough to think this encounter with Jack was more than rotten luck on both their parts. He had no delusions they'd send each other Christmas cards or keep in touch. And yet, he did care what happened to her. After what they'd shared during those mad, wonderful weeks in

Kentucky, he'd never be able to completely erase her from his heart.

But if he was doomed to carry the memory of her forever, he'd rather her image be softer, healthier, more peaceful, instead of the stressed to the limit, waxy-pale, driven woman she'd become. Maybe Lucy was right, Jack wouldn't be won over by something as simple as lasagna, but if he had enough guts, he could try something else. He could talk to Jack. Maybe even tell her something close to the truth. And maybe, just maybe, she'd decide to forgive him.

Jack hesitated outside the blue painted door, its brass anchor knocker emblazoned with the name Pepperell in Old English script. She figured China would faint dead away when she found Jack on the doorstep. The woman had tried a dozen times to get Jack to visit the "new family headquarters," a cluster of small houses and apartments that kept the brothers within shouting distance of one another.

China's own lodgings sat directly atop the pub that now took up most of her time and energy. After years of living at the lighthouse with only her sons and husband to talk to, she was reveling in the captive audience that came to Cap Ramsey's every night to hear her tales.

China had used every wile at her disposal to convince Jack to visit—tried to lure her with boxes full of old family photos and heirlooms generations of sea captains had brought back to Maine in the holds of their ships. Baubles and curiosities to dazzle and amaze the wives and children they hadn't seen for so long.

Jack had used every excuse she could imagine in order to avoid passing through this door. After all, she was working on a book about the lighthouse, not the people in it. She'd thought nothing could break down her stubborn decision to avoid the Pepperell home. But the shots she'd taken of Lucy had cracked her reluctance to show the human side in the book, and today Jack was desperate enough to put in at any port as long as it was as far away from the lighthouse and Tom Brownlow as possible.

She hated the fact that she was avoiding the man and his daughter, but she'd be damned before she lost a whole day's work because of it. At least here, she could convince herself she was gathering background for the book.

The door swung open, and China stared at her, the older woman's hair still wild from her morning adventure with her grandsons, her cheeks windburned bright pink.

"Well, bless my soul, I'd be less surprised to find the old pirate Ramsey on my doorstep."

"I suppose I've been considering what you said. The more information I have about the lighthouse's past, the truer I'll be able to paint its image in the present."

China's keen gaze narrowed. "Trying to avoid that handsome Tom Brownlow and his baby girl, are you?"

Jack wanted to argue. There wasn't any point. "I'm not used to having people around. Guess I've lost my knack for casual conversation."

"Not much casual between you and that man if you ask an old woman like me. And I'd wager the two of you didn't do much talking when you knew each other. Probably barely came up for air."

"China—"

"Don't 'China' me. I wasn't always sixty, you know. And the captain and I didn't have eight babies by talking to each other. Something purely crackles between you and that Brownlow man."

Jack was stunned to find herself blushing as if China had caught her parking with Tom on the Old Line road. Worse still was the knowledge that China had read her so easily. In an effort to hide just how much that fact disconcerted her, Jack wandered past China into the room beyond. Spices she'd smelled in places like Morocco and the Orient filled the air, every inch of the forest of shelves that walled the room crammed with knickknacks of every shape and size.

"There's something between Tom Brownlow and me, all right. Irritation. I could have strangled him when he wouldn't let Lucy go exploring with you. The kid's facing so much right now. Why shouldn't he let her go with you?"

"It's hard to know why a soul with as much trouble as Tom Brownlow's makes the decisions it does. It's more dangerous still to judge him. You're wise in the ways of the world, Jack. You must have sensed the decency in him or I can't imagine you'd even have let him through the lighthouse door to begin with."

"It was storming. Even if I wanted to push him straight down the hill in his car, I couldn't let him drive with the little girl."

"I know you well enough to be sure that if you wanted the Brownlows gone, you would have found a way to make sure that's what happened." China moved to her small, galley kitchen, put a copper kettle on the stove for tea. "Have you stopped to wonder what it was about the two of them that made you decide to let them stay?"

"The child is going blind. I'm not a complete heel. Anyway, it doesn't matter why I let them stay. What matters now is why Tom wouldn't let Lucy *go*. It's all the kid can talk about—getting to know this place. Of everywhere in the world, Mermaid Lost is the one place Lucy Brownlow wants to see before she loses her sight forever."

"And you know Tom Brownlow's heart, know his life well enough to pass judgment on it? Tell the girl's father what he must do?"

"You know as well as I do that exploring the cliffs would be the best thing in the world for a child who's going blind. Sure, there are risks, but there are ways to minimize them. It would make her strong, build her confidence, allow her to store up memories of sights she'll never see anywhere else, creatures she's only glimpsed in books, adventures that will still give her a thrill of excitement, even after her blindness won't let her clamber around on cliffs anymore."

"It's easy to see it your way," China said, preparing a blue-and-white teapot with deft fingers, warming the cold pot with hot water, dumping it out, then measuring loose tea leaves with a practiced hand. "Perhaps we should try to see it from Tom Brownlow's point of view as well. Maybe the man wants to spend every moment he can with his baby, doesn't want to waste even one morning. Maybe he wants to see her face shine when she pokes among the wonders she'll find along the sea edge. Maybe it made him nervous—my knowing the little girl's mama. I swear, the child looks so much like her mother, for a heartbeat, I thought I was staring into Laura's face again."

"The fact that you knew Laura should have made him more at ease about letting you take Lucy, not less so."

"You think so, do you? But then, you didn't know Laura Willoughby."

Bitterness welled up in Jack, surprising in its strength. "Oh, I learned enough about Laura the one time I met her. I saw just how many people she could trample over without ever once losing that wide-eyed look she had—like a fairy-tale princess someone had dumped in the woods. I just had the good sense not to play her games."

Jack stopped, appalled at herself for venting to any-one at all, but especially China, who craved the kind of emotional closeness Jack dreaded. The older woman's eyes glowed bright in wrinkled pockets of flesh, wise and sympathetic, the eyes of someone who had lived long enough to see heartache in all its varied forms.

"Forget I said anything." Jack swore, still astonished at her outburst. "I never—never blow off steam like that with anybody."

"Except Ziggy," China finished softly.

Jack swallowed hard, missing her crusty, bighearted mentor so much the grief felt brand-new.

"I'm honored, then, to have you trust me so much," China said. "Ziggy Bartolli was a fine man. A friend worthy of trusting with your heart's deepest hurts. But he's gone, Jack. He won't be coming back. You've got the rest of your life to live. You can't be holding in feelings all that time. Tell me. Talk to me. If Ziggy trusted me with his secrets, surely you can trust me with yours."

"I just want—want to get this infernal book done. Keep my word to Ziggy. And get the hell away from here. It was hard enough before. But now—"

"With Tom Brownlow and his little girl here?"

"This is crazy, China. I didn't sign on for this."

"Sign on for what?"

"To see him again. Stay under the same roof with him. And with his daughter. She looks so much like Laura, the first time I saw her it was like—like my lungs were on fire. I couldn't breathe. I wanted to shove them out the door, storm or no storm. Let them take their chances. They weren't my responsibility. Coming to the lighthouse without so much as a phone call—they deserved to have the door slammed in their face. Especially since the last time I saw Tom, he—" Jack stopped, stalked to the bank of windows on the far side of the room.

"You cared for him once."

"Unfortunately it wasn't just hot sex, although that part was great." Jack tried to take refuge in humor.

Even if she hadn't admitted the truth, China would have figured it out, she reasoned. It was a no-brainer that she cared about Tom Brownlow on some level, at least *had* cared—past tense. Otherwise he wouldn't have had the power to slip past her guard, get her blood boiling with anger, impatience, and maybe, just maybe, the tiniest whisper of remembered pain.

"It was all a long time ago. Why should it even matter anymore?"

"Maybe you can tell me."

"I don't know," Jack admitted, turning to look full into China's weathered face.

"Do you want me to tell you what I think?" China asked.

"Ziggy would have just spit it out. He wouldn't have bothered to ask. Go on, tell me."

"You've business between the two of you that isn't finished. You've got a chance to figure out what that is, if you'll take it. You say you're long over whatever hurt there was between you, and yet, look at yourself, Jack. You're nothing but raw nerves."

That was the problem, Jack admitted. What she was feeling now wasn't echoes of some old affair. It was too fresh, too new, too damned dangerous even for her, the biggest adrenaline junkie east of the Mississippi. But she'd rather be eaten by a dozen crocodiles than admit it.

"And you think I'm so edgy because of a man I

haven't seen in years?" Jack asked. "I wish it were that simple, China. I really do. This is just the way I am. So restless my feet hurt when I try to stay still, so edgy I have to keep moving so I can never catch up."

Catch up to what? The question hung between them, one Jack didn't ever want to answer, especially to herself. Did China sense it? The older woman had the grace not to ask.

"As for Tom, he's got plenty of troubles of his own. Secrets. Things closed up so tight inside him I doubt anybody could reach them. Not that I'd want to," she amended hastily. "I've spent more time wanting to throttle him than anything else."

"That's what happens when you fight so hard against what your heart knows is right. A few hours fighting and then a night sorting things out in bed would do wonders for both of you."

"That's not funny! I'll admit the guy is sexy as hell, and I'm not above, well, jumping between the sheets if I thought it was worth it—which it hasn't been for a very long time."

"Years, according to Ziggy."

"Glad my old buddy spared me the trouble of having to tell you about my own lackluster sex life."

"Jack, you and I, we feel as much as any other woman. We just try to hide it with bluster and humor and pure downright stubbornness. But I've come to care about you, child. Maybe even before I ever met you. When Ziggy used to talk about you."

A lump formed in Jack's throat. She wasn't used to people caring. Wasn't comfortable with it. Then why was it that some part of her suddenly wanted to cry out all her frustration, all her loss, all her anger on China's ample bosom? Instead she turned away, clenching her jaw until it ached.

"I've only seen Tom for a few moments," China said gently, "but for generations we Pepperells have had a gift of seeing clear to a man's marrow at only a glance. When your life depends on judging a man's character, choosing whether or not to sign him on as a hand on your boat, you learn to be quick to see what a person is made of. Now I don't know what hurts lie between you and Tom Brownlow. And I'm not certain how Laura Willoughby figures into the mix; though, having known the girl long as I did I can make a pretty good guess. But I can tell you this— there's goodness in that man. A fineness of spirit I've seen precious few times in my sixty years. Whatever temper sparks are flying between you right now, and whatever happened in the past, don't be too hard on him now. He's carrying the weight of the world on his shoulders, what with his baby going blind. You're not the kind of person who'd make his burden heavier, even if he steps on your toes a bit as he stumbles along the road."

Jack rubbed her temple with her fingertips, regret nudging her hard at the memory of Tom's stricken face when she'd accused him of being like her father. A man she knew Tom had loathed because of the stories she'd confided to him.

"I know you're right," she admitted. "I should be ashamed of myself, getting so mad at a man who is going through something so terrible. But it just—just made me crazy when he told Lucy no. I know how she felt—confused and hurt and angry, not understanding. Wanting the adventure so bad she could taste it and yet helpless to change his mind. And it's not like she can do what I did, tell herself to be patient—she'll be able to climb all the cliffs she wants to when she's grown up. Lucy only has a tiny window of time."

"Maybe this is none of my business, but will you indulge an old woman just this once, Jack?"

Jack shrugged, nodded.

"It's always dangerous to assume you know how someone else feels—even someone as young as Lucy Brownlow. What you really know, what makes you chafe and burn isn't what she feels, it's what *you'd* feel if *your* father had told you no. Ziggy told me something about your father, the kind of man he was. The way he treated you, trying to keep you under his thumb. No wonder it made you fearsome angry—wild-spirited creature that you are. But Lucy isn't you, Jack. And Tom Brownlow isn't your father. What's between the two of them, the love and the trust and even their weaknesses—those are Lucy and Tom's alone. And we don't know them well enough to even guess what they feel."

That's not exactly true, Jack thought. She knew how Tom felt about his daughter. She'd seen the love, the fear, the pain naked in his eyes when she'd discovered him keeping vigil beside Lucy's bed. Would a man who sat at his daughter's bedside night after night to keep her from being afraid be thoughtless enough to deny that little girl pleasure just because he had the power to?

And as for Lucy, she'd seen the trust in the child's face as she reached for her father's hand. The wonder Lucy wanted to share with him as she chattered about the pictures Jack had taken, the magic of having her picture in Jack's book.

"You've given me something to think about," Jack admitted to China. And she did think, through the hours she and China pored over the old woman's treasures, sorted through boxes of photographs, unsmiling Victorians and stiff-shouldered Edwardians, each one of them stalwart in their own way, posed before the light tower. Generations standing firm before the sea's wildest fury.

The dinner crowd was lining up at the pub below by the time she left China's attic, but in spite of the knots in her shoulders and the aches in her back there was a spring in her step. She locked her booty in the car, then straightened, peering down the little row of shops, their windows glistening with welcoming light. She had one more errand to do. It was a crazy idea, she thought with more hope than she'd had since she'd buried her best friend. But then, maybe it was just crazy enough to work.

At any rate, she was going to do her best to ease some of the worry from Tom's face and put the sparkle back in Lucy Brownlow's smile.

9

Jack slung her camera bag over one shoulder, then hefted a boxful of old photographs and journals China had packed up for her at the end of the afternoon. With her left hip, she bumped the car door closed, then sneezed for about the hundredth time since she'd climbed up to the Pepperell attic hours ago.

Her eyes felt gritty from dust, her hands dry and powdery from sorting through three lifetimes of memories. Considering the success of her mission, she might have felt like a treasure hunter who'd just discovered the mother lode except for the fact that her stomach had a knot in it roughly the size of Manhattan.

Okay, so she wasn't looking forward to her first encounter with Tom after the explosion between them that morning. Usually she thrived on confrontation, lived for it. But somehow, the "in your face" attitude she'd perfected during years of fighting for the best angle on a story didn't have the same appeal when it was aimed at a guy who was barely keeping his head above water.

She wasn't exactly *sorry* for challenging him when he'd refused to let Lucy go exploring the beaches of Mermaid Lost with the Pepperells. She wasn't even sure she had been wrong to question his decision. But she wasn't quite as ready as she had been to paste Tom Brownlow's picture next to Mussolini's in the encyclopedia. At least not yet.

Her life on the road had taught her plenty of lessons: how to fight her way out of a jam; how to tell someone to go to hell so they'd be looking forward to the trip. She'd learned when to up the ante and when to change tactics. But she'd never quite gotten the hang of backing down from a stand she'd taken. Not even if she was dead wrong—and she wasn't saying that she *was* this time.

Jack paused for a moment, midway up the crushed-shell sidewalk, her gaze fixed on the lighthouse door. She'd always been great in a fight. But in this kind of situation she hadn't the slightest idea how to handle herself.

Stay out of it. Don't make things worse than they already are for Tom, she told herself. *Decisions he makes about Lucy are none of your business.* It should have been simple.

It would have been except for the images of Lucy Brownlow that kept flashing in her mind like slides in a projector carousel. Lucy's eyes gleaming with eagerness as she looked at Jack's camera. Lucy's cheeks pink instead of pale as she climbed about the cliff top with all the innocent anticipation of a nestling bird just waiting to learn to fly. Lucy's soft brow crinkled in thought, wondering if she'd remember what green looked like a dozen years from now.

Jack should be avoiding the kid as if Lucy had the plague. At the very least she should be coolly polite, try to stay out of Lucy's way as much as possible.

But there was something about the kid. Something beyond the fact that she was wearing Laura Willoughby's face, staring out at the world with Laura Willoughby's eyes. Something Jack couldn't turn away from.

Lucy had a quality so compelling, she hadn't been able to resist stopping on her way back to the lighthouse to pick up the surprise tucked into her jacket pocket. Even if Lucy could never go roving with the Pepperell clan, Jack hoped the gift she'd gotten for the little girl would help make her days here at the lighthouse all the more exciting.

It was the only plan Jack could come up with. Better than doing nothing at all. The present had also helped her to avoid going back to the lighthouse for another hour or so, picking out just the right accessories, getting everything perfect. The only thing left to do was to find just the right way, just the right time to slip the package to Lucy. And that would definitely *not* be until the smoke cleared after the gunfight at the O.K. corral.

"Might as well stop putting off the inevitable," Jack grumbled under her breath. "Just go in and see what kind of attitude Tom throws at you."

Sucking in a deep breath, Jack marched to the door, then tried to maneuver her way to the brass knob—no small feat considering she had the box and camera bag to contend with. She'd just brushed the cool, polished surface when the door swung wide on its own, nearly pitching Jack, the box and the bag in an avalanche over Lucy.

The kid was just the first onslaught, the second wafted into Jack's nostrils, filling them with the luscious aroma of tomato sauce and cheese. In an instant she decided to revoke Tom's pardon from the dictator's club. Any man who would use food that fantastic-smelling to punish a starving woman didn't deserve any mercy.

It was almost eight o'clock. He and Lucy must have eaten hours ago. There could be no reason to keep what smelled like lasagna warming in the oven except to torture Jack.

"You're lucky my grandma's not here or you'd be in big trouble," Lucy warned. "Whenever *she* tries to keep stuff warm for somebody who's late, she gets real mad and she burns stuff up until it's hard as a rock just so they won't do it again."

"But I'm not—not late. I'm not supposed to—"

"I know," Lucy said with a stern nod that almost made Jack laugh. *"That's* why Daddy and me are letting you slide this time."

Tom actually intended to let her eat that heavenly smelling stuff? Jack thought, stunned. What was he? Crazy? They'd been biting each other's heads off earlier.

"You sure have a lot of stuff. Come on, let me help you." Lucy grabbed the edge of the box, almost tipping it out of Jack's grip entirely.

"Better not, kiddo!" Jack warned instinctively. "It's heavy!"

Lucy rolled her eyes with such a long suffering expression Jack couldn't help chuckling. "I'm going blind, not losing my muscles," the little girl said.

"Right you are. Stick it on the hall table." Jack released her hold on the box. She hoped the container of fragile old books and photos made it safely to a table, but she knew China would be the first one to agree that Lucy's self-confidence was far more precious than any inanimate object could ever be.

Hauling her camera bag over to a cane-back chair, Jack had just started to set it down when she felt the

weight of Tom's gaze on her back. Completely unexpected, a tingle ran, like the light brush of a fingertip
down her spine. An awareness even deeper than
before, though she wasn't sure why—perhaps because
of China's insights into the man's heart, or the memory
of how generous he'd been, how tender and wild and
splendid when he'd shown her just how soul-shattering
making love could be.

She released her hold on the bag, then turned. Tom
filled the kitchen door, the plain apron tied around his
waist only making him look more masculine. Biceps
that had earned him scholarships as a most unlikely
star quarterback bulged the sleeves of his polo shirt,
cloth the color of hot chocolate matching the hue of his
eyes.

He looked more mouth-watering than the lasagna
smelled. The thought jumped into Jack's mind all on its
own. Okay, so she was starving. She wasn't dead. Tom
Brownlow had definitely shaken her libido out of
hibernation. For an instant, the wicked part of her
sense of humor wondered what he'd look like serving
the lasagna wearing nothing *but* his apron—providing
Lucy was on the other side of Mermaid Lost, of course.
The image was so vivid, so sensual, for the second time
in two days, Jack didn't have any idea what to say.

Tom broke the silence, his voice soothing, a tone
she'd never expected to hear again. "Considering the
surgeon general's stand on smoking, a peace pipe was
out of the question. I figured I'd try lasagna instead."
He cleared his throat, glanced away, his cheekbones
just a shade darker. "Do you still love pasta as much as
you used to?"

He remembered.

Jack braced herself against the knowledge, her own
memory spinning back in time. He'd made her lasagna

after her first rabies shot. The stuff had been pure heaven. She'd told him if the vet school thing didn't work out, he could open a restaurant.

She'd kissed him, full on the mouth, threaded her fingers through the silky strands of his hair. Even now, years later, her mouth still went dry at the memory of how much she'd wanted him.

He'd tried to draw away even though Jack could feel every fiber in him wanted to keep kissing her forever. "Wait—promised I wouldn't."

"I didn't promise *I* wouldn't," she'd whispered, craving for the taste of him—something strong, something fine, something good. Someone different from anyone she'd ever known. Like Galahad, but she'd wanted him to throw his vow of chastity out the nearest window.

He'd drawn away, cupped her cheek in his hand, warm, so warm, she could feel it to her toes. "It's not that I don't want to, Jack," he'd said, voice rough with regret. "It's just—I don't want to hurt you. I promised myself . . . wouldn't rush into anything again after—" His eyes darkened with sadness, self-condemnation. "I made a mess of things the last time I cared for someone."

Jack remembered the parts of her body his kiss had been melting suddenly feeling chilled. "You're in love with someone else?"

"No!" he cried, then repeated softly, "No. I never was in love with her. She wanted me to be. Needed someone to—I don't know. She seemed lost. Maybe I thought I could save her. But I didn't ever love her. I promised myself that if I ever took a chance on love again, it would be the real thing. I'd be sure before I—" He stopped, shrugged. "I care about you. And God knows, I want you. But I won't risk hurting you."

"It's my risk to take. I'm not asking for guarantees.

I'm not even sure if I want forever. Why should you have to be?"

"Because you're precious to me, Jack. You've got such a big heart and you run into life headfirst. No fear. I'd hate myself forever if I were the man who made you afraid."

Her chin had bumped up. "I don't believe in being afraid."

"I know. You're so . . . brave. So free. Maybe that's why I—"

"You're what?"

"I might be falling in love with you, no matter how hard I'm trying not to."

The memory faded, bittersweet. She'd wanted to give him everything inside her, let love for him flood every corner of her heart. When they parted, she'd vowed that she'd never give away so many pieces of herself again. Not that Tom had wanted her to give so much. He'd been so careful, so tender, so strong. And she'd believed in him, like she'd never believed in anyone before.

Was he remembering all that now? Jack's cheeks burned. She couldn't look at him, let him see how vivid the memories were in her own mind. She busied herself by taking off her jacket and laying it beside the camera bag, the package in the jacket pocket thudding dully against the hard wood surface.

"You don't have to feed me to make peace, Tom," she said more abruptly than she intended. "I mean, it's really thoughtful of you, but it's not necessary. I can get a little, well, vocal with my opinions, and—"

"It's one of the things I respected most about you. I always knew exactly where you stood. No games. No manipulation. Just the truth, plain and simple, whether I wanted to hear it or not. It meant I could trust you. Know that you believed what you said. Over the years I came to value that even more than I did when we . . . first met." He cleared his throat as if acutely aware of Lucy standing there, watching him with curiosity in her expression.

"So you liked Jack a lot when you took care of her dog?" the child asked intently.

"Yeah. She was very brave and very kind."

Jack felt the compliment as if Tom had touched her with his hand, the way he used to, long and lingering, as if he didn't ever want to draw away.

He wiped his strong, tanned hands on the apron. Jack didn't want to see the wounds life had left in his eyes.

"Go ahead and wash up. I fed Lucy. She squawked, but I didn't want her staying up too late. I want to make the most of the day tomorrow since today was a bit of a dud."

Lucy sidled over, hugged one of her dad's long, jeans-clad legs. "I've got to go to bed so you two can make up. Daddy's really sorry he got mad. But you yelled, too."

Jack chuckled. "I have a habit of doing that. Unfortunately, sometimes before I stop to think."

Lucy started toward Jack, longing in her pixie face. She stopped halfway across the floor, put her hands behind her back.

Something in the little girl's eyes made Jack's throat tighten. "What is it, Lucy?"

"It's just, at home I'm used to having lots of people to hug. Grandma and Aunt Debbie and Gracie. It's hard to get used to just having Daddy. Don't worry, though. I'm not going to grab you or anything. I know you don't like kids much. Bet you don't like hugging much either—just 'cause you're not used to it."

If Lucy had begged or pleaded or pouted, Jack could have resisted. It was the quiet understanding in the little girl's eyes that she was helpless against.

"I suppose we could try it," Jack said unsteadily. Lucy put her small, warm arms around Jack so gently, as if Jack were something that might shatter at a touch.

Jack folded her arms awkwardly around Lucy, not quite knowing how they should fit together. It was terrifying, realizing how small the child really was, how fragile in a world Jack knew had little mercy.

Jack wanted to gather Lucy even closer, hold her tighter, the instinct to protect the child that had flared earlier that morning striking Jack with something she wouldn't admit was dread.

Jack patted Lucy on the back, trying to figure out the fastest way to put space between them again without crushing the kid's feelings. But almost as if on signal, Lucy drew away, peering up at Jack.

"Daddy, she knows the secret code," Lucy said. "How you and Grandma and Aunt Debbie all pat me three times when you're finished hugging. Maybe we're kindred spirits, you know, like in that book you read me. *Anne of Green Gables*. A kindred spirit is someone who likes you just the way you are in here," Lucy said, patting her heart. "They understand stuff without you even telling them. Like me not just hugging you 'cause I wanted to when I knew you were nervous."

"Nervous?" Jack protested. "I've faced down lions that ate half a village for lunch. Why would I be nervous about getting a hug from you?"

Lucy cocked her head like a curious little bird. "I don't know. Maybe you'll tell me sometime."

Jack tried not to flinch at the mere idea of telling this innocent kid about the dark places inside her.

"Better get up to bed, Lucy," Tom suggested. "Jack's starving and I want to get this apology stuff out of the way. It's never any fun to admit you've messed up. Even when you're a grown-up."

"People who like you will still like you even if you do mess up as long as you're sorry, right, Jack?"

The little girl was looking for reassurance. But how did Jack feel about Tom Brownlow? Afraid, excited, off balance. The way she had when she'd walked on thin ice, not knowing whether she'd reach the exquisite glacier formations on the other side or plunge into ice-cold water. Dear God, Jack thought with a rush of pure panic. Was she in danger of losing her heart to him again? It took all her self-control not to let Lucy see how shaken the thought had left her. Cold and warm at the same time, like a thawing someplace deep inside her she'd been determined to keep frozen.

"It'll be fine, kiddo," Jack said as evenly as she could.

Lucy started up the stairs as if a mountain had just tumbled off her narrow shoulders. But she'd only taken a few steps before she slowed, some other concern obviously troubling her. She paused, peeped around the doorjamb, her face suddenly pink. Jack was astonished to realize at that instant just how far she'd be willing to go to wipe away the worry from Lucy's earnest features.

"Daddy?" She drew out the last syllable, a secret code between them Tom completely understood.

"It's okay to leave the light on."

Jack ached at the tenderness, the strength in his voice.

"I'll be there when you wake up."

Lucy disappeared up the stairs. Her worry lines smoothed away, her face so serene because of Tom's few words of comfort that it awed Jack.

Jack wasn't sure why the question formed on her lips. Merely a seasoned journalist's thirst to understand? "What does it feel like to have someone trust you so completely?" she asked, turning to face him.

She expected Tom's features to warm, his mouth to soften into a smile, as if his daughter's love were a diamond cradled in the palm of his hand and she'd just told him it was beautiful.

His face tightened, his smile suddenly brittle. "What does it feel like? Terrifying. And wonderful," he amended. But shadows still clung about his eyes.

"Sit down. Better eat before you vanish all together." He was trying to change the subject. She let him off the hook. The awe and the dread mingling in his eyes had been answer enough. "You're thinner than you used to be." A crease deepened between his brows. As if he were worried about her?

Jack forced a careless smile. "All that running around the globe, chasing terrorists, hunting down rogue warlords in their dens. Hard to find a McDonald's on the corners I hang around on."

"I suppose."

She'd been crazy in love with him once. But that was a long time ago. Before their innate differences had begun to rear their ugly heads. Before Laura swept in and wrapped her tentacles around him. But Laura was out of the picture now, Jack reasoned. Why couldn't he have been strong enough to cut free of her eight and a half years ago when it would have done some good? When Jack and Tom could have had a future together. Before they'd both turned into different people, taken completely different paths. Before it was too late.

But if he had, there would have been no Lucy, Jack thought. And a world without Lucy would be a much darker place, she realized with an ache. Whatever pain the child's birth had cost Jack, she was suddenly glad. Glad there was a Lucy, and glad the little girl had Tom to love her.

Jack carefully folded the ache in her heart away, determined not to let Tom guess what was going through her mind.

She must have succeeded, because he smiled as he dished a gooey square of lasagna onto a waiting plate. Seemed he was taking this "fattening her up" idea seriously. The serving of pasta could feed a family of four and leave all of them too full to ask for seconds.

Jack grabbed a fork and took a bite. She couldn't stifle a sigh of pure ecstasy. "Remind me to recommend you to the CIA. You could be a great tool in interrogations. Give a half-starved prisoner one bite of your lasagna and then threaten to take it away. They'd confess anything to get their hands back on the plate."

Tom chuckled, dishing out a serving for himself. He ate in silence, letting her savor the pasta. She'd devoured most of it before he spoke again. "You ever learn how to cook? I could give you the recipe." He smiled, trying to drive the frown lines from between his brows.

"I'm still hopeless in a kitchen, but over an open fire, I can do a decent enough job." He rose, gathering up his empty plate and putting it in the sink. He lingered there for a long moment. Avoiding the conversation they were both dreading? Jack wondered.

"Anyway," Jack said. "We're not here to talk about food, are we?" She finished her last bite of lasagne and put down her fork. "There are things we both need to say. We'd better say them so you can head up to Lucy's room. Let me go first—"

"Better let me, this time." Tom quietly closed the

kitchen door, then pulled out the chair across from Jack's and sat down in it, a glass of iced tea in his hand. "I know why you reacted the way you did this morning," he said. "My decision not to let Lucy go with the Pepperells made no sense."

Jack shrugged. "It didn't have to. It was none of my business. I might as well be a stranger to both of you. It's just that Lucy adored exploring this morning before you came outside. Her whole face lit up, and she told me . . ." Jack hesitated, not wanting to cause Tom pain, wanting even more to help him see just how much the adventure with China and the boys would have meant to Lucy. If he understood, Jack was sure he'd act differently if Lucy had another chance to go.

"She's trying to memorize colors, landscapes. What green looks like. How far away it is where the sea and the sky melt together on the horizon. She's saving it all up, Tom, for . . . later." Jack surprised himself by softening the last words. Lucy was going blind. Tom knew that and so did Jack. Jack had made a life's work of not flinching from reality. What was it about this man and his little girl that made her hedge the blunt truth?

"I know what she's doing," Tom said. "I've watched her for months, now. She stares at something, so intense it's like she's trying to burn it into her memory. She talks about it, tries to describe whatever she's looking at in words, doing it over and over again, trying to get it just right, so that the words will make a picture in her mind."

"If that's the case, it seems like a day of exploring with China and the boys would be just the kind of adventure you wanted Lucy to have."

"It is. Except for one small detail." He lowered his gaze to the tablecloth, as if the nautical ropes and knots printed on its navy blue surface held the perfect words to express what he had to say. "I haven't made it a secret that I wasn't happy with Lucy's choice of Mermaid Lost as our first stop on this trip."

"Bet you were thrilled to death when I opened the door, huh? I've never seen somebody so anxious to run."

His gaze clouded. "The truth is, I was grateful you were here and that you wanted me the hell out of here."

"But you fought so hard to stay—for Lucy."

"I fought for her to be able to see the place. But the truth was, I was looking for any excuse to put Mermaid Lost and everyone within a hundred miles of it behind me."

Jack winced inwardly, not sure why it should bother her so much. Tom said seeing her again hadn't been so traumatic, and yet, he'd been acting edgy as if he'd been walking barefoot on a knife blade ever since he'd come to the lighthouse. How deeply had he cared for Laura if her mere aura in a place could still unsettle him so?

She was used to facing hard questions head-on. She reverted to that instinct now. "You must have come to care about Laura very much, if it bothers you so much to come to a place she loved."

"I wish it were that simple. A dash of heartache, a few old wounds ripped open." He winced, apology flashing in his eyes. "I'm sorry, Jack. I don't mean to minimize the pain I caused you. I doubt you could ever understand how—how ugly things can get. How many lies people can tell. How many mistakes they can make to cause an innocent little girl to suffer."

"Don't tiptoe around me, Tom. You, above anyone, should know I'm not made of glass."

"No. I know what you're made of, Jack. Courage

and honesty, defiance and determination, with such a big heart nothing could turn you away."

Her throat closed at the sudden, stark yearning in his eyes. The truth was far different now. Her time with Tom had changed her all those years ago. She guarded her heart now, with the fierceness of a temple lion. And she turned away anyone she feared might touch her too deeply. That was, she thought uneasily, since the Brownlow SUV had driven up the lighthouse road.

She shivered a little, far too aware of the weight of Tom's gaze on her face, that intuitiveness filling his dark-brown eyes, regret softening that sensitive yet unrelentingly masculine mouth. Jack would've been tempted to duck and run if she wouldn't have looked completely ridiculous. But she couldn't shake the feeling that somehow he could read her mind.

"At least, that's how you were *before* I hurt you," he said. "You'll never know how sorry I am that I did. But I can't deny the truth. That I'd give ten years of my life if heartache and regret was all that lay between Laura and me. There's so much more, Jack." He dragged one hand wearily over his eyes.

"You don't owe me an explanation." Jack wished he'd take the escape she'd offered, turn the conversation back to lasagna and the fact that she wasn't eating enough to suit him. She'd always made damned sure she was *not* the type of person other people confided in—unless they were complete strangers caught up in some newsworthy strife and she was dead sure she'd never see them again.

She groped for something to say that would let them both off the hook nice and easy, without any wounds, without feeling bound together by whatever confession Tom was so determined to make. "It's no wonder you're edgy here, Tom. Doesn't take a rocket scientist to figure it out. This lighthouse was Laura's special place. Everywhere you look, there has to be another reminder that your little girl is going through life without her mother."

"You think I need this place to remind me of that? I'm aware of it every day. When I chaperone her school field trips and see other kids' reveling in the kind of attention only moms can give. I see it at Lucy's dance class where all the other kids' moms sit stitching sequins on their daughter's costumes, each glittery bead holding so much love."

"I doubt Lucy runs out onto the stage in ballet shoes and her 'Save the World' tee shirt," Jack said, squirming under the quiet misery in Tom's rugged face. "You adore that kid. I know you make sure she's got every bead or feather or rhinestone costume doodad that she needs."

"Yeah. I hire someone to do it all."

"See!" Jack cried in relief. "I bet Lucy's costume is as perfect as any performer who ever opened with Baryshnikov. All the other girls are probably dripping doodads all over the stage. They're probably lucky if their costumes make it through one lousy performance!

"But when their sugarplum fairy crowns or their swan tails fall off, they have their mothers waiting in the wings with needles and threads, spare feathers and hugs to make even the worst disaster fade away. To make them feel like the most special little girl who ever slipped on ballet shoes.

"You think that kid of yours walks on water. Anyone can see how you adore her! There are probably plenty of girls in that class who envy Lucy like crazy for having a dad who loves her like you do. I know I would have." She hadn't meant to confess the last, dredge up the secrets she'd shared with him under the covers of his big, soft bed. Old wounds her father had left long ago.

"Thank you for that," he said with a wan smile. "I love her so much, Jack. But sometimes I'm not sure that will be enough."

"Enough for what? Plenty of kids in two-parent homes get shoved aside every day, shown without words that they aren't nearly as important as the PTA meeting or the job or the card club that meets on Friday nights. Plenty of kids spend their time at home just bracing themselves for their parents' next criticism, knowing that no matter how they try to brush their hair or pick out the right shirt or get the piano piece they've run through a jillion times right, they just won't cut it. Just because you've got the right gender of bodies in the 'mommy chair' and the 'daddy chair' at the kitchen table every night doesn't mean that everything is Norman Rockwell perfect, or that the kid sitting across from them is getting the love they need. Trust me. I spend my life peeling back layers from the first appearance of things. I guarantee you, Tom, things are rarely as picture-perfect as they seem. Maybe it's true that Lucy doesn't have a mother in her life. Even so, Lucy's one of the lucky ones. I'd stake my life on it."

Tom angled his face away from her, his eyes suddenly overbright. His voice roughened with emotion. "I do love her. I'd do anything to see her happy. Keep her safe. And, believe it or not, that's what I was trying to do this morning. There are things around here a lot more dangerous to Lucy than tumbling off a cliff."

In spite of the oven-warmed kitchen and the bright lights driving back every shadow, Jack felt cold.

"There are things Lucy doesn't know about her mother. Things I've done everything in my power to keep from her. At least for as long as I can."

Jack noted the grim set of Tom's jaw, the regret that carved deep lines in the rugged planes of his face. And it chafed her to realize that she'd sensed even eight and a half years ago that Laura would take such a toll on the man who had married her to give a child his name.

Even from her one brief meeting with Laura, something about the woman had made Jack uneasy. Besides the fact that Laura was determined to take the man Jack loved. Laura hadn't seemed exactly evil. Jack had just sensed the woman could be dangerous to herself and anyone who tried to help her, like someone drowning in the surf, flailing about for anyone to hold on to, not noticing that she was dragging her rescuer's head under the surface along with her own. The question that troubled Jack was this: What was it about Laura that had made Tom willing to sacrifice so much?

Had he cared about Laura more than he'd been willing to admit even to himself? Had his need to ride in, a white knight on his charger, been more exciting to him than the adventures he and Jack had planned? Or had it been Jack's failings, somehow, that had destroyed their relationship? Her stubbornness, determination not to be swayed, even a little, from the path she'd chosen. Had the problem been her fear of compromise? Terror of slipping under someone else's control? Giving anyone else power over her—even someone she loved. Was *that* what had made Tom choose Laura over Jack? Had he figured that if she really loved him she would fight harder to keep him?

God knew, she'd been hurt and angry in the hours that followed Laura's grand entrance. But she hadn't let Tom see how deeply it cut her to discover that another woman was carrying his child. The instant Laura had blurted out her disastrous news, Jack had realized just how dangerous a mistake she'd made in the weeks since Tom Brownlow had entered her life. She'd come face-to-face with her own vulnerability, that soft, aching center inside her that was as susceptible to heartache and loss as any other woman was, no matter how good she was at concealing it from the rest of the world. But she hadn't had the courage to let the man she loved know it.

"Jack?" Tom's voice shook her from her thoughts. "Do you remember the night Laura burst in on us, told me that she was pregnant?"

A month ago Jack would have brushed the question off. She and Tom had only known each other for two weeks. A mere blink in a lifetime. But here, now, with Tom sitting across the table from her and the soft, warm imprint of Lucy's hug still surrounding her, it was harder to deny the truth. Did she remember the night Laura Willoughby had destroyed her far-too-fleeting dream?

Every detail. They'd made love until their skin glowed with it, the tangle of passion their favorite remedy for increasingly frequent arguments. But for once, they hadn't been able to exorcise their differences even with mind-shattering sex. Their differences of opinion still stood, like shadowy ghosts in the room. Maybe she should have guessed even before the unexpected knock sounded on the door that the dreams they had woven together could never come true.

She and Tom had been in the middle of a ridiculous argument, whether or not she'd still go deep into the bush when she was pregnant. She'd been so damned stubborn about it. Hell, she didn't really even *know* if she'd want to go into such wild country pregnant—that was, if she ever got pregnant in the first place. She'd just be damned if she was going to let anyone else tell her not to try. Even if that someone was the man who hoped to father her child, someone who loved her, feared for her, wanted, like any man, to see the mother of his child safe.

But she never gave an inch—no, not Jack Murphy. She'd been chin-up, eyes sparking, hands-on-hips-defiant when the knock on the door came. She'd been the exact opposite of the woman who stood in the apartment corridor, soaked with rain.

Laura Willoughby, looking like Desdemona moments before Othello went for her throat. An exquisite, fragile fairy princess three months pregnant and desperately in need of saving.

10

Jack closed her eyes tight and dragged herself back from the memories, feeling as if she'd been teetering on the edge of a cliff. But in those few unguarded moments, she'd glimpsed more than she could bear, shadows of that night in Tom's small apartment in Kentucky.

The desperation in Tom's face, the shock that turned his skin white, his dark eyes into wells of broken dreams. His chin jutting up as if he would welcome any distraction from the chaos roiling in his mind, even the clean, honest pain of a fist crashing into him full force.

And during that endless, agonizing night, Jack had been tempted a dozen times to strike him, knock some sense into him.

At least wait and get a paternity test, she'd begged him. *Why destroy your whole life when you're not even sure the baby is yours.*

Maybe she had been grasping at straws, searching for anything that could keep her from losing the dream of the life they'd planned together. Maybe she hadn't been that much different from Laura after all.

She hadn't *really* cared about anything but her own future. Hadn't really considered the baby as much more than a doll. She had no experience with infants back then, no idea how fragile they were, how helpless in the hands of whoever was caring for them. Now she was older, wiser. The thought of Lucy in inept hands made Jack's stomach clench. Tom had known the danger way back then. God, he must've thought her to be acting like a self-absorbed jerk. Still, couldn't they have found a better way? A middle ground where their love could have survived? Couldn't Tom have been a part of Lucy's life without marrying Laura?

Not if he was in Africa with Jack.

The realization staggered her. She remembered the expression on Tom's face, hurting but resolved. His voice a quiet ache as he said that their dreams lived in different places now. *Try to understand, Jack. She can't handle a baby alone.*

Why not? Jack had argued. Her own mother might as well have raised her alone. Women did it all the time. Couldn't he help Laura with the child and not marry her? Couldn't they figure out some better way to handle things than Tom flinging himself on a land mine? Condemning himself to a life with a woman he didn't love?

Jack had tried hard to cling to fury in the weeks that had followed Laura's catastrophic reentry into Tom's life. The fragile fairy princess, the poor little rich girl Jack was certain would suck the very joy out of Tom's life, tear up the astonishing sense of serenity that surrounded him, cage him in a life that would rob him of all the adventures he'd wanted for his own.

Tom had known how Jack felt even back then. There was no sense in raking through it all right now.

Especially since time had proved Jack so horribly right.

Or had she been? Was it possible Tom would have been far more miserable married to Jack? An ocean away from his child? Married to a woman who'd continually fight him anytime he tried to caution her, protect her from what he saw as danger? Strange, after years of blaming Laura as the villainess who caused Jack to lose Tom, Jack suddenly had to wonder. What if the problem that had destroyed their relationship had been a far simpler one—one that came from inside Jack herself.

Jack opened her eyes to find Tom peering across the table at her expectantly, still waiting for some answer to his question of moments ago. Did she remember the night her world had crashed and burned? Only every miserable detail, now that he'd brought it up again. Not that she was willing to share that with him.

"It was a long time ago. So much life has crowded in between. But I don't suppose anyone ever forgets their first love. Of course, it was only two weeks. It was ridiculous to think it was something that could last."

Tom's mouth softened. He smiled for an instant, tender. "You were sure about it then. So sure about everything. God, I envied you that. But for once, I was sure, too."

They'd both been young then, innocent, their whole lives before them. For those two weeks anything had seemed possible, the whole world shining and new, just waiting for them to conquer it.

He paused, cleared his throat. "I'm sorry. I didn't mean to dredge up old memories. We were such different people then. Sometimes it's hard to remember the man I used to be."

He glanced away and Jack could feel his sudden

loneliness. After a moment he spoke again. "When I told you I was going to marry Laura, I didn't go into the reason why very much."

"She needed you. I didn't, as I remember," Jack said, trying to be flippant to hide the unexpected gnawing ache the memory of his rejection had awakened in her. In the end, Tom had chosen the fainting, helpless little damsel in distress over a strong woman like Jack, just as her father had said any man would. She'd been stunned at how disillusioned she'd been, how much Tom's defection had hurt. Sweeping the memory back where Tom would never see it, she flashed him an ironic smile. "You were right. About me, anyway. I got along just fine."

Did you?

Tom hadn't said anything, but the question echoed between them just the same, his dark eyes searching her face. Jack swallowed hard, fighting off the almost physical sensation, as if he were touching her, running his fingertips over her cheeks, her temples, her throat, to reassure himself that she *had* been fine, just as she'd claimed. His gaze cut too close, read her too clearly. She shot him a grimace edged with irritation.

"We knew each other for two weeks. Even if my life had been a disaster after that, it wouldn't have been because of you. Anyway, I thought we were supposed to be talking about Laura, and whatever it was that kept you from letting Lucy go off with the Pepperell boys to play."

A flash of something darkened his eyes—old pain, regret? The idea that those two weeks still held so much power over Tom's emotions surprised Jack. Maybe it shouldn't have.

"I guess I was just trying to lead into things, and got

distracted. The last thing I ever wanted to do was hurt you. I mean, back then," he amended.

"No big deal. If you're looking for absolution, you've got it. I just look at those two weeks as an aberration. A kind of detour on the path of life. I got back on track in no time, ended up doing what I always wanted to."

"Wish I could say the same," Tom said. "The detour Laura and I took ran us both right off a cliff."

Jack tried not to remember the way Laura had clung to Tom in his small, student apartment, how she'd cried and apologized, insisting at first that she wasn't going to ask for anything from him. She'd manage with the baby alone, somehow. Yet, once she had the baby, she wouldn't be alone anymore. There would be just the two of them. She just hoped she could manage . . .

It had been a speech worthy of a heroine in some 1930s melodrama. Jack had wanted to wring her neck. Especially when Laura had turned on the tears—a delicate sniffling that only made her look more helpless and innocent and alone. Anyone who was miserable enough to cry should look like hell when they were done—that was Jack's theory anyway.

A surge of old frustration welled up in Jack. "I just never understood it. She waltzes back into your life, pregnant, and you don't even ask for a paternity test. You never even question it. The woman was wrecking all of our plans and you didn't even try to—" Jack stopped, heaved a sigh. This was crazy, raking all of this up again. For what? Tom had made his choice.

"I didn't need a paternity test."

"Of course not. Laura would never have cheated on you. That kind of thing happens to other guys."

"Lucy is mine."

Jack winced, suddenly aware of what she was saying, how much the mere suggestion Lucy could be another man's child would wound him. "I didn't mean to question Lucy's paternity now. I mean, with that dimple it's obvious she's your daughter. But back then—"

"There was no point in taking the test," Tom explained. "The reason I broke up with Laura was that I caught her flushing her birth control pill. When I confronted her, she confessed that she'd been trying to get pregnant for the past two months. She'd had an infection as a girl, and the doctors said she might be infertile. She wanted to have my child, but didn't think it possible, so I didn't have to worry."

Fury blazed red-hot in Jack's formidable temper. "What a crock of garbage! She got pregnant on purpose! Trapped you. You should have told her to go to hell for manipulating you that way." She sucked in a breath, froze, thinking of Lucy. Her shoulders sagged. "But it wasn't that simple, was it? How could you leave Lucy with someone who would manipulate, lie, scheme."

"Thank you for understanding that much. But there was even more about Laura that you didn't know." Tom met Jack's gaze levelly. "Laura's an alcoholic. Has been for as long as I've known her, even though, back then, I didn't recognize the signs. She said her parents had always served cocktails in the evening. It was no big deal, just a way to relax. When she'd had too much, it was just because she was lonely, scared. But when she was with me, she didn't need the liquor. She said she felt strong enough to face anything."

Jack's reaction must have shown in her eyes. Tom shook his head. "I know now how stupid I was, but it made me feel important, like Sir Lancelot or something, riding in to slay the beautiful damsel's dragons. I just hadn't figured out that sometimes damsels don't want their dragons slain. Sometimes the dragons are terrific excuses not to fight back on their own. Once while I was dating Laura, my mom cornered me when I was visiting home. We talked for a long time about marriage, about what it means to share your life with someone. I realized that Laura's dependence on me wasn't a good enough reason to marry her. That you had to be partners, respect each other, nurture each other's strengths. I was considering breaking up with Laura even before I saw her dumping her pills. That finished me. I broke up with her, knowing it was the best thing I could do for myself. As for the pregnancy risk—maybe I believed her about the fertility problems because I was too scared not to. I prayed she'd get her balance back, but I couldn't be responsible for choices she made."

"Makes a lot of sense," Jack said. "Too bad you didn't take your own advice."

"When I met you, I realized everything my mom said was true. You made me proud just to be with you. Made me want to be better than I was so I could deserve you. The whole world seemed to open up instead of narrowing the way it had been until all I could see were Laura's problems, Laura's pain, Laura's insecurities. God, I felt so damned lucky, like I'd just escaped out of some long, dark tunnel."

Jack didn't want to hear about how wonderful things had been for those two brief weeks. Dwelling on them could only remind them both of things they'd tried hard to forget. "If you'll remember, we were fighting plenty on our own."

"We had some bumps to work out. Doesn't everybody? I'm sure in time we would have found some compromise."

"Are you? Then you didn't really know me very

well. Back then, compromise was the vilest word in the dictionary as far as I was concerned. I wasn't about to knuckle under to anyone. Not even you." Jack winced inwardly, thinking how lonely that fierce determination had left her over the years. Isolated. The way she'd been so sure she wanted it. At least until Tom and Lucy Brownlow had stumbled back into her life. The thought terrified her. She rushed to change the subject to something safe.

"Just . . . just tell me about Laura. The rest doesn't matter anymore."

Was that hurt that sprang into Tom's eyes? He obviously still hadn't learned the art of self-protection. How to keep things from jabbing too deep, slicing too close, where they could hurt you.

"Laura was determined to keep the baby, not give her up for adoption."

"Of course she wouldn't. She'd schemed like crazy to get pregnant. Without the baby she wouldn't have any way to hold on to you."

"The thought of an innocent baby living in the kind of chaos that surrounded Laura—it made my blood run cold. I'd chosen to have sex with Laura. Even with her on the pill, I should have used protection. If I had, she couldn't have, well—even if she tried to trick me, it doesn't mean I'm not responsible for a child I've helped make."

"More information than I need to know," Jack warned, holding up one hand.

"I'm sorry. Maybe I'm trying to justify things to myself. Why I made the decisions I did. Insane, isn't it? Eight and a half years later trying to convince myself I did the right thing? Especially when I know I just did what I had to do. Even if I could turn back the clock, go back to the beginning, even if I knew every bit of pain and misery ahead, I wouldn't change a thing. Lucy— Lucy was worth everything I've gone through."

Jack's throat tightened at the memory of Tom with his daughter. "She's beautiful," she said. "A great kid. And, as Lucy pointed out, I'm not big on the twelve and under set."

Tom chuckled, a rough, weary sound. "She likes you, too. It surprised me, how much. She's not a kid who warms up to strangers easily. She's always careful—a little wary. Learned early that things could fall apart in a hurry, and she was always trying hard not to step on the cracks. One of the few lessons Laura taught her before she disappeared."

Tom fingered the rim of his iced tea glass, stared at the melting ice cubes, thoughtful. "Funny thing was, at first, I thought Laura had been right. That she *would* be able to pull things together as long as I was there to support her. From the time we got married, all through the pregnancy, Laura just glowed. She blossomed under all the attention she got from my family. She fixed up the nursery, bought all kinds of baby things. I kept myself busy with work. Maybe more than I should have. But vet school is tough. Demanding. Laura knew that as well as I did.

"Anyway, Laura seemed so much better, I remember reassuring my mom, insisting on how well Laura was doing. Mom said she was glad, but she still looked worried. I didn't understand it. Figured that if Laura was so happy and together just planning for the baby, she'd be overjoyed once the baby actually got here."

Jack didn't want the words to hurt. She'd known the instant Tom had chosen Laura that he would try to make the relationship work. For the sake of the child he and Laura were bringing into the world. But in spite of those characteristics in the man she'd so briefly loved, Jack had managed to imagine he was missing her, wishing he was with her. She'd hoped in her heart of hearts that when he closed his eyes at night, he imagined it was her head cradled on the pillow beside him.

"When Lucy was born six months after we were married it was the most humbling moment of my life. She was so perfect, so tiny. When I held her in my arms, I knew that I could actually be happy. I wish to God Laura had felt the same way. Then, maybe things would have turned out differently."

"She wasn't thrilled with motherhood?"

"The instant Lucy came onto the scene all the attention that had been on Laura shifted. Lucy was the queen of the world. My parents and brothers and sisters were crazy about her. And I adored her. I wish you could have seen her, Jack." His eyes glowed at the memory.

Jack felt a pang of envy. Envy because she was sure her own father had never looked like that when he'd thought about her. Envy because she would have given anything way back then to be the one to lay that beautiful little daughter into Tom's loving arms. Strange, it should cause her such a twinge. She'd given up the idea of motherhood years ago, and it wasn't as if it had been one of her burning desires, anyway. Except for those two weeks when anything had seemed possible.

Even marriage wasn't something she'd ever considered again. Tying herself down to a man, giving up her independence wasn't for her. She had to be able to dash off to any hot spot in the world at a moment's notice. What few lovers she'd had, had little choice other than adapting to her crazy schedule. Husbands were a whole different matter.

But Tom wasn't thinking of the life he and Jack might have shared. He was lost in the joy of remembering the life he'd lived—at least the part in which Lucy had burst on the scene.

"Lucy was beautiful from the moment she was born," he said. "Not like other babies. When you talked to her, she'd look up at you with these wide, solemn eyes, almost as if she understood what you were saying. Then, all of a sudden, she'd grin or laugh or crow. It was like pure sunshine, something all the more precious because she didn't go around flinging smiles and gurgles at everyone who passed by. She made you feel special."

Jack imagined a tiny, baby Lucy, with those great, too-wise eyes, and that smile that made you feel warm inside even when you were trying hard not to. The image tugged hard at her heart.

"Laura changed after the delivery. Post-partum depression, I figured. I remembered my sister Debbie going through it. It was just a phase, I told myself. Be patient. Any new mother is tired after all they've been through. I thought that maybe if I just gave her time to rest, everything would level out. I took over all the chores I could, handled everything involving Lucy from the moment I got home until I left for work in the morning. Not like it was some great sacrifice. I loved every minute I got to spend with my daughter."

He shrugged, guilt softening his voice. "Maybe that was part of the problem. Laura had to know I didn't love her. At least not the way she wanted me to. But I loved Lucy, with nothing held back."

"You talk about your love for Lucy as if you deserve some kind of blame," Jack said. "Laura knew you married her because of the baby, not because of some burning passion between the two of you."

"I don't know what she thought—or hoped our marriage would be. Whatever it was, she was disappointed. She got more emotional, less stable. I didn't want to see it, but she'd started drinking again."

Tom closed his eyes for a moment, ran his fingers through his dark hair. "Lucy was nine months old when I found the first bottle of whiskey hidden in the bathroom closet. How many more I found in the next three years I can't even guess. I did my best to get Laura the finest help available. She was my wife. Lucy's mother. I tried to stand by her."

"You could never have done anything less."

"I suggested we move closer to my parents so Mom and Debbie could help Laura. That way she wouldn't be so isolated. And," he admitted, "family could look in on Lucy during the day. But Laura wouldn't hear of it. It would make her look like a failure. She couldn't stand to have anyone know she'd fallen off the wagon. She promised she'd straighten out herself. If I would just pay more attention to her, help her through the transition, she was sure she could give up the booze once and for all this time."

"I've known my share of alcoholics in the press corps. Sometimes people try to blot out the ugly things they've seen with a bottle of Jack Daniel's. There was one old guy in France who'd hang out at the press bar to talk about the good old days when he'd covered the First World War. Ask him about the Pulitzer he'd won and he couldn't even remember the year. Ask him how long he'd been sober and he could tell you to the day. He was prouder of that achievement than any award he ever got."

"I don't think I believed Laura's promises even then," Tom confessed, "but I couldn't give up on her. It was one thing to give up hope my wife was going to get better. But to give up on Lucy's mother—All I could think of was my little girl growing up without a mom. What it would be like for Lucy. How much she would miss. I got Laura help during the day when I was gone. She went through rehab. I believed Laura when she said she was so much better. Would never drink again because she didn't want to hurt her baby. What she really did was get better at hiding things from me."

Considering what Tom had shared about Laura's efforts to trick him into getting her pregnant, Laura had been good at hiding her manipulative ways from the beginning of their relationship. It was easy to imagine how good she could be at it when indulging in her addiction was at stake.

"Lucy had just turned three when Laura had her first car accident. She'd been drinking, of course. Hit a telephone pole. When I got to the police station, the cop who'd answered the emergency call said there was something I needed to know. He was a dad with kids of his own, he said. And if one of his babies had been in that car . . ." Tom swallowed hard.

"Laura hadn't even told the cops the baby was with her. The rear windows in the car had that sun glare stuff on them, so you couldn't see in the backseat. The tow truck guy heard Lucy crying just as he was hauling the car up with the winch."

"My God," Jack breathed, thinking of Lucy. Three years old? She must have been so scared. "Was Lucy hurt?"

"No, thank God. But it was the middle of summer. If the tow truck guy hadn't found Lucy and she had been closed up in that hot car much longer, she could have died."

Outrage surged through Jack, loathing for the

woman who'd forgotten Lucy that day. What kind of parent could just forget a child like that? Jack had to admit that even Frank would never have done that.

She and her father had had a miserable relationship most of her life, but she'd never doubted that if a building were on fire, he'd hammer his way through the walls with his bare fists to get to her. Of course, he'd probably have accused her of setting the fire afterward, and yelled her half-deaf, but not until she was safe.

"I told Laura that the marriage was over the minute she was released from jail. I wasn't going to take any more chances with Lucy. I'd been a fool to close my eyes as long as I did.

"It was one of the hardest things I've ever done, abandoning Laura like that. Maybe I wasn't in love with Laura, but I cared about her. She was drowning and I couldn't so much as reach out a hand. The only thing that would save her, she claimed, was if I took her back. But I'd already tried that so many times. How could I do it again, after what had happened?"

"You did the right thing. You have to know that."

"Laura fell apart. Things got ugly, Jack. So ugly. But I held firm. I had to protect my daughter. I'd failed her once already. I took Lucy and rented one of the houses on my mom and dad's farm and started my vet practice. Meanwhile, Laura's drinking got worse. It was as if she thought that if she were enough of a mess I would rush in to rescue her. But why wouldn't she? I always had before. Six months later I got a phone call. Laura. Hysterical. Why hadn't I helped her? She'd begged me to. It was my fault she'd—"

Tom stopped for a moment, steadied himself. "She'd gotten behind the wheel again, so drunk she could barely see. But this time she wasn't so lucky. She crossed the center line, plowed into a woman head-on. The woman died, Jack. Laura killed her."

Fierce protectiveness welled up in Jack. "It wasn't your fault. You tried to help her. Damn, isn't that just like Laura to kill someone and try to blame you? Was Laura hurt?" Jack wasn't sure she'd be sorry if it were true.

"She was banged up, but a twenty-minute trip to the emergency room and she was okay. At least physically. But emotionally—"

"Nobody can just walk away from an accident like that."

"They convicted her on charges of vehicular manslaughter and driving under the influence. The judge sentenced her to fifteen years."

"So that's the reason Laura isn't in Lucy's life. The reason you looked so strange when I asked if your wife was with you."

"Lucy thinks her mother is off writing children's books somewhere, and that's why Laura never comes to see her. I play into the charade by buying Christmas presents and birthday gifts and writing 'love Mom' on the tags. Lucy doesn't know her mother is in prison."

Jack winced, as an image flashed into her mind, Lucy's wistful face when she'd talked about her mother. What would be worse for such a sensitive, loving little girl? Believing that your mother was too busy writing to bother coming to see you or knowing that your mother was behind cold steel bars because she'd killed an innocent person? Jack wished she knew the answer.

"You did what you thought best for Lucy," Jack said. "That's one thing I'm absolutely sure of."

"I thought so, too. Now, I'm not so sure. Laura might be paroled in the next few months. She's sent letters, telling me she wants to see Lucy once she gets out. And she has that legal right. She doesn't know yet—about Lucy's failing eyesight. I don't know how she'll react. But either way, I'm in real trouble here. What's going to happen when she tells Lucy where she's been all this time? That I've been lying. What will that do to my little girl, Jack? How will she ever trust me again?"

Jack's fists clenched at the hopelessness in Tom's voice. "Lucy will understand everything, at least when she's older."

"But what about now? This is when she needs me the most."

Empathy welled up in Jack, and she didn't even try to quell it. Maybe the man had made mistakes. But he'd paid for them in blood. And she had to admit, she felt better, now that she understood why he'd married Laura. Not to save Laura, but the child who would come into the world with no defenses at all. And he'd been right to fear for Lucy. The child had come close enough to disaster even with Tom standing guard. If he hadn't been there—

"I'm sorry, Tom. About everything. I won't say I wasn't mad as hell at you years ago. I might even have had one or two petty moments when I hoped Laura made you a little bit miserable. But you didn't deserve this. Not any of it."

"I made my own choices, wrong or right. If I have to suffer because of them, well, that's just the way it is. But Lucy had no choice in any of this. I've tried so hard to protect her from all the ugliness, but I won't be able to for much longer. It's all coming apart, Jack, all the secrets, all the lies. That's why I was afraid to let her go off with the Pepperells this morning."

Tom folded his hands together, almost as if he were

trying, in some way, to hold back the storm about to engulf his little girl. "No one back home knows anything about what happened, so I've been able to keep Lucy from finding out the truth about her mother. But here—Laura was their crowned princess at Mermaid Lost for years. Her family spent summers here until she was eighteen years old—the summer Seth Pepperell got too attatched to her for her daddy's comfort."

He met Jack's gaze, his eyes filled with misery. "The chance of someone who knew her keeping up with news about her is easy to imagine. I can almost hear them saying 'You'll not guess what that girl's been doing now.' Laura herself sent a dozen copies of our wedding announcement back to Maine. And she'd been in the society pages plenty of times before that. It's possible people here know about the accident, and if they do, God knows what could happen. I feel like I've been walking through a minefield ever since I came here."

"That's why you were acting so strangely this morning. No wonder."

"I guess what I'm trying to say is this: I don't want Lucy to find out about Laura because someone slips up and 'poor baby's' her about her mom being in jail. I know I'm going to have to face up to the choice I made not to tell her. And the day of reckoning is going to be soon. But not until after this trip, Jack. Is that too much to ask?" His eyes pierced her, begged her, as if it were in her power to grant his desperate plea.

Jack wished she could erase Laura from their lives. But she couldn't. Laura was Lucy's mother, and there was nothing Jack or Tom could do to change that. And as for any chance Laura would ease carefully back into Lucy's life, doing as little damage as possible, that was a faint hope knowing Laura's history. The woman had been self-absorbed her whole life. How much chance was there that she had changed?

"I know Lucy wanted to go exploring with the Pepperells," Tom said. "But I just couldn't risk it. Please try to understand."

She did understand. Down to the very marrow of her bones. He had every right to make the decision he'd made in an effort to protect his daughter from news that could damage her so deeply. The only sensible thing to do, Jack reasoned, was just let it go, not press him.

It wouldn't be the end of the world if Lucy didn't get to poke around in China's rooms over the pub, if she didn't get to drink out of the ancient blue-and-white teacups and peer through the pirate telescope the Pepperell boys adored.

Tom had given a damned good reason why he didn't want his daughter running loose around Mermaid Lost. And yet Jack couldn't help but remember the rare eagerness in Lucy's face, the delight that had bubbled through her for just a moment before Tom's resounding *no* had swept it away.

"I do understand why you're worried. Really, Tom. But China would never hurt Lucy. Even if she knew about Laura's conviction, which I'm almost sure she doesn't. China's easy to read, and blunt as they come."

"Jack, I don't trust her—can't trust anyone where Lucy is concerned. She's too precious. As for this China you're so crazy about, she adored Laura if the stories I heard were true. How good a judge of character can she be? The last thing Lucy needs is a bunch of pretty lies to break her heart when Laura comes on the scene!"

"You're wrong about China. She'd never do anything to hurt a child. Maybe she felt sorry for Laura, but how can you blame her for that? You felt sorry for Laura, too."

"Damn it, it's not the same!"

"Isn't it? Just because you felt sorry for Laura didn't mean you weren't fully aware of her flaws. Knowing how intuitive China is, she probably had the girl figured out long before you did. And if you're worried, just tell her, point blank, no stories about Laura. I'm sure she'd honor your rules."

"How can you be so sure? Maybe it would just make her more determined to defend poor misunderstood Laura to a motherless child. Maybe she's just senile enough to slip and say something even if she doesn't intend to."

"China—senile? I'd give a pile of money to see you say that one to her face. Tom, I understand why you wouldn't want Lucy running around with just anybody here in the village, but couldn't she visit China? Couldn't she spend a little time with the boys? See all the souvenirs the Pepperell family collected from around the world?" It seemed so innocent a request, Jack thought suddenly, and yet, what if Tom were right?

Lucy would have to face up to that disappointment someday, anyway, Jack told herself. Maybe it would be better if she had something warm and beautiful, something nostalgic and bright in China's memories of her mother, so that she wouldn't only see the broken, addicted, needy woman Tom had described Lucy's mother to be.

And yet, no matter how much Tom wished it weren't so, Laura was Lucy's mother. The only one she'd ever have. And far too soon Lucy was going to have to meet her, whether Lucy spent time with the Pepperells or not.

There was one possibility, Jack thought. One solution that would answer the needs of both Lucy and her father. But she'd have to be out of her mind to do it. Jack needed seclusion. Concentration. Lucy and Tom were already invading her space. But then, if that were true, a few more pirates running around wouldn't make much difference.

"China and the boys could come up here to the lighthouse," she suggested, hardly recognizing the sound of her own voice. "That way they would be far away from the village."

Tom almost looked choked up, his voice rough with gratitude. "Haven't we imposed on you enough? You've got work to do and I promised we wouldn't interfere."

It was true. She had to finish the book. And she would. Maybe she could get some great shots of Cal Pepperell and Lucy to give the project even more life. And even if it didn't work out that way, there would be other days, other times she could snap the rest of the shots she needed.

"Jack, you don't have to do this," Tom insisted. "You've already gone above and beyond to be kind to us."

"I told you, I always have my own self-interest at heart. I'm thinking of including pictures of China with all her trinkets from lands afar in the book. What better way to do it than to have her showing teacups to a little girl?"

"You're not fooling me, Jack. You're not doing this for yourself. You're doing it for Lucy."

"And for you," Jack said. "Believe me, Brownlow, someday you're going to thank me for it."

Tom moved closer to Jack, so close his shadow fell over her, his breath stirring the wispy tendrils of her hair. He cupped her cheek in his hand, tipping her face up so he could see every nuance of expression, every flicker of eyelash, tremble of lips. "You are so . . ."

Beautiful, Jack wanted him to say. *Sexy. I've missed you so bad my body aches for you.*

The way mine does? a voice in Jack whispered.

But whatever attraction Tom was feeling, he didn't voice it. His tone just a little raspy when he questioned Jack. "You trust this woman?"

"I trust her with my life. More than that, I can tell you this. If Lucy was my little girl, and she was losing her eyesight, I'd want her to get to know China. She's such a strong woman, has weathered so many storms. She makes you feel as if you can stand up to the wind and rain, too. Of all the people in the world, she's the one who can help your little girl understand the strength she can find inside herself."

"But Lucy's already found someone to do that. You."

Jack's cheeks burned. "No. I'm the worst example in the world for a little kid."

"Lucy doesn't think so." He swept his thumb over her cheekbone, tender movement sizzling along Jack's nerves, the touch so familiar, so strong, so full of long suppressed yearning. "Help me, Jack. Just while we're here at the lighthouse. You've never been afraid of anything. I want that, need that kind of courage for my little girl. And you're the only one who can give it to her. Maybe that's why God put you here at Mermaid Lost. Why Lucy and I had to come here. Maybe you could be the key she needs. Help me."

Jack looked into Tom's face, his eyes so dark and hot and intense, his lips parted as if he were longing to taste her, to share a bit of the heavy load he carried, just for a little while.

What had he claimed? That she'd never been afraid?

Well, he was wrong. She was terrified now. Terrified she'd let Lucy down.

"Will you help me?" Tom repeated, and this time she couldn't look away.

"Yes," she promised, knowing that when Tom and Lucy Brownlow drove away from Mermaid Lost, they might both take a piece of her heart with them.

11

Jack stood at the window, peering out at the soft night sky. She'd done so on six of the seven continents, in five-star hotels and in no man's lands where she'd wrapped herself in blankets and nearly froze to death because lighting a fire would reveal their position to the enemy. She was used to long nights, the loneliness that came during endless hours when she felt like she was the only person awake on the planet.

Yet tonight was different from all the rest, she thought, pressing her hand against the cool, smooth pane of glass. She'd looked through a window into another man's world, listened to him as he spilled out the secrets that were poisoning him, felt a bond sizzle to life between them, awakening softer, more feminine parts of her she'd long thought cold and unshakable as stone.

It astonished her, humbled her, the trust Tom had offered her, telling her so many things, baring so many places where his spirit was raw and bleeding. And the reason why he'd shared it was most astonishing of all.

He'd cared. It mattered to him what Jack thought of him. He respected her enough, not only to tell her truths Jack doubted he'd shared with anyone else, but he'd had the courage and the confidence in her to ask her for help as well.

She shivered, remembering the supplication in his whiskey-rough voice, the burning intensity in his eyes, the heat in fingers that touched her cheek, the pulse of her throat. She'd thought that pulse would explode, it felt so good to be touched by him, there, in that tender, hidden spot. Felt so good to know from that touch what his lips hadn't dared confess. That he still felt that burning thrill between them, that knee-shaking welcoming home of passion after so many years.

He might have gone on with his life, Jack knew with sharp satisfaction. But he hadn't forgotten her. Hadn't stopped wanting her. And she sure as hell hadn't stopped responding to him. They'd stepped over some invisible barrier tonight from which neither of them could draw back. Realization that the need was still there, the spark, the hunger. And a trust as dangerous as it was precious.

How did Tom feel now that he'd shared his pain? Jack wondered. Was it just like Ziggy always tried to convince her? Like lancing a boil? A mind-numbing relief, a pouring out of emotions repressed for too long? Ziggy had always claimed your heart was like a closet you had to clean. You had to get rid of the ugliness time and again to make room for other things, like light and laughter and goodness.

She'd always ignored his advice. But this was one time she hoped he was right. She wanted Tom to be free of as much of the burden he carried as possible. Wanted to wash away the troubles Laura had left him with, the doubts, the dread, the damage.

Maybe she couldn't change what had happened. Not in the two weeks that they'd be together here in Maine. And maybe she couldn't keep Laura from disrupting her daughter's world once they returned to their everyday lives. But she would do her best to make the rest of Lucy and Tom's stay here special.

Jack went to her jacket, took a package out of the pocket. She smiled at the camera she'd chosen so carefully. Lucy might not always be able to see the pictures she took with her eyes, but Jack would make certain she would see them in a far deeper way. She'd see them in her heart.

"Dad! Dad!"

Tom jolted awake at Lucy's shrill cries. He staggered to his feet. "It's all right, Lucy. I'm here." He raked his hand across sleep-fogged eyes. "You don't have to be afraid."

"Afraid? I'm not afraid! Look what I found on my pillow! A camera of my very own! Jack gave it to me. I know she did."

"A camera," he echoed, looking into Lucy's luminous face. Her blanket lay abandoned on the bed. In its usual place, she cradled the camera tight against her chest. Tom stared, a slow rage burning under his breastbone.

"I have to go tell her thank you. I'm going to be real real careful with it."

"I know," Tom said stiffly. What the hell had Jack been thinking, giving a camera to a little girl who was going blind? One more thing Lucy would have to throw into a corner once her eyes went dark. But Lucy was over the moon.

She hurried out of the bedroom without pausing so

much as to slip on her bunny slippers, her bare feet padding against the wooden floor.

"Jack! Jack, where are you?" She called until the stone walls rang. Tom followed the streak of pink-and-white nightgown down the stairs into the kitchen. Jack was at the table, pictures arranged in careful order before her. At least they were until Lucy flung herself at Jack in ecstasy and banged into the table in her enthusiasm. The pictures scattered, but Jack didn't even notice. She gave Lucy a sincere, if still awkward, hug.

"You put a camera on my pillow."

Jack feigned confusion. "A what? A camera? I don't know what you mean. My camera's still in my camera bag."

"Not a camera for you. A camera for me! You sneaked in while Daddy and I were sleeping and you put it on my pillow."

Lucy gave Jack a conspiratorial wink. "Daddy always says I never have to be scared of robbers and monsters and stuff because he'd hear 'em and wake up. But once, this big picture in the living room fell right off the wall and made a bang so loud Grandma heard it all the way next door, but Daddy didn't even wake up!"

Jack turned her smile on Tom. "If I were one of the monsters from the closet, I could have eaten you up and you wouldn't even have noticed until you woke to find me picking my teeth with your shinbone."

Lucy giggled.

Tom looked straight into Jack's eyes. "You shouldn't have done it," he said, so evenly Jack stiffened.

"It's nothing," Jack insisted, looking confused. She turned back to Lucy. "So, what did you think of your present, kiddo?"

"It's awesome. But it—it doesn't look like the ones my friends have." A worried crease formed between her eyebrows. "It looks lots fancier. What if I break it?"

"You won't break it," Jack said. "It's really sturdy, the best camera I could find for an eight-year-old aspiring photojournalist who is going to spend the next two weeks banging around the beach."

"Will you show me how to use it? I don't know much about cameras, except Uncle David has one with all kinds of buttons and stuff you can stick on it. He uses it at Christmas, but I can't touch it."

"You can touch this one all you want. I'll show you how to use every button, how to load rolls of film. I'll even teach you the way the best photography teacher I ever had taught me. We'll play the color game. You try to find something that's the bluest blue you can imagine, or something redder than anything else."

"Is that the way you learned how to take pictures in college?"

"I went to college and learned photography, but that's not where I learned the color game. Photography is something you keep learning about your whole life."

Lucy sobered, her chin setting with determination. "I won't be able to take camera lessons with a professor when I'm in college. I've got to learn everything right now."

"Lucy, go check out the instruction manual in the box," Tom said. "Jack and I need to talk."

Lucy looked from one adult to the other nervously. "You can talk with me right here. Jack, what's this little red thing—"

"Now, Lucy!" Tom snapped a little more harshly than he intended. Lucy flinched at his tone, then turned and fled.

Jack shoved her chair back from the table and stood up, her eyes angry, confused.

"What the blazes is this all about?"

"Why don't you tell me? Just how insensitive can you be, Jack? What the hell were you thinking, giving Lucy a camera?"

"I was thinking she'd have fun with it while she was here. She could take pictures to remind her of Mermaid Lost."

"Pictures she may not be able to see next year!"

"But she can see them now. She can have fun now. Maybe it will help her remember the things she wants to so desperately. Maybe it will help her think about what green looks like and how the sunset gets all orange."

"Maybe she'll just love the hell out of photography, and it will end up being one more thing she loses when her eyesight fails. She's already going to lose so much! Why add anything else? She's not strong enough."

"She's plenty strong enough!" Jack fired back. "And last night you said you wanted me to make her even stronger. Have a little faith in the kid."

"I don't want her hurt."

"You can't stop her from going blind. But you can do what you claim you're trying to do. Give her experiences. Make sure she misses out on as little as possible. That's what I was trying to do. She loves that camera, Tom. She'll have the time of her life taking pictures around the lighthouse. And you're going to have a good time helping her."

She faced him down, so much more like the woman he'd loved his legs felt unsteady. Had their tempers always been the flipside of that fearsome attraction that had flared up between them? he wondered suddenly, thinking of the times the two of them had settled their differences in his wide, quilt-covered bed. Jack had made him feel so alive. And this morning, there had been something fresher, something brighter in his daughter's small face, as she clutched the gift Jack had given her.

Joy far too rare and precious to squander by continuing an argument Tom already knew he'd lost.

"So what are you waiting for," he grumbled, not ready to capitulate entirely. Wishing he could ease some of his painfully taut nerves the way he once had, by grabbing Jack in his arms, kissing her until neither one of them could breathe, neither one of them could deny how good it felt, neither one of them could remember what they'd been fighting about.

Tom's loins tightened, his heart thrumming hard against his ribs as he imagined backing Jack up against the kitchen wall, pinning her there with his body, feeling every inch of her, so fiery fierce for a woman so small. He wanted to kiss her until they melted in a pool on the floor, wanted to skim his hand beneath her blouse, find her breast, suckle it. Wanted to feel her legs open wide, ready for him, her hips thrusting against his hard shaft in that secret dance that had driven him wild with need.

A drop of sweat formed at his temple, trickled down the side of his face.

"Well, what are you waiting for?" he rasped, painfully aware of the fire in Jack's eyes that matched the one in his own.

"What?" Jack choked out, cheeks red as if she'd been party to every reel of his own personal fantasy.

"You better get out and help Lucy take pictures, or all she'll end up with are a bunch of blotches that look like aliens. I'm rotten with a camera."

"You're good at other things," Jack said, turning to gather her own equipment from the counter.

Oh, lady, Tom growled inside himself. *If only you'd let me show you just how good.*

It was easy to imagine, safe, Tom thought, doing his best to hide the stiffening in his shorts. Because with Lucy around as a chaperone, sex was a chance neither he nor Jack would dare take.

Sun dappled the stretch of beach, splashing the two children clambering about on the rocks with gold. Tom watched with hungry eyes as Jack leaned over a tidal pool, her willowy body lithe and slender, and somehow exotic, even in a simple pair of khaki shorts and a white tee shirt.

It was as if Jack carried with her some essence of those faraway places she'd loved, as if she smelled of cinnamon and ginger and tasted of honey dripped over bread that would taste rich and foreign to his tongue.

She'd softened, somehow, during her time with Lucy, the camera seeming to cast its own kind of spell, putting both the withdrawn woman and shy young girl at ease, creating a bond between them that made Tom grateful and made him ache. They looked so natural together, there were times he could almost forget Lucy was Laura's daughter, and that Jack would soon waft out of their lives as quickly as she'd drifted in.

He'd tried to forget how fleeting this time would be, whenever he touched Jack's hand. Tried to just enjoy the sensation of having a woman around to talk to, to share things with, to appreciate, something beautiful, and unexpected in his world.

Jack had her world to return to, and he had his. There was still nowhere to meet in between, even if he were rash enough to imagine a life with her in his bed. He just did his best to be grateful for her now.

Lucy blossomed under Jack Murphy's hand. Cal

Pepperell, Lucy's new partner in crime, wasn't your "average laughing-at-cooties kind of boy," Lucy had informed them at bedtime the night before. One of the highest compliments he'd ever heard his daughter utter about a member of the opposite sex.

In the five days since Tom had served Jack a dinner of lasagna and painful truths, Cal had become as much a fixture on the cliff as the lighthouse itself, another "kindred spirit" Lucy had managed to find. The two of them explored every nook and cranny Mermaid Lost had to offer, played pirates and shore patrol, looking for enemy subs during World War II, while Tom and Jack had lain on China's picnic blanket, talking about life, about hopes, about Lucy's zest for adventure.

He'd told her about the wildlife rescue he'd worked toward for years—a remote place in the mountains where he could care for hawks and eagles and other wild things, and ease them back into their natural habitat. A place he judged far too dangerous for Lucy, now. How could he take her someplace totally unfamiliar, where if she got lost, he might never find her?

How could he not give Lucy a chance to try? Jack had asked. But he couldn't be angry with her anymore—not about this, anyway. Her faith in Lucy touched him, warmed him, gave him more hope for his daughter's future than he'd dared to have for a very long time.

He'd followed with the flashlights and binoculars and sunscreen while Cal had shown Jack all his best "special places" in the area so she could take pictures of them. Tom knew just how amazing the spots had been by the rolls of film Jack had used and the smile she'd shined on the little boy again and again.

He shaded his eyes with one hand to get a better

look as Lucy scampered back to Jack, brandishing her precious camera. Small and easy to operate though it was, the top of the line camera made him a bit nervous. He didn't have to see the price tag to know it was way more expensive than the kind a person would usually entrust to an eight-year-old. But Jack had insisted it was the right camera for the job.

Most kids had forever to putz around with cameras, starting with the simplest one imaginable and working their way up, Jack had told him. But Lucy needed to take a lifetime's worth of pictures in the next few months. Jack had made certain she had the equipment to do it.

He still grinned when he remembered Jack's saucy wink, the way she'd told Lucy she figured *he* was the one who needed glasses. Or maybe a hearing aid, considering how easy it had been to sneak into Lucy's room without waking either one of them, slipping the camera right on the pillow.

The thought of her so close to where he'd been sleeping made Tom's mouth go dry. He wondered if she'd paused for a moment, looking at him in the soft glow of the lantern on Lucy's bedside table, and remembered how it had felt when every inch of his body had been hers to touch, to tease, and he could make her cry out from needing him so badly.

Maybe it was a good thing we didn't end up in Africa, she'd teased him, while Lucy scampered just out of hearing. *I would have had to spend all my time keeping the crocodiles from making you their lunch.*

She'd laughed. A real laugh. When Tom had let an answer flash into his eyes—a far more X-rated opinion of exactly what she'd have spent all her time doing. And Tom's heart hurt when he realized that it was the first time in eight and a half years that he had heard that sound. Even her smiles had seemed stiff at first, brittle. Lucy had explained in her infinite wisdom that "Jack's smiles were just out of practice." But Jack was getting the hang of it now.

He'd forgotten how amazing her smile had been. Even with her skin buffed by time and hardship and endless hours in the sun, he still thought Jack's was the most arresting face he'd ever seen.

"Daddy!" Lucy cried. "I need some more film. Cal trapped a starfish on this real cool rock. Jack says if we catch it just right it'll be a perfect 'orange.' "

So they were playing the color game again, Tom thought, amused. It was an everyday occurrence since he and Jack had buried the hatchet.

"Daddy!" Lucy yelled. "Hurry up and come down here!"

Tom shifted the camera bag hanging on his shoulder and picked up the mini cooler on the sand beside him and headed toward "party central."

"Jack's going to develop these right when we get home," Lucy enthused. "And she said I could help. And she knows the perfect thing to take a picture of for blue. Just guess what it is!"

"Uh, the sky? It's blue. Maybe the ocean if you can get the light just right."

"That's too easy. We're trying to find special junk, not what everybody else would think of right away. You gotta think what you want to say in your picture. Use your creativity."

"That's a new word."

"Well, I have to use all mine up now, make all the pictures I can. I'm not like Cal. He can just take pictures of dirt if he wants. He'll have plenty of time to get this whole photography thing right later."

Tom's heart twisted. "You're doing a terrific job,

Kitten. I bet they'll be the best pictures any eight-year-old ever took."

"Jack says she'll even put one in the book she's working on, and she'll give me a photo credit." She enunciated the last word so precisely Tom had to stifle a chuckle. "So, see, Daddy, I *will* have my name in a book. And I won't have to wait to have Mom put it on hers."

Tom fought to keep his smile pasted to his face. "Just wait until you tell Grandma and Aunt Debbie. They'll have to buy a dozen copies."

"You can have all the copies you want," Jack said, coming toward them. "I'll see you get some. I have to get some for my partner's wife, anyway."

"Who's your partner, Jack?" Lucy asked. "Is he the one you played the color game with?"

Tom hated the shadow that passed over Jack's face.

"Yes. Yes, he was."

It's a game a friend and I used to play sometimes, Jack had said. But the loss and the fierce admiration that flickered in her eyes whenever she mentioned her partner made Tom suspect that this "friend" had been much, much more. A jealous knot tightened in his gut.

Had Jack been in love with this friend? Had she been in love with other men in the time since she'd stormed away from the tiny apartment? Eight and a half years was a long time—a lifetime. He'd been so wrapped up in Lucy he hadn't really stopped to think about it before.

Jack had been traveling the world, working with real-life adventurers, men who risked death every day. She'd spent weeks with freedom fighters, rebels trying to save their countries from oppression. She'd pitched tents beside naturalists and animal behaviorists who had devoted their lives to saving endangered species.

Men who could match her in courage and commitment to a cause they believed in. Men who risked their lives every day. Far more fitting mates to a woman like Jack than a simple veterinarian, a single parent who'd moved next door to his parents so his daughter would always have family nearby.

Tom couldn't help but feel a sense of loss about the life he might have had, a twinge of embarrassment at the safety, the security, the blandness of his world when compared with the excitement of Jack's.

Even given the chance to go back in time and do things over, it wasn't as if he would change a thing. He just needed to find a way to change the subject right now, banish the presence of this faceless man from this perfect afternoon. But Lucy's curiosity won out.

"What was your partner's name?" she asked.

Jack hesitated for a moment. "Ziggy Bartolli."

"That's a funny name."

"We called him that because he was the best out of all of us at dodging bullets. He always knew just when to zig and when to zag."

Lucy's eyes widened. "You mean people shoot guns at you when you're playing the color game? That would make it lots harder."

"No. They didn't shoot at us while we were playing the color game." Jack laughed. "But there were lots of other times when they did."

"For taking pictures of lighthouses and stuff?" Cal asked, astounded.

"I don't take pictures like the ones I'm working on now very much. I take pictures for the magazines and newspapers. Pictures of faraway places where bad things are happening. I always hope that once I show how bad things are, someone will want to help the people who live there."

"Are you ever scared?" Lucy asked, fiddling with the strap on her camera.

"Usually I'm too busy trying to get the pictures to be scared. The bullets don't even seem real. But other times . . . yes, Lucy. I'm scared."

Jack felt her cheeks warm. She could feel Tom's gaze on her.

"Daddy tries to keep my scary stuff away at night. My cousins say that makes me a baby, having to have Daddy there. They say it's silly to be scared of the dark."

"I'd like to see them say that to you with me around." Cal scowled, grinding his grubby fist against the palm of his hand.

"Lucy, why didn't you tell me they were teasing you?" Tom asked, a little bewildered.

"Because they call me a baby, say 'run to your daddy and cry.' " Lucy's mouth worked, as if, even now, she were trying not to let them make her cry. "If I told you, I'd just be proving they were right."

Jack surprised herself by reaching out and taking hold of Lucy's hand. "In all the time I've been a photo-journalist, I've worked with lots of different kinds of people. One thing I've learned is that 'dark' isn't the same for everyone. Some people only see shadows in the corners that aren't scary at all. Other people see monsters so big they take up the whole room. But this much I can promise you—everyone will be scared sometime. Even the bravest person in the whole world. Your cousins will find that out for themselves someday. Lucy, listen to me," Jack said, meeting the little girl's gaze, holding tight to her hand. "You're not a baby just because it helps you to have somebody with you when you're scared. It's only natural to want someone to love us. Help us feel safe when life gets all crazy."

She felt Tom's eyes on her, thoughtful, deep, suddenly achingly tender, as if he suspected the truth, that there were times even Jack wished there was someone she could reach out to hold. Jack swallowed hard, wondering for just an instant what would happen if she reached out to him.

She pulled herself away from the tempting image, forcing herself to concentrate on the little girl before her. Lucy nibbled her lower lip and tugged at her glasses. "I bet you don't have somebody guarding you all night so the monsters won't come. I bet you're so brave you chase them off by yourself."

Jack's cheeks burned, but she couldn't ignore the shame that flooded Lucy's small face. "The truth of the matter is that I *did* have someone who helped me chase away nightmares when I was traveling all over the world."

"You did?" Lucy peered up at Jack, her freckles like a sprinkling of ginger across her upturned nose. "Did your daddy go everywhere with you just like mine does?"

The notion was so incredible Jack had to chuckle. She pictured Frank shivering near a campfire in the Khyber Pass, cursing Jack to high heaven because the snow was starting to fall.

"No. Ziggy used to help me," she said, as matter-of-factly as she could.

"Ziggy your partner, right?" Lucy asked. "Is Ziggy a boy?"

"A man. Yes."

"Is he your boyfriend?" Cal asked.

"Is he?" Lucy echoed, looking so dubious it surprised Jack. It was as if the answer mattered to Lucy a lot. Jack felt Tom's gaze on her, solemn, probing, maybe dreading her answer more than a little?

The realization unnerved Jack, made her feel off balance.

"We were best friends. Partners. That's all," Jack said, but her eyes were on Tom. "Ziggy had a wife he loved very much. She was so brave, Lucy. She walked through the desert with her sisters, came to a place where she didn't even know the language. She didn't know anyone."

"Can I meet her someday?" Lucy asked. "And Ziggy who ducks bullets like the Lone Ranger?"

"You can meet Shaara, his wife. But Ziggy—Ziggy isn't here anymore."

"Oh. Is he running around making a different book like my mom?"

"No." Jack's lungs burned, and for a moment, she wasn't sure she'd be able to get the words out. "Ziggy died."

Lucy's eyes rounded. "You mean he didn't zag when he should have and a bullet got him?"

"Yes."

Tom reached out surreptitiously, squeezed Jack's hand. He wanted to ease the wound he sensed in her, the grief. But somehow, the touch only made Jack tremble, as if he were shaking the foundations of some wall she'd built around herself to keep from coming apart.

Jack pulled away from his touch and shifted her gaze back to the little girl.

Tom ached at how much effort it took for Jack to force briskness into her voice.

"Lucy, the light's starting to fade. Come on, kiddo, let's get that picture!" Jack insisted.

Lucy scrambled to do as Jack asked, taking frame after frame, adjusting things ever so slightly as Jack suggested.

But it was as if a gray veil had fallen over the day. The sun glittered, the waves glistened, but the rare light that had shone in Jack's eyes was gone.

Cal Pepperell's stomach felt all hot and churny he was so mad inside. How could those cousins of Lucy's have been so mean to tease her like that? He'd never been around girls much. They said his hands stank when he'd been helping his dad on the fishing boat. But Lucy was real nice, and his grandma said there was something wrong with her. Lucy was going blind.

Sometimes Cal scrunched his eyes real tight, to try to see what it would be like. But even with all the imagining he could do, he couldn't think how scared Lucy must be, or how brave she was, still smiling and laughing no matter what.

"Cal?"

He jumped, surprised to find Lucy standing close to him. He wondered how she got there, so quiet without him hearing.

"Did you cut yourself or something?"

" 'Course not."

"Oh. Your face looked all scowly for a minute. Daddy went back to the lighthouse to get some more pop and Jack's taking a few pictures of her own. I supposed I ought to let her. I mean, she *does* still have to get that book of hers done. And you and me can't be in *all* the pictures." She plopped down on the ground next to him and leaned back, propping herself up on her elbows. She was settling in for a "long quiet." Cal liked those times they didn't say anything almost as much as times they talked. It felt good just to be quiet with Lucy. His brothers were always making so much noise they scared all the birds and animals away. Cal bet a seagull could take a piece of popcorn right off of Lucy's hand and not get scared.

"It's funny," Lucy said after a while. "I thought I knew just what Mermaid Lost would be like. 'Cause my mom, she wrote this story about it, see. And I've read it and read it tons of times. But Mermaid Lost isn't like I expected at all."

"How come?" Cal stiffened, worried that this place he loved so much had disappointed her somehow.

"It's beautiful," Lucy said, as if she knew what he was thinking, and wanted to make him feel better. "Even more beautiful than I imagined. I love the water and the sound of the waves and the wind feels so good on my face. And I like you. Best of anything here. But I thought I'd get to see the pirate ghost and the light-house would be all haunted. I thought I'd be able to see all the shipwrecks mom wrote about."

"They're under the water, except for that old steel hull."

"That shows how much I know." Lucy smiled. "I thought the wrecks would be sticking out of the water, like, well, like in a ride at Disneyland or something. Silly, huh?"

"You couldn't help it if you thought that. I mean, if you read about it in a story, it's no wonder you thought it was real."

She got quiet again, but it was different this time, like something was building up inside her. Her cheeks were pink underneath all those freckles when she turned to face him again. "Can I tell you a secret?" she asked soft, so that even the seagulls couldn't hear. "Promise you won't tell?"

"Cross my heart."

"Know why I wanted to come here so bad? I was going to find the treasure. The pirate treasure that's on one of those ships. Mom wrote all about it in her book. I figured that if I did find it, it would make a great ending for her story. My mom could have all the money and she wouldn't have to stay far away being a writer anymore. She could come live by me. I haven't even seen my mom once since I was three."

"Oh." Cal grunted. He hated not knowing what to say. His mom was always around. At his hockey games, at the kitchen table when he was doing his homework.

"I read about lots of treasures," Lucy continued. "And even if I didn't find any, I thought, well, if I'd been in the crashed ships, maybe my mom would want to talk to me, want me to tell her all about it. That way, she could put it in her book, even if she never saw it herself." Lucy looked down until all Cal could see was her eyelashes on cheeks that got really red. "It's silly, isn't it? Thinking maybe she'd want to see me? Why would she want to after all this time?"

Cal swallowed hard, hating the sadness that tugged down the corners of Lucy's mouth. "Maybe she doesn't know about what you're like. About how—how special you are. Not like other girls. If she did, I bet a whole army of ghosts couldn't keep her away."

"You think so? I don't know. I just—I'm getting kind of scared. The doctor said my eyes could break just like that. And if they do, it will be too late. Everybody else I know has a mom who wants to see them all the time, Cal. Some kids even get sick of how much their mom wants to see them. Why not me?"

"Maybe your mom is just—just—" *Stupid* was what he wanted to say. But Cal doubted calling Lucy's mom names would make Lucy feel better. "I wish I could find a way to help you," Cal said. "I'd do anything if I could."

"You can't make me a fish so I can breathe under-water." Lucy sighed. "And you can't make my mom love me. She can't even like me if she doesn't even want to see me."

"If I was a pirate I'd make her look at you," Cal said fiercely. "And she'd have to love you then, or I'd make her walk the plank and get eaten by sharks."

Lucy smiled at him, and Cal's cheeks burned like fire.

"Or I'd take all the treasure and dress you up in diamonds and rubies and pearls and put a sparkly crown on your head. You'd be so beautiful she'd have to notice you then."

Cal took hold of Lucy's hand, the way he did his little brothers' sometimes when they were sad. But it didn't feel the same. It made his stomach all jumpy, like he'd swallowed a netful of butterflies.

"Cal, before I have to go away again, can I take a picture of you?"

"For the game you and Jack play? What color would I be?"

"Not a color. A word. Brave."

"I'm not that brave."

"You make me feel brave. Like I can be—I don't know."

"You know what I think? I think you're the best girl I ever met. I think any monster that ever tried to get you would run away 'cause you've got this light inside that can never get dark. If you stayed here forever, I think—I think I'd marry you someday."

"Even if I can't see?"

"Yeah. We'd get one of those dogs that can open cans and lead you everywhere. And we'd teach it how to make spaghetti. I like spaghetti lots, do you?"

"Yeah."

"And I'd let you share my mom, too. She'd like to have a girl around."

Lucy squeezed his hand. "That's real nice, Cal. It is. But I . . . I kind of want a mom of my own."

Cal nodded, understanding. But he wished with all his might that there was something he could do. Maybe he couldn't make Lucy's mom love her, but maybe, just maybe, he could find a way to get her to those wrecks.

"Lucy, my dad and Uncle Asia, they go diving sometimes. They've got masks and oxygen tanks and all kinds of stuff."

Lucy sat up straight, her eyes round and excited. "Do you think they'd let us borrow it?"

"No way. They'd say we're too little."

Lucy looked like a balloon that got popped.

"But people didn't think a pirate should be coming to Mermaid Lost, either, and Captain Rake Ramsey did it anyway 'cause he loved my great-great—well, I can't remember how many 'greats'-grandmother so much. I got pirate blood right inside of me. And you're real smart, too. We can figure it out together. Don't you think so? We just can't tell anybody. Especially not grown-ups."

Lucy looked worried. "I always tell my dad everything. Well, almost everything. Do you think they'll be mad?"

"When we come up with tons of pirate treasure? Heck, no. We'll even give them the stuff your mom doesn't want."

"I'm not sure . . ."

Cal wasn't either. He figured he'd be in big trouble when his dad found out. Dad didn't spank very often, but for this, Cal figured he'd probably make an exception. "Do you want to get your mom back?"

"More than anything."

"Then it's the only way. I'll let you know when I get stuff ready."

"Okay," Lucy said.

"Bet we'll have to do it at night, or someone will catch us," Cal said after a moment.

Lucy's face got whiter, her freckles standing out like dots from a Magic Marker. "I'm sorry," Cal said softly. "I know you're scared of the dark. But the grown-ups would catch us if we tried it in the day."

"You'll be with me all the time, won't you? Promise?"

"Promise." He held her hand real tight until he heard Lucy's dad in the distance, calling their names.

12

Something was coming. Jack could feel it in her bones, even though the sky seemed clear. Was it weather? Or something harder to put your finger on? That almost imperceptible ripple in the air that was a journalist's bread and butter. The intuition one felt when a "situation" was about to blow.

Trouble was, she could be sensing anything from an earthquake three continents away to a coup in Tibet. Or it could be something on a far more personal level, where the only ground shaking was the patch under her own feet.

Her instincts had been sizzling like downed power lines ever since she and Tom, Cal and Lucy had explored the beach three days ago. It was absurd to imagine anything that could be lurking at Mermaid Lost to give her this sense of unease—except a sudden awakening that still had her reeling.

The days had spun out, each easier and warmer than the last. "The Four Musketeers," as adventure-loving Cal liked to call the four of them, falling into a closeness that Jack both relished and felt uneasy about.

Maybe that was why she felt so on edge. It was such a long time since she'd had this sensation of camaraderie with anyone besides Ziggy, and even that had been full of boundaries that a couple of eight-year-olds didn't hold with. Jack had been used to blowups and excitement in her work every day, and yet, was it possible that, once the adrenaline rushes were stripped away the days seemed far more tedious, gray, marching on to the next assignment?

It hadn't seemed that way until fate had thrown her into a room with a little girl with clear-framed glasses, a boy with a pirate's smile, and a man who, with every day, every heated glance, every brief, knee-melting touch was changing her somehow, widening her point of view, softening the edges she'd thought so much a part of her, and making her want . . . and want, and *want*.

Jack's heart squeezed, and for the first time she was glad she'd come to Mermaid Lost, glad she had the book to finish. It would be filled with images of people she'd come to love in spite of herself. China and the Pepperell boys, Cal and Lucy. Ziggy and Shaara. And Tom. She'd been in such a hurry to get away from this place. Now she was glad she'd have something to hold on to, something to remember it by.

A dull ache formed in her throat at the impending loss. It was surprising how quickly she'd started to listen for the sound of footsteps, children's laughter, the low rumble of Tom's voice. Touches so tender they made her feel precious, rare. She'd wanted to pull away, tell him how independent and tough she was. He knew that and wanted to treasure her anyway. She smiled, knowing she'd treasure this time together, too, before they each returned to their own, very different, worlds.

She hugged her arms around her waist, unable to deny the yearning deep inside her as she thought of the undeniable emotion in Tom's dark brown eyes whenever he looked at her—desire, yes, but maybe far more.

A longing like hers, and a quiet, painful understanding of the differences between them. And it wasn't as if there were middle ground somewhere, a compromise that made sense.

There was no place for Tom and Lucy in her world of jetting around the globe, dodging machine-gun fire. And as for Jack zinging back and forth from assignments to Tom's Kentucky farmhouse—that was as ridiculous as imagining him in warlord country in Somalia. He needed someone who would be there with him when things got tough at home. And if Lucy was finally going to get a mother, it should be one who'd be around, not popping in whenever there wasn't much happening on the world political front.

So would the world end if you turned in your press badge?

Jack stiffened, stunned at the whisper deep inside her. For a moment possibilities rippled through her imagination. Then crashed, suddenly to a halt. Photojournalism was her job and she was good at it. Her photographs elicited reactions in people no one else could get in just the same way. Her talent gave her the power to change people's lives—just not the course of her own.

It saddened her, and yet steeled her resolve. The most important task she'd ever undertaken lay before her. The one tangible thing she could send with Tom and Lucy to remember her by, and if she did it right, they would understand all the things she couldn't bring herself to say.

She crossed to the big table she'd set up in the corner of her bedroom, the place she worked at late into the night. Two days ago China had brought a package up to the lighthouse, an order from one of Jack's favorite catalogues. Soft blue, like the sea, the book cover glowed, an empty square cutout waiting for the perfect picture—the one Jack hadn't found yet.

Lucy's book. Her color book. Jack ran her fingers over the cover with a rare reverence. Of every job she'd done in her long and successful career, this, Jack knew, was the most important.

Ziggy would think so, too.

She went to the drawer, surprising herself by taking out the medicine bag Ziggy had left to her. It made her feel closer to him. And somehow, tonight, she needed that. She slipped it under her pillow, lay down on the bed for just a moment. The glue had to dry on one of the pages she'd been working on anyway. Pages of Lucy and Cal huddled over books dug out of China's vast library—treasure hunter books, with pictures of the grinning divers dripping in gold chains and mountains of gold ingots.

The perfect food for imaginations.

Jack closed her eyes, wishing she was eight again. She'd have done more than dream like Cal and Lucy, she thought with a smile. She'd have found a way to those wrecks if it killed her. No wonder her parents hadn't ever taken her on vacations.

She felt her body relax into the mattress, felt herself start to let go. She curled one hand around Ziggy's medicine bag, remembering things he'd saved. A fragment of the Berlin Wall, a small stone from Tiananmen Square in Beijing. A few lines Nelson Mandela had smuggled out of prison. A tiny length of leather from the sandals Shaara had worn on her trek out of the desert.

But there wasn't any way to tuck a child's smile into the leather bag, or a man's kiss, or images of a future that might have been. Jack couldn't remember the last time she'd cried, but tears came, hot and slow and deep.

Somebody was crying. Lucy sat up in bed, listening to the sound come from far away. Was it the wind? Or maybe the ghosts Cal had told her about? She wondered with a delicious shiver. She wished the ghost wasn't so sad.

She blinked the sleep from her eyes and glanced over at the big easy chair Jack had made Daddy drag in from the living room so he could sleep better. It looked like it was working because he was snoring away real quiet. Jack was right. A whole tribe of crocodiles could come in and eat him and he wouldn't know what had happened until he woke up in their stomachs.

Lucy stiffened as another sound drifted down from upstairs. It sounded like it was coming from Jack's room. But Jack would never make a sound like that. Jack wasn't scared of anything. Not even tigers or bombs or jumping out of airplanes.

If it wasn't Jack, then it had to be a ghost, didn't it? Lucy reasoned. There wasn't anyone else in the lighthouse but them. At least not anybody alive.

She glanced at her dad again, trying to decide if she should wake him up.

If it *was* the ghost, she might be able to talk to it. Ask it where its treasure was. But she wouldn't be able to ask if her dad was there. Besides, she doubted ghosts talked to grown-ups much anyway. It was pointless to talk to people who didn't believe in you.

Creeping out of bed as quiet as she could, she stuck

her feet into her bunny slippers. She didn't want to start shaking because she was cold. The ghost might think she was scared of him.

Ever so quietly, she started up the stairs, trying not to notice the weird shadows that poked through the lacy iron stuff the steps were made out of. If the ghost squeezed through one of those holes and yelled boo, Lucy just knew she'd pee her pants.

Lucy made her way to the bedroom where Jack was staying, and pressed her ear against the closed door. She bit her lower lip, wishing she knew what to do.

Lucy opened the door just a tiny bit, wincing when it creaked on its hinges. "Jack?" Lucy called softly, edging into the room. "It's me. Lucy."

The light by Jack's bed was still on, making the whole room glow. Jack's work was scattered on the table, like she was just taking a little break. But the break wasn't doing her much good. Jack looked up, her face all shiny with tears, and she looked like she wished the roof would cave in on her she was so embarrassed.

"Lucy," Jack stammered, scrubbing the wetness away. "What are you doing up here?"

"I—" Lucy searched for the right words to say. "Thought I heard a ghost."

"Oh." Jack shoved back the tendrils of hair that were sticking to her forehead. She tried to fake a smile. "I'm sorry if I scared you. Sometimes I just get a little, uh, restless, when I'm sleeping."

Lucy looked her over carefully, trying to be brave. "Daddy says everybody cries sometimes. It's nothing to be ashamed of."

Jack stared at her for a moment, like she'd just got splashed with cold water. Lucy held her breath. "Is that what your daddy says?"

"Umhumm. Sometimes it helps to talk about it. I

used to cry when the sky felt too dark. Lots and lots of dark I can never get out of. Someday it won't be a nightmare anymore. Someday it will come true."

Jack scooted over, patted the bed next to her. Lucy climbed up and Jack cuddled the blankets around her. "When that happens, you'll still be able to make light inside you, Lucy. I'm sure of it. The dark will never win."

Lucy nibbled at her thumbnail, thinking. "Will your dark win? The dark that was making you cry tonight?"

"I don't know. It's been with me for so very long now. And it's gotten worse, ever since—" Jack stopped, looked away. Lucy knew what she was thinking. That she was telling a kid something important. Grown-ups thought kids didn't understand stuff like that. Or else they wanted to seem like superheroes and not let kids know they couldn't jump tall buildings in a single bound or pound their fists through brick walls.

Jack was going to change the subject. Lucy knew it. And once Jack did, she wouldn't change her mind. Whatever secret she'd been about to tell would get hidden again, deep inside where no one else could see.

"Last summer, I got this splinter," Lucy said. "I *hate* getting splinters dug out so I hid it from my grandma. By the time it got so sore, I couldn't stand it. It was all red and puffy and had lots of pus around it. I think secrets get infected just like that."

"Do you?" Jack looked at her, all funny. She reached out to touch Lucy's hair. Lucy sat real still, the way Daddy taught her with wild animals he took care of, so she wouldn't scare Jack away.

It worked. Jack took a deep breath, and stroked Lucy's hair. It felt so good Lucy got brave enough to lean her head against Jack's shoulder.

"I've got secrets that make me sad. Things that are my fault. Like my mom leaving me."

"That's not your fault, honey."

"How do you know for sure? You don't know my mom. I must have done something bad to make her go away."

"No. There are lots of reasons grown-ups go away that have nothing to do with their children."

"I wish I could ask her. You know, look right in her face, like I'm looking at you. Then I'd know for sure that she didn't go away because I was bad or ugly inside or—or there was something wrong with me."

"Oh, sweetheart."

"But I'm running out of time. Pretty soon it'll be too late. I'll never know for sure."

Jack held her close, wishing there was something she could say.

"Know what's hardest of all about my secret?"

"What?"

"I can't tell my daddy. He looks all sad whenever I ask about Mom. He thinks I don't know how he feels, but he gets this fake smile and changes the subject. Grown-ups must think kids are real dumb to fall for fake smiles instead of real ones."

Jack winced, remembering the pain in Tom's face as he spoke of Laura, and the heartbreak he couldn't keep away forever from his little girl.

"You could tell him how you feel. Your dad loves you."

"I can ask him anything but that."

"Lucy, I don't know a lot about, well, about little girls. I told you that from the very beginning. But I do know this. Any mother would have to be crazy not to adore you. You're something special, Lucy Brownlow."

Jack wanted so bad to see the lines smooth from Lucy's face, wanted to feel as if she'd comforted the little girl, inept as Jack was at comforting anyone at all.

"You're so rare and precious and—and worth every bit of loving in somebody's heart."

"But you're not my mom." Lucy regarded her with sad, solemn eyes. "I wish . . ."

"Wish what?" Jack urged, feeling as if she'd do anything in her power to give the child whatever her little heart yearned for. But Lucy's clear green eyes were easy to read. For an instant the child's dream pierced Jack's heart—a little girl's bed, a story half finished, good night hugs and kissing the bad dreams away. Tom waiting in the master bedroom a few doors down, ready, eager to make love once Jack slipped back between the sheets of their own wide bed.

Lucy regarded her solemnly. "I can't tell you my other secret. I can tell you one of my wishes, though," Lucy offered, snuggling close in Jack's arms.

Jack braced herself, waiting for the wish no one could grant, the wish Jack was sure was the most important one Lucy could imagine.

I wish I wouldn't go blind. I wish I could see forever.

"I wish my daddy would smile again. A really true smile without so much sad inside."

Jack did the only thing she could think of, held Lucy, quiet, leaning her cheek against the little girl's hair.

She heard the slightest sound beyond the doorway, strained to hear what it was. The salt breeze against the windowpanes, the creak of the old house on foundations two hundred years old, or maybe Lucy's words had made even a pirate ghost weep.

13

Tom stumbled down the winding staircase, his bare feet quiet against the lacelike iron. His lungs burned with the effort not to make a sound. They couldn't know. Neither Jack nor Lucy could guess that he had overheard the wounds Lucy had revealed to Jack, the secrets his little girl had not wanted him to know.

But he'd learned of his daughter's secret heartache in the minutes after he'd awakened to find Lucy gone from her bed, and set out in search of her.

He would never have believed Lucy would have the courage to brave the lighthouse's dark corridors, the wrought-iron staircase with its ghostly shadows holding strange terrors for a child in the night.

But something about Jack had given Lucy the courage to face the dark hallway alone. Made Lucy care about reaching her new friend more than she cared about the nightmares that usually so terrified her she'd begged him to stay and stand guard.

The courage of his little girl touched Tom, the memory of Lucy and Jack holding each other amid the tangle of blankets astonished him, awed him. Terrified him.

Lucy had depended on Jack so openly, with every fiber of her mother-hungry heart; Jack, so tough, so guarded, holding Lucy in her arms. For the first time ever, he wasn't the one Lucy reached for, wasn't the one she turned to for comfort, wasn't the one trusted with her deepest secrets.

It hurt, filled him with the surprising sensation of envy and concern.

Tom's hands curled into tight fists as he made his way back into the bedroom he and Lucy had shared since they'd come to Mermaid Lost.

When had Lucy and Jack grown so close? Sometime during the hours they'd spent photographing every nook and cranny of the lighthouse and its surroundings? Of course Tom had known Lucy liked Jack—what kid wouldn't? A woman who treated children with respect, taught them how to use a real camera, listened as if their opinions really mattered.

But he hadn't realized the bond the two were forging had gotten so deep. Dangerously deep. Especially for his motherless little girl.

His little girl who thought it was her fault her mother deserted her. His little girl who had spent God alone knew how long, searching inside herself for any tiny flaw that would explain why her mother didn't love her.

And most devastating, still, learning the truth—that the one thing Lucy really wanted to see before her sight slipped away wasn't the bright chaos of Disneyland or the castles of England, not the Eiffel Tower or the Statue of Liberty. The one thing Lucy wanted to see was her mother's face.

Tom's jaw clenched. He hurried to the bathroom

across the hall and shut the door quietly behind him. Crossing to the sink, he turned on the faucets, full force. Flattening his hands against the white porcelain, he hung his head down, shoulders sagging as hot steam poured upward, dampening his face with sweat. Sweat, not tears, he reassured himself, fighting the burning sensation in his eyes.

He'd caught just a glimpse of Lucy and Jack from the shadowy doorway where he'd stood. Lucy, perching up on Jack's bed, her little pink nightgown askew, her curls a tangled halo around her solemn angel face.

I can't tell my daddy, Lucy had confided to Jack. *He looks all sad whenever I ask about Mom.*

Tom couldn't deny it was true. He'd tried his best over the years to pretend Laura's absence away. It had been his own personal masquerade. No. He'd drawn Lucy into his conspiracy of silence and locked all of her questions away.

But then, wasn't his reaction one thing at least that Jack should understand? Silence about pain?

Of course he wanted to heal the hurts in his precious little girl.

But what stunned him was discovering he wanted to reach out to Jack as well. The fierceness of the need stunned him, cast him off balance. He'd told himself again and again in the past five days to leave the past where it belonged. Jack was a different person than the girl he'd loved a long time ago. She was determined to isolate herself from emotions so powerful they scared her, heart-ties that could hurt far more deeply than any bullet could ever pierce.

Every time attraction stirred in Tom, he'd told himself he was just falling prey to old memories of how much he'd loved the girl he'd known so many years ago. In fact, he hadn't even been certain his growing fascination with Jack had anything at all to do with his memories of her. It was possible he'd been using those memories to help him draw closer to the man he'd been way back then, before Laura had stumbled, sobbing, back into his life, before choices he'd made drove him from the path he would have chosen forever.

It might have been easier if he could believe that, instead of suspecting, fearing the truth. That some part of him was tempted to fall in love with Jack Murphy all over again.

He raked his fingers through his hair, remembering how good she had tasted when he'd kissed her, the jolt of excitement, so exotic, so intense, that had rushed through his body. Jack's own flavor of magic, that silent dare that tested a lover to see if he was strong enough, passionate enough, brave enough to make love to a woman as exceptional as she was.

No coy games, no feminine flutters of indecision, no mock shyness or bald seduction. Just a kiss that was everything it seemed to be—fiery, honest, filled with the very essence of the woman Jack had become.

He wasn't a saint, dammit. He wasn't a monk. He was a man who hadn't made love to a woman in longer than he could remember. And there was no denying that Jack had reminded his body in no uncertain terms how good it felt to explore a woman's mouth with his own. How luxurious a woman's skin felt under his hands, how hard his passion would drive inside him at the sounds of pleasure that would answer every sweep of his fingers, swirl of his tongue, thrust of his sex inside her.

But even more insistent than physical need was his need to hold her, listen to her, let her trust him. Share wounded places in each other's souls and sooth them.

Know that there would always be someone to listen when things got too hard or lonely or bleak.

Did Jack ever crave those things the way he did? Or did she mean it when she claimed she liked to be alone? Except for her partner—the one who had died. But then, Ziggy would have been plenty safe for Jack to confide in. No danger of falling in love, having to commit. Ziggy was married to the woman Jack was finishing the lighthouse book for. And for all her grumbling years ago about Tom's sense of duty, she had a rock-hard core of honor in her that would never have permitted being involved with another woman's husband. Or would she?

How much did he really know about her now? The one thing he was sure of was that he still wanted her physically with a hard ache that knotted inside him whenever he saw her, smelled her hair, brushed her hand.

A soft knock on the closed bathroom door made Tom all but jump out of his skin.

Was it Lucy, returned from her adventure?

Scooping up handfuls of water, he splashed his face, then dried himself furiously with the towel. Looping it around his neck, in an effort to look casual, he opened the door.

He froze. Lucy wasn't standing before him, cheeks flushed, desperate to explain what she'd done. Jack stood, her hands clasped in front of her, an exotic, silk tunic covering her from collarbone to ankle. The moss-green fabric rippled about her body, clinging to breasts still high and firm, the perfect size to fit the cupped palms of Tom's hands.

"I wasn't sure what to do. Lucy fell asleep up in my room. I didn't want you to worry." Jack hesitated, emotions racing across her features. "But then, you already knew that, didn't you? That Lucy came up to my room?"

"Yeah," Tom said hoarsely.

"In fact, you know a lot more than that."

Tom paced across to the bedroom. The lantern that was Lucy's night light glowed, throwing golden light as she followed him. "I, uh, heard Lucy go up the stairs," Tom explained. "Couldn't believe it. She's been so skittish about the dark. I followed her up, heard—well, heard enough. When I got the idea for this trip we'd take together, it seemed so simple. Lucy could see all the things she wanted to before it was too late. I could think of a million places I wanted her to experience. Mountains and rivers, the ocean. The tower of London, Disneyland. Places. Things. But she doesn't want that, does she?"

"It's easy to understand why a little girl would want to see her mother."

"Easy? Not for me. Hadn't I built a perfect world around her? Given Lucy everything in my power, everything she wanted and more. What *I* wanted her to have. I tried so hard to make it up to her."

"Tom, the fact that Laura was a rotten mother isn't your fault."

"But the fact that she's *Lucy*'s mother is. I had a choice, Jack. I could've thought with my head instead of my hormones."

"It's not like you planned for her to get pregnant. It just happened."

"Yeah. It happened, all right. It happened to my little girl. And now—what the hell am I supposed to do?"

"Do what you promised. Let Lucy see what she wants most to see."

"Are you crazy? You think she should spend whatever time she has left to see disillusioned and miserable? Because that's what seeing Laura will make her.

Lucy thinks she's sad because she doesn't have a mother? Wait until she comes face-to-face with the mother that she has! Why couldn't it have been you? Even if you'd left us behind, gone off to do what you had to do, Lucy could still be so proud of you."

He choked into silence, stunned at what he'd just said aloud. He gave a ragged laugh. "Do you know how many times I tortured myself with that? Asked why Laura, why not you? I loved you."

Jack stared back at him, stricken, her emotions stripped bare. She came to him, laid her fingers along his cheek. "I'm sorry. I'm sorry for all the hurt you've suffered. Both you and Lucy. You deserved so much better. If I could—could wave a magic wand and turn Laura into Mommy Wonderful, I'd do it in a minute, and I know you would, too. But it's out of our hands. It's inevitable that Lucy is going to meet Laura again. The only question is whether it's going to be sooner or later. Why fight it, Tom? Don't you think Lucy has the right to choose?"

"She has such a little time left. She should fill herself up with beautiful things. Not—not ugliness, not betrayal. Not prison walls where her mother's lived for five years. What would it do to Lucy to see that horrible place? And Laura in it? What will it do to Lucy to realize that Laura's been behind bars all along, and I knew it?"

"She'll find those things out anyway."

"But she won't see the prison, Jack."

"She'll see it in her mind, maybe even worse than the reality. And she'll believe you kept her away from it to hold on to your own lies a little longer. That protecting yourself was more important than keeping your promise to her, that you'd take her to see the things she wanted most in the world."

"I wish Laura had died. In that accident."

"No you don't. Most other people would. But you—in spite of everything, you've always got that crazy hope that somehow, people will heal, get better, have a second chance to get things right. Even Laura."

Tom wanted to argue, wanted to rage at the injustice of it all. But there was nothing more to say. Jack was right about so many things—the inevitability of Laura crashing back into Lucy's life, the resentment Lucy would feel toward him for keeping secrets, the betrayal years of lying to her would bring.

"I can't do this, Jack. Can't you see? I can't take Lucy to see her mother in prison. She's scared of the dark when it's outside her world, in the hallways and in the shadows that hide under her bed. How do you think she'll feel when she finds this other kind of darkness, the kind that gets inside you and colors everything it touches? Fills you with suspicion and dread and doubt?"

"She's stronger than you think. She came to me through the dark."

"But when she got to you, she knew she'd find light. She won't when she finds her mother. She'll find everything I spent her whole life protecting her from."

Tom hesitated for a moment, then succumbed to the need thrumming deep in his veins. He framed her face with his hands, his fingertips dipping into silky hair, savoring velvety skin, his soul hungry for the honesty, the inner strength and courage ever present in Jack.

"Why now, Jack? Of all the people in the world, why did I find you here, now?"

He felt her throat work delicately, her breath quicken, warm and moist where it touched his skin.

"I don't know," she whispered.

"I needed . . . someone so badly. To talk to. To listen.

I've been alone for so long. But there wasn't anybody strong enough, anybody close enough, anybody who could look all the ugliness in the face and not turn away. There wasn't anybody like you."

Her eyes widened for a heartbeat, like an animal who had just scented danger. Her reaction cut, down deep. "Tom . . ." she drew out his name, a gentle warning.

He drew back just a whisper, tried to harness the secret longing that had been welling up inside of him from the moment he first saw her framed by the green painted door of the lighthouse. Or was the truth, he wondered, that the need for her had never left him at all?

"I know," he said. "You can't turn back the clock. Can't change—everything in just a heartbeat. You've got your life and I've got mine. What I meant to say was that funny as it sounds, if I could've chosen any-one in the world to—to share this time with, I would've picked you. You always did make me feel stronger, braver, as if I could handle whatever hard knocks fate wanted to dish out. And make no mistake, there are going to be plenty of bumps ahead."

"Bumps both you and Lucy will get through. I can't count the number of times I've shot the rapids on rivers in Africa and South America in these little bark canoes that look about as sturdy as a dry leaf strung between toothpicks. I was sure I was going to be killed. And I got plenty bruised up and shaken and lost some of my gear a couple of times. I even took a header over a waterfall once in the Amazon and lost the rest of my party for three days. But somehow I managed to hold on to my waterproof camera bag."

"Pure stubbornness?"

"No. I wasn't going to be turned back by a tribe of overgrown rocks and a river with an attitude and fish who considered me haute cuisine. But you, Tom, you've got something far more important than work to see you through. You've got your love for Lucy to hold you up when the water gets rough, and Lucy will have her love for you. You'll hold on to each other all the way through it because you love each other too much to let go."

"Lucy and I against the world. That's the way it has always been when you get right down to it. And yet . . ."

He hesitated, his gaze caressing her face, the need in him radiating through every inch of his body. "Is it so terrible to wish you and I could help each other while we're all here at the lighthouse? You've got pain, too, Jack, wounds you're trying to heal. I feel it. Know it. Would it be so wrong to lean on each other just a little while we're here?"

"Not wrong," she murmured, wary, but not trying to pull away. "But it could be dangerous."

"Or exactly what we both need right now. Maybe fate knew what it was doing when we both ended up on the doorstep of Mermaid Lost. Maybe it knew that we both needed a little more strength than we had by ourselves. Maybe it was giving us a chance to make peace with ourselves and with each other, so that when we walk away, finally, finally, we can really let go."

"Can we? I'm not sure. Things are already so tangled, and I don't want to make them worse. And yet . . . I'd be lying if I said I didn't wonder—"

"Wonder what?"

"How it would feel to—let someone close enough to touch me again. Let *you* close enough. Sometimes I feel like I've been cold so long, alone so long, I'll never be able to get warm."

"Do you want to find out?" He waited for her answer,

feeling as if he were dangling from a wire. The slightest touch of a breeze would send him plummeting down. But he wouldn't take anything Jack wasn't ready to give, wouldn't force her to cross lines she wasn't willing to cross.

It seemed an eternity had spiraled out between them before she gave the slightest nod of her head. Tom's heart thudded hard against his rib cage. He breathed in the scent of her, sunshine and shampoo, and some exotic perfume permeated with spices and musk and flowers so rare he knew he'd never even heard of their lush, lovely blooms. Green silk rippled in a sheath around her lithe body, softening it into curves where it had seemed too thin before.

Tom's breath caught, his eyes drifting closed as he dipped his head down to kiss her.

The contact shot sensation to Jack's very toes. Was it possible that this could be even better than she'd remembered? she wondered, dazed. She'd assured herself a hundred times in the years she'd tried to forget Tom that her memories were sweetened beyond reality by a young girl's first infatuation, that sense of being in love, not just with the first man of your dreams, but also in love with love itself.

She'd told herself the kisses of other men felt as if they were lacking because she'd been so much younger with Tom, in age, in experience. A babe who'd stumbled into the woods and found them beautiful. An innocent who didn't realize how much danger lurked there as well.

Tom's mouth explored hers as if it were his first time and he wanted to learn every bit of her by heart. Softly, so softly, he searched every curve and hollow and crease of her lips, his kiss brand-new, and yet devastatingly familiar in its strength and tenderness. Jack sank deeper and deeper into the sensations, awed. How could he do it? Give so much in a simple caress in which most people gave so little of themselves?

He didn't even bother to try to hide how vulnerable he was, how much he needed her. The kiss stripped him naked, and he had the courage not to scramble back to where everything was safe and sure.

Jack wished she could be half that brave.

She wanted to lock her hands around the nape of his neck and pull him tighter against her, melting together bodies, lips, sharing breath, sharing strength. She wanted to fall into bed with him and try, just one last time, to recapture the magic of those weeks they'd shared under his warm, soft quilt.

But they weren't two naïve kids anymore, who thought they could dive under the covers without consequences. When the price tag for this one night came due, Jack knew it would turn out to be far more costly than either one of them could afford.

She drew away, ever so gently, hating the sense of loss that seeped into her very bones as the warmth in him faded away.

"What—what is it?" Tom asked, sounding a little dazed, his eyes still misted over with need so compelling that Jack had to look away or cave in completely. She struggled to steady her breathing, to find the right words to explain.

"Oh, Tom," she said with a sigh. "It's wrong. It's just wrong. Kissing you."

"Because it's been so long since we broke up? Because it was over then, and you don't want to dredge it all up again? I guess it's hard to blame you. I'm the one who betrayed your trust. I let you down. Why would you want to risk even so much as a few clandestine kisses. Even if those kisses were the most incredible . . ."

He paused, stuck his hands into his pockets like a kid who didn't want to be too tempted to touch something precious, after he'd been warned he might break it. "I'm sorry," he grumbled.

"Don't be. Just let me try to explain. You and I, Tom, we can never be just a 'summer fling' to each other. And considering the lives we each lead, we can't ever be anything more than we are."

"So what are we to each other, Jack? Painful memories of what might have been, what never was?"

"What are we? Friends. I care about you, Tom. Maybe too much. Not just because of the past. But because of the man you've become in the years we've been apart. That's the problem. The last thing either of us needs is more hurt. And Lucy—if she thought we cared about each other, she might not be able to help hoping—"

She didn't finish. She didn't have to.

Tom didn't need to hear the words to imagine the hunger that would flare in his daughter's eyes. Hunger for a mother who would hold her and talk to her and teach her wondrous things. But no point in dreaming. Perfect as Lucy thought Jack was, Jack was a mother Lucy Brownlow could never have.

Jack would never be able to stay in one place long enough. She craved excitement, new places, new people. Spent most of her time traveling, racing from one place to the next, rarely stopping to rest, let alone put down roots.

As for Lucy—just as Jack's world would be expanding again the moment she left Mermaid Lost, Tom feared Lucy's world would soon be getting smaller. Limited to the places Lucy could commit to memory. Six hundred and thirty steps to Grandmas house. Sixteen stairs to her school.

Tom raked his fingers through his hair. He hungered to touch Jack with the kind of need that was bone deep. Needed to feel warmth and life under his hands, her heartbeat's soft thud when he crushed her against his chest. Sex—oh, yeah, he wanted to make love to her until they were both too exhausted to think about anything else.

He wanted to kiss her throat, her breasts, feel her long, sleek legs twine together with his under cool sheets with the salt air wafting through the slightly open window.

But she was right. They could never be just a fling to each other. And even if they were reckless enough to seek comfort in each other's arms for just these few short weeks fate had thrown them together, there was Lucy to consider. A frightened, fragile little girl whose world was already about to crash down around her.

Tom crossed to the easy chair, sagged down into it, feeling overwhelmed, oddly helpless, uncharacteristically resentful. What did fate have against him, anyway? Why did it seem like every time he got close to something good, something *he* needed, it always conflicted with something someone else needed even more?

He heard the brush of footsteps nearing the chair. Saw Jack's bare feet framed against the hardwood floor. Such beautifully shaped, utterly feminine feet to have carried her so far from the world he knew.

"Tom, I wish this could be easy."

"Nothing ever was between the two of us. It wasn't easy. But it was—God, Jack, how do we even try to describe what it was? Do you know how hard it was, learning how to keep from thinking about you every minute of the day? If I hadn't had Lucy to consider, nothing on earth could have kept me from finding you."

He could see his words were hurting her, and yet, there was just a hint of something else in her eyes, pleading for him to say more.

"I swore I'd block you out of my mind, out of my heart," she shared. "Pretend you hadn't even existed. I made sure I was so busy I barely slept or ate. Prided myself on the fact that no one would ever know I'd fallen prey to that disgustingly weak female flaw—a broken heart."

"You have the strongest will of anyone I've ever met."

"Not when it came to us. I think Ziggy knew within the first ten minutes of meeting me that in spite of all my bravado and my claim that the career was the only thing I'd ever wanted in life, I was running away from something just as much as I was running to it. He called it my 'lamebrained version of running off to join the French Foreign Legion.' "

"Was it everything you wanted, Jack?"

"Not everything. But it was enough. After a while it got easier, learning how to be without you. I was good with a camera. Really good. And I had so much to learn. I liked the unpredictability of it, never knowing where I'd end up next. You have to keep your wits sharp, so sharp. That helped me most of all."

He should be glad she got over him so quickly. Should be thrilled that she'd buried herself in work she loved, exploring lands she'd only visited in her imagination. But it hurt, imagining Jack focusing that laser beam intensity of hers on pretending he'd never existed in her life at all.

"And then everything changed. In an instant. One bullet out of all the guns that had ever shot at me. I couldn't pretend anymore, act like it wasn't real. Or that I didn't care."

"Your partner?"

"He died trying to save me. He had this—this wonderful joy in life. A wife who adored him. A future. He was dreaming of building a house here at Mermaid Lost and retiring. Who knows, maybe he would have had some kids. Any way you looked at it, he would have had a flock of them around him. Ziggy was a kid magnet everywhere we went. I used to tease him that he carried as much candy as he did film. Called him on it, once. Told him the kids didn't even have milk. The last thing they needed was candy. Ziggy just winked and told me everybody's life needed sweetening, sometimes more than bread or water."

Jealousy burned Tom at the love and respect in Jack's voice. Maybe Jack and Ziggy hadn't been lovers. But from what Jack had said, Ziggy was the man she'd shared her life with, her secrets with, her vulnerabilities with. Now he was dead. How much had that hurt her? The pain, the guilt, the grief still shadowed her eyes.

"You must miss him." It was not easy for Tom to admit this.

"He was . . . my best friend. It's still hard to imagine the world without him."

"It's difficult when a part of your life ends. Especially when you weren't expecting it." He'd found that out for himself. When he'd lost Jack. When he'd had to abandon Laura to keep his daughter safe. When the doctor had given him the news that Lucy was going to lose her sight. "Nothing is ever quite the same. But you can't throw away the good parts because the bad parts hurt."

Jack smiled, her face softer. "Like Gracie?"

"Gracie?"

"I'm still having trouble believing that you kept her after I left. Lucy told me the whole story, about how she'd gotten her dog. It sounded like some Pet Planet talking-animal show on television. The kind people get all sentimental about."

Tom smiled. "It was. That's Lucy's favorite story of her whole childhood, and she wasn't even born yet."

"Laura couldn't have been quite as enthusiastic about hearing it."

"No. I told her Gracie had too many medical problems to place in a home, that if we took Gracie to the shelter they'd have to put her down. Most of it was true. The neglect had messed up Gracie's system but good. But it hadn't damaged her heart. Once Lucy was born, Gracie guarded her with a faithfulness that awed me. Amazed me. It was as if the dog had stored up a lifetime of love just to give to my daughter. And Lucy needed it, Jack."

Jack smiled, her eyes soft. "I'm glad Gracie was there to help. She always looked like she was just hoping to find somebody to love."

Isn't that what we all want? Tom thought. *Gracie was just luckier than most of us.*

"What did Lucy say when you told her that you were the lady in the story? The one she calls 'Gracie's Angel'?"

"I didn't tell her. I don't think she needs to know. She's already—I don't know—looking at me as if I were more than I really am, you know? Like she's making me into some kind of hero or something. It's a bad idea, putting people on pedestals. They always fall off. And when they do, they usually do a lot of damage on the way down."

"You're telling me." Tom couldn't keep the desolation from showing in his face. "I'm about to take one hell of a long fall."

"Don't fall any farther than you have to. Do what

you can to make things better for Lucy. At least *think* about what *she* wants."

"It's too soon for Laura to come back into her life. Lucy's eight years old. How can she know how badly things are going to fall apart once she sees her mother again? I owe it to Lucy to give her a summer to remember. Her 'Lighthouse Summer.' She kept calling it that, over and over before we left Kentucky." He got to his feet, suddenly so restless he couldn't keep still.

"I never should have come here. I knew it from the beginning. I could feel it—something was going to go wrong. But I expected it would be something from the outside, some kind of gossip Lucy might overhear or some scrap of the truth she might stumble on. I never guessed that the danger would come from inside my little girl's own head."

"It's come from her heart. This longing to see her mother."

"What good is any of it going to do? The trip? Time with me? The pictures you two have been taking? In the end Lucy's special summer is going to turn into one more nightmare. One more bundle of regrets I'll end up carrying with me forever."

Like the pain of losing you, Tom realized, his heart even heavier.

"In the end," Tom said, "I think you were the lucky one. You had your work, so far away from where we fell in love, our time together probably didn't even seem real. You got on with your life, ended up with the work you wanted, the life you'd planned. It had to be easier to forget—"

"It should have been. I've never been able to understand why—

"Why what?"

"Even when Africa was singing its songs to me,

somehow you were there. Sometimes even here, when I close my eyes, I can see it all so clearly. The raw beauty of a pride of lions teaching its cubs to hunt. The scent of the river on the wind. The sun hot on the back of my neck. I miss the people in the war zones I've photographed. The way they still try to make their children laugh."

Tom tried not to let her words hurt him. The new wistfulness in her voice sounded as if she were already longing to be a thousand miles away. When he and Lucy first arrived, she'd seemed almost battle-shocked, as if she wanted to burrow herself away, blot out the rest of the world and never come out. The tone in her voice now made him afraid for her.

"You miss your work for the press? Even though your partner died doing this job?"

"Ziggy made one fatal mistake."

"And you're so perfect, so damned good that could never happen to you?"

Pain flashed in Jack's eyes, so naked Tom's breath caught in his throat.

"It should have happened to me! I was the one who should have been shot. I should have died in that damned helicopter. Not Ziggy."

"Don't be crazy. I know it's hard to lose someone you love." There, he'd said it out loud. Admitted that Jack loved Ziggy—even though it was as a friend. "But you can't change the way things work out in a situation like that. You can't change places."

"Can't you?" Jack blazed back. "What do you know about what it's like out there? You can go from dead boredom to terror in five seconds. Be running for your life."

"And sometimes people don't make it. You had to know that before you picked up your first press badge.

It's terrible that Ziggy died, but it was a risk he chose to take. It wasn't your fault, Jack."

"It was, dammit! I fell. He ran back to get me."

Oh, God. Tom's heart twisted, so much was making sense now. Jack—brave, independent Jack—who charged into danger without thinking of herself. What had it cost her when someone else had taken her bullet?

Tears gleamed in Jack's eyes, her lips trembling even though he could see how hard she tried to stop them. He took her hand, waited, silent. He'd been a doctor long enough to know you had to be patient when poison spilled out.

"He swore he wouldn't play hero if we ever got into real trouble. I made him promise. I was a woman, and there were plenty of men who wouldn't even work with me. What was it my father used to say? Chivalry will get a man killed."

"Wouldn't you have gone back for him if the situation had been reversed?"

"No! We promised each other—"

"You would have gone back for him no matter what, Jack. I know you. Know your courage. Your heart. You would have charged after him the same way you charged into that burning barn to save Gracie. Hell, you'd have gone back into machine-gun fire to help a total stranger."

"You think I lived this long pulling crazy stunts like that?" she demanded, trying so hard to be tough.

"Yes. And I'm glad for it."

"Ziggy had so many people who loved him. The funeral was so packed, people spilled out of the building." She stopped, shrugged. "It left such a hole, tearing Ziggy out of the world. It wouldn't have if I were the one who was gone."

"Jack, you don't believe that."

"I'm not feeling sorry for myself. It's just the truth. Sometimes, I forget he's dead. I hear some offbeat joke I want to tell him. See something tacky in a store that reminds me of his goofy sense of humor. Once he gave me this gorgeous Tiffany's box for my birthday. I pulled back this elegant tissue wrapping and a dozen bloodshot eyeballs rolled out. They were gumballs. He almost died laughing."

Jack paced to the window, pressed her hand against the glass. "The night he died, he'd found some way to get his hands on some Swiss chocolate bars. I still don't know how he did it. We ate them while we were waiting for the helicopter that was supposed to fly us out. I was still licking the wrapper when the first shot blasted into the tree inches over my head."

"And then?" Tom asked gently.

"Mayhem. We were running through the jungle. Running. Could hear the sound of the copter coming in spite of the gunfire. We were close. So close." Jack's fingers curled into her palm. She didn't want to talk. Didn't want to tell anyone what had happened. Or maybe that was the thing she wanted most. She could taste her own sweat, smell the gunpowder, feel the burn in her muscles as she ran the way she had so many times before. Running for her life—she'd always known that's what it was. She'd just never realized it might also be running into death.

She turned to Tom, trying to put horror into words.

Close, the warlord's men were so close . . . Jack thought. Couldn't Ziggy wait till they were off the ground to gloat? Instead of tempting fate? He'd make the helicopter first. Ziggy always said it was every man for himself in this business—that's why he'd never even been nicked by a stray bullet. But Jack knew he went ahead so he could help haul her into the plane when they had to take off. A torn rotator cuff she'd gotten in a wrestling match with a camel made it hard to hang on sometimes.

Ziggy vaulted into the copter, wheeled and flashed her his usual grin. "Beat'cha again, Murphy. Maybe women *shouldn't* be allowed in war zones." An extra nudge to speed her already aching legs. Jack's lungs burned, her jaw clenched. Gunfire sprayed up pebbles at her feet, but she didn't even feel them cut her skin.

Damn Ziggy, he knew just how to tick her off—

Suddenly Jack's leg was on fire, she stumbled, fell. Tried to scramble to her feet. Her camera strap broke, and she felt her precious Leica crash to the ground. The rebels were closing in on them. She heard the copter's blades speed up. Then Ziggy was beside her. Hard hands grabbed her, dragged her. Hit. She'd been hit. She could feel the blood running down her leg, could feel the blazing gash the bullet had dug.

"I got'cha, princess," Ziggy said, the familiar smell of cigars and good bourbon muting the sickly sweet stench of blood. Jack flew through the air, into the copter. She hit with a thud. Ziggy disappeared for an instant, then reappeared, the Leica in his hand, a triumphant grin on his face.

He lunged through the helicopter door, but in that instant, triumph shattered into surprise. Eyes rounded with shock under salt-and-pepper brows.

"Ziggy?" Jack swore, shoving away the copilot, who was attempting to wrap a tourniquet around her leg. "Don't even try it! If this is your idea of a joke to distract me—"

"Never could stand to . . . be upstaged," Ziggy said, but his face was so pale. Oscar caliber actor though he was, even he couldn't make his face that gray at will, could he? He tossed her the Leica, sagged back against the helicopter's interior.

"Hey, Jack, I'll show you mine if you show me yours," he quipped, but it wasn't funny anymore. Jack stared in horror as blood spread in a grim stain across his barrel chest.

"Ziggy?" Jack croaked, her own pain fading, her head spinning.

The copilot swore, the helicopter lifting off, strange, weightless, surreal.

"He's hurt!" Jack scrambled toward Ziggy, putting pressure on the wound, gathering him in her arms. "Got to stop the bleeding, stat!" She ripped open his shirt, her stomach heaving at what she saw.

"Helluva way to avoid a deadline, huh?" Ziggy said with a wan smile.

"Why did you turn back for me?" Jack demanded, trying to assess the damage, staunch the alarming flow of blood. "Dammit, that was the deal! We swore— every man for himself! I could've made it to the helicopter on my own. And even if I couldn't have—"

"That's the trouble with you, Murphy. Always insisting on making it on your own. Being alone . . . not all it's cracked up to be."

Sky whirled beyond the open helicopter door, clouds blurred by the tears burning Jack's eyes. She heard the pilot on radio, demanding an ambulance be ready when they landed.

"You're going to make it, Ziggy," she said, more to herself than to him.

Ziggy grimaced, the first sign he'd shown of pain. "We've both seen enough of the world to know those guys on the ground are dragging out their doctors' kits for nothing. It's over, Jack."

"No."

"You're a . . . hard woman, Murphy. Can't a man even . . . die without you . . . arguing with him? Want to . . . give you something." He patted one of his pockets, dragged out a leather bag.

"No," Jack shook her head, horror jabbing deep, the small bundle making this suddenly, terribly real. "I don't want it. Keep it for yourself. You always said it was magic. So prove it. Live!"

"It is magic. Remember what . . . told you. This is what . . . hope looks like. Want you to have it."

It was junk. Just a bunch of junk Ziggy had collected over the years. He'd always tried to get her to see beauty in the conglomeration of stuff, but she'd known it for what it was. A scrap of yellow felt, a leaf pressed into a little book, a broken link of chain. Junk. Ziggy Bartolli's treasure. She let him slip it into her hand.

Tom wasn't sure exactly when he'd closed the space between them, taken her into his arms. He held her, just held her as she cried.

He wished he could take all her pain away. Knew she would never let him.

He hadn't gotten over Jack the first time he'd had to let her go. When he'd barely been a man and she'd been so damned young and eager and full of plans. It had been hard enough then, to watch her walk out of his life.

How could he hope to get over her now?

Jack chewed on the cap of her pen, trying one more time to come up with good copy for the array of photographs she'd fanned out across the coffee table. She grimaced. Good thing she hadn't made up her mind to be a print journalist all those years ago. She'd still be working on her first article, at the pace she was going.

Words were slippery little suckers. You had to wrestle them into submission if you wanted them to say exactly the right thing. And it was vital these words be perfect. Someday the words would be the only thing Lucy had left.

But her concentration kept being broken by thoughts of the night she'd confided in Tom, the strange sensation of intimacy between them, an understanding when their eyes met. Knowing the truth about wounds they'd both tried to keep hidden. Secrets they'd now shared.

It would have been easier to put those unaccustomed feelings from her mind if Lucy had been around as usual, but Cal's father had taken the kids out for the day on his fishing boat. The strange thing was that she already missed the little girl, even though Lucy had only been gone a few hours.

She'd boarded the boat when the sky was still slate-dark. Jack had tagged along to see Lucy off under the pretense of getting a picture or two if the sun decided to peek out a bit early. She doubted either Lucy or Tom had bought her story, but she didn't care. She'd wanted to see Lucy launched on her great adventure. And to be on hand in case the little girl ended up needing a little nudge to overcome any nervous jitters.

Lucy had been adamant that she wanted to take the trip with the Pepperells alone, and Tom, after much worry and consideration, had thrilled Jack by letting the little girl have her way.

He was trying so hard to give Lucy room, make her feel as if she could handle things herself instead of waiting for her father to sweep in and save her. Lucy was taking baby steps toward independence and Jack was so proud of her.

And of Tom.

Every time Lucy struck out on her own, her buddy

Cal in tow, Jack watched Tom. There was no way he could hide the worry lines etched into his face, or disguise the restlessness that all but drove Jack crazy during whatever time Lucy was gone.

He worked on the lighthouse property, digging up half-rotted stumps, attacking them with an ax he'd found in a nearby shed.

Jack knew Lucy's blossoming social life at Mermaid Lost was a big adjustment for Tom. Maybe it was giving him just too much time to think, though he'd shown no signs of relenting about letting Lucy meet her mother until there was absolutely no way that he could stop it.

The man had plenty on his mind, that Jack knew for certain. Unfortunately, with everything else Tom was dealing with, she was uncomfortably sure there was something else on his mind as well. The touch of fingers, so fleeting, the warm brush of lips, the softly glowing light that had made the cozy lighthouse bedroom seem so right for that brief time the two of them had taken shelter inside it.

He'd made no secret he wanted her. She'd made all kinds of excuses, rationalized with a brilliance she might have been proud of except for the fact that she was on tenterhooks, too.

It was dangerous to want someone to make love with you so much—especially when you kept telling yourself it would only happen just the one time.

It wasn't that she was unfamiliar with men attempting to seduce her. Something about a woman succeeding in a man's world, fiercely independent and sure of herself, made plenty of drop-dead-gorgeous men want to tame her.

Those few times in the past years that she'd actually risked having a lover, she'd had her exit planned almost before the first kiss. The experience had left her so dissatisfied with them and with herself she'd given up on sex altogether. But somehow those few moments in the lighthouse bedroom with Tom had left her skin tingling, her libido clamoring and her cool decision not to let things get out of hand seem like stark insanity.

Except that she knew she'd been right to put on the brakes. And Tom knew it, too.

The phone buzzed insistently, surprising Jack into dropping her pen. She muttered under her breath. Doubtless another call from back in Kentucky—Lucy's aunt or grandmother or uncle calling to check in, using one excuse or another, when all concerned knew they just wanted to hear Tom and Lucy's voices.

What would it be like to be able to make someone's day by just saying "hello"? she wondered as she heard the muffled sounds of Tom answering the phone in the other room.

She grabbed her fallen pen, and went back to work, dead certain the call wasn't for her, when the door to the kitchen swung open, Tom holding the portable phone toward her with a bemused frown.

"It's for you," he said. "Some guy named Wasserman."

"What th—" Jack exclaimed, getting up from her chair. She grabbed the phone.

"How the hell did you get this number?" she demanded.

Her boss chuckled. "You know how ruthless I can be. I conned your mother out of the number after I couldn't get it from Shaara Bartolli in spite of the fact that I was using my best tricks. The woman's a rock."

"I'm on leave. Remember, I told you to just imagine I'd fallen off the edge of the earth for the next few months."

"But this is important. It's the story of a lifetime."

"Yeah, like I've never heard that before."

"Remember your buddy Mustapha? The one who tried to marry you?"

"Don't you mean 'buy' me? For a bunch of mangy camels, no less."

"Well, he's been lighting a few fuses in his corner of the world. We've gotten reports he's bought a few little war toys from some guys pillaging what's left of the Soviet Union's old stash. I'd sure like to know if it's true. And you're the only Western journalist whose head the guy wasn't always sizing up with his scimitar."

"I told you I can't go. Send Klaus Koenig. He's better than you give him credit for."

"He doesn't have your secret weapon!"

"I'll give it to him, just this once."

Abe choked on the other end of the line. "What're you going to do? Dress Klaus up like a woman? You know Mustapha was crazy about you because you're a chick."

"I let you think that, but he didn't want to marry me for my gorgeous body or my Cindy Crawford face, surprising as I know that is."

"Then why . . . I mean what made him so crazy about you?"

"Basketball."

"Basketball?"

"The guy's crazy about pro basketball in America. Tell Klaus to forget packing even a change of underwear. Stuff his suitcase with autographed pictures of Michael Jordan and every Jordan tee shirt you can find and Mustapha will welcome Klaus like his long lost brother."

Abe swore, long and loud.

"I've heard the words before, Abe," Jack said, "so I

hope you won't mind if I hang up the phone before you go into the next verse."

"Murphy, don't you dare hang up. We have things to get settled."

"They are settled. I've got promises to keep. Until I see them through, I won't be taking any calls from you. Don't pout. Maybe I'll get lucky and have everything taken care of before there's another world crisis!"

"I hope so. There's no one else in the business like you. I already lost Ziggy. The agency can't afford to lose you, too."

Jack chuckled. "Don't worry, I'll be out getting shot at in no time."

Abe was quiet for a moment. "Aren't you missing it? The job, I mean?"

"It's my life."

She turned off the portable phone, started to hang it up. Tom still stood in the doorway, his brow creased with concern.

"Everything all right?" he asked.

"It was my agency. A story that just can't wait."

"You're leaving?" He stiffened, his eyes dark. She was jolted by the awareness that he didn't want her to go.

"I should be heading for the airport right now," she said. "It's a great story. It'll get lots of play in the news."

"You should be going, but you're not?"

She turned away, uncomfortable with the emotion in his handsome face, uneasy about what he might think her refusal to go on assignment meant. About him. About her. About these feelings for each other neither of them could seem to control.

Emotions that could only lead to a hell of a lot of pain once they did the inevitable and walked out of each other's lives. She didn't want to make it harder for Tom, make the pain of separation worse.

And what about her? How hard would it be when the time came to leave him? What was the real reason she wasn't heading off for a ride on one of Mustapha's camels? She probably had more than enough photos of Mermaid Lost to satisfy Ziggy's editor. And it was past time for her to get back to work before she lost her edge.

She shrugged, hoping Tom didn't notice her cheeks were getting warm.

"I can't leave now." She made it sound so simple. "I've got this book to finish. Besides, I'm not up for all the high drama right now."

"Isn't that what you're job is all about?"

"Not danger kind of drama. Uh, a more personal kind. This guy and I have a history. A romantic one, no less."

"What?"

"He offered to marry me. I forget how many camels I was worth."

"That's not funny!"

"Anyway, I told Abe that I've got promises to keep. It's not like it's that big a deal. Believe me, there'll be another 'story of a lifetime' when I'm done."

But it was a big deal, at least to Tom. He jammed his hands into his jeans pockets, unable to hide the sudden tension in his body. *What's the deal?* Jack wondered. It wasn't as if she were leaving. For now, at least.

Tom's eyes lasered in on her. "These shoots of a lifetime you're talking about. They're always dangerous, aren't they?"

"This one's not as dangerous as other missions I've gone on. Come on, Brownlow, you can't get the kind of photographs that win you Pulitzer prizes by taking shots of the local garden club."

She gave him a wry smile. "Don't look so worried. I can take care of myself."

"It only takes one slipup. One bullet. One plane flying in too close."

Tom winced. He'd reminded her of her partner's death. He hadn't wanted to. But he just couldn't help himself. It hurt him to think of her out there alone, imagine something happening, Jack injured, maybe dying, with no one to tell her . . .

What? That he loved her? He'd lost that right eight and a half years ago.

Tom turned away, forcing himself to remember. This time at Mermaid Lost was an illusion. Jack would soon be chafing to get back to the work she loved. It was just a question of when.

True, she seemed to be enjoying her time with him and Lucy. And she obviously cared for China and Cal. But this wasn't her world. A vacation, a duty, an aberration, maybe. But Jack Murphy didn't belong on this deserted stretch of Maine coast. She could never be part of the life Tom would return to. A neatly clipped lawn, Saturday ballet lessons and PTA meetings.

Be careful, Tom warned himself. The time was coming when Jack would hand Lucy the pictures they'd taken together, then she'd head off for her real life on continents that he would never see.

It was a nasty trick of this lighthouse, making it seem as if they all belonged together. But Lucy was too young to understand the transience of life. Tom could only hope she'd gathered enough of Jack's knowledge and strength and courage to think it was worth the loss the child would suffer when they went their separate ways.

And what about him? What would he feel when he watched Jack walk away again? He curled his fingers tight into the palms of his hands, closed his eyes. He expected to see images from eight and a half years ago, Jack's eyes bright and savvy and eager to embrace life, not filled with ghosts of things she had seen, people she'd lost. He'd expected to find in his consciousness the young woman from his past, but that wasn't the Jack Murphy who haunted him tonight.

It was the older, more world-weary Jack that tugged at the vulnerable places in his heart. The camera-wielding soldier who had fought injustice wherever she found it. Jack returning from battle, forever changed by what she'd seen.

Strange, the Jack he'd found here at the lighthouse was slowly easing the other Jack aside. An eager girl unable to hold a candle to the woman she'd come to be.

If things were different, he thought, putting a name to his yearning.

He stopped. There was no sense in raking up dreams that couldn't come true. Some things hadn't changed, in spite of the understanding that had grown between them.

They were as far apart as they'd ever been. Except for this small space in time when the lighthouse made the world stand still, and they could share at least a moment, before returning to their own separate worlds.

But maybe it was time to stop wasting those moments. Just maybe.

"Jack?"

She looked at him, and he surprised himself.

"You've been here for weeks. Have you dipped your toes into the ocean even once?"

"I've swum in oceans before. They're cold."

"Well, I just thought maybe we could head down to the beach. Walk. Wade a little. It's a gorgeous day outside. Shame to waste it." He felt heat rising in his cheeks. He sounded like a kid fishing for his first date.

"Having a tough time hanging out on your own, Dr. Brownlow?"

She smiled at him suddenly, her features warming with empathy. "Well, yeah. But that's not the main reason. I'd really like to spend some time with you, Jack. No big deal. Just a walk. We don't even have to go near the water if you don't want to."

Warning signals blared in Jack's head. But the simple truth was that she wanted to go with him.

She shoved her work across the table and shrugged. "I've been ready to tear my hair out today, anyway. My copywriting stinks. Maybe someday I'll get a real job."

Tom chuckled, the rich sound making the nape of her neck tingle.

He reached out to take her hand and for the first time since she'd come to Mermaid Lost, Jack went out the lighthouse door, leaving her camera behind.

14

❖

Sunlight warmed Tom's shoulders as he strode down the deserted stretch of beach, Jack keeping pace beside him as if they'd never been alone. Warm golden rays drenched her hair, the breeze buffing roses into her cheeks, her eyes full of intelligence, anticipation, and yet, most alluring of all, just a touch of shyness.

The past hour had been pure heaven. Talking about nothing. Talking about everything. Sometimes just pausing to be silent and watch a seagull dive-bomb the waves. They'd laughed themselves breathless at a rock throwing contest Jack had challenged him to. She'd been so intense, so determined as she'd lobbed her pebbles over the water that he'd been tempted to let her win.

"It's a biological fact men have more upper body strength than women," he'd explained, almost apologetically. She'd sent him a killing glare and hurled another rock. It had taken three more rounds of throws before she'd surrendered.

"Still a little competitive, are we?" Tom had teased. "It's only a stupid game, Jack."

She'd slugged him in the arm, then strode out down the beach double time. He'd been the one who finally admitted he'd had enough.

"You know, we're not in training for the Navy SEALS or anything," he'd gasped, grabbing the hem of her tank top to put on the brakes. They'd walked on for a while in silence, with a rare sense of camaraderie that didn't demand any words.

"When was the last time you took a walk just for fun?" he asked impulsively.

"June of 1983, I think."

"Not funny."

"No. It's not, is it?" she asked, a pensive light stealing into her eyes. "I guess when you make your living with a camera, you know a great shot can come up when you least expect it. You try to be ready."

"Doesn't that take a lot out of you? Being on call like that all the time?"

"Aren't you? On call, I mean?"

"Not the way you are. Sure, I have to be ready in case there's an emergency. But watching you, listening to you—it seems like you go through life always being afraid you might miss something."

"I do miss things all the time. Plenty of them. Guess I never realized how many until I came here."

"Things like?"

"Like taking a walk in the middle of the afternoon for absolutely no other reason except that I want to. Or listening to kids talk about pirate treasure. Or talking to someone else about things that matter."

"So what do you do in your time off? I mean, you spend your time in the most interesting places in the world."

"Ziggy used to say I was the only person alive who could walk through the Champs de Elysées and not be moved to tears by how beautiful it is."

"Was he right?" Tom asked tenderly. He stopped beside the beached wreck of the sailboat, leaned against what remained of its hull. His heart thudded hard. The wistfulness in Jack's tone was new. So was the regret. As if she were looking at the world a new way, might want something different than the life she planned to return to.

"I thought he was full of bull. I knew how beautiful it was. I was taking pictures of it, wasn't I?" She made a face. "But he was right. I wasn't seeing the whole sweep of the place. I was breaking it down into neat little rectangles that would look good in a six-page magazine spread."

She turned her face toward the old World War II wreck that seemed like a crouching beast in the distance.

"Funny, isn't it? You never know just how much time you're going to have to notice things are beautiful. Ziggy should have had another thirty years. And Lucy should have had a lifetime. Want to hear something crazy?"

She leaned against him for a moment, the trust touching Tom's heart.

"Maybe sight is wasted on someone like me."

"How can you say that? Look at the images you capture on film! You see things no one else sees, Jack. Make people feel when they see the pictures you've taken."

"Part of me wishes I could give Lucy my eyes."

"I wish I could, too." Tom swallowed hard, his throat suddenly tight.

"Everything she sees is so wonderful, so fresh and new. Beautiful in a way that I'll never be able to see."

Tom cupped her cheek in his hand. "The first place you should look is in the mirror."

"What?"

"To see what beautiful is. You are beautiful and compassionate."

"Compassion is your strong point, and Ziggy's. Not mine."

"Who let us stay at the lighthouse? Gave Lucy her own camera? Who took a walk today just so I wouldn't be alone?"

"That's not why I came. I wanted to."

"I'm glad." Tom kissed her forehead, his arms cradling her close as the salt air ruffled her silky hair against his cheek. "But you're not fooling me, Jack. Underneath that tough, never-say-die exterior, you have more heart than anyone I've ever known." He tipped her chin up, his smile so sexy, so sincere, it warmed her to the tips of her toes.

"Don't worry," he whispered. "Your secret's safe with me."

A car horn blasted from the lighthouse road above, and Tom pulled away with a shaky laugh. "Fishing trip must be over," he said. Jack was stunned to see regret in his dark eyes. "Guess I'd better get back up to the lighthouse."

"You go ahead," Jack told him. "I think I'll stay here for a little while."

She watched him retrace their steps down the beach, one set of footprints where they had made two. The wind tousled his dark hair, plastered his shirt against the muscles of his shoulders, his jeans molding to his narrow hips and long, runner's legs. He stopped near the old boathouse to flash her a smile and a wave of the hand, then broke into a jog as he mounted the path that climbed the steep hill.

Jack watched him until he disappeared, wishing with all her heart that the things Tom believed about her were true.

Cap Ramsey's Pub rang with laughter, Seth Pepperell's fiddle filling the dim, smoky room with jigs that dared every toe in the place to tap along in time. In the dining area around the handsome oak bar, families with kids sat at tables adorned with red-checked cloths and the best sandwiches this corner of Maine had to offer.

Tom did his best to seem engrossed in the music. But his real attention focused on hiding his restlessness from the woman across the table. Jack. She'd always had the power to stir him up inside, knock him out of his comfort zone, make him want more of himself and the world.

And ever since he'd kissed Jack in the moonlight streaming in through the lighthouse window, the turbulence inside him grew more insistent by the day. Secrets shared, emotions voiced, yearnings years old resurfacing at last. It might have been the kind of closure they both had needed for so long. They'd shared so much with each other, he should have felt more relaxed in spite of their disagreement about granting Lucy's wish. He should have been relieved, now that Jack knew why he'd chosen to marry Laura when what he'd really wanted to do was gather Jack into his arms and hold on to her forever.

But instead of a sense of putting the past to rest, the feel of Jack's skin and the taste of her mouth haunted him even more relentlessly than they had years ago. But then he'd barely been a man. Too young to know Jack's worth, appreciate her strength, understand that love isn't just every man's due, but rather, something rare. If you were given one chance, just one, to seize it, you were the luckiest person on earth.

Love like that didn't come with second chances. Jack's warning rang so true—"We can never be just friends," she'd said. "And we can never be anything more."

She was right. Tom knew it. And yet, he couldn't help but imagine what it would be like to have a future with a woman like Jack, to be loved by her, to wake up and see her face the first thing in the morning and the last thing at night.

But there lay the problem. With Jack, there would be plenty of times she'd be gone, doing the work she'd committed her life to. Emergencies that would send her bolting away from him to the most dangerous places in the world. She'd lose herself in flushing out the most dangerous drug lord or religious fanatic of a leader, take any risk necessary to tear the story she needed from all too often blood-soaked ground. But when she returned to her job this time, she didn't even have that partner she'd adored to travel with her, watch her back. She'd be alone, terrifyingly vulnerable, often in lands that held all women in contempt and loathed Americans in particular.

Men would shoot at her, try to ambush her, and God forbid they ever got their hands on her. They'd beat her if she didn't cooperate, and worse. She could be murdered, dumped into a ditch and lost forever. It might be weeks before Tom even knew she was missing. Months before he knew she was dead. And he might never be able to find her body, bring it home to be laid to rest in the gentle Kentucky rain.

His stomach pitched at the images tormenting him ever since he pulled from the lighthouse bookcase an autographed copy of the autobiography Ziggy Bartolli had written. Tom had leafed through pages showing the kind of lifestyles he and Jack had lived. Surely she had to be getting sick of all that by now—the strain, the exhaustion, racing around the globe like a gypsy with no place to call home. He'd seen the weariness in her from the first moment he'd laid eyes on her in the lighthouse doorway. And the danger she continually put herself in—there was no denying it since her partner had been mowed down by machine-gun fire. That fate couldn't possibly be what Jack wanted for herself.

And maybe, just maybe, Tom could offer her a far different one. A home where he could make certain she was safe, a little girl who adored her, and a husband who would do anything to see her happy. Anything except watch Jack race off into danger again.

Selfish bastard, a voice whispered inside him. *That's who Jack is, what Jack does.*

But it was one thing to take so many personal risks when you were on your own. It was another thing entirely to do it when a child was depending on you. Surely Jack would understand that if he ever—

Ever what? Gave way to the emotions clamoring inside him? Jack had made it clear she didn't want to stir up old feelings. How had she put it? "Complicate things even more."

Too bad she hadn't said that before he'd kissed her. Before he remembered it was possible to feel the very essence of a woman all the way to your toes. Before touching her, tasting her, had made him face just how lonely he'd been all these years, without a woman in his life, in his bed. He'd always thought the ache he felt was because Lucy didn't have a mother. He'd never realized a large part of that raw emptiness was his very own. The need to wake up to a drowsy feminine smile, to feel a woman's hands on his body, to be able to share worries and joys and the precious strand of days that made up a lifetime.

Not wanting Jack to guess the thoughts running through his mind, Tom shifted away from her, turning his gaze with paternal concern to the table for two in the corner, where Lucy and Cal were holding some kind of kiddie war council.

The children perched on the edges of their chairs, thick ironstone plates of hamburgers and fries barely touched as they murmured in intense conversation Tom couldn't begin to hear over the din of the Saturday night crowd of tourists and locals.

A low, feminine chuckle drew his gaze back to the woman who sat opposite him, her white shirt outlining her figure in a most distracting manner. "Jealous, Dad?" Jack asked with obvious glee. "You've been watching the kids like a pirate captain anticipating mutiny."

Tom couldn't quite erase the frown line drawn between his dark eyebrows. "I'm glad she's got a friend her own age. She spends too much time around adults, being an only child and living out in the country the way we do. Sometimes I think it's hard for her to connect with other kids. I guess I'm just not used to being on the outside this way. I've always been the one she tells secrets *to*. Not guards secrets from."

Jack surprised him, covering his hand with hers and giving his a quick squeeze that made his mouth go dry. "You know, I think you're both doing great, all things considered. You've eased up on the boundaries a lot for her. And she's feeling better about herself because you've shown your faith in her. Anyone can see she's feeling more . . . capable. As if she can still handle things on her own."

Tom grimaced. "I have zero delusions about the changes in her. But they're your doing, not mine. She's not hanging around on the fringes of life anymore. She's back to plunging in headfirst. Sometimes I wonder if that camera you gave her had some kind of spell on it or if maybe her buddy Cal has some magic of his own. Maybe it's just this place. Maybe it's as special as Lucy thought it would be."

"Maybe you're just doing what you've done all of Lucy's life. Given your daughter what she needed the moment you knew what it was."

The words should have cheered him, but a silence fell between Tom and Jack, a long moment Tom knew they were both thinking of the one thing Lucy wanted above all others. The one thing he was still determined to deny her for as long as he could.

The local crowd roared a request as Seth played the first few bars of a tune. "A dance! We'll have a dance, China!" an old salt yelled from the far corner of the room.

"Does your grandma dance?" Lucy exclaimed. Lucy's face lit up with admiration as the sixty-year-old woman made a show of casting aside her apron and stepped into the center of the scuffed wood floor.

"Nobody dances like Grandma," Cal claimed proudly. "She says an old sailor with three wooden legs taught her everything he knew."

"Three legs? How could he have three legs?" Lucy queried.

"Dunno," Cal shrugged. "Are *you* gonna tell her she's lying?"

China took a quick bow, greeting customers and friends alike. An overhead light turned the older woman's face into that of an ageless elf, and she flashed an irrepressible grin at her fiddling son. In a moment they were off—the music rollicking, China's feet flashing, her heels bang-*banging* on the floor.

Lucy started clapping furiously, and Cal stomped his feet in time, as if he could barely stand the challenge of staying in his seat. In the end, he couldn't. He leaped off his chair to join his grandmother, but he didn't go alone. He grabbed Lucy's hand, half dragging her out onto the makeshift dance floor as well.

Jack threw back her head and laughed as Cal capered around, Lucy, as ever, more solemn, doing her best to imitate China's steps.

Tom's heart squeezed as Lucy's shyness fell away bit by bit until she was laughing as much as Cal. God, Tom thought, he was feeling damned old. He wished he could join them—discard all his worries and dread about the future along with the stray French fries on his nearly empty plate, and dance as if he were young enough not to know how hard-edged life could be.

But he wasn't a kid anymore. And the troubles he faced now weren't the kind you could escape, even for a little while. He thought he managed to stifle a sigh, and yet, he must not have. Jack looked at him sharply from beneath thick, dark lashes.

"One of the first things you learn when you're going into a foreign land is to follow the customs of the natives. That means, if they eat worms, you eat worms. If they dance, you dance. Come on, Brownlow. Time for you to be polite."

She was out of her seat in a heartbeat, tugging him toward the dancers. Cal whooped when he saw them approach, Lucy giving an extra skip of delight. China dove in, guiding them through dances her grandfather might have enjoyed, spinning, reeling, toe-tapping dances that left them all breathless.

Tom clasped Jack's hands when they spun around. Do-si-doed with her, and "danced her down the hall," swirling her in circles, one arm at her waist, the other holding tight to her hand. He could feel the life in her, as if something she'd thought dead was awakening in her, too. And he wished that the music would go on forever.

One of the violin's strings snapped and the melody ended midmeasure with a twang. Seth erupted in a string of curses worthy of generations of sailors.

Lucy ran to Tom, flinging her arms around his legs, breathless with laughter. "Oh, Daddy, wasn't it just great? Isn't Cal's dad the best fiddle player you ever heard? And his grandma—she dances better than anybody in the world, I'll bet."

"You danced pretty darn well yourself, Kitten!"

"I love it here, Daddy. So much. You don't hate it anymore, do you?" she finished in a hushed voice for him alone. "I know you didn't want to come here when I asked. But see, everything turned out perfect, didn't it? Just like I dreamed it would be."

Tom picked her up, held her for a long moment, loving the change in her, the eagerness where she'd been so careful, the delight where she'd been subdued. "I'm glad we came to Mermaid Lost," he said. And he was. No matter what else was to come.

"Daddy?" She wriggled free, too big to submit to public displays of affection for too long. "Daddy, you want to hear the most wonderful thing of all?"

"Sure, sweetheart."

"Cal's grandma asked if I could stay here all night. She said she'd get out the trunks from the attic, the ones with all kinds of old clothes. And I could dress up in them and she could tell me and Cal stories about shipwrecks and how things were when she was a little girl."

Tom gaped at her. "You . . . you want to stay here overnight?" he asked, scarcely believing his ears. Even before the trouble with Lucy's eyes had begun, she'd been a little reluctant to go on the overnights other kids her

age seemed to love. It had taken plenty of encouragement to get her to even try going, though most often
she'd had a decent enough time.

Since she'd been losing her sight, Lucy had refused
even to stay at her grandmother's in the dark. She'd
had to be in familiar surroundings with her pink blanket and Laura's tattered notebook and Tom close
enough to make her feel safe.

"Daddy, I know I've been a real baby about stuff
lately. And," her gaze dropped, color flooding her
cheeks, "between me and you, I'm not positive I won't
get scared. But if I do, I can call you up on the phone. I
really want to try, at least try, Daddy. If I don't do it
right now, when I'm feeling brave, I'm scared I'll be
sleeping with you standing guard in my room even
after I'm all grown up and married."

"Ah, so you're talking marriage, now? I hope that
doesn't have anything to do with Cal?"

Lucy slugged him playfully. "Don't be ridiculous. I'm
not getting married anyway. It just makes it harder
when people go away."

Tom's grin faded. He hugged her again. She might not
need the hug, but at the moment, he sure did. "Lucy,
we've talked about it before. You know lots of people
who are married who love each other—Grandma and
Grandpa, Aunt Debbie and—"

"I don't want to talk about it anymore," Lucy said,
frowning. "I just want to know if I can stay here, with
Cal and his grandma. His dad and mom live right next
door, too, so they can tell me all about diving under the
water."

Tom's eyes narrowed. Why was he feeling so uneasy?
He should be over the moon with Lucy summoning up
the courage to attempt an overnight.

"What's up?" Jack asked, approaching with Cal in

tow. "You guys look way too serious to be planning another round of dances."

"Lucy wants to stay here in town tonight with Cal and his grandmother," Tom said, unable to keep the doubt from his voice.

"Excellent!" Jack actually hugged Lucy without hesitating. "That's real brave of you," she whispered in the little girl's ear, just loud enough for Tom to hear. "I know you can do it."

"See, Daddy?" Lucy exclaimed, as if Jack's stamp of approval was even more important than his impending verdict on the matter. "Grandma China said she can put in my eyedrops and everything."

Tom winced as Lucy's smile suddenly faded, her eyes wide and pleading and for an instant, just a little bit scared, the way they were in the first instant when he turned on a light in a dark room.

"Do you think I can do it, Daddy?" she whispered. Tom forced a smile.

"Of course you can, angel. You're the bravest girl I've ever known."

"I haven't been brave, not for a really long time," Lucy said, never one to let an untruth slide past. "But I'm trying to be brave now. Like Jack. And China. And you."

"I'm not that brave."

"I saw you with that lion that got hurt at the zoo. It could've bit your head off. Everybody was scared, but you went right in the cage and made that lion better."

For an instant Tom considered telling her the truth—that the lion had been darted with anesthetic before he'd entered the compound. But it was nice to see the hero-light in Lucy's eyes.

"I bet you could have been a pirate if you'd lived

way back then. If you were, where would you have put your treasure?"

"I suppose I would have hidden it under the floor-boards in the captain's cabin, in a big wooden trunk with a lock on it as big as a man's fist. And I would have swallowed the key so that no one else could have gotten inside it."

He expected Lucy to laugh. Instead she got even more thoughtful than usual.

"I suppose it could happen that way. If the pirate turned into a skeleton, the key would still be right there, wouldn't it? You could reach right through his ribs and grab it."

"I hadn't thought of it like that, but I bet that's true. Maybe you and Cal and Jack and I should go treasure hunting tomorrow. See if there are any stray skeletons lying around with keys in their stomachs."

Lucy's cheeks turned bright red, her gaze darting away. "It's just a—a story, Daddy. About pirate trea-sures, you know. They'd be way underwater, and . . . well, it's not like I'm a fish or something. I can't go swimming down there to look."

"No, you can't, thank God. Or I have a feeling you'd be underwater before I could catch you by your flipper."

"Daddy?"

Lucy hugged him.

"You know I love you more than anybody in the world. Even more than Cal or his grandma or Jack."

"I'm glad to hear it."

"I've made you worry lots and lots lately, haven't I?"

He couldn't deny it outright. She'd know he was lying. "You're my angel girl. I love you. That gives me worrying rights. It's in the contract parents have to sign at the hospital when they pick up their babies."

"You're joking, huh?"

"Why?"

"Or else my mom didn't sign the paper you did. But maybe if she got to know me, she'd like me. Even enough to worry just a little bit."

Tom set Lucy down, and tried to hide his sudden edginess. "I'll take Jack back to the lighthouse and pack a bag for you. Then I'll bring it back down here."

"Don't forget Mom's book and my blanket," Lucy pleaded sheepishly in his ear. "I can't sleep without them, you know."

"Yeah. I remember."

"Do you think Cal will laugh at me?"

"No. And nobody else will, either, with him around."

He kissed her cheek, then turned to Jack. "Suppose we'd better take off."

Jack nodded, then turned to Lucy. "Have a great time, kiddo. You can do anything you put your mind to, Lucy. Anything you dare to dream. Don't ever forget that. And one little overnight, well, that's a piece of cake."

"Yeah. Just one little overnight," Lucy echoed. Her gaze turned to the window, and the sweep of sea-kissed night beyond.

15

Jack curled up in the Adirondack chair, the night wind washing over her in silky cool waves. She'd offered to ride back to the village with Tom, he'd looked so bereft when he'd come out of Lucy's room, her bundle of necessities in hand. But Tom had grimaced, insisting he'd rather she stay right where she was, waiting for him in the moonlight. He wasn't fooling her, though. He needed some time alone to sort things out, get used to how quickly Lucy was changing.

I tied everything up inside the blanket, like a hobo's pack or something. he'd explained. *That way, no one will have to know it's her security blanket. It might save her from getting teased about it.*

Jack reassured him as best she could, reminding Tom of the high praise Lucy had lavished on her new friend; if Cal didn't laugh at cooties, he probably wouldn't laugh at Lucy's blanket, either.

Tom hadn't looked convinced. But then, he had spent the past eight years worrying about his daughter, a habit that must have grown even more intense in the months since the doctors had handed down their diagnosis.

Jack turned, alerted to the approach of Tom's car by the crunch of the shell drive, the pinpricks of headlights joggling up the bumpy road. She stood up, waved until he flashed the lights to show he'd seen her.

Tom parked the car, then strode toward her, a tall shadow, shoulders hunched just a little against the wind. Even in the dimness, she could see the flash of his smile, knew he was working hard to keep it pasted on his face.

"So, how goes the grand adventure?" Jack asked, clambering up to meet him.

"China has already got the dress-up trunk out and was showing Lucy the pieces that were Laura's favorites when she was a little girl. Lucy should be over the moon."

"Should be? Is she having a case of pre-sleepover jitters?"

"She looked a little preoccupied, as if she had something on her mind. And when I left she hugged me tight enough to break a couple of bones. It worried me."

"Knowing Lucy, she's probably worried about how *you'll* get along without *her.*"

Tom glanced away, shoved his hands deep into his jacket pockets. "Maybe you're right, and she's feeling it, too. The strangeness of tonight, no matter how good it is for both of us. It's always been the two of us. We've never really been apart that much. Even before we got the news about Lucy's eyes. And since then—I haven't wanted to leave her for an instant. I'm afraid that the moment I turn my back it will happen, she'll go blind. I want to—to be there for her, Jack. When things get dark."

"Even you can't be with her every moment. You'll be there for her when it counts, Tom."

"I can't be sure—"

"There are no guarantees. But if you keep hovering over her, waiting for the worst to happen, aren't you going to lose a big part of the joy of the day? Get tired? Maybe even a little resentful?"

"Resentful?" Tom shot back, defensive. "With Lucy?"

"It has to make you mad as hell, what's happening to her. You're not a saint. Doesn't it scare you sometimes, knowing how much Lucy depends on you?"

"Of course. But I've got no control over what's happening."

"Try convincing yourself of that. You've set it all up in your mind, how it all has to happen. Lucy can't go blind unless you're right there with her. She can't see Laura until she's had these few perfect weeks you've planned. And as for you—right now, you can't allow yourself to want anything at all just for you."

"I don't want anything except for Lucy to be well. And for you to—" He stopped, paced away, stopping just at the edge of the cliff.

"For me to what?" Jack prodded.

"Talking isn't going to help anything, Jack. It'll only make things harder between us. That's the last thing I want to do."

"Tell me, Tom. Whatever it is, I want to know."

"I don't know. For you to—to trust me enough to tell me what's happened to you. You know everything about Lucy and me. Even things about Laura."

"You heard about what happened with Ziggy. That night that Lucy came up to my room."

"If you hadn't loosened up with her first, I'm still not sure you'd have told me anything." She could feel the intensity in him, the sensitivity so rare in a man. "I just wish I'd been the one, Jack. The one you opened up to first." He paused, swallowed hard. "You know, the first night I showed up at the lighthouse door, you looked like a different person, so changed, I could hardly believe it was you. In the past you were always so lit up inside, so full of life, energy, eager for whatever the future could throw at you. All those years without you, I tried hard to believe you would never lose those gifts. Is it so strange that I want to understand what changed you?"

"Where's the Jack who leaped tall buildings in a single bound went to?" Jack made a stab at being flippant. "I guess I charged into one too many burning barns, arrived too late at too many sites where people were starving. Saw one too many mothers, facedown in the dirt, sobbing over another son's grave."

She folded her arms tight across her breast, as if trying to ward off a chill. "Yeah, I got what I always wanted, all right. Adventure, my camera, respect. I just didn't know the baggage that came with the world I chose."

"Baggage?"

"I take pictures. Rolls and rolls and rolls of film, so many I can't even keep track of the number I've taken. That's the way it's supposed to be for photojournalists. Snap the shot and then on to the next one, and the next and the next. Rarely a moment to pause. The thing they forget to tell you in photojournalism classes is that it's easy to clear out a portfolio, sort through mountains of shots so you have one, just perfect, just right. But even after the shots you dumped are long gone and the pictures you've printed and saved so carefully are obsolete and lining birdcages with the rest of the newspaper, even then, the photographer who took those pictures will be playing them over and over again in his mind. The images never go away. No matter how much time passes. No matter how many other pictures you've taken in between. It's like the images get branded inside your head, and just when you least expect it, the projector will flick on and it will come flooding back, the horror, the hopelessness, the fear that nothing will ever really change."

"You were always so sure your pictures would change the world, had that kind of power. I remember you leafing through clippings you'd kept as a kid, showing me images that had changed the world. Martin Luther King Jr. preaching from his pulpit, the kids at Kent State."

"They shot King. And those students. And if anything much has changed because they gave up their lives, I've yet to see it."

"Baby steps, Jack. People can only take baby steps toward change. Even so, you should be proud that your photos are nudging them in the right direction."

"You know what's worst of all? Feeling as if no one is ever shocked anymore, horrified by what they see. Sometimes I think I'm the worst of all."

"I don't understand."

"I'm numb to it, Tom. I used to crawl into the very marrow of whatever story I was trying to tell with the photographs I was taking. Didn't hold anything back."

"The way you didn't hold anything back with me."

Jack gave a weak grin. "I always was a slow learner, I guess. But this—this was even more dangerous than opening up with you. Sure, you had hurts and disappointments, and I can only imagine the kind of hell Laura put you through before she was dragged kicking and screaming out of your lives.

"But the things I've seen, you can't even imagine." Jack shuddered. "For a while, I cried a lot. In secret, of course. But even that couldn't wash away what I saw every day, what I heard. It was as if I was inside the skins of the mothers grieving at the riverbank for children the crocodiles had snatched away and eaten. I would feel and feel and feel until it hurt too much, all the time, and the only thing that dulled the hurt was to hide away in my mind where none of it was real and none of the people I ached for so badly could touch me. I just shut down. It was easier. What a thing to be good at. Capturing other people's pain so well on film that you stop feeling your own."

"Jack." He breathed her name.

Tom reached out to her, and Jack stepped into the warm circle of his embrace. She felt his arms close tight around her, drew in the scent of him, burrowed her face against his chest. One large hand eased up, his fingers delving through the waves of her hair, massaging her scalp gently, so gently, as if by force of will alone he could drive back a different sort of darkness from the kind in Lucy's nightmares. Instead of Lucy's horrible, black nothingness, a relentless army of haunted faces, eyes that had seen too much, just like Jack's own.

"I didn't want to come here to Mermaid Lost," Jack confessed. "My partner had been trying to bulldoze me into it for years. Ziggy said I needed a break from the ugliness I was seeing every day, something to help me remember that even though parts of the world were messed up, and some people were suffering cruelly, not everyone was. What was the point of spending your whole life staring at the worst human beings could do to each other, people trapped by poverty or dictatorships or warlords or terrain so unforgiving barely a blade of grass can grow on it let alone a child? If we wanted to give those people hope, Ziggy insisted we had to take breaks to remind ourselves what kind of world we wanted to give them. We had to 'wash our eyes clean' or we'd lose our edge, sink into the darkness ourselves."

The moon drifted out from behind hillocks of clouds, silvery light touching Tom's handsome face. His dark eyes, so intense, so full of feeling, so desperate to ease her pain. His poet's mouth, drawn in lines that understood far too well what she was saying, how lost she'd been in a world he could only imagine. "Your friend sounds very wise," Tom said after a moment.

"I didn't think so. I didn't have time to waste 'recharging my batteries' or whatever Ziggy called the breaks he took from the job. There was always a disaster waiting somewhere for me to capture on film. And as long as I kept running at warp speed, I wouldn't have to feel how—how empty I was inside. The violence, the pain, the hopelessness was eating me up inside."

"I wanted to believe you were happy," Tom murmured, voice rough with regret. "But some part of me always knew . . . facing so much human misery day after day wouldn't be that easy, not for you."

Jack squared her shoulders. "I'm good at what I do."

"I know. You're one of the best. I followed your work, at least part of the time. 'The Soul-Catcher' one magazine called you. It carried a five-page spread, a collection of pictures you'd taken over the years. Faces of people from all over the world. I can still see their images. It was as if you'd captured their souls in that frozen moment, and their eyes reflected every atrocity they'd ever seen.

"One photo in particular still haunts me. A woman with a red shawl draped over her head, her face barely visible beneath its shadow. Three little girls were clinging to her, but her eyes were so hollow, like empty graves."

"Not empty graves," Jack said. "The graves you saw in her eyes held her husband and son. She dug with her bare hands to bury them after they were executed on the road by soldiers.

"There were a dozen instances of aid being offered to her. She was able to bring her daughters to America." Jack felt a vague stirring of satisfaction.

"Because of you." Tom's voice resonated with admiration. Jack was glad in that instant for the darkness, hiding the heat of her blush.

"There were at least ten photographers in the refugee camp that day. Someone else could've taken the picture."

"Maybe. But it wouldn't have been the same. You do have a gift, Jack. Something rare and wonderful that opens people's minds, changes their lives."

Jack looked away, wistful. "I just wish . . ."

"Wish what?" Tom urged.

"Wish it got easier. I wish I'd taken Ziggy's advice and learned how to, well, just to *be*. But I don't know how anymore, Tom. How to be still and serene and just listen to the quiet. No matter how hard I try, even here at the lighthouse, with you and Lucy nearby . . . Sometimes it gets so—so noisy inside my head I can hardly bear it. I always feel on edge, like something's going to happen. Something bad. But I'm all alone, and there's nothing I can do to stop it."

She gave a little gasp as Tom moved suddenly, scooping her up in his arms. He carried her to the chair she'd abandoned a while ago. He sank down into its generous wooden seat, angling Jack so that she was curled up on his lap.

"We'll sit together, then, and be quiet, the two of us," he said. "Just for tonight, Jack, you don't have to be alone."

She looked up at him, his square jaw, his soulful dark eyes, his mouth that could have belonged to a poet or a warrior king. He meant just to hold her, Jack knew, for as long as she would let him.

Like the cliffs that dropped off from the land's edge, he'd stand strong, whenever someone might need him. And somehow, he sensed that she needed him now.

Yet, what about his sorrow? His confusion? The wistful loneliness he was trying to conceal?

"What are you thinking about?" she asked. "Lucy?"

"No. At least not the way I usually do. Jack, I've been thinking about us, wondering . . . I suppose it's crazy, but you did ask."

"Wondering what?"

"Do you really think things turned out the way they were supposed to? That we never belonged together? All the love we felt for each other was just some kind of lie? If I'd found a way to keep my daughter and still marry you, would you have been less happy than you are today?"

"Happy? I wouldn't call myself happy."

"Satisfied, then. Proud of what you'd accomplished. Would you have thought it all a waste if we'd done what we'd planned, traveled to Africa—me, to study animals, you to photograph . . . I don't know, life, instead of so much death."

Jack hesitated, thinking, wanting to give him the truest answer she could. "There would've been plenty of death on those research projects. Poachers, messy little wars. That's why the species are endangered, you know?"

"I'm not saying it would have been perfect, that pristine kind of 'Animal Wonderworld' kind of glow, where the lions never catch the cute baby giraffes and eat them. But there would have been life, Jack. Clean, real life. And I would've been there, every night to make love to you, to make you talk to me, to listen so you wouldn't have to bottle up all the ugliness inside, carry it around all by yourself."

Jack's throat ached. "I don't know how our relationship would have worked out. Maybe it doesn't matter. We took different paths. Lived different lives. Became different people than we would have if Laura had never changed things between us."

"You know what's craziest of all?"

Stop him, Jack thought. Don't let him keep saying things that hurt, filled her with loss, taunted her with might have beens.

But she couldn't help herself, some part of her wanting this closeness. Knowing it couldn't last. "What's crazy?"

"I thought I loved you then, as much as any man could ever love a woman. I was so sure there couldn't possibly be anything more than what I felt at that moment for you."

Jack's eyes burned, memory welling up, that wild, magic roller coaster of emotions that had burst to life inside her. Love so complete she'd hardly believed it could be real. But it had been real all that long time ago.

"I used to tell myself I hadn't really loved you," Jack said. "I was just a kid in love with love. But now, I guess I'm amazed at how lucky we were to find each other even for that little while."

"Know what I think? I think we were just dumb kids. I had no idea how amazing you would become when you grew into a woman. I just wish I could have a chance to love you again."

Jack touched his cheek, her voice cracking. "Tom . . . we're just so different. Our lives—"

"I know. The other night, you said you didn't want me to get hurt, that if I touched you, it wouldn't be a simple thing. But it never has been simple between me and you. I loved you eight and a half years ago. I loved you when I first saw you glaring at me through the lighthouse door. But now that I've come to know the woman you grew into, Jack, I love you even more. So it doesn't really matter whether we make love while we still have the chance, or whether we walk away from each other with just a few stolen kisses to hold on to—there will never be another Jack Murphy in my life."

"I spent so much of my life determined not to feel anything that might leave me open to hurt that I strike out at anyone who even tries to get close to me. A legacy of my years with Frank, I guess. Loving was dangerous. Surrendering any power to a man left you helpless, vulnerable, made you weak like my mother had been all those years. I swore I'd never be like her."

"You're not like anyone else in the whole world, Jack. You're just . . . you. You could never be weak. And any man who would use the love you gave him against you should be hanged."

"Remind me to give you a rope next time Frank is around." Jack tried to joke, but failed. "I just want you to know that it was a miracle you were able to break through my defenses, even when we first met. Even way back then I was determined never to need anyone."

She splayed her palm across his chest, felt his heartbeat race under her hand. "But you changed all that," she confessed in awe. "You made me dare to believe someone just might be able to love me just the way I was. And made me trust that if I got up the courage to open my heart to you, you'd never use my love as a weapon against me to hurt me on purpose, or manipulate me or hold me back from reaching for whatever dream I wanted for my own."

"You say that as if that quality is something rare. It should be the very least you expect from someone who really loves you."

"And yet, we both know that love usually doesn't work out that way." Jack closed her eyes for a moment.

"Give me another chance, Jack. To show you." Tom cupped her cheek with his hand, as if he could feel all the fragile, broken places inside her, and still thought her beautiful. He didn't even try to kiss her. And Jack knew from the look on his face that he wouldn't. She knew how much he wanted her. He'd laid his soul bare.

It was up to her to answer the fearsome longing on his face, to say yes or no. Whatever memories they'd have to take out and hold like photographs a dozen years from now, would be of her choosing.

She closed her eyes, not wanting to imagine how it would feel when Tom drifted back out of her life again. Maybe that was the problem. She didn't need her imagination at all. She *knew* every burn of loneliness, the sleepless nights, the wrenching emptiness of reaching for his pillow and finding him gone. But it would be worth all that pain off in some not so distant future to feel the power of Tom's loving now. She wondered if he was counting the cost as she was.

But he was murmuring things against her throat, sweet things, things that made her thighs melt, her heart pound, her center burn and ache.

"I've wanted you so much, Jack. For so long. Never forgot the feel of you under my hands, so soft, so strong, sleek and warm and eager. And the taste of you—it's never stopped driving me crazy, so wild and clean and honest. I know things are confusing right now. Neither of us know what the future might bring. But right now, I don't care as long as we have tonight. Do we, Jack? Do we have tonight?"

Jack sucked in a shuddering breath, took the most dangerous leap of her life. She kissed him, heard a groan sound deep in his throat. "Make love to me, Tom," she whispered. "Give me something beautiful to hold on to when you're gone."

He levered himself up from the chair, still holding Jack in his arms, but she wasn't about to let him throw his back out carrying her all the way to the lighthouse like some movie hero. She wriggled free, but wrapped one arm tight around him, unwilling to let him go.

Golden light glowed through the lighthouse window, welcoming them home. She was breathless by the time she reached the top of the winding iron stairs. She grabbed Tom's hand, led him into her room.

The bed was piled with China's pillows, dripping with crocheted lace, the linens soft and cool as Jack turned back the covers. It felt so right, so easy, now that she knew what she wanted. Maybe neither one of them could keep this love they had forever, but she could slip the memory of one perfect night into the medicine bag Ziggy had given her, her first, tiny scrap of light to ward off the darkness.

An idea flashed into her mind and wouldn't let go. She turned to Tom with a shy smile, grabbed the top button of his shirt. She saw his eyes widen expectantly, knew he was waiting for her to unfasten it, bare the skin beneath. Instead, she gave the button a sharp tug.

Tom laughed when the stitches didn't let go. "Uh, you slide the little round thing through the buttonhole. That's the way it works," he teased.

"But I wasn't trying to unbutton it. I wanted to tear it off."

Tom looked at her, askance. "Oh. Well, you could try again."

"I wasn't trying to do some big, sexy, show kind of thing. Tarzan and Jane. I wanted the button so I could keep it. To help me remember tonight after . . ."

She didn't say it aloud. Both knew the likelihood of what they were facing. Brief hotly intense weeks together, a difficult parting, but maybe, please God, a kind of closure. Healing where they'd both once had open wounds.

Tom's gaze softened. He grasped the button and tore it off himself. Ever so gently, he put the mother-of-pearl disk into her upturned palm. He closed her fingers over it. She took the button and slipped it into the soft leather medicine bag. She struggled to remember Tom's smile in her heart.

"I won't need any help to remember you." He dragged his knuckles gently along the slope of her cheek. "You're so beautiful."

"I thought I was too skinny." She winced, knowing she'd just let him see how much his assessment of her had stung.

"You looked so . . . starved, when I first saw you here. I thought it was about food, but now, I know better. You were hungry for something else. A little peace, maybe. A little quiet. Someone to touch you."

"Not just someone. You."

Tom unbuttoned her shirt, slid the cloth off of her shoulders, the cool air touching her skin, but she felt warmer than she could ever remember. They'd danced this dance before, the slow stripping away of barriers between them, the nurturing of the fire rising in their bodies.

Jack fumbled with Tom's clothes, filled with a desperate need to see his body again, a mouth-watering landscape of shadow and rough silk, rippling muscles and masculine heat strong enough to melt the icy chill that had held her prisoner for so long.

But when he stood before her, naked, she caught her breath in awe. His body had changed, like so much else had in the years they'd been apart. His broad, athlete's shoulders had filled out, his chest a wedge of well-honed muscle dusted with golden brown curls. His torso tapered into narrow hips, his legs long and hard with a masculine beauty that made Jack's mouth water.

She would never have believed he could have grown even more rugged, stronger, more shatteringly sexy than he had been—sheer perfection, like a Greek statue of Adonis come to life. But in the ensuing years his body had developed to its full promise. Moonlight stroked silvery fingertips over the shape of a man toughened by hard work, honed by life's challenges, taught compassion through scars that marked his spirit, not his skin. A body, a spirit, a man even more beautiful than the Tom she had known before.

Jack caught her lip between her teeth, a rare shyness stealing over her. The years that had polished and perfected every inch of Tom's body hadn't been nearly as kind to her. Soft curves had grown firm and taut as she'd mastered the roughest terrain, her skin weathered by exposure to the elements that no mere sunblock could tame.

Not that it had ever bothered her until now. She wanted Tom to take the same wild pleasure in her body as she did in his, wanted to feel like silk to Tom's hands, rich and luxurious, warm and elegant, lovely and feminine.

Jack wanted with all her heart to be the way he remembered. But she'd traveled too long and too far.

The thought that she might disappoint him somehow cinched a knot tight in her stomach.

Tom must have felt her stiffen, sensed as she drew away in spirit if not in body. A troubled expression creased his brow. "What is it, Jack? What's wrong?" he asked, stroking her hair. "Have you . . . changed your mind? We don't have to go through with this if you don't want to."

She knew how much the words cost him.

Her cheeks burned, and she felt raw, foolish. "I'm . . . different. Everything about me." She swept one hand up the length of her body, then shrugged, averting her eyes from Tom's probing gaze. "I'm not—"

"What?"

"Young and soft and—maybe it would have been better if we'd never started this. If you remembered me the way I used to be."

"You think—think you were more beautiful then?" he asked, incredulous.

"Even you can never convince me that the words 'beautiful' and 'Jack Murphy' belong anywhere in the same sentence."

"You're so wrong. The day you stumbled into the vet clinic, full of soot, stinking of smoke, bits of straw tangled in your hair—right then I knew you were the most beautiful woman I'd ever see. But now I know I was wrong. You're so much more beautiful now."

His gaze traced her body with such reverence, such sincerity, Jack could almost believe him. "Everything about you is richer now, Jack. Warmer, deeper. I cherish every little scar, every line, every change in you. You were a girl when I first made love to you. You're a woman now. Wise, because you've seen the world. Compassionate because you know life's not easy. Strong because you had to be, to survive."

He kissed her throat, her shoulder, her lips. "Jack, you make me feel so—so honored that a woman like you would want me to touch you, kiss you." He gathered her up in his arms, and carried her to the bed. "Just this once try to see yourself through my eyes. You're more than I ever dared dream of. Far finer than I deserve."

Jack swallowed hard, so moved by his praise she could barely speak. "You're the one who—who's fine, Tom Brownlow. Rare. You have so much love inside you and you're not afraid to—to—"

"What, love?"

"Give everything. Every bit of yourself. Keep nothing held back to be safe. I've traveled all over the world, and never once have I met any man as generous-hearted as you."

"Ah, Jack . . . I'm not generous. You're just so easy to love."

"No I'm not," she said, refusing to be dissuaded. "I never have been. I've been prickly and full of walls. Tom, fill me up with memories tonight," she begged. "I need . . . need things only you can give me."

Tom groaned, his features contorting with hunger so deep that just the sight of it made Jack's knees go weak.

She offered herself up to him, gathering his hands in hers, filling his palms with the weight of her breasts. The ripe mounds were one of the few places the sun had never seared or the wind blistered. There, at least, she felt delicate, womanly, the sensitive globes the essence of her femininity, of all she wanted to desperately to give him.

He cradled them like treasures, his thumbs skimming the hardened points of nipples that fairly begged for him to taste them.

His mouth swept over her in silken fire, burning her

with pleasure, searing away doubts and ugliness and scars eight and a half years old. It was as if he were washing her spirit clean, somehow, ridding her of the darkness, soothing away bruises left by the rough patches in life.

His hands couldn't get enough of her, cupping her breasts, skimming her waist, dipping lower to where her body ached for him. His mouth devoured her by inches, tracing her shoulder, her neck, with devastatingly sensual nips, soothing strokes of his tongue until at last, he found her nipple. His lips parted over the hardened nub, his tongue tracing a circle about its edges, as if to warn the tender flesh of the onslaught to come.

Jack gasped as his lips latched upon her, firmly, hungrily, drawing her nipple into the melting heat of his mouth. He suckled with fevered sweetness on nipples that throbbed and ached. She stroked his hair, the sweat-damp satin of his bare shoulders, memorizing every hollow and curve to keep forever.

He flung one long leg over her body, drawing her tighter into his embrace, as if he wanted to fuse them into one being so that nothing could ever drag them apart. Jack felt the hard length of his penis swelling against her hip, and she undulated against it, wanting him to know just how good he felt, just how much she wanted him inside her.

"You feel . . . so good," Tom gasped, arching against her. Then he stopped, pulled away. "I want you so badly. I don't want this to be over, Jack. Not ever."

Jack trembled at the tenderness in him. Trusted him with all the bruised places inside her. "Don't stop," she pleaded. "Make love to me, Tom. Please. I need you."

His gaze locked with hers with a heat so intense her hands trembled. He covered her with the hard warmth of his body, framed her hips with his hands. "Jack," he whispered. "I've been dreaming of this forever . . . touching you again, loving you. I can't believe—"

His voice cracked, and he buried his face in her breasts. "But you're *real*," he said fiercely against her skin. "You're here in my arms again and you want me."

He raised his head so he could look into her face. Nearly sent her over the edge with words alone. "I want to see you," he moaned. "I want to see you when I come inside you."

Passion flooded his rugged features, his jaw clenching in exquisite pleasure as the tip of his penis sought out the soft opening to her body.

She cried out as he entered her inch by precious inch, taking care not to hurt her even now. But he was hurting her, every cell in her body that had been numb for so many years coming suddenly, excruciatingly to life.

She couldn't stand the pain of it, the pleasure, the madness or the magic. The slow shimmering healing that blossomed in the deepest reaches of her soul.

Tears sprang to Jack's eyes as he filled her completely, drove himself inside her body until it seemed he touched her very soul. He buried his face against her breasts, murmuring words of praise, words of passion, words of love so real they stunned Jack, humbled her.

"I feel as if I've been waiting for you . . . for a thousand years," he said, his voice catching. "But I'd wait even longer, Jack. I'd wait forever." He reached between their bodies, touching the dewy place that was burning for his attention, his hands and body urging her to lose control, daring her to reach farther, strive faster, fly higher until she thrashed in his arms, dizzy and gasping and desiring even more. Sensation clenched her in its fist, she was wild with the need for release. The place where their bodies joined seemed pure heaven, absolute torture, a wild racing tingle spreading through her veins like wildfire. Jack clutched at his shoulders, sleek and sweat-damp, stroked the silk of his hair, the beard-roughened curves of his face. She smoothed her hands down to the curves of his buttocks, reveling in the flexing of muscles rock-hard with need of her.

"Tom," she cried his name again and again, as he filled her, and he loved her as if they'd never been apart.

Her hips rose up in frenzied need to meet him, her head tossing on the pillow, low moans tearing from her throat as she strained for the wild release his loving promised.

"I love you," he rasped. "I love you."

He thrust deep, his mouth taking hers in a fierce, wild kiss. Jack exploded, Tom crying out as he came in a world-shattering rush of fulfillment. They clung to each other, strained tight together, neither wanting to let go. But the climax, so complete, drained the strength out of their muscles. Tom surrendered at last, collapsing against her, his weight pressing her deep into the mattress.

They made love again and again, until they knew every secret of each other's bodies, had whispered every secret of their souls. Both of them excruciatingly aware that the night was flying past on swift, dark wings.

"I don't want to ask for too much," he murmured, as the tide of need rose again. "But this may be the only night we have. I want to love you a lifetime's worth."

Jack looked into his face, so familiar, so infinitely precious, hers alone for such a short time. "A lifetime's worth," she echoed, wishing they had forever. Knowing they never would.

* * *

Lucy shivered in spite of the pink blanket wrapped around her, her arms aching from holding on to the sides of the dinghy Cal was propelling through the waves. Diving gear she and Cal had lugged to the boat before anyone else was awake tangled around Lucy's feet, the tubes and masks and oxygen tank looking hopelessly confused and way too big to fit kids their size.

Even the sky looked cold and gray and disapproving, as if the angels Grandma always said were watching over Lucy were all scowling at the very same time because she was breaking the rules. But the angels couldn't really complain, Lucy reasoned. They hadn't been doing a very good job on their own. She must have prayed a million times year after year, begging to see her mom. The angels sure hadn't made her appear.

Lucy chewed at her lower lip, her nerves tingling, heart pounding as another wave smacked against the wooden hull, splashing her in the face with cold, salty water. Her eyes stung and she swiped at them with the back of her already damp sleeve.

Maybe this wasn't such a good idea, she wanted to say. The ocean felt lots bigger and meaner than it had when they'd gone for a ride in Cal's dad's great big fishing boat. Maybe they should go back and wait for a better day—one where the waves weren't so high and the wind wasn't pulling so hard. Only trouble was that once she got off this boat, she wasn't sure she'd ever be able to make herself get back on the thing again.

"I've been thinking and thinking," Cal said, "and I've got it all planned, how we're going to do this. We'll have to tie on right over there."

Cal pointed to a steel mast from the old World War II wreck that thrust out of the water. "Yeah. That mast there will be the best place. The pirate stuff has to be close by. Once when I was out fishing with dad, he drove the boat close to the wreck so I could see it real good. Dad said on a clear day he and Uncle Asia can see the wooden ships under the water, almost close enough to touch. Anyway, I asked a whole bunch of questions and found out that even if the pirate gold is too deep for us to reach, we might be able to get your mom here another way."

"What's that?" Lucy asked, trying to hide another shiver.

"I heard the Nazi's had gold, too. Secret gold they hid all over the world so they could escape from the good guys once they lost the war. Maybe that gold is still a secret 'cause it's in the ship that wrecked here. We'll be famous if we find it." His eyes sparkled eagerly.

"I don't want to be famous," Lucy said, through chattering teeth. "I just want to find treasure so that my mom'll hear about it in the newspapers and decide to come find me. And when she does, she'll hug me and kiss me and tell me how much she missed me while she's been gone."

Cal braced himself against the wind, the boat's small motor working hard to push against the waves. "I bet by this time tomorrow every newspaper in Maine'll be here trying to interview the kids that found the treasure. But when your mom comes, we'll just let Jack take the pictures."

"Jack will probably be really mad at us 'cause she didn't get to come with us," Lucy said in a subdued voice. "But she'll be glad, too. She wants me to be brave and have adventures. I heard her tell my dad so."

"And your dad—what about him?"

Lucy hushed, her ribs suddenly squeezing too tight. "He'll be madder than I've ever seen him."

"Even if we find the treasure?"

"Yeah. Dad doesn't care about treasures. He just cares about animals and people and me. He'd freak if he knew I was out here."

"If we're famous, our dads can't ground us forever," Cal suggested hopefully. "I mean, think how it'd look in the newspapers."

"I don't think my dad would care what anyone else said. He'd do just what he thought was right. But even if he did ground me, it wouldn't change anything. I'd still have the treasure and if my mom came to see me, I know he'd let her. I wonder what she'll be like?"

Cal smiled his special smile that always made Lucy feel better. "If she's your mom, she'll have to be nice. All moms are nice to their kids. It's some kind of rule or something."

Lucy shrank against the wooden plank seat, hoping Cal wouldn't see. "I'm scared my mom doesn't know that rule. It's been five whole years since she's done any mom stuff at all. Maybe she doesn't remember how."

"Bet it's like riding a bike," Cal said confidently. "You never forget it. Grandma rode my brother's once, and she didn't fall off once. But then, Grandma can do anything."

Lucy closed her eyes, remembering the way China had made her laugh and told her stories and served her cambric tea in a cup all the way from across the ocean. "Will she be mad when she finds out we're gone?" Lucy swallowed hard. "Maybe she won't like me anymore."

Cal snorted in disgust. "I'm the one she'll be mad at. You're a guest, she'll say. You don't know any better. But I'm a sailor's son, and I've got pirate blood in me. I know what the sea can do."

"What can the sea do?"

Cal got really still and wouldn't meet her eyes. "Don't worry. I won't let it hurt you."

She huddled deeper in her pink blanket, hating the way splashes of water were making it damp. A big wave crashed against the side of the boat, shoving the motor out of the water for a moment. It roared like a hungry lion. Lucy bit her lip to keep from crying out.

Their boat rocked crazily, and her stomach ached a little as Cal steered the dinghy closer to the big steel mast.

"We'll just tie the boat up, and then try to figure out how to use all this stuff," Cal said. "Can't be that hard if my Uncle Asia uses it. Hey, you *can* swim, can't you?"

"In a pool. With lifeguards. And a shallow end where my feet can touch," Lucy admitted defensively, eyeing the unruly waves as if they were the mouth of some kind of sea monster.

"Um, and there's one more little thing," she said. "I don't like to get my face wet."

Cal shot her a momentary glare of disgust. "You might have wanted to tell me that sooner. If we go after that treasure, we're going to have to get in the water, you know."

"That's why I brought my blanket," Lucy said, her cheeks burning. "I won't be scared as long as I can hold on to it."

Cal didn't laugh. He just nodded, apparently satisfied with her plan. "Lucy, do you think your mom will like me?" he asked all of a sudden.

"I don't know. I'm not even sure she'll like me. But I'll never know if I don't get to see her."

Cal's brow furrowed in concentration as he pulled up close to the iron mast and flicked off the motor. The boat almost turned over as he lashed it to the post with a rope. "My Uncle Asia taught me this sailor's knot,"

Cal boasted proudly. "He says it wouldn't pull loose if a hurricane came busting in."

A groan rose up over the sound of the water. Lucy choked. "Was—was that the pirate telling us to go away? Hidden treasure places have curses, you know. In Egypt, King Tut's tomb had curses so bad the guy who found the treasure died. I read it in a book at school."

"Well, even if that was the pirate making noise, he could hardly kill me. I mean, we're related. It just wouldn't be polite, you know? Besides, Grandma would be really mad. She'd come out and kick his butt."

"But the pirate might kill me. I mean, I'm just a regular kid."

Cal grabbed up the bagful of treasure hunting gear Lucy had helped him pack hours ago: a waterproof flashlight, a thick burlap sack to put all the gold in, and some old keys he'd found in a drawer in his grandma's kitchen, just in case one of them might fit the lock on the treasure chest once they found it.

Cal flicked on the flashlight and looked at the slippery, dark piece of ship sticking out of the water, and for a second Lucy almost thought he was as scared as she was. But then he just shrugged as if he wasn't scared at all.

"Guess we'd better get started," he said. "We want to find that treasure before everyone wakes up and finds out we're gone. If they get here before we're done, they might steal our idea and try to get the treasure before we do."

He stepped onto the rusty chunk of hull and balanced the flashlight on a broken piece of railing. Then he held out his hand. For a minute Lucy's feet wouldn't move and her stomach felt like Jell-O. She was being silly, Lucy knew. Jack wouldn't be afraid of a rocky little boat and a few splashes of water in her face.

"C'mon, Lucy," Cal urged. "Don't you want to see your mom? I thought the treasure was the only way."

"It is," Lucy said faintly, making herself grab onto Cal's hand.

Lucy clutched at her blanket, stepped off the boat. But just as she let go of the dinghy, her shoe slipped. Lucy screamed as she slid toward the water. Rough iron scraped her knees and elbows as she skidded down the hull's curved side, the blanket tangling around her. Cold, splashing waves scrabbled at her like hands, pulling her head under. She kicked, and fought until her head popped up where she could suck in a choking breath.

"Lucy! Grab on!" Cal yelled against the wind.

She clutched at his hand, felt his stubby nails dig into her fingers.

"You have to use both hands!" he cried. "Otherwise I can't hold on!"

Panic jolted through Lucy as she gulped in icy water.

"Let go of the blanket!" Cal begged. "Lucy, you have to!"

The sodden pink mass was clinging to her legs now, so heavy it was pulling her under. Lucy's fingers clenched on her precious blanket one last time, desperate to hold on. Then she let it go. She grabbed onto Cal with both hands. Twice he slipped, and almost fell into the water himself. Twice, he fought his way back up on to the slippery hull and struggled to pull her out. But the waves were like a kid's hand, holding on to a brand-new toy. They didn't want to let go.

Lucy jammed the toe of her tennis shoe onto a little ledge in the metal. She shoved with all her might. With a thud she landed in a heap beside Cal on the part of the rusty old deck where the waves couldn't reach them.

Lucy struggled to catch her breath, her heart sinking

as the flashlight beam lit up a puddle of pink blanket drifting away. She tried not to cry.

"I'm sorry you lost it," Cal said solemnly. "But I'm glad I didn't lose you. That could've been you floating out there." He almost looked like he was crying, but Lucy knew that was impossible. Boys didn't cry. Especially boys as brave as Cal.

He turned his face away from her, but instead of making things better, he sounded a whole lot worse. "Lucy?"

Cal's voice got all trembly. She blinked the tears out of her eyes and turned to look at him. His face was all white under his bright red hair.

"It's okay about my blanket," she said, even though she knew it wasn't.

"That's not the only thing we lost. My bag of stuff slipped off when I was trying to get you back up here. And you know that knot Uncle Asia taught me? Maybe it only works in a hurricane. It sure didn't work here."

Lucy cried out, cold all the way to her toes. The little boat was floating away, off all on its own. They were stuck, she realized, her stomach turning over. Stuck on the haunted pirate ship way out in the ocean and nobody even knew they were gone.

16

❧

Purple and peach clouds scudded across the horizon as Jack stepped out into the new morning, the brisk breezes chasing the dawn into the sky. But for once she wasn't even thinking about grabbing her camera, no matter what kind of shot she could have made. Underneath the soft folds of her navy blue sweat suit, her whole body was still buzzing from the night she'd spent with Tom, making love until their muscles burned and their hearts were full.

Barely two hours had passed since Tom had fallen back against the pillows, his dark hair tousled from her fingers, his face so peaceful it made Jack ache with tenderness. He'd closed his eyes—just for a moment, he'd promised. But in no time he'd been fast asleep.

It was as if his very bones had melted, his muscles relaxed, his features almost serene, the beauty of him all the more bittersweet because of the shadows that still remained. Reminders of the challenges he faced, and the certainty that as soon as he woke, they'd come flooding back to him in a rush.

Jack wished she were a sorceress, like the ones in the Arthur legends she'd read as a kid. Then she could build an enchanted wall around him and make certain he could sleep until the weariness that haunted him was gone.

Unfortunately, Jack knew that the most likely thing to disturb his precious sleep was Jack herself. She was bubbling up inside, like an underground spring that had just found the earth's surface.

It was as if Tom uncovered the place where her fire for life had burned until all the pain she had seen had left nothing but cold, dead ashes. Tom had rekindled her passion, encouraged the tiny tongues of flame until she could feel them again, inside her. And she'd needed to run out into the dawn, drink it all in, the shapes she'd failed to see magic in, the colors that had faded for so long.

Jack shoved a tendril of wind-tossed hair away from her cheek and grinned. Yes, she'd been so restless there had only been one thing to do. Throw on her sweats, lace up the worn running shoes she'd ignored for far too long, and head out into the fresh, new morning.

She checked the double knots in her laces, and set out at a brisk pace along the narrow path that led down to the nearest stretch of beach. She'd never been an exercise junkie, had suffered through her workout as a simple survival tactic. When your life might depend on outrunning angry drug lords or trying to reach a bomb shelter before half the street blew up, it made sense to stay in shape.

But today, she couldn't wait to run. Every muscle in her body protested, more from hours of lovemaking than abandoned workout schedules. But in spite of the knots she needed to work out, she loved the feel of her legs pounding out a smooth rhythm. The wind buffeted her face, energy pulsing through her veins as she'd never imagined it could again.

In every dull twinge, she could feel the hunger in Tom as he'd taken her over the edge, as if he could never get enough of her. She could remember the way his hands had devoured every curve and hollow of her body, how he'd made her feel beautiful, the most desirable woman he'd ever seen. He'd given her a night she would never forget. Maybe the only one the two of them would ever have.

Jack couldn't completely quell the pain that caused her. It was doubtful they'd find the privacy to indulge in any more passion-hazed nights once Lucy came back to the lighthouse. And yet, in spite of that fact, Jack could hardly wait to see the little girl, hear all about her adventures with Cal and China. Lucy had made it through the whole night, without her father standing guard, Jack thought with fierce pride. The little girl might just carry that renewed sense of confidence back to Kentucky, make up for so much of the fun she'd missed.

But even if Lucy does all those things, you won't be there to see it, Jack, a voice inside her whispered. Her pace slowed, her grin fading, a deep sense of loss shadowing her heart.

"No point in thinking about it now," she chastised herself. "The time to say good-bye will come soon enough. And when it does, you'll do the only thing you can do. You'll let Tom and Lucy go."

Maybe she could ask Lucy for her secret before the little girl vanished from her life forever. Find out how Lucy had mustered up the courage to face down what she'd feared most. What had it been that had made her take that final leap of faith? Love for her father? The lure of China's house packed with treasures and tales of

Lucy's mother? Or Cal's unfailing friendship, bracing her courage?

Or had Lucy's catalyst for facing down the darkness been something else entirely? Jack wondered. Some secret force that had hovered in the strained, secretive curl of Lucy's bemused frown last night in the pub when the child thought no one was looking? Whatever had spurred Lucy's fit of daring this time, Jack could only be grateful for it. Lucy would need all the courage she had to face the future that lay before her—her failing sight and the mother who had the power to shatter her new confidence by disillusioning her one more time.

Distracted by her thoughts, Jack cried out in surprise as a spasm of pain shot up her right calf. She swore under her breath, stumbling to a stop, rubbing the rigid muscle with her fingers in an effort to loosen it. But as her gaze swept down toward her leg, she glimpsed something strange out of the corner of her eye, something caught on some rocks along the shore.

"What the heck?" she murmured to herself, staring at the strange lump of what looked like pink fabric.

In a heartbeat, she was back in Africa, and the women were wailing for the newest victim of crocodiles or lions or poisonous snakes. Even here, danger could lie waiting. Her mind filled with stories of kids pulled out by the tide, or people falling out of boats, and washing up on shore.

She ran, heart pounding, across the last stretch of beach, relief flooding through her as she reached the pink bundle, saw that it wasn't covering the twisted body of some child. Jack sagged to her knees to catch her breath. She'd obviously been on vacation too long, letting herself get crazed over nothing.

It was nothing but an old pink blanket some kid had

probably lost. Thank God it couldn't be Lucy's! The little girl would be a wreck—

Wreck—the word drove into Jack's consciousness
like a cold blade.

She froze, her gaze locking on the frayed square of
cloth, her memory filling with images of Lucy, the little
girl's earnest chatter. Pirate treasures her mother had
written about in Lucy's precious book, Lucy's desperate
need to connect with the woman she couldn't remember. The secrets she and Cal had been jabbering about
in the pub last night, just before Lucy came up with her
astounding proposition to stay at Pepperell's overnight.

What had given Lucy the courage to brave the dark? Jack
thought wildly. *Not Laura's imaginary treasure. Please
God, not that.*

Jack grabbed the sodden cloth, desperately untangling it from of a hunk of driftwood. Lucy's blanket had
had something special, hadn't it? A bunny embroidered on one of its corners.

"Please, God, it can't be Lucy's," Jack pleaded as she
wrestled with the blanket. "Don't let it be—" Her fin-
gernail tore, but she barely felt the sting as she scrabbled to get the last corner untangled from the branch
that had washed away. The wood snapped, the blanket
falling into her lap. Jack looked down, her stomach
plunging to her toes.

Lucy's embroidered one-eared bunny stared past
her, its woebegone eyes fixed on the ocean beyond.

Tom started awake at the sound of a door banging
hard against a stone wall, Jack's yelling out his name
from two floors below in a voice that made his blood go
cold.

He snatched up his pants on the run, jammed his legs
into them as he made his way down the spiral stairs,

almost killing himself in the process. He expected to meet her racing toward him, spilling out whatever had struck panic through her voice. A panic he would've doubted Jack Murphy capable of mere hours ago.

But she stayed in the kitchen, talking to God knew who on the phone, what few words he could catch tightening the dread in the pit of his stomach. Something about boats and the Coast Guard and rescue and the ocean getting rougher by the moment.

He raced down the hallway, rounded the corner into the kitchen. Her back was toward him, desperation radiating from every muscle in her body, the sight of her filling him with an even darker foreboding.

"What is it?" he snapped. "Dammit, Jack, tell me!"

She turned to face him, the phone still clutched to her ear, her face ashen pale. "It's Lucy," she said. "I called China to check—Lucy and Cal, they're gone."

"No way." Tom shook his head in denial. "Lucy wouldn't—it's still almost dark. Where would she go?"

"They might be at Cal's house across the street. China ran to check in case the kids had gone over there."

"They have to be close by, playing some kind of game or something," Tom insisted, confused.

"China?" Jack choked out, her attention once more fixed on the person at the other end of the phone line. "Oh my God. Diving equipment gone? But they couldn't possibly—two kids—right. In the boathouse by the beach. They have to—have to be out there somewhere." She hung up, wheeled to face Tom.

"Seth Pepperell's dinghy is gone," Jack said. "He thought it had pulled loose in the wind. Some diving gear is missing, too. But Lucy and Cal are nowhere to be found. The kids must've taken the dinghy and—"

"No!" Tom cried, unable to wrap his mind around the fact that his little girl might be out somewhere on that vast sweep of water that edged the horizon. "Lucy's scared of the dark, and the water—she won't even get her face wet. Nothing on earth could get her into some rickety little boat."

"Seth grilled Cal's little brother. Said Cal had been talking about a secret mission, pirate gold, even saw a book about it that Lucy had with her," Jack said. "It had to be the book Laura wrote about the ships wrecked off Mermaid Lost."

Tom's hands shook as he remembered Lucy's questions the night before—about pirate skeletons and keys to treasure chests, a strange, burning intensity in her small, pale face. No. It couldn't be. He wouldn't let it—

"They could be hiding somewhere," he said with faint hope. "You know the kind of tricks kids like to play."

Jack met his gaze, her face taut with fear. "Tom, they're out there somewhere, on the ocean. I found this on the beach." She slid a mass of pink cloth off the oak table, held the dripping wet bundle toward him. In a heartbeat Tom knew what it was.

"Oh my God."

"The Pepperells are heading to their boats, calling the Coast Guard. But we're closest to the wrecks. China says there's an old boat of Asia's in a shed down on the beach. She's not sure if the motor will work, but we've got to try," Jack said, grabbing jackets and blankets and a first-aid kit from a closet with instincts honed over years of dealing with crises. "They'll be cold when we find them."

When? a voice in Tom warned. Didn't she mean *if* we find them?

Tom yanked a sweatshirt over his head, then snatched the bundle of cloth from her arms and ran out the lighthouse door, Jack right behind him. Wind struck his face, and he could see whitecaps far below, the outline of the shipwrecks in the distance.

How long could two kids stay afloat in water like that? They rushed down the path, hit the beach running to where a weather-beaten shed crowded close to the cliff's edge. The boat inside barely looked seaworthy. Jack grabbed its prow. He hefted the end weighted down by an ancient motor, splinters from the battered hull jamming into his hands.

For a moment he thought it was too heavy. The two of them would never get it to the beach, but Jack was stronger than she looked, her reflexes sharp. And right now, adrenaline was rushing through their veins. They wrestled the boat to the water at an amazing speed.

The hull splashed into the waves, two pairs of oars jammed tight under the flat board seats in case the motor failed them.

"Get in!" Tom yelled over the roar of the ocean, and Jack scrambled over the boat's side. He shoved the little craft hard against the current, driving the waves to shore. By the time he'd hauled himself, gasping and wet, into the boat, Jack was fitting the iron pins of the oars into the metal hasps meant to hold them.

"Row," she ordered. "I'll get the motor running."

He started to argue, but she was already working on the motor with the intensity of a neurosurgeon. "I spend lots of time in Third World countries trying to get outdated equipment to work with nothing but duct tape and hairpins. When's the last time you tried to start an engine built in 1953?"

Tom surrendered, centered himself on a seat, stroking with the oars as hard as he could, knowing that rowing was the only way he was going to get to his daughter. There was no way Jack was going to get that relic of an engine started. Even if she'd had a workshop full of extra parts it would take a miracle. Hell, there probably wasn't a drop of gas in the battered red tank on the boat's floor!

But for once luck was with them. Jack's weird collection of talents was enough. The motor sputtered and choked, coughing up a black cloud of smoke. Then, all of a sudden, the engine came to life. The boat bobbled awkwardly, throwing Tom to the far side of his seat, until Jack got the motor wrestled into place. The propeller dug into the water. The craft surged forward, against the tossing waves.

Tom propped the oars back into the boat in case they were needed again, but the old motor clung tenuously to life. In spite of the antiquated machine's efforts, it seemed to take forever before the boat nudged beyond the cliff's edge, and Tom could make out the dark outline of the abandoned metal ship's hull against the horizon.

"Can you see anything?" Jack yelled against the wind.

Tom shielded his eyes with one hand, straining to see. His heart leaped as one small figure clambered up, the red-haired boy waving furiously, shouting words that were carried away by the wind.

"Somebody's out there," Tom called back.

"You saw them?" she cried. "Both of them?"

Tom swallowed hard. "Cal . . . Cal's there for sure. I thought I saw a shape that might be Lucy, lying on the hull, but I don't know. She didn't move, Jack. What if she's hurt?"

What if she's dead?

He saw his own worst fear flash into Jack's eyes.

"Cal will take care of her," Jack insisted fiercely. "And she's strong. Stronger than you think."

Tom wanted to believe that. But all he could think of

was the little pink blanket Lucy hadn't been able to surrender when most kids had long abandoned their own. What the hell had he been thinking, letting her stay overnight with Cal? He should have known something was up. He should have guessed. But for once, his full attention hadn't been focused on his little girl. He'd been thinking of Jack, dreaming of Jack, imagining what it would be like to hold her in his arms.

The wood hull of the boat struck hard against the metal hull, a dull ring echoing hollowly, like a broken bell. Jack grabbed a length of iron mast protruding from the wreck. She held the boat fast as Tom leaped over its side. A low cry tore from his throat.

"Lucy . . ." He fell to his knees beside the small, miserable heap of humanity that was his little daughter. She huddled tighter into a ball, clutching her knees against her chest, burying her face where he couldn't see it. Tom grabbed one of the blankets from Jack, tried to wrap it around Lucy, but his little girl resisted.

"Lucy, are you all right? Are you hurt?"

"She's just cold," Cal said, his own voice giving an unmanly quiver. Jack must've found a way to secure the boat, because she'd clambered up onto the ship's hull, and was wrapping Cal's shivering body in a jacket.

"Later," Jack cried, touching one ear. It was impossible to hear any more shouting against the wind. All four huddled close, the adults chafing feeling back into the kids' chilled fingers.

A horn blasted, startling the huddle of people on the wreck's rusted hull.

"It's Seth," Jack said quietly. Tom looked up to see the large aluminum fishing boat pulling up alongside. China herself helped manage ropes and lines and life vests, maneuvering the children onto the safety of the wide metal deck with Jack's help. They bundled the kids into more blankets, poured cups of hot chocolate from a thermos to warm them, Asia tying his old boat onto a metal cleat so it could be towed behind.

Jack and Tom got the two badly shaken children into the shelter of the boat's small cabin, out of the worst of the wind.

"How did you find us?" Cal asked. "The water kept getting rougher and nobody knew where we were."

"Lucy's blanket washed up on shore. Jack found it." Tom stroked her damp hair, desperate to feel the life in her, needing to feel her arms clutching tight around his neck. "I've got you safe, sweetheart," he soothed, his own voice breaking. "Everything is going to be okay."

"No, it's not going to be okay," Lucy sobbed, raising her tear-ravaged face from her arms. "It's never going to be okay. I didn't find the treasure."

"It doesn't matter," Tom tried to comfort her, sensed he was failing. "I'm not mad at you, Lucy. Nothing's more important than having you here, now. Safe."

"But it does matter. It does!" Lucy wailed. "I'll never get to see her, now."

"See who, sweetheart? Tell me."

Lucy shook her head fiercely. "No. I can't—"

"You can tell me anything, angel," Tom urged.

But it was Cal who answered. He pulled away from Jack, bracing his feet on the deck with the instinct of generations of sailors, his soft chin tipped at a belligerent angle. "Lucy won't talk 'cause she thinks you'll get mad at her if she tells you why we had to come here."

"There's no good reason on earth for the two of you to come out here!" Tom snapped, unable to forget that without Cal's "help," Lucy would never have been able to put herself into this much danger.

"Tom," Jack cautioned, but he couldn't shut down

the anger boiling up inside him. The kid was glaring as if *Tom* were responsible for this, somehow, as if he were the villain.

"You could've gotten yourselves killed! For what?"

"The treasure," Cal insisted.

"There is no treasure!" Tom cried, exasperated. "There never was."

Cal faced him without flinching, hands on hips, an overlarge jacket flowing off his narrow shoulders like some superhero's cape. "Lucy had to find out for sure. It was the last chance. The only way."

"Only way for what?"

"To get to see her mom before her eyes got worse and it was way too late."

"What the—" Tom stopped just in time. "You're not making any sense."

"You're not listening!" Cal flung back, so furious he almost toppled into the cabin wall. Tom grabbed Cal's arm to steady him, but he just pulled away, glaring at Tom all the more fiercely.

"Lucy just wants to see her mom before she goes blind. Any kid would! But you won't even let her talk about her mom without making Lucy feel bad. And her mom's even meaner than you or else she's real greedy or something. 'Cause Lucy's got to find the treasure. Her mom won't come see her any other way."

Tom reeled inwardly, barely registering Jack's hand touching his shoulder, trying to brace him somehow, against the words Cal Pepperell had just said. But nothing could keep Tom's heart from shattering as he looked down at his woebegone little girl so pale against the green seat cushions. "Oh my God. You risked your life because . . ."

"I—I'm sorry, Daddy." Lucy's face contorted, tears streaming down her cheeks. "I just want to see her.

Just once. So I can know if she loves me a little or maybe she doesn't at all. I have to—have to know."

Tom sagged onto the seat beside her, gathering Lucy into his arms, his eyes burning, as he buried his face against the blanket wrapping his little girl. God in heaven, if Lucy had drowned it wouldn't have been Cal Pepperell's fault. It wouldn't have been anyone's fault except his own, Tom thought.

Seth entered the cabin. The iron-willed Cal finally fell apart the instant he was caught up in his father's strong arms. But for once, Lucy didn't want Tom's kind of comfort.

His heart hurt as Lucy kept her face turned away from him as the fishing boat headed back toward its docking place.

Tom looked up at Jack, desolation filling his eyes.

"This was my fault," he said. "It's my fault those kids came out here. My fault they almost drowned."

"Tom, don't—"

"It's true! Did you hear what Cal said? Lucy wanted to see her mother, but I wouldn't listen. Couldn't stand to . . . I told her she could tell me anything. Promised I'd keep her safe. But I didn't, Jack. Not this time." He buried his face in his hands. "I could have lost her, because I wouldn't listen. Because I was afraid she'd hate me. Because of mistakes I made, and Laura."

"We got to them in time, Tom."

"Because of your quick thinking. If you hadn't found Lucy's blanket, God knows how long it would have been before anyone realized they were gone. Anything could have happened."

"But nothing did. It won't help, imagining every terrible thing that could have happened. Blaming yourself. Just be grateful Cal and Lucy are safe."

"I'm going to do a helluva lot more than that. I have

to make things right. Don't you see? I have to do whatever I can to—to give her . . . what she wants."

"She wants to see her mother," Jack said gently.

"I know." His voice filled with resolve and with dread. "We'll leave just as soon as she's well enough after everything she's been through."

Jack should have been relieved. God knew, she was humbled by Tom's courage. Instead, something hard, cold, knotted in her chest as she thought of the lighthouse, empty of Tom's kisses and Lucy's hugs. Jack's world wrapped up in isolation again, the independence and solitude Jack had been so certain she loved.

No, Jack wanted to argue. *You can't leave yet. It's too soon. I'm not ready to say good-bye.*

But against the sound of the waves, Mermaid Lost whispered warning.

Tom and Lucy Brownlow had never been hers to keep.

17

~~~~~~~~~~~

Tom peered in at his daughter, who cuddled under a mound of blankets in spite of the fact that the day was warming bit by bit. Lucy didn't feel the change in the weather, see the sky, now free of clouds, or hear the wind murmuring softly where hours earlier it had whipped the waves into a noisy frenzy. She slept, exhausted, subdued after her adventure hours before.

The doctor China had called had surprised Tom by making a house call, the cheery mother of two sympathizing with all her heart. But even Dr. Evan's tales of her twin sons' myriad of "near misses" had done little to lighten the guilt that weighed on Tom.

His throat ached, his whole being shaken by how close he'd come to losing his little girl forever. But in spite of his resolve to honor Lucy's wish to see her mother, it wouldn't be a simple undertaking.

He couldn't just take Lucy by the hand and escort her into the prison visiting room without giving her some kind of explanation, preparing her somehow, if it were possible to prepare an eight-year-old for the fact that her mother had killed someone.

Tom heard a sound from the doorway, turned to see Jack entering the room.

"Come on into the kitchen," she said. "I've got lunch waiting on the table. It's not lasagna, but it should keep you on your feet, anyway. You're going to need all the energy you can get once Lucy wakes up."

Tom smiled weakly. "Thanks, but I'm not really hungry."

"I didn't ask if you were hungry. I said you need to eat. They're two different things entirely. Don't look as if I'm trying to poison you. I promise this isn't one of my famed war photojournalist specials like volcanically fried rats or grubworm jelly. Just some of the turkey lunch meat you stuck in that weird drawer in the refrigerator that I never know what to do with."

"I can't leave her."

"It's not dark, Tom. And we'll hear her the minute she starts to stir. Come on. She's going to need you when she wakes up and you're not going to do her any good dead on your feet."

He couldn't argue with Jack there. Surrendering, he followed Jack into the kitchen. He sank down into a chair and took a drink from the glass of milk Jack had waiting for him. It tasted like dust.

"Some day, huh?" Jack said, obviously trying to spur conversation. If there was one thing Tom felt less like doing than eating, it was going through a verbal instant replay of what had happened that morning. But no matter how reluctant he was to relive the events of those nearly disastrous hours, he was half-crazy from the effort it took to try to bury the emotions boiling through him.

In the end, he couldn't stop himself from rasping. "Dear God, Jack. What have I done?"

Her eyes met his with stark honesty. "You've raised an incredible daughter all by yourself. Been the most spectacular father any little girl ever had. You've given that child so much love that she'll never have to ask herself how her daddy felt about her."

"A lot of good that love did her today." Tom gave a raw snort of self-disgust. "Lucy was so desperate to see her mother that she risked her life in that harebrained scheme. You warned me she had her heart set on seeing Laura. You tried to convince me to talk to Lucy about it openly, work things out between us. But did I listen? No. I just rattled off all the reasons why being honest with my daughter was impossible and kept pretending that everything was just fine. I was far more worried about trying to protect myself. I had to keep my standing as some kind of hero in Lucy's eyes."

"You were trying to protect Lucy, too. Maybe you did make a mistake by putting off talking to Lucy about her mother for so long. But you can make other choices now if you want to, decide whether to take Lucy to see her mother or not. It's up to you. But no matter what happens next, you've done the best job you could, Tom. Made the best choices you were able to under impossible circumstances, knowing damned well that it didn't matter which path you chose. Lucy would still wind up losing in the end."

Tom's hands balled into fists. Seething at the injustice of it all, he surged up out of his chair, paced to the window. "It isn't fair," he snarled. "Dammit, Lucy's never hurt anybody. She doesn't deserve the kind of kick in the gut meeting her mother is going to give her."

"Maybe she doesn't deserve it. But that doesn't

mean she won't be able to handle the truth." He heard the soft scraping of Jack's chair being shoved back, sensed Jack closing the space between them. She came up behind him and wrapped her arms around his waist, pressing her cheek against his rigid back. Tom gritted his teeth at the thought of how much he'd miss Jack's touch once she was gone. He softened against her, melting into her warmth, her strength.

"Lucy is stronger than you think, Tom," Jack insisted, her breath warm through the fabric of his shirt. "Look at how she faced down her fear of the dark, took off in that teensy little boat with Cal. Think of how determined she's been to get what she wants."

Tom gave a caustic laugh. "Is that supposed to make me feel better, considering how close she came to killing herself?"

Jack released him, grabbed his arm and pulled him around to face her. "As a matter of fact, it should make you feel fantastic," she said in the tone that seasoned warlords had come to respect. "Lucy is everything her mother could never be. Strong, independent, full of so much compassion. She learned all that from you."

"It wasn't enough. My loving her. She wants Laura." Tom hated the vulnerability stark in his voice.

Jack's features softened with empathy, but she didn't back down. "She doesn't want Laura. She wants the mother she's dreamed up in her imagination. Some perfect composite character out of all the moms in all the storybooks she's read."

"I wish to God I could give that to her. But I have no idea how Laura is going to react to seeing Lucy again. She's had no contact with us for years." Tom dragged his hand across his face. "Jack, last time Laura was in Lucy's life, she was such a mess."

"She was sick, Tom. Hitting rock bottom with a

booze bottle in her hand. It's tough to get bottles of scotch in prison. And part of her sentence must have been some kind of treatment for her alcoholism. Hell, if you get a DUI, you have to have counseling. And there's always the chance that accident might have been the slap in the face Laura needed to come to her senses."

And if Laura did? A voice in Jack taunted. What if Tom wanted a mother for Lucy so badly Laura could win him back? The thought of Laura chatting over morning cereal with Lucy, or lying in bed with Tom, made Jack sick to her stomach. Tom had already shown that he'd sacrifice anything for his daughter eight and a half years ago. But forgive Laura? Let her take her place again in their lives? The mere thought was ridiculous. Laura had almost killed Lucy. Surely Tom would never take another chance with his daughter. Any doubts Jack had should have been put to rest by the disgust on Tom's face.

"So you think she's going to walk out of prison and turn into Rebecca of Sunnybrook Farm? Come on, Jack."

"I don't know what Laura will be like after years behind bars. But I do know what it does to someone to know that they're responsible for another person's death."

"What happened to Ziggy was part of the job description, a risk he chose to take. Laura plowed into a complete stranger because she drank and didn't have the sense to give someone else her keys."

"All I'm trying to say is that the experience changed me, Tom. Cut all the way to the bone. Maybe it changed her, too."

"The two of you are nothing alike," Tom snapped, anger flaring.

"We both made mistakes. That's the simple truth. And I know that right now you're tearing yourself apart, asking yourself if you're about to make another. There's no way to know what's going to happen. Laura's reaction is beyond your control. And, the fact that Lucy is so dead set on seeing her—Tom, you can't control that, either. If Lucy had all the time in the world like other kids—time to grow up, get wiser, stronger, before seeing Laura, maybe you could play it safe, put that meeting off as long as possible. But Lucy's running out of time."

"You think I don't know that?"

"I know you do. You're aware of every moment, counting the sunsets, the sunrises, and you're wondering how many more times she'll get to see those colors. But what you *don't* know is how powerful the bond between you and Lucy is. Even if all this ugliness about Laura coming to light causes Lucy to pull away from you, it will only be for a little while. It's impossible to give anyone as much love as you've given Lucy without imprinting yourself on the other person's soul. That's your gift. Giving a depth of love so rare you're impossible to forget. God knows, I spent eight and a half years trying."

She almost looked away. She wanted to. He sensed it as color crept into her cheeks. In spite of his anguish, his heart squeezed with a tenderness that pained him.

"Trust that love," Jack urged. "Nothing so paltry as Laura and a few tangled up lies will ever be able to ruin the relationship you and Lucy share. Your daughter will come back to you. I promise."

She believed it with all her heart. Tom felt the conviction in her, so fierce, so true. And he couldn't help remembering the pain she'd tried so hard to hide whenever she spoke of her own uncertain childhood, the father's love she'd never been able to count on.

"I wish I could be half as sure as you are. She's my whole life, Jack. It's been just the two of us for so long."

"I know."

"No. You don't know. How could you when I didn't even know until these past few days."

"Know what?"

"About the loneliness that came from raising Lucy on my own. Never having anyone to share with—the worries, the laughter, the memories that will be all I have left once she grows up and goes away. I never let myself admit how much I wanted a woman in my life, in my bed, in my heart."

Emotion flared in Jack's eyes, heat, frustration, regret, her face suddenly brittle. "You deserve somebody wonderful, Tom. I know you'll find her someday." The words in which she handed him off to some imaginary woman might have stung if he hadn't seen the sense of loss that haunted her features.

"I'd never even try to find anyone now. There'd be no point. I knew it a long time ago, and these past weeks, here with you, well, they've confirmed what I've known deep down all along. I'll never find anyone to fill that empty place in my life, Jack. Because no woman on earth could ever compare to you."

Her eyes glistened with aching regret. She trailed her fingertips down his cheek. "You're the finest man I've ever known."

"Just a fine man?" Tom asked, burning questions churning inside him. "Or a man you could love?"

Jack drew her hand away, curled her fingers into her palm as if to protect something too fragile to touch. "You know the answer to that. I have loved you."

"In the past?" Tom asked, knowing that could never be enough. "What about now?"

"I do love you." Jack's heart thundered at the truth

of it, her hands trembling at a world suddenly full of possibilities. They were both so much older this time, wiser. Knew each other so well. They could make a relationship last if they could find some middle ground. "Tom, I know things are crazy, our lives are so different. But if we both want to make our relationship work, then we can find some way to sort things out. Our lives might not be like most people's, but we can make it wonderful, do things our own way. Even when I'm on assignment, I could call, send letters. And when I do get home, I'll make up for the time lost."

He regarded her with eyes suddenly dark, confused. "I thought you were tired of your job. From everything you said—it was draining you, exhausting you. You won't have to go through that anymore."

She stared at him. "I won't. You've taught me something, you and Lucy and Mermaid Lost. Washed my eyes clean, just like Ziggy used to say."

"Jack, I thought you understood. Lucy needs you full-time, a mother who will be there for her. And I— I'll need you, too. Don't you deserve a life? Happiness? Away from a job so grim it came close to destroying you?"

Disbelief surged through Jack, anger throbbing low. She fought to find a scrap of patience. She loved Tom. Loved Lucy. She didn't want to lose them. But she couldn't lose herself, either.

"Tom, I can't just throw away my talent, my gift. What if I told you to stop being a veterinarian and you saw some helpless animal hit and bleeding by the side of the road?"

"That's different," he insisted.

"No, it's not. You see wounded dogs and cats and horses and you fix the places that hurt. I see wounded spirits in people the rest of society might never even notice, and I show the world where it hurts. Maybe I was too intensely focused on my job in the past. Tunnel-visioned like Ziggy said. But my work is important."

Temper flared in Tom's eyes, rare, hot. "Complete strangers are more important than Lucy and me?"

"That's not fair!" Jack fought for balance. "Tom, we're not twenty anymore. We know that if we want something badly enough we have to work at it, and that life is full of trial and error, not some kind of perfect fairy-tale ending."

She held Tom fast, trying to let him see into her very soul, see the truth that lay beyond walls and boundaries and fears so entrenched in her heart she'd thought it would take a miracle to dislodge them. But then he'd come back into her life, more than a miracle—love nearly twice lost. "Isn't love worth every challenge we have to face?"

"I'll do anything for you. Anything except watch you march off into some war zone to be killed. Anything but face Lucy and tell her that the first mother she can remember, the woman who was supposed to adjust her bridal veil and cry over her high school graduation got gunned down on some street in Tehran." His face contorted with desperation, desire, dread. "Marry me, Jack. I'll make a new life for you back in Kentucky. I swear, it will be more beautiful than anything you can imagine. I'll be faithful to you, take care of you. Give you anything you want, as long as you stay with me."

"If you love me, Tom, trust me. I know we can make it, in spite of all the tangles, the difference in our worlds. I want to be your wife. Lucy's mother. The three of us can travel to the most interesting places in the world. It will give Lucy even more chances to experience life, whether she's sighted or blind. And when I need to 'wash my eyes clean,' I'll have a home to come back to, to heal."

Jack closed her eyes, their future together burning too bright, too vivid. So real she could see Tom's head on her pillow, see him building kites with Lucy, feel the tug at her heart as he waved good-bye while Jack climbed into yet another plane, camera in hand. Knowing she could leave, secure in the knowledge that when her assignment was through, he'd be waiting to take her in his arms again.

Tom wanted a future with her, too. She'd seen it in his face. Surely he'd see reason. He'd compromise. He just needed a moment to think about how much she loved him, how much they'd all lose if he turned away. Surely God wouldn't throw Tom back into her life, let her fall in love with him again, open her heart enough to love the little girl who had cost her a future with Tom eight and a half years ago. Surely God wouldn't make her start to feel again just so he could snatch it all away.

Jack opened her eyes, praying she'd see the answer she needed so badly.

Her breath caught at the sight of Tom's stiff, white features, the passion in his eyes eclipsed by fierce, stubborn regret.

"Tom, I don't want to go off into the sunset alone. But you can't ask me to be someone else. I'm a photojournalist. It's what I do, Tom. It's who I am."

"Lucy needs someone who can stand by her when the light finally goes out. Not just a drop-in mom who's great at playing 'Madam Wonderful,' and surprising her with cameras and making books full of memories from perfect summer days. She needs someone she can count on when all she sees is darkness and she's terrified and lost."

"I will be there for her. Maybe not every moment like—like most mothers. But there are other things I can give her. Adventures and courage and an understanding of a world most people don't even know exists. I can show her mountain gorillas in the wild, instead of some glossy magazine. I can make sure she meets people like Jane Goodall and Nelson Mandela. And there's one other thing I can give her. She'll never wonder if I'm taking care of her because I have to. She'll know she matters so much to me I'll work like hell to be a part of her life. And yours, dammit. I love you, Tom. Don't throw this second chance away."

"What other choice do I have? There are some things I can't compromise on, Jack."

"But I can? I can throw away my life's work?"

"Dammit Jack!"

"Remember when you dumped me eight and a half years ago? Maybe I understand now, why you had to marry a woman you didn't love, in order to give your daughter your name, and a father who would love and protect her. But I don't understand why you're throwing our love away this time. Because things aren't just the way you want them to be? Because I might get shot or killed and it might hurt Lucy? You could be hit by a bus crossing the street, Tom. You can't protect Lucy from life. Can't guarantee she'll never be hurt. Love hurts. You know that. I know that. Lucy knows it, too. Let's show her that love is worth the pain, the struggle, anyway. It's worth the risk, Tom. It's taken me a lifetime to figure that out. You're the one who taught me."

"It's impossible, Jack. I should have let things stay as they were. I guess I just—I thought you had changed."

"I have changed," Jack said softly. "But you—you're

still trying to make the world spin just your way. It won't, Tom. It never does."

Tom's jaw clenched as he turned and walked away. Jack listened to his footsteps as he crossed to Lucy's room. He might as well have been a thousand miles away.

18

~~~
❦
~~~

For the very last time, Jack closed the book she'd made for Lucy, locking in the colors they'd captured forever on enchanted summer days. From a rectangle in the center of the cover, Tom and Lucy grinned out at the world from the top of the lighthouse tower, the many faceted lens behind them catching the sunset and throwing beams of color all around them. Blue and orange, grapefruit pink, shimmering gold, almost as if Jack had captured the brilliance, the rarity, the colors of the love the two had for each other.

A love that was being tested even now, Jack thought, her heart aching for the man and the child locked in intense conversation in the bedroom below. What would Lucy think, feel, when Tom told her the truth about the mother she'd never known? How much would it cost them both?

She closed her eyes, remembering all too clearly Tom's face, his eyes fiery with intensity, his body so close to her, so hot and hard and real. "Marry me," he'd pleaded, every place he touched her burning with need. "I know you love me. Love Lucy."

She'd wanted to. Wanted to kiss him until her knees buckled, wanted to make love to him until she couldn't move. She'd wanted to sweep Lucy up into her arms and make angels dance in the child's solemn eyes. *I'm going to be your mom, now. I've never been a mom before, but I love you so much I'll learn how.* She'd wanted to bind Tom's heart to hers forever, give him all the love she'd kept hidden deep inside her. Make him laugh. Make him smile. Make sure he wasn't so terribly alone anymore. She would have done anything to give Tom the future they both wanted so desperately. Anything except the one thing that would doom their relationship before it even began. Surrender the very essence of who she was. Sell herself out for a marriage, the way her mother had. The way Tom had when he'd wed Laura.

No. If there was one thing Jack knew for certain, flinging yourself into marriage on the wings of some great personal sacrifice you didn't really want to make all but guaranteed that love would crash and burn. What was the point of loving someone else if you couldn't be yourself?

But Tom thought I was tired of my job. Exhausted by it. Drained.

And I was. Until I let myself fall in love with him. Opened my eyes to the beauty of life as well as the pain. Love that makes even the worst suffering worthwhile. He made me understand why the refugee woman with the red shawl I glimpsed for just a few moments on the road had the strength to walk as far as she did to build a future for the children of the man she'd loved and buried. He helped me to see, not just the fragility of a child, a hostage to fortune, but also the joy, everything wondrous in life distilled to its purest essence.

*He helped me to find the courage to let myself open up, be
vulnerable. Not feel as if I had to pretend I was made of steel,
impenetrable, solitary, always in control.*

*Yes, a voice whispered inside Jack. And then he took it
all away. He demanded courage from me, a breaking down of
walls, a letting go of the shore, sailing in deep waters far from
the sight of anything I'd known before. And then, just as I
reached out my arms to everything his love had promised me,
he turned coward. Too afraid to take the last, terrifying step,
letting go of control, trusting in each other and the fate that
had brought us together not once, but twice.*

Jack bit her lower lip, but the slight sting couldn't
banish the taste of Tom's kisses, the sweet, seeking sensation of his tongue parting her lips, stealing inside. His
hands rediscovering every curve and hollow of her
body, all the secret places she kept hidden so well, the
vulnerable, womanly places, so tender, so eager, soak-
ing up his life-giving touch as greedily as a field parched
by sun and drought far too long. A Jack Murphy no
other man had ever seen.

She expected the thought to make her feel better,
but it wasn't as easy as it should have been to close the
door on these past few weeks. Once China had warned
that people who came to Mermaid Lost carried the
spirit of the lighthouse away with them. But Jack knew
she wouldn't be haunted as much by this place as by
the man and child who had shared it with her. She
didn't need China's pirate ghosts anymore. When she
left the lighthouse, she'd be carrying ghosts of her own
in her heart.

She glanced tenderly at a manila envelope tucked
under the conglomeration of photographs that still
remained, those that would comprise Ziggy's gift to
Shaara. The old Jack would have convinced herself she
was only keeping doubles of Lucy's prints in case she

wanted to put them in *Lighthouse Summer*. But the new Jack wasn't so easily fooled.

She was keeping those precious images of Tom and his daughter for herself, so that someday, when enough time had passed to dull the pain of losing them, she could take out those pictures and remember that once, just for a few short weeks, she'd known what it meant to love and be loved in return.

A timid knock sounded at the door. "Jack?"

Lucy. Jack's heart squeezed at the forlorn tone of the little girl's voice.

"Come on in, kiddo," Jack invited. Lucy crept across the room, her eyes welling up with tears, but she didn't climb onto Jack's lap, no matter how much Jack knew she wanted to.

Jack couldn't bear it. She opened her arms to the child, gathered her in, warm and tearful and so very wounded inside. She wanted to hold on forever. Knew in that moment how precious motherhood could be.

Jack closed her eyes, breathing in the scent of baby shampoo in Lucy's hair. Memory stirred, a dark, Christmas Eve night in her parents' New York apartment. Hot cocoa on the kitchen table, no one else awake. Her own mother trying to explain why she'd stayed in her hollow marriage. Jack had been well into her twenties then, thought she was so worldly-wise. She wasn't about to be duped by her mother's lame excuses. And yet, now, years later, the words made so much more sense. Painful sense, yes. Tragic in some ways. But Jack understood far better now that she was going to lose the little girl she loved as her own.

If I'd left your father I would have had to work full time, would have had to split up your holidays, your summers, your life. I wanted to be with you, Jacqueline. Childhood disappears so fast. It's far too precious to miss.

But she'd stayed even after Jack had grown and gone, too worn out with life and unhappiness to bestir herself to divorce. Or had her mother and father come to some kind of understanding after so many years? Comfortable in their misery? Her father controlling her mother's life, her mother, passive-aggressive, mounting her resistance so quietly few people would ever have guessed how effective it really was.

One thing Jack knew for certain: over the years their toxic relationship had convinced her marriage wasn't worth it. Tom had shown her possibilities far different. At least that was what Jack had believed. Until he'd laid down the one condition she could never agree to. Not even for him. And especially not for the precious little girl she held. If there was one message she wanted to leave to Lucy, it was that it was impossible to be true to someone else unless you were true to yourself first. If only it wasn't the hardest thing Jack had ever done.

"Daddy and I have to go," Lucy quavered. "He's putting the stuff in the car."

Jack kissed the crown of Lucy's head. "I've got something for you. Remember all those pictures you took? And all the times we talked about colors and how they looked?"

"So I could remember." But she looked crestfallen. "I probably still will forget."

"I hope not. I made this for you."

Jack handed her the book. Lucy stared at it, smoothing her small hands over the angles and planes, running her fingertip around the edges of the photograph on the cover.

"Open it."

Lucy did, seeing the writing on the pages, the images, quotes from the hours she'd spent on the beach, roaming the cliffs, exploring the ocean.

"What's this itty-bitty tape thing for?" Lucy asked, touching the cartridge Jack had stowed in a small pocket at the back of the book.

"Remember how I talked into my little tape recorder sometimes?"

"So you could remember what time you took the picture and where it was and who the people were in it. And stories and stuff that you didn't want to forget. You said it would help you write those lines that are always under pictures in magazines, telling what the picture's supposed to be about."

"Well, I did the same thing with your book. Told about the days you spent here, what it looked like, smelled like, tasted like. How the wind sounded. I've got a couple of spare recorders, too, so you can take this one."

She slipped the miniature tape recorder into Lucy's shirt pocket.

"Did you make the tape? You know, say all the stuff on it?"

"Yes."

Lucy's mouth wobbled into a smile. "I'll be able to hear your voice, then, won't I? When I'm listening to the colors?"

"Yes."

"I've got presents for you, too." Lucy rummaged in the pocket of her shorts, dragged out several crumpled objects. "Remember when you told me about the special bag your friend Ziggy made? Where he kept all the stuff that made him feel happy?"

Jack thought of the small leather bag that held all the magic in Ziggy's generous heart. "I remember," she said.

"I've got two new things for you to stick in it. First, this." She extended a scrap of pink satin, one edge frayed and worn, the other smooth, as if sharp scissors had just snipped it. "It's part of my blanket," Lucy admitted, blushing. "It helped you find Cal and me when we were lost out in the water. Maybe, if you ever feel lost, it'll remind you that someone will always be looking for you. *I'll* always be looking for you, even if I can't really see."

Jack's throat closed, her eyes burning at the generosity and courage in Lucy Brownlow's heart. "I'll treasure it forever," she said, meaning it with all her heart. She rose and retrieved Ziggy's bag, slipped the scrap of blanket inside it.

"Here's something else, too." Lucy gave her an object no bigger than Jack's thumbnail. A tiny photograph carefully cut into the shape of a heart. Jack's eyes narrowed to focus and Tom's face smiled back at her— younger than he was now, less troubled, but still so honorable, so strong, so full of compassion. A man who'd devoted his life to healing other creatures' pain.

"It's the picture from my locket," Lucy said.

"Oh, sweetheart, it's—it's wonderful, but I can't take this. It belongs to you."

Lucy shrugged. "It's hard for me to see real little things anyway. Besides, I'll have the real daddy with me all the time. And you'll be far away in the desert or the jungle or somewhere. You might need something to remember us."

"I don't need this picture or even your scrap of blanket to remember you and your daddy, Lucy. I could never forget you." *Because I'll carry you in my heart.*

"Maybe you could come and see us sometime at our house in Kentucky. You could meet my dog, Gracie. She's real smart and she likes to carry this stuffed hedgehog all over. We call it her baby."

"She's lucky to have a girl like you to love her."

"Yeah. Daddy would like it if you came to see us, too. Even if he is acting funny. He doesn't mean to be—"

Lucy stopped, at a loss to describe Tom's current mood. But then, she didn't have to. Jack sensed every twist of guilt, every ache of loss he'd suffered since he'd asked her to give up her career to marry him, and she'd told him no.

"It's because of me that Daddy's sad," Lucy confessed.

Not entirely, Jack wanted to comfort her. But how could she tell this hurting child about the scene in the kitchen earlier that day? About how Tom had asked Jack to share the rest of her life with him and with Lucy, loving them?

How could she explain to Lucy the reasons she couldn't let herself be forced into giving up such a big part of who she was, even for a love greater than any she'd ever imagined could be real? She loved Tom for who he was. She'd never ask him to be someone else, live someone else's life, give up a part of himself that had defined who he was, in his own mind, his own heart. And when he'd asked all that of Jack, she'd had no choice. She'd had to tell him no. He had to love *her*. The Jack who dashed around the world, camera in hand. The Jack who could cook over an open fire, but not on a stove. The Jack who could show Lucy mountain gorillas in the wild and marvel at a world so wide one person could never see it all. Tom had to love those parts of her, too, if there was ever to be any chance for them to build a life together, a home Jack hadn't even known she'd longed for. Someplace warm and safe and familiar and beloved to rest her wandering feet.

Jack tried hard to hide her thoughts from the little girl who sat, quietly puzzling something out in her mind. "It's not your fault your daddy is sad, Lucy. Sometimes, things just don't work out the way we hoped they would. We can't help wishing they'd turn out differently."

After a moment, Lucy adjusted her glasses, then turned to look at Jack, a fine line of worry between the child's delicate brows. "You mean, about my mom? My dad told me the truth about her," Lucy said. "She's not off writing a book like you are. She's in prison 'cause she had too much to drink and ran her car into another lady. That lady died. My mom must be real bad."

"People make mistakes, Lucy. Your mom made a big one. She didn't mean to hurt anybody, but she did."

"Daddy hurt me. He lied."

"You lied about what you and Cal were up to the night you sneaked out to the pirate wrecks."

Lucy flushed. "I'm a kid. It's different for daddies."

"Daddies have a tough time of it. They have feelings just like everyone else does. They get scared and desperate and confused and yet, we expect them to be really strong and never cry and always do exactly the right thing for us, even though they can't read our minds. It must be hard, don't you think?"

Lucy stared solemnly at her hands, her wounds obviously still too fresh.

"Your daddy loves you more than anything in the world. And you trusting him—that means everything. Why do you think he lied this time?"

"I dunno. I just know it's wrong."

"I know you're a lot smarter than that," Jack said. "Think, Lucy. I know your dad made you mad, hurt your feelings. But has he ever done anything like this before?"

"No," she admitted faintly.

"Then why would he do it now? He told you some pretty heavy stuff about your mom, didn't he? Things that were hard to hear even when you're eight years old, almost grown-up, really. How hard do you think it would have been for you if he'd told you about your mom when you were younger?"

Lucy frowned, considering with all her might. "You mean when I was still a baby? I don't know. There's lots of stuff for me to understand. Did you know about my mom, too?"

"Your dad talked to me about it. He was so worried. He wanted you to have a perfect summer to remember always. He didn't want to hurt you or make you sad. He was afraid you wouldn't understand why he lied."

"What—what did you tell him?"

"That he's really lucky. He didn't tell you the whole truth, and that hurts. It might take a while for the sting to wear off. But it will in time. You're a smart, strong young woman, Lucy Brownlow. You might not always be good at seeing with your eyes, but you'll always see clear as can be with your heart."

This time Lucy didn't ask. She wrapped her arms around Jack's middle and held on tight. "You know what I like best about you?" She muffled the question against Jack's shirt.

"What?" Jack barely squeezed the word past the lump in her throat.

"You just ask questions about what I think and how I feel about stuff. Other people tell kids what they should think. They say stuff like 'You shouldn't feel like that. You shouldn't be sad or mad or scared.' But it doesn't matter if you should or you shouldn't. You feel that way, whether you're s'posed to or not."

At least she'd done that much right, Jack thought,

grateful, remembering all the things her own parents had told her she "shouldn't" feel. Jack grimaced, remembering the times her mother had told her "You don't hate your father, Jack. Don't say that!" But she had hated Frank. Maybe this time with Tom and Lucy would give her the courage she needed to better understand him. Had Frank wanted the kind of relationship with his daughter that Tom had? Wanted hugs and frilly dresses and ribbon bows in softly curled hair, a china doll who looked at Daddy like a hero? Had Frank longed to see adoration in a soft, sweet daughter's face? Instead she'd defied him at every turn, so strong-willed nothing could move her from the path she'd chosen. But was the truth in her behavior far from defying Frank? Had she been fighting for his respect all along? And Frank, hard-edged, a bulldozer with a press badge—had he been relating to her the only way he could? Scared to show weakness, scared she might be killed in the world he knew too well? But they'd just been too different to understand each other. Or maybe, in some ways, too painfully alike. Unwilling to let anyone see the tender sides of their hearts.

The two of them had been in a standoff for most of Jack's life, neither one willing to blink first. But time was running out. The lines on her father's face were getting deeper, his hair, grayer, his eyes, once sharp and intelligent, vaguer now, a little confused, like an aging lion about to lose its harem in the wild. Time didn't give a damn how smart you were, how talented, how stubborn. It came for you, all the same.

Maybe Frank was supposed to be the grown-up. But what could Jack lose by reaching out first? Her pride? Maybe that didn't matter quite so much anymore when compared with a chance to make peace. Let go.

Stop letting Frank's screwed-up opinion of her rule her life even now, when she was grown. Maybe she hadn't had a father like Tom Brownlow to teach her to love herself. But she could teach herself, give that love and approval to herself right now.

"I'm scared, Jack," Lucy confided in a whisper. "China and Cal's daddy and everybody says I look just like my mom. Maybe the bad stuff that put her in prison is inside me and I didn't even know it."

"There's no bad stuff inside you, Lucy. You may look like your mom, but you have your daddy's dimple, right here." She touched Lucy's left cheek. "And you share more important things with your daddy, too. Things that prove you're Tom Brownlow's daughter, down to the center of your precious heart. You have his gift for loving people and animals, loving the whole world and seeing all that's good and beautiful and right instead of the dark places. You'll never lose that, Lucy. No matter what. And there's another thing you'll never lose."

"My blanket?" she asked sheepishly.

"Well, you might keep it forever. And if you do, that's just fine. But I was thinking of your daddy. Your mom is sick, sweetheart. I hope she's better now, and that when you meet her it's something good. But just remember, no matter what happens, you'll always have your daddy. I wish—" *I could be there for you, too. Love you and hold you and help soothe the hurting.* Jack stopped, horrified at what she'd almost confided to an eight-year-old, who had enough confusion and heartache to work through on her own.

"What do you wish?" Lucy asked.

"I don't know," Jack evaded.

Lucy looked up at her with eyes far too wise for such a little girl.

"You wish you had somebody like my daddy to love you, too?"

But he does love me, Jack's heart cried out. *He swore it. Wanted me to be his wife.*

Not enough to let me be myself. Make my own choices. Not enough to trust me with my own life.

How could he trust, surrender control, considering everything that had happened in his life? The disaster with Laura—he thinks he should have stopped it from happening. Lucy's blindness—he thinks he should be able to heal it.

He hasn't figured it out, yet—that none of us really have any control at all. We just have to let go and love and trust and hope that will be enough.

Tears welled up in Jack's eyes, but she turned away so Lucy couldn't see. The child was already wrestling with disillusionment because of Tom's attempt to protect her.

"Lucy?" Tom called up the stairs.

"Up here, Daddy."

Jack heard Tom's heavy footsteps on the iron stairs, his tread slow and disheartened. He'd carried a heavy heart into Mermaid Lost the night he'd first come here. He'd carry another heartache away.

"I'll never forget you, Jack," Lucy said. "Please come and see me sometime. Maybe you'll get tired of being by yourself all the time, and you'll want to take pictures of things like dogs and kids and horses instead of bombs and sad people. If that happens, you could come visit Daddy and me. Maybe you could even rent the old farmhouse at Grandma's. There's nobody in it right now. And then I could bring Gracie to come see you and pretend that you're my mom. Won't you at least try?"

"You're my favorite little girl in the whole world. And I love you—so much. Maybe that isn't exactly the way you wanted it to be, but it's more than we had before we both came to Mermaid Lost, isn't it? Let's just try to be really grateful for the time we did get to have together, okay?" Jack saw from Lucy's face that the little girl already knew what Jack couldn't bear to tell her. She wouldn't be coming to Kentucky. It would only make the separation harder if she did.

Lucy gathered up her book, hugged it tight against her chest. "Well, I'll have this anyway, won't I?"

"Forever and ever."

And Jack would have the little packet of pictures she'd kept, that and a heart full of regret. Tom entered the room. "Kitten, we've got a long way to go. I called your mom. She knows we're coming."

"Good luck, Lucy," Jack said, hugging the little girl good-bye.

"I'll always remember colors because of you. And I'll remember something even more important. To keep on going no matter how scared I get. Just like you, Jack."

Jack fought to keep the smile on her face. Knowing that this time would be the hardest she'd ever faced—going on without Tom or Lucy in her life. She'd do it. She had no choice. But the prospect was bleak and hard-edged and lonely.

Tom appeared in the doorway, dark shadows under his eyes, his face taut and pale. Like a man on his way to his own execution, Jack thought, her heart aching for him.

"Lucy, you'd better go check and make sure I put your blanket in the car," Tom suggested. "Wouldn't want to forget it."

"You'd never forget it, Daddy. But I'll go check anyway. Besides, I have to say good-bye to Cal. He promised he'd come before we had to leave."

Lucy gave Jack one last hug, so hard, it was as if the little girl was trying to imprint the feel of it in her memory.

Jack almost cried out when Lucy let go. But the little girl flew from the room, drawn by the chugging of an engine—the Pepperells arriving en masse to say good-bye.

Tom stood awkwardly in the room, not meeting Jack's gaze. He crossed to where her green silk tunic hung on a Shaker peg on the wall. He touched it, and breathed deep as if taking in the scent of her. Saying good-bye.

"I talked to Lucy about Laura."

"Lucy told me."

"I don't think I'll ever forget the look on her face."

"It was a shock."

"That her mother's in prison or that her father's a liar? I wish I knew which one of those facts cut her the deepest."

"She's a smart kid, Tom. You've both got plenty to adjust to. But in the end, I think she's going to surprise you with how resilient she can be."

"I hope you're right. I never wanted to hurt her."

"She knows that. She doesn't want to hurt you, either."

"I suppose that's just the way it happens sometimes when you love someone so much," Tom said, letting the folds of her tunic slide from his fingers. "It hurts."

Jack averted her eyes, aware of just how much.

"How . . . did it go with Laura?" Jack switched to a safer subject, knowing that whatever Tom said, she'd be able to read the truth in his eyes.

"She'll see Lucy this time. But, she's changed her tune about wanting to be in Lucy's life now that she knows about Lucy's problem. She says she has enough problems of her own to work out once she's paroled. She doesn't think she can handle seeing Lucy once she goes blind."

A knife twisted in Jack's heart. She wanted to rage at Laura, scream at her, demand to know how the woman could turn her back on Lucy when she needed a mother so badly.

"Jack," Tom said slowly. "There's something I need to say. Part of me always knew you'd have to go back to your real life someday. I wish I had the courage to love you and still watch you put yourself in so much danger. But I've already made so many mistakes. Let my daughter in for so much pain. Losing you would be more than either Lucy or I could handle."

"But you are losing me. By choice, Tom. It doesn't have to be this way. Dammit, don't be so stubborn you throw our chance away."

"You call me stubborn? Hell, Jack. It's almost funny! I don't want to bury you the way you did your partner!"

"You would be burying me alive, by forcing me to choose between you and my work. It would be different if it was my own decision, Tom. I'm willing to compromise, work out something we can both be satisfied with. But I won't be bullied or manipulated into something I don't want to do. I don't want to end up hating you."

"You hated me for eight and a half years, didn't you? Now I've given you one more reason." He stunned her, snatching her against him, hard for a moment, kissing her, passion rising, a brief, fierce explosion of desperation that left them both shaken. Tom pulled away, his breath ragged in his throat.

Jack touched her burning lips. "Good-bye, Tom."

He stormed out the door, out of Jack's life.

Jack crossed to the open window, tears streaming down her face as she hid behind the curtain and listened. She ached as China pressed one of the precious blue-and-white teacups into Lucy's hand. And she strained to hear Cal as he gave Lucy a present of his own.

"I wish we could have found that treasure you were looking for," Cal said shyly. "But maybe you could take this instead, and just imagine there's lots and lots of them."

Lucy looked down. "I never saw money like this. It's cut like a piece of pie."

"They call it a piece of eight. A pirate coin," he explained. "My dad gave it to me for Christmas a few years ago. I want you to have it."

"You'll be a really great sailor someday, like your dad. Maybe you'll need this."

"Naw. I think I'll be a pirate and get lots of my own."

Jack saw Lucy give Cal a kiss on the cheek, saw the boy blush. Knew that if Lucy ever needed him, Cal Pepperell would charge through stormy seas to reach her, just like the pirate captain whose blood ran in the little boy's veins.

What would it be like, Jack wondered, to have a life filled with love? She'd come so close to finding out. Now she would never know.

Was Tom right? Was she being stubborn? Unreasonable? Was she the one who was throwing their future away? What the hell did it really matter what she did with her camera if she ended up alone? No Lucy to make her smile? No Tom to make her heart race? No home where the three of them could laugh and love and help each other grow? But there wouldn't be room enough for Jack to grow in the life Tom offered her. And when someone didn't have room to grow the way they needed to, they withered, died in a way far worse than a quick, clean bullet.

But knowing that didn't stop the pain, the loss. Tears ran down Jack's face, unchecked as she listened to the laughter and the tears and the loving farewells far below her. She stood at the window watching them, an outsider again.

But this time she didn't want to be.

19

---∞---

Jack fingered the small leather medicine bag hanging around her neck, wishing some of the power of it would heal her. But it seemed Ziggy's talisman had the power to "wash eyes clean," not soothe aching hearts.

Two weeks had passed since the SUV had disappeared down the lighthouse road, two weeks that had been an agonizing mix of solitude and silence. Even China hadn't made her usual visits to pester Jack, only dropped off what was needed at the lighthouse and hurried off.

Not that Jack had anything to say. Ziggy's book was on his editor's desk, and she was just waiting for the okay, staying at the lighthouse until she got it, in case there were more pictures needed, or adjustments in text to be made.

Not that she didn't have hundreds of other shots for the editor to choose from, Jack admitted to herself grudgingly. But somehow, she wasn't as eager to leave Mermaid Lost as she should have been. Because once she locked the green painted door and handed the keys over to China, it was over. The magic summer she'd shared with Tom and Lucy.

Empty as the rooms here were, she could still imagine they were in the next room, Tom throwing together a pan of lasagna, Lucy cuddled up with her blanket and a book, or playing some secret game with her buddy Cal.

Jack wondered if the little boy felt as lost as she did.

She'd been so desperate to hear another voice, she'd even called home, and when she was done talking to her delighted mother, she'd said something that had shocked them both. *I love you. Tell Dad I said hi.*

It was the first time she'd called her father something other than Frank since she was ten. It had felt good, though. Strange, and yet—maybe it was time to do what she could to mend bridges. She'd never have the kind of relationship with her parents that Lucy had with her father, but maybe it was time she ditched all the old anger and resentment, tried to find out just what kind of bond she could make it.

Maybe she'd stop home before she checked in with her agency. Then, back to the smell of gunpowder and blood and danger. Tonight she should head down to the pub, let China know when she'd be heading out.

The pub was quiet after the lunch hour rush, a few tired, windburned tourists kicking back at secluded tables, showing off the antiques they'd purchased from the shop down the block.

Jack made her way to the bar that was China's small kingdom, as the old woman buffed a beer mug to a shine.

"So, you finally decided to join the world of the living?" China gave her a keen glance.

"I just wanted to tell you I'm going to be leaving day

after tomorrow," Jack said, surprised at the bite in China's tone, "if you want to rent the place to someone else."

"I think I'll leave it empty for a while. I need a rest."

"From the housework?"

"No. From worrying about the damn fool tenants." China glared.

Jack stared at her, taken aback.

"You know what, Jacqueline Murphy? You're the biggest fool who's come to Mermaid Lost since my idiot of a great-great-grandfather ran his ship onto the rocks after his wife had done her best trying to save him. She should've beaten the daylights out of him with the nearest broomstick. And, God knows, it's taking all the self-control I have not to knock some sense into you. That man loves you and so does that little girl. And what's worse, you know it!"

"China—"

"You like to be alone, oh, yes, haven't I heard that a million times. But it's high time you stopped spouting quotes off like a lunatic parrot and really think about what you're doing! I've been alone ever since my Henry went to his maker. It's been years since I've heard him swear when I stuck my cold feet on him in the winter. I've not felt his hands on my skin or watched him stitch a fishing net together as if he were weaving it out of gold. But at least I remember what it felt like to be loved."

"Not everybody is as lucky as you are. Not everybody is meant to have a husband and a family."

"And I suppose you're going to tell me you're one of those people? Just try it!"

No pirate had ever challenged an enemy more fiercely.

"Sure, there are women who live their lives alone," China snapped. "There are even women who like it, thrive on the independence. And you've built a hell of a career, earned respect, done good with the work that you've done. No one could ever deny that. But I saw you with Tom and Lucy. And no matter how prickly you tried to be, you couldn't hide how much you wanted to belong to them."

Jack wanted to just leave things where they were— let China think she'd refused love. It would be far easier than admitting the truth. That she'd been ready to marry Tom, be a mother to Lucy. But in the end, the love she'd offered hadn't been enough. At least not for Tom.

"When you're as old as I am, lived and worked and raised men for sixty years, you get to know a little bit about them," China blustered. "Tom Brownlow is one of the finest I've ever met. He's the kind of man to stand beside you in a storm. I don't understand why you don't grab on to Tom and Lucy and never let go. Fall down on your knees and thank God that a man like that loves you. I don't know why you don't take that little girl in your arms and give her the mother she's breaking her heart wishing for. But I'm just wasting my time, aren't I? You know what you want. Know who you are. Some hopeless case with a heart so cold and withered you might as well be dead. Well, all right, then. I give up. Maybe you're right and you *are* just as hopeless as you say. Because if you can't love Tom and Lucy Brownlow, you can't love anyone at all."

Jack met China's gaze, tears burning her eyes. "He didn't want me," she choked out.

"What the devil?"

"He asked me to marry him. And I wanted to. I love him. Love Lucy. But that wasn't good enough."

"Of course it is! Why, child, you've got enough heart for a dozen women if you'd only trust yourself."

"I did. I do. Tom's the one who walked away."

"I don't believe it. Any fool could see he's in love with you."

"He's in love with a person who doesn't exist. A Jack Murphy without a camera, without a career, without a chance to change things in the world. He'd marry me, all right, as long as I gave all that up."

"He tried the sweet, demure, weak little half-wit before. You'd think he'd know better!"

"He doesn't want to have to bury me."

"So he'll bury himself and his little girl, and try to hold back the darkness with his bare hands, will he?"

"It's what he wants."

"Did you tell the man you love him?"

"Yes."

"Tell him the secret for choosing a mate that the Pepperell family always knew. Don't choose a fool who won't tell you when you're heading for the rocks. You have to choose someone who'll stand strong beside you in a storm. Because the storms will come, whether you will it or no. You make him see that, Jack Murphy. You've got fight in you and strength and now you've got love, too. You're strong enough to guide them through the storm. Like the lighthouse. Of course you can't change who you are. But don't leave him out on the sea all alone. Be there, even if he's trying to sail through on his own."

20

❧

Lucy was climbing a tree again, a bright pink bandanna tied in a rakish blindfold around her eyes, her book-laden backpack hanging over her shoulders, weighing her down. Tom watched from the window of his clinic as she felt her way from branch to branch, fighting the urge to go out and haul her down, or at least, be there to catch her in case she fell. But he knew he couldn't run interference for her this time. The adventures she'd been going on lately were too important—a legacy, in a bittersweet way, from her brief visit with Laura.

Tom watched as Gracie paced around the tree trunk, as nervous as he was, but if Lucy had seen, she'd think the dog anxious to hear her read aloud from the book she carried—a copy of *Lassie Come Home* she was determinedly using to teach herself braille.

I have to show myself I can do things myself, even in the dark, Lucy had insisted. *That way I won't be scared.*

Because she'd seen what fear could do when she'd looked into the face of her mother. And so, by God, had Tom. Laura still looked out at the world as if she were waiting for the sky to fall, and was expecting someone else to ward off the blow.

And Tom had sensed that even when she walked out of those iron-barred doors, she still wouldn't be free. She'd always be so afraid, so fragile, so self-absorbed that she'd never really live.

He felt sorry for her, even more so because she couldn't put aside her own problems long enough to reach out to her daughter.

Lucy had known within minutes of seeing Laura that all the dreams she'd spun about building a relationship with her mother would never come true. One more disappointment he'd feared would scar his little girl. And yet, instead of shattering Lucy, it had strengthened her. *I'm not like her at all, Daddy,* she'd said after hours of intense thought. *I'm like you. Jack said so.*

"Jack said so." How many times had she quoted Jack Murphy in the past two months? So many times, it was as if they could both feel her presence, hear the sound of her voice, daring Lucy to be braver, strive harder, urging Tom to let her try.

She'd been just the person Lucy had needed. A woman who'd learned to fight back in a world that tried to take things away from her. Defy a society that tried to make her dependent instead of self-sufficient and brave.

Jack wouldn't surrender. Wouldn't settle for less than she deserved. Wouldn't let anyone stop her from being herself.

Not even the man she loved.

Tom's heart twisted. He fingered a photograph Jack had sent to Lucy from Rwanda. Jack stood against a backdrop of rich, rain-soaked green, an infant gorilla cradled in her arms. How strange to realize he'd never seen a picture with Jack *in* it before. As if she didn't exist except for peering through the viewfinder of her camera.

Jack looked so much more at ease with herself, not stiff. She was laughing as the baby gorilla tried to feed her part of its lunch of leaves. He could still see the loss in her eyes, the determination. Had she set her tremendous will to getting over him? The jerk who'd tried to change her? The thought made him ache inside.

Whatever she felt about him, she hadn't forgotten Lucy. More and more pages had come for Lucy's color book. Places his daughter would likely never see. Words of encouragement Lucy drank in like parched ground drank in rain.

He'd helped with spelling as Lucy had written back to Jack. And hadn't been able to resist sneaking peeks at the correspondence that had sprung up between the two of them. It awed him, humbled him, hurt him to know just how much Jack loved his little girl. How generous Jack could be, writing this way after he'd asked her to marry him and then turned away. *A second time*, he thought in self-disgust.

She'd gotten on with her life. It's what she'd needed to do, wasn't it?

"Thomas?" His mother came bustling through the door joining house and clinic, a dishtowel in her hands. "Tell that child to take that blindfold off her eyes right now! I'm scared to death she's going to break her neck."

"But Lucy's not scared. She's going to learn how to climb trees whether she can see or not. That's worth risking a few bumps and bruises."

"But she could get hurt! I swear, since you two got back from that lighthouse, it's like she's a different child!" In spite of her agitated words, she relaxed as both of them watched Lucy settle herself on a likely-looking branch. Lucy pulled her blindfold askew for a moment to see where she was, then grinned, so pleased with herself that she glowed.

"She's growing up," Tom said. "Getting stronger. The other day she told me she was going to leave her blanket in her bed all the time, instead of dragging it around the house with her. And she's actually gone to two overnights instead of pretending there was some reason she couldn't go. I haven't had to stay up with her at night since we got home. She still keeps a nightlight on, but when she wakes up now, she isn't crying."

No, I'm the one who can't sleep now, Tom wanted to say. *Because I keep reaching out, wanting to feel Jack's body beside me, kiss her mouth, stroke her hair. I keep remembering the love in her eyes when she begged me not to throw her love away. When she said my losing her this time was my choice. Mine . . .*

His mother laid one work-worn hand on his arm. "And the doctor? What does he have to say?"

Tom ached for a moment. "She's lost a little ground. But her attitude is a dozen times better. She took her Color Book with her last time, showed it to everyone. He wanted to copy it for some of the other kids."

"I can see why. It's an amazing book. The woman who made it for Lucy must be remarkable."

"One of a kind. I love her, Mom."

"That accounts for some of the changes in you, then. Why don't you go spend some time with her? See where it leads? I could watch Lucy. It's always hurt me, Tom, knowing you're alone. You were never meant to be."

"It's too late. I made her choose between Lucy and me and a career she's worked her whole life to build."

"That doesn't sound like you."

"Her work is dangerous. I was afraid— Dammit, Mom, I don't want to make any more mistakes."

"And if you don't even give your love a chance—

isn't that a mistake? There's a saying in the Talmud that I love—it says that when we die we will be held accountable for every allowable pleasure we denied ourselves. You've already sacrificed far too much joy out of a sense of responsibility or duty, Tom. If you love her, love her. Do this for yourself."

"It's too late. You don't understand."

"But maybe she does." She touched his hair, tenderly, the way she had when he was young, but her smile was sadder than he remembered, tempered with the knowledge that it was far harder to heal wounded hearts than bruised knees. Did a parent ever stop wishing they could protect their children from hurting, no matter how old they got, no matter how inevitable the pain? Tom wondered.

Or was the plain truth that sometimes love hurts? It just didn't matter because love was also life's blood and air to breathe and hope to hold on tight.

Or was the trick not to hold on tight? But rather, to have the courage to trust love and let go?

He watched his mother walk away, then crossed to the desk where Lucy's most recent letter was waiting. A half-dozen photos Lucy had taken were spilling out of the carefully addressed envelope. Her letter was filled with new adventures.

Tom knew that when Jack read it, she'd feel proud.

But what was she feeling about him? It had taken so much courage for her to open up her heart a second time. And he'd hurt her again.

Any other woman would never forgive him for that. But Jack was made of stronger stuff. She didn't buckle under pressure, didn't turn away when things got too harsh or dark or hopeless. And she didn't give her love easily. Was it possible that made it more resilient? More lasting?

He picked up Lucy's Harry Potter pen, and added one short line to her letter. A hastily scrawled line that said everything he dared. "I'm sorry" sounded absurd. "I was wrong" far too late.

And yet, he had to tell her the truth, somehow. Let her know what he felt. Maybe heal some of the hurt he'd dealt her, rejecting her the way he had.

I love *you*, Jack.

He underlined the word, hoping it said so much more.

Tom went to a crate where some orphaned puppies squabbled with each other, ready for another feeding. Thankful he had Lucy to help. In the past two months it seemed like every bitch in thirty miles had whelped—most of them in the middle of the night with complications that took a doctor's hand.

He was grateful that he was busy. It distracted him from thinking too much about the postscript he'd written, and the ominous silence that had descended in return. Jack hadn't written—either to Lucy *or* him. And as he watched the evening news he tried not to imagine Jack in the midst of the chaos on the screen, cameras revealing violence as it erupted.

It was terrifying to think Jack was out there somewhere. It was worse that he didn't know where she was. A letter, a phone call. He would have been so damned relieved, just to know she was all right for the time being. It was driving him crazy that she might be in danger. It was far worse not knowing where she was.

And even the cutest batch of orphaned pups in the world couldn't change that. He gathered the fuzzy brown-and-white bundles into a basket, grabbed the bottles and carried the lot of them outside to where Lucy was waiting in her favorite tree.

Lucy heard the tiny yapping. Down the tree she pelted, delighted with her brood of adopted babies.

She plopped down on the grass, lifting the smallest of the puppies gently, nuzzling it under her chin. "C'mon, Gracie!" she called to the Border collie sunning herself on the front porch. "Time to teach my babies how to be dogs."

Tom couldn't help smiling, the pup Lucy was holding whining piteously in protest at the idea, obviously preferring to be an adored furry idol instead of a mere dog.

"Shh, don't cry," Lucy said, slipping the nipple deftly into the little orphan's mouth. "Try and be brave like Jack. You don't have to be sad because you don't have a mommy. I don't have a mommy either, and I'm just fine."

Tom watched her, trying to believe that it was true.

He grabbed up two puppies himself, ready to feed them at the same time, but before he got them settled in, he heard wheels crunching on the gravel drive. Someone hoping to catch him at the clinic, no doubt.

He squinted, trying to see the car more clearly, his heart lurching. It was an old blue Mustang, like the one Jack had driven into Kentucky years before. But it wasn't possible. She couldn't still have that car. And she was off on assignment somewhere. He was sure of it.

Even so, he turned to Lucy and bundled the puppies back into the basket. "Sweetheart, take the babies inside."

"How come?"

"Please, honey. Just do it." *So you won't have to see me fall apart if she's just come to visit. So I can pull myself together before . . .*

Before she gets out of that car—

Lucy did as she was told, heading inside, Gracie following in her wake.

Tom waited.

The Mustang pulled to a stop. The door swung open. Jack unfolded her long legs and got out. Tom's heart turned over.

Whatever these months had been like for him, they'd changed her as well. But not by painting darker shadows under her eyes or making her pale and more haggard.

Her skin glowed, cheeks blushed with color under eyes still sharp with intelligence and strength, and yet, softer, somehow, deeper.

"Jack," Tom rasped. His heart threatened to beat its way out of his chest.

She came toward him, so strong in herself, so beautiful, so wise.

"I got Lucy's letter while I was in Kenya. It didn't matter."

Tom's heart sank.

"I was coming to Kentucky anyway, the minute I got back to the States."

"Lucy will be glad to see you. You'll be so proud of her, Jack. She's grown so damned much. She's so brave, now. So strong. She's not afraid anymore. Not the way she was."

"I always had faith in the kid."

"I know. I was the one who didn't have faith. In Lucy. In myself. In our love. I tried to make things safe. Control things I couldn't control. Pretend if I tried hard enough, worked long enough, I could keep bad things from happening. But I couldn't keep Laura from drinking. I couldn't keep Lucy's sight from starting to fail. And I couldn't keep myself from loving you."

"You said you loved me before. As long as I met certain conditions. I'm here to tell you that I'm going to hold you to that note you wrote. You're going to have to love me, Tom. Just the way I am. Camera, press assignments, stupid stubbornness and all."

"And if I said I would?"

"It's not a question, Brownlow. I'm telling you straight. I love you. I love Lucy. We're going to make a life together. And you're just going to have to like it. I've spent the time since I left Mermaid Lost working things out at my agency and in my own head. And I've been going on assignment, to prove to myself my plan would work, before I came and set you straight."

"You did?" A smile spread over Tom's face.

"I'm going to freelance. Take assignments I want. Sell the pictures as I go. That doesn't mean I won't be going into dangerous situations. It just means I'll have a little more control. I figure summers you and Lucy can come with me—we can do great nature spreads, and she'll get to see more of the world."

"I see."

"And as for you—you're just going to have to trust me—my skill and my determination. I'm not going to do anything stupid, Tom. Not when I have you to come home to. You always knew I was strong. Let me be strong for you and Lucy. Maybe you don't have enough faith to think we'll have years and years to love each other. But I have enough faith for both of us. Together we can stand up to the storm. Maybe everything will go crazy around us, but our love will be like the lighthouse, Tom. Nothing will shake it, not even if we live a hundred years."

"I'm sorry. I was so stupid. I love you so much the thought of you hurt somewhere off in some war zone where I couldn't reach you was terrifying. I just didn't realize that living without you would be even worse. Marry me."

"What's that people say about the third time being

the charm? You'd better hold to it this time or you'll be sorry."

"I'm already sorry for all the time we missed. Forgive me, Jack. I love you. You. Just the way you are. No matter what happens."

He kissed her, his mouth closing over hers, hot and filled with passion. Jack trembled, melted into his arms, delighting in the raw familiarity of his touch, the hunger in it, the telltale hardening where his hips pressed tight against her own.

Who knew? Jack thought in that instant. Maybe they'd have a baby of their own someday. A brother or sister for Lucy. Maybe that would be wonderful. But no more wonderful than the little girl who had first won her heart.

She kissed Tom fiercely one last moment, then pulled away. "I don't want you to think I couldn't kiss you forever, but I—I need to see Lucy. I've missed her so much!"

Tom laughed, leading her inside. Lucy sat cross-legged on the living room rug, murmuring to the puppies. "Don't cry 'cause your mommy's gone. I'm your mommy now."

Jack's throat ached at the sight of Lucy, so small, so precious. "I was wondering if you might need a mommy, too."

Lucy bolted up, gently lowering the puppy into the basket.

"You came back!"

"Yeah. I thought I'd try my hand at this mommy thing, if you'd help me."

"I don't know anything really about mommies," Lucy confessed. "Mine wasn't anything like I thought she'd be. I liked you so much better, that I didn't even care when she didn't love me. 'Cause I knew you did. Even if you were far, far away. But this is so much better!"

Lucy ran at Jack, certain of welcome as she gave her a hug.

"This is Gracie. You two have to meet."

"Actually, we already have." Gracie's ears pricked up, her tail wagging, but not with the usual friendly greeting she gave to strangers. The collie tipped her head at an angle, then bounded toward Jack in a rush.

Jack went down on one knee, gathering the dog into her arms.

"Jack's the one who saved Gracie from the fire," Tom said.

Lucy stared, astounded. "You're Gracie's angel? Why didn't you tell me?"

Jack shrugged. "I didn't want you to think I was—was some kind of hero. Thought it would just make it harder when we had to leave Mermaid Lost."

"It was hard. Real hard. But it doesn't matter anymore. You may be Gracie's angel, but you're my mom."

"And my wife," Tom growled, low in his throat.

"And now you'll be here, even when it's dark," Lucy enthused, "and you can help me—"

"I'm the one who was in the dark," Jack told them. "No colors, only gray. You helped me to see again, feel again. Dare to take a chance to love."

"But you take chances all the time, jump out of planes and everything."

"Loving is a lot scarier to me, Lucy."

"I'll hold your hand," the little girl said, clutching tight to Jack's fingers.

"I won't let you fall," Tom promised.

Jack gathered them into her arms, heart pounding, as she embraced the greatest adventure of her life.

Visit the
Simon & Schuster Web site:
www.SimonSays.com
and sign up for our
mystery e-mail updates!

Keep up on the latest
new releases, author appearances,
news, chats, special offers, and more!
We'll deliver the information
right to your inbox — if it's new,
you'll know about it.

SIMON & SCHUSTER
A VIACOM COMPANY
www.SimonSays.com

POCKET BOOKS

SONNET
BOOKS

2350